HARUKI MURAKAMI
MANGA STORIES

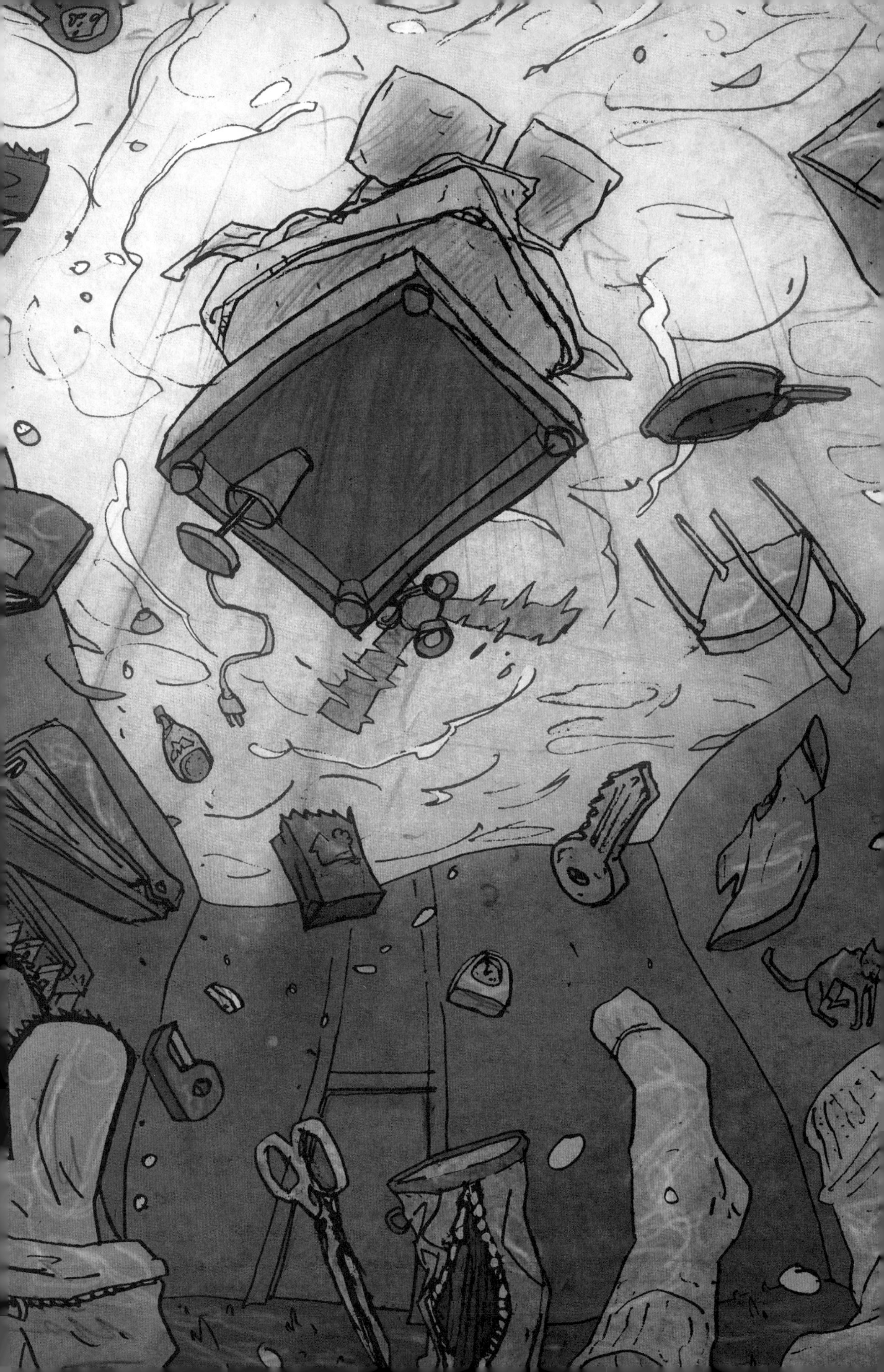

HARUKI MURAKAMI
MANGA STORIES

Adapted by **Jean-Christophe Deveney**
Illustrated by **PMGL**
Original onomatopoeia by **Misato Morita**

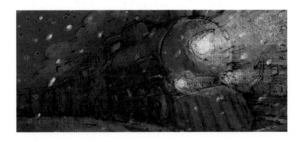

TUTTLE Publishing

Tokyo │ Rutland, Vermont │ Singapore

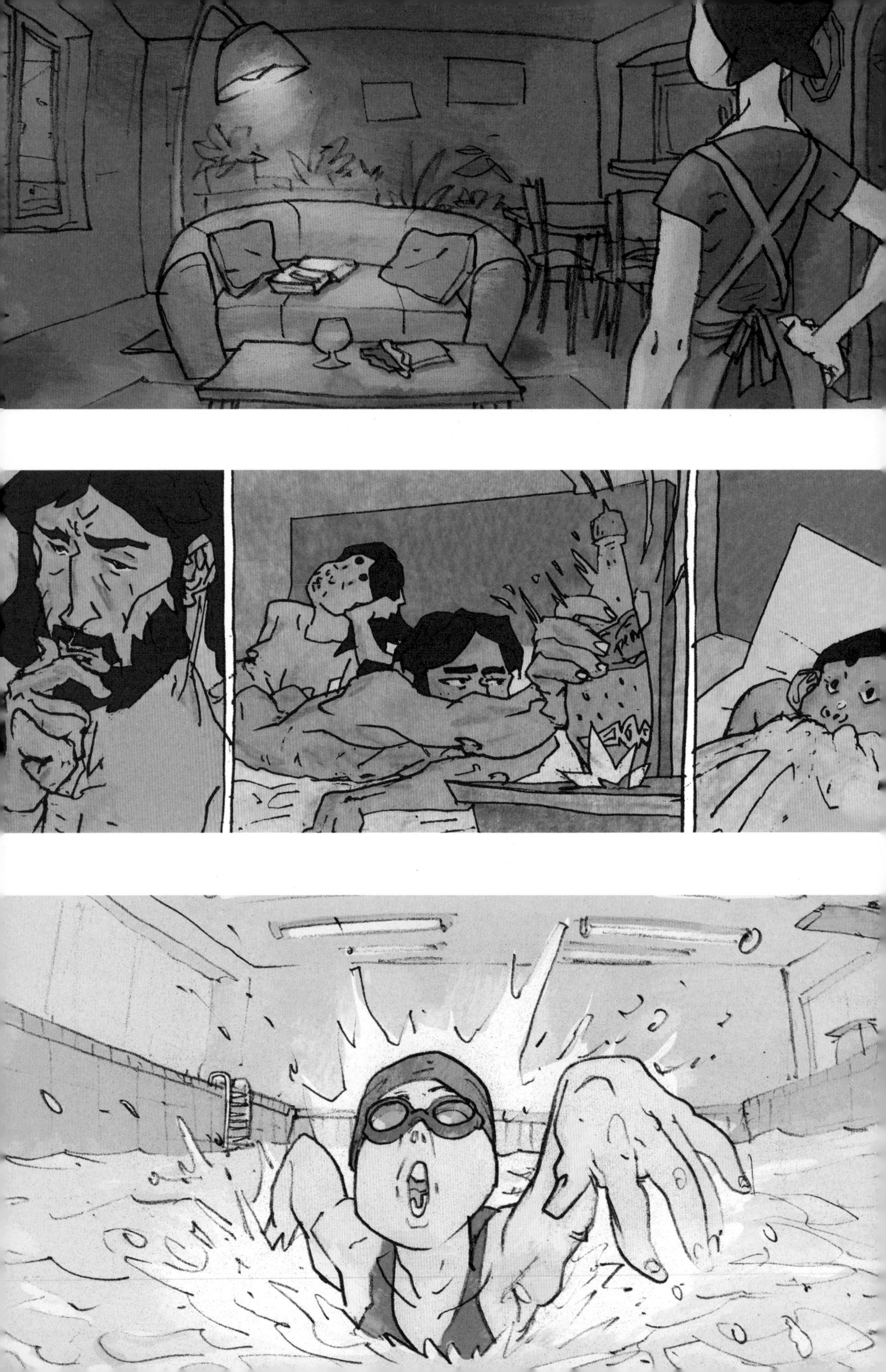

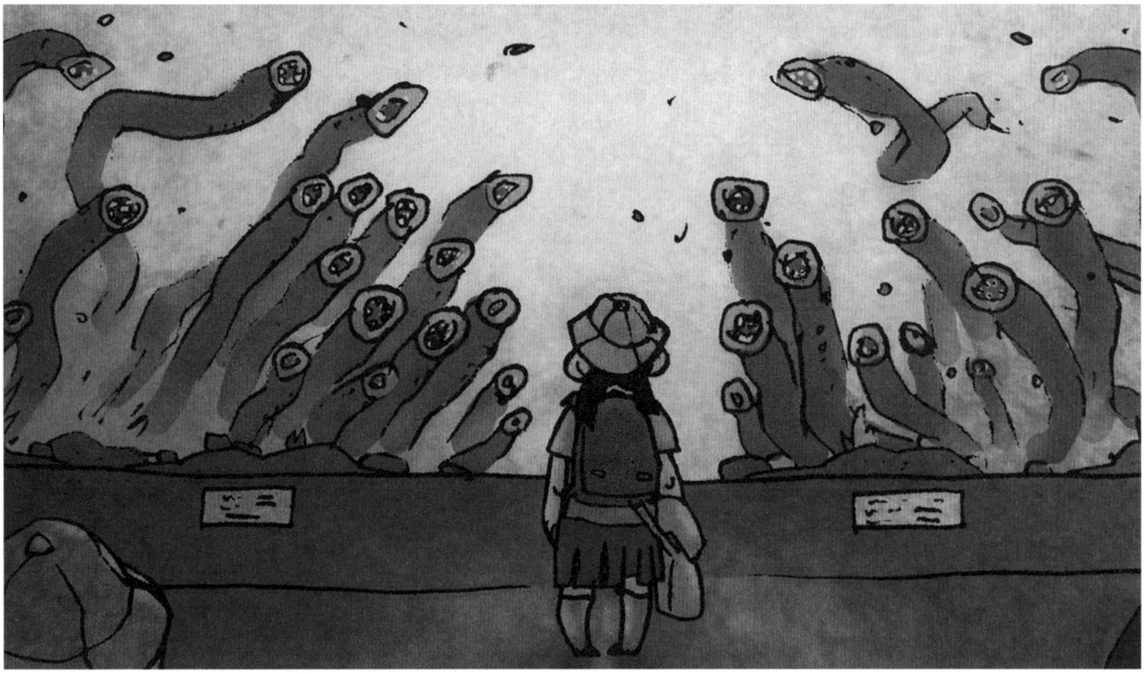

CONTENTS

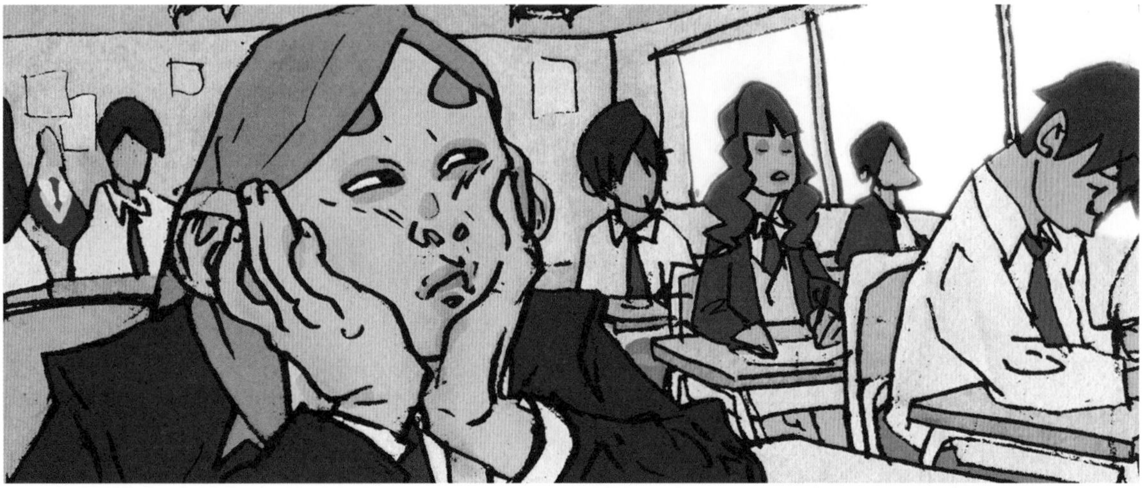

SCHEHERAZADE

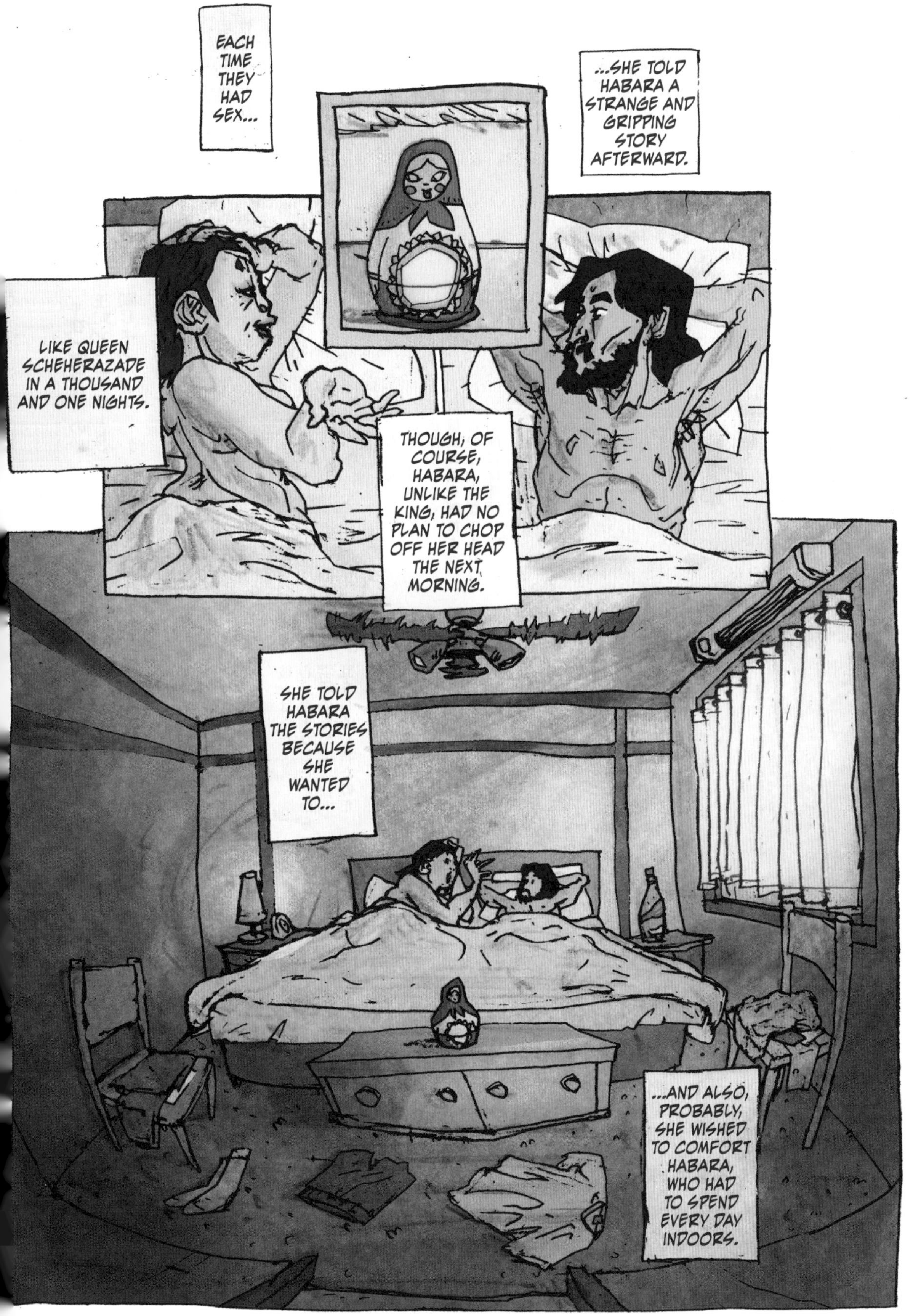
EACH TIME THEY HAD SEX...
...SHE TOLD HABARA A STRANGE AND GRIPPING STORY AFTERWARD.
LIKE QUEEN SCHEHERAZADE IN A THOUSAND AND ONE NIGHTS.
THOUGH, OF COURSE, HABARA, UNLIKE THE KING, HAD NO PLAN TO CHOP OFF HER HEAD THE NEXT MORNING.
SHE TOLD HABARA THE STORIES BECAUSE SHE WANTED TO...
...AND ALSO, PROBABLY, SHE WISHED TO COMFORT HABARA, WHO HAD TO SPEND EVERY DAY INDOORS.

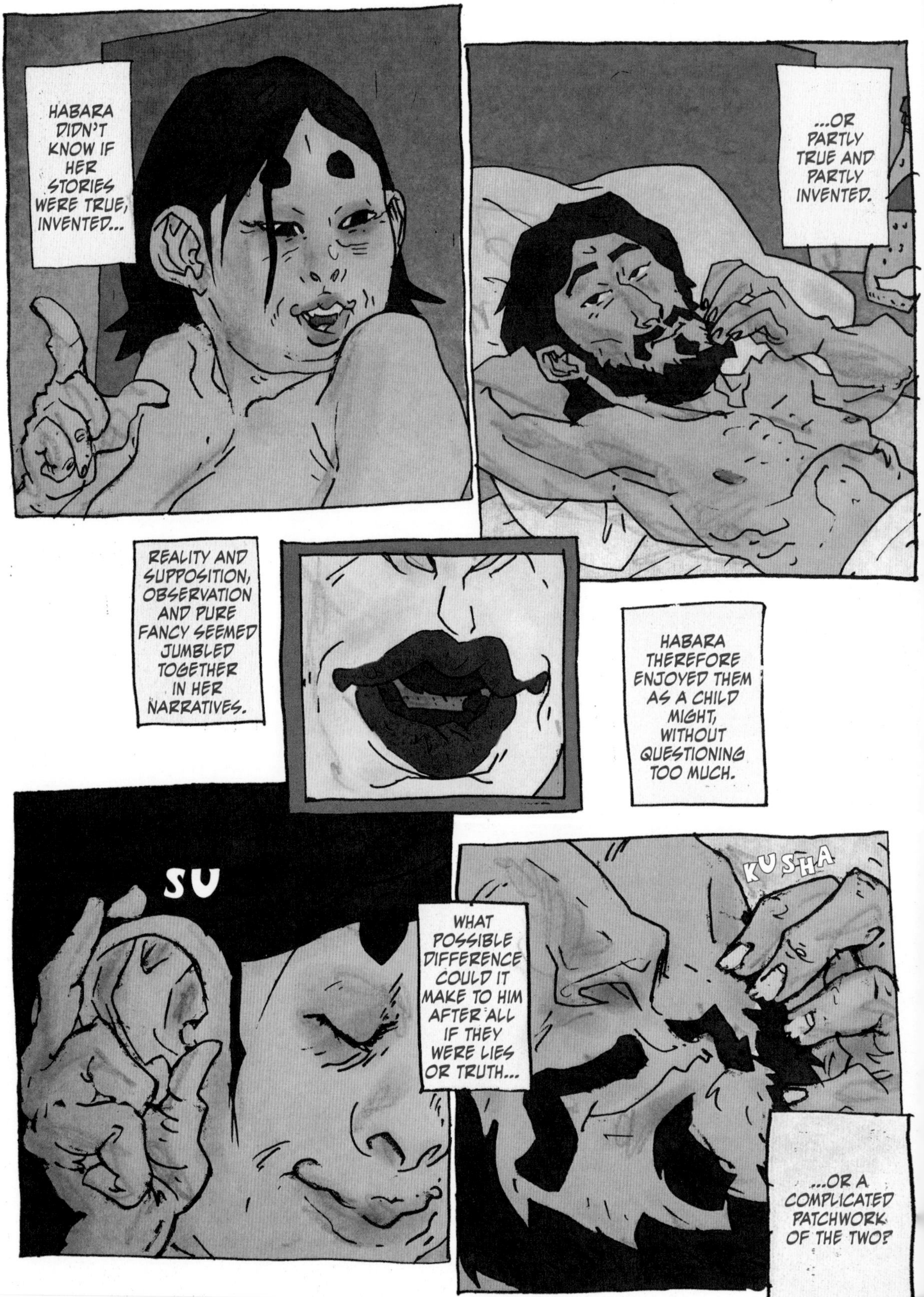
HABARA DIDN'T KNOW IF HER STORIES WERE TRUE, INVENTED...
...OR PARTLY TRUE AND PARTLY INVENTED.
REALITY AND SUPPOSITION, OBSERVATION AND PURE FANCY SEEMED JUMBLED TOGETHER IN HER NARRATIVES.
HABARA THEREFORE ENJOYED THEM AS A CHILD MIGHT, WITHOUT QUESTIONING TOO MUCH.
SU
WHAT POSSIBLE DIFFERENCE COULD IT MAKE TO HIM AFTER ALL IF THEY WERE LIES OR TRUTH...
KUSHA
...OR A COMPLICATED PATCHWORK OF THE TWO?

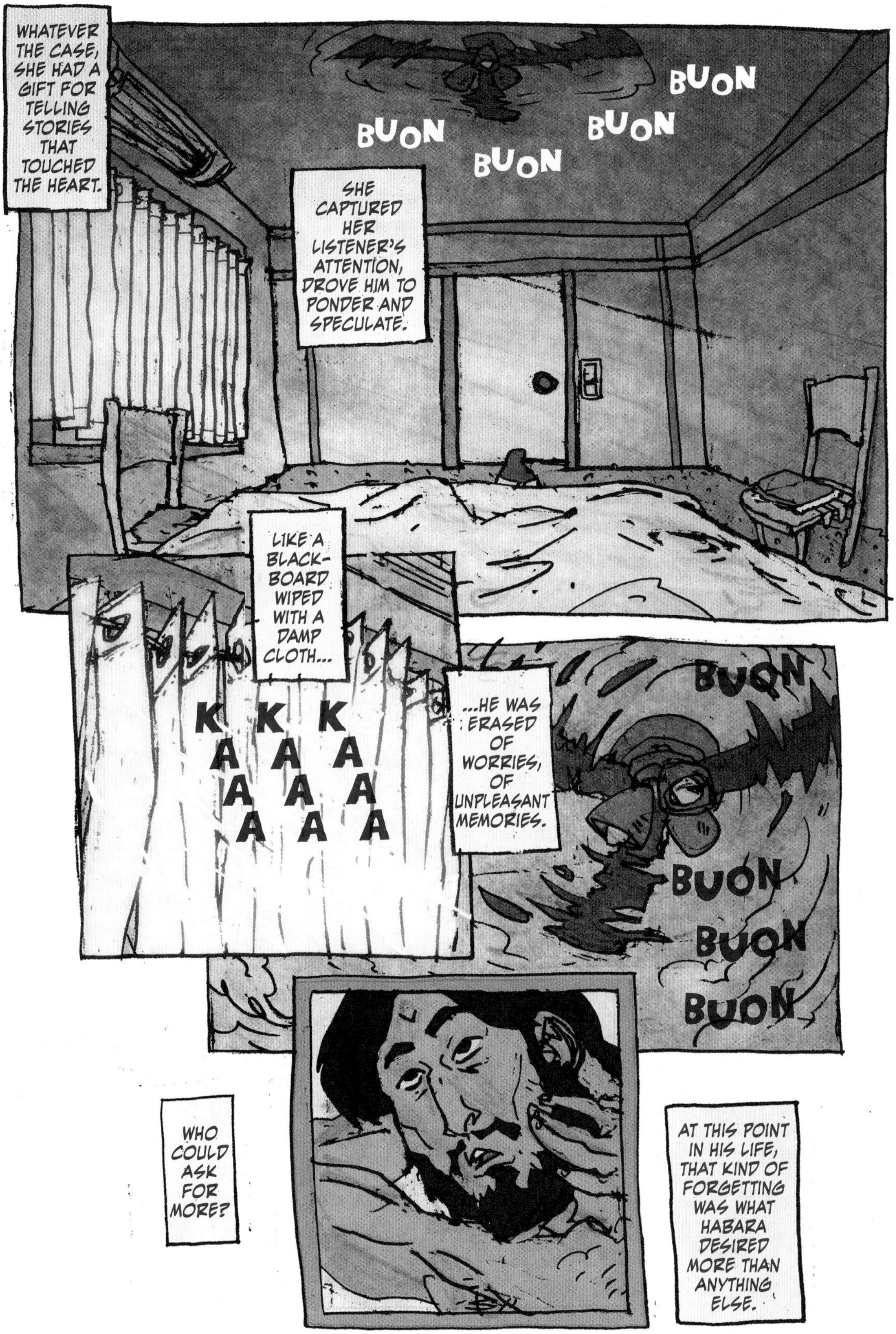

WHATEVER THE CASE, SHE HAD A GIFT FOR TELLING STORIES THAT TOUCHED THE HEART.
BUON
BUON
BUON
BUON
SHE CAPTURED HER LISTENER'S ATTENTION, DROVE HIM TO PONDER AND SPECULATE.
LIKE A BLACK-BOARD WIPED WITH A DAMP CLOTH...
KKK AAAAAAAAA
...HE WAS ERASED OF WORRIES, OF UNPLEASANT MEMORIES.
BUON
BUON
BUON
BUON
WHO COULD ASK FOR MORE?
AT THIS POINT IN HIS LIFE, THAT KIND OF FORGETTING WAS WHAT HABARA DESIRED MORE THAN ANYTHING ELSE.

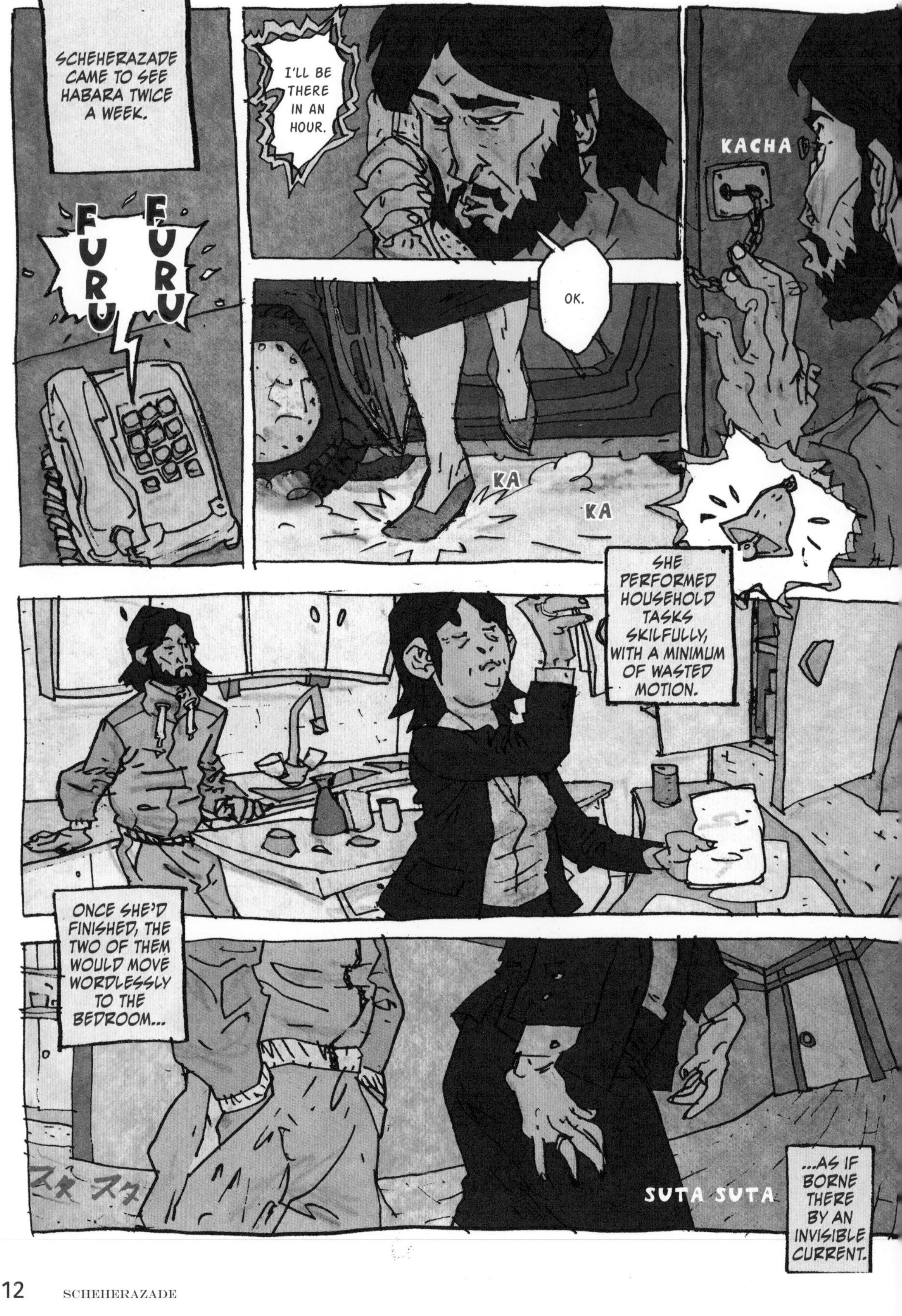
SCHEHERAZADE CAME TO SEE HABARA TWICE A WEEK.
I'LL BE THERE IN AN HOUR.
KACHA
FURU FURU
OK.
KA
KA
SHE PERFORMED HOUSEHOLD TASKS SKILFULLY, WITH A MINIMUM OF WASTED MOTION.
ONCE SHE'D FINISHED, THE TWO OF THEM WOULD MOVE WORDLESSLY TO THE BEDROOM...
スタ スタ
SUTA SUTA
...AS IF BORNE THERE BY AN INVISIBLE CURRENT.

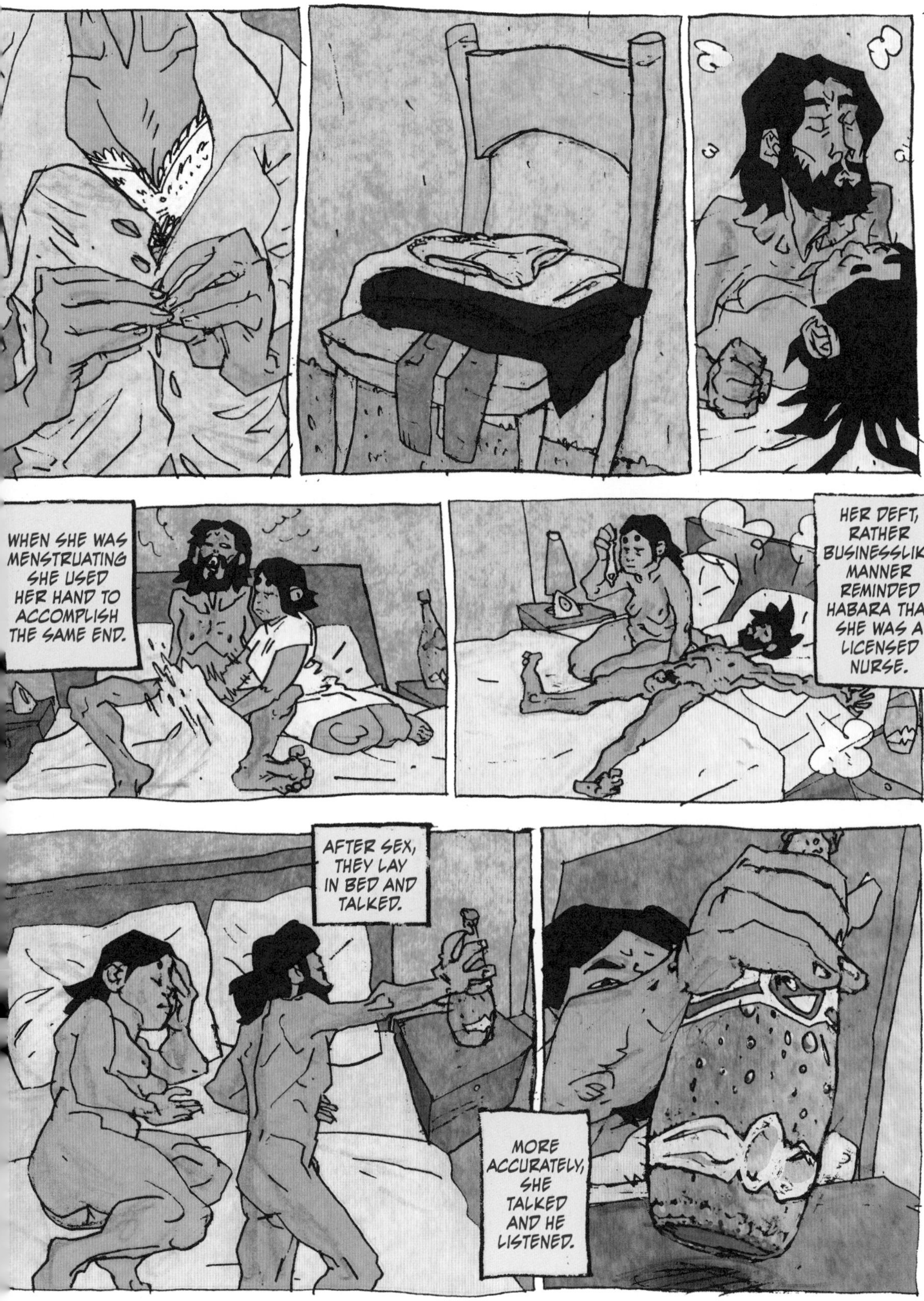

WHEN SHE WAS MENSTRUATING SHE USED HER HAND TO ACCOMPLISH THE SAME END.
HER DEFT, RATHER BUSINESSLIKE MANNER REMINDED HABARA THAT SHE WAS A LICENSED NURSE.
AFTER SEX, THEY LAY IN BED AND TALKED.
MORE ACCURATELY, SHE TALKED AND HE LISTENED.

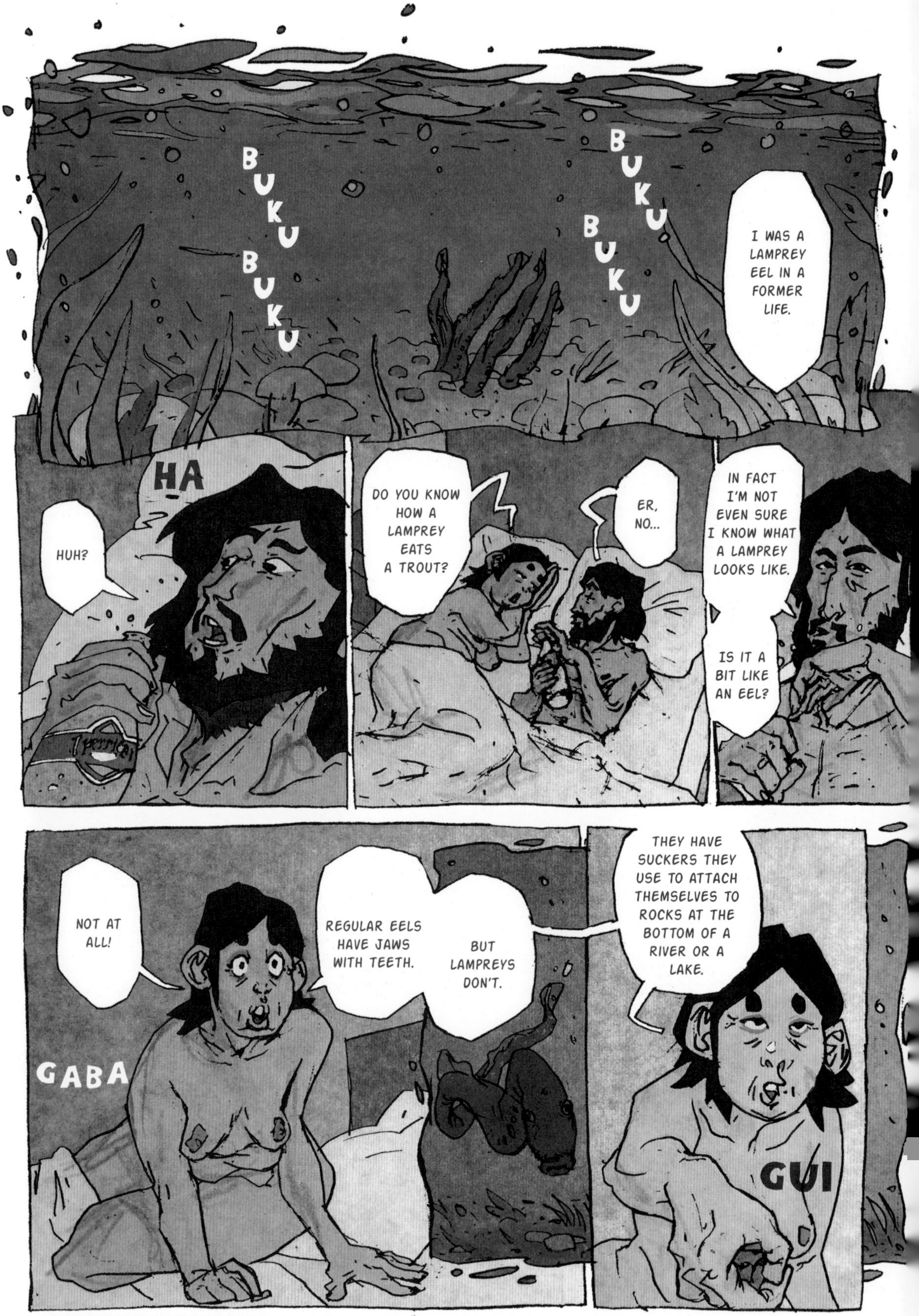
BUKU BUKU
BUKU BUKU
I WAS A LAMPREY EEL IN A FORMER LIFE.
HA
HUH?
DO YOU KNOW HOW A LAMPREY EATS A TROUT?
ER, NO...
IN FACT I'M NOT EVEN SURE I KNOW WHAT A LAMPREY LOOKS LIKE.
IS IT A BIT LIKE AN EEL?
NOT AT ALL!
GABA
REGULAR EELS HAVE JAWS WITH TEETH.
BUT LAMPREYS DON'T.
THEY HAVE SUCKERS THEY USE TO ATTACH THEMSELVES TO ROCKS AT THE BOTTOM OF A RIVER OR A LAKE.
GUI

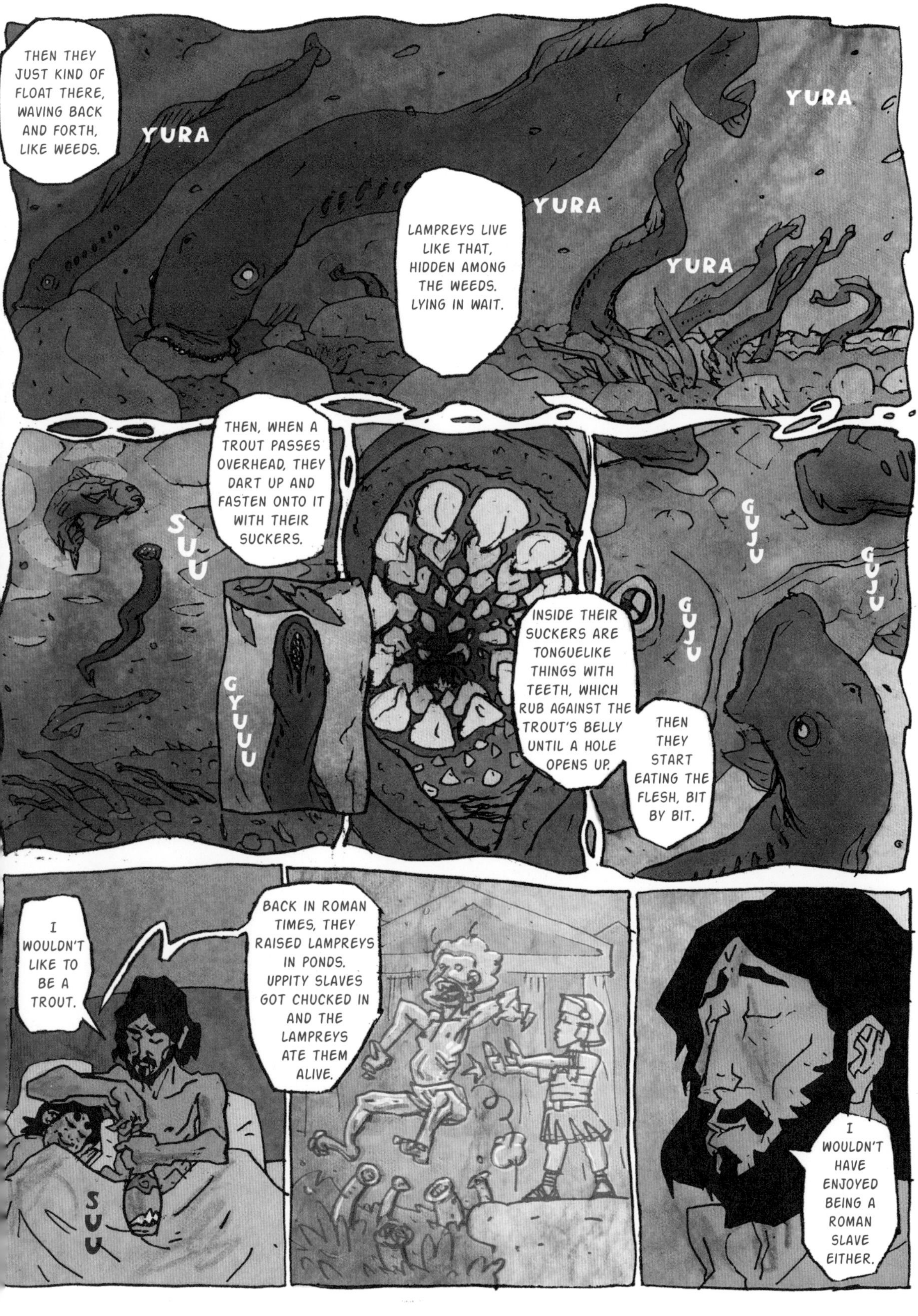
THEN THEY JUST KIND OF FLOAT THERE, WAVING BACK AND FORTH, LIKE WEEDS.
YURA
YURA
YURA
LAMPREYS LIVE LIKE THAT, HIDDEN AMONG THE WEEDS. LYING IN WAIT.
YURA
THEN, WHEN A TROUT PASSES OVERHEAD, THEY DART UP AND FASTEN ONTO IT WITH THEIR SUCKERS.
SUU
GYUUU
INSIDE THEIR SUCKERS ARE TONGUELIKE THINGS WITH TEETH, WHICH RUB AGAINST THE TROUT'S BELLY UNTIL A HOLE OPENS UP.
GUJU
GUJU
GUJU
THEN THEY START EATING THE FLESH, BIT BY BIT.
I WOULDN'T LIKE TO BE A TROUT.
SUU
BACK IN ROMAN TIMES, THEY RAISED LAMPREYS IN PONDS. UPPITY SLAVES GOT CHUCKED IN AND THE LAMPREYS ATE THEM ALIVE.
I WOULDN'T HAVE ENJOYED BEING A ROMAN SLAVE EITHER.

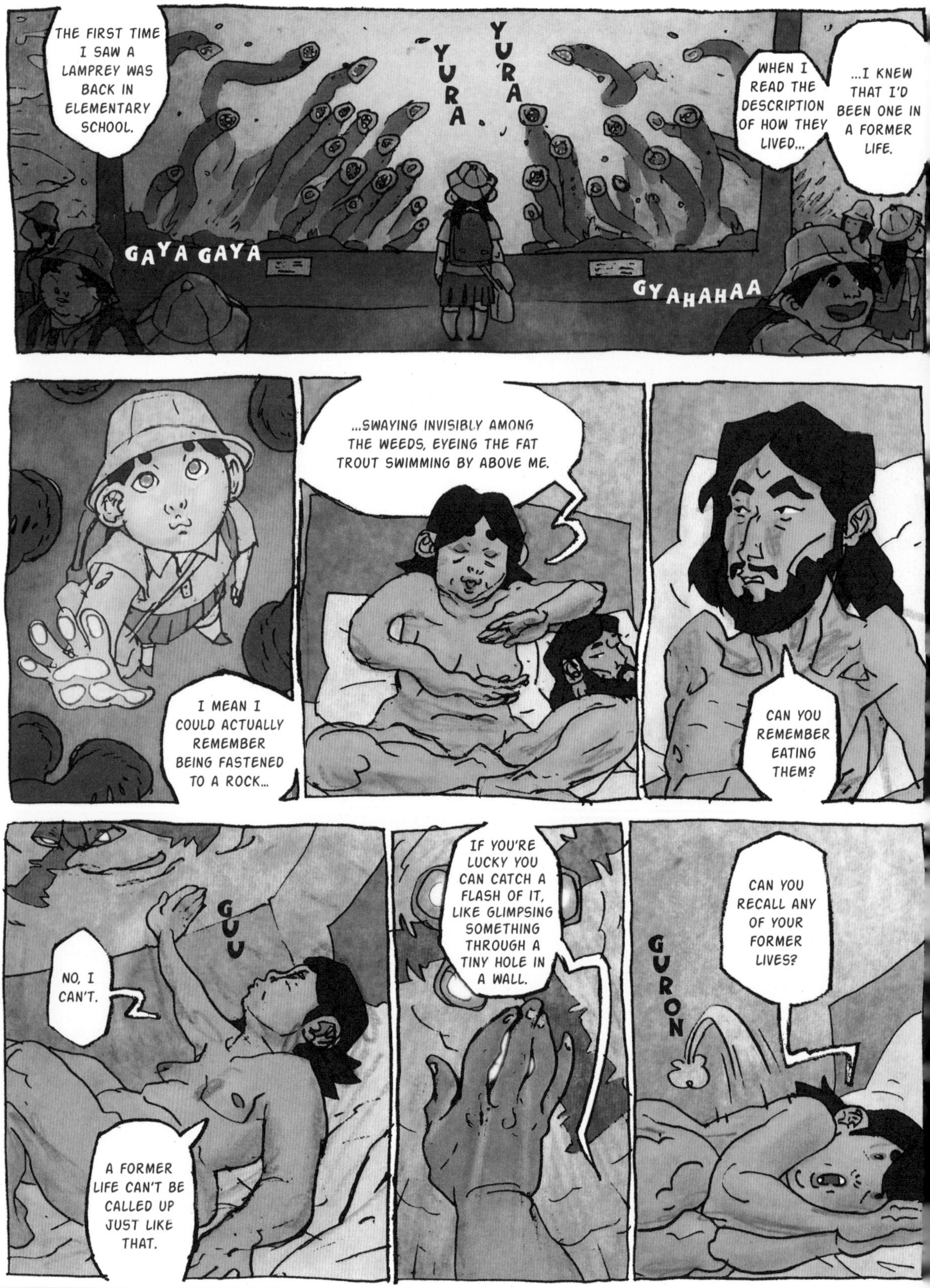
THE FIRST TIME I SAW A LAMPREY WAS BACK IN ELEMENTARY SCHOOL.
YURA YURA
WHEN I READ THE DESCRIPTION OF HOW THEY LIVED...
...I KNEW THAT I'D BEEN ONE IN A FORMER LIFE.
GAYA GAYA
GYAHAHAA
I MEAN I COULD ACTUALLY REMEMBER BEING FASTENED TO A ROCK...
...SWAYING INVISIBLY AMONG THE WEEDS, EYEING THE FAT TROUT SWIMMING BY ABOVE ME.
CAN YOU REMEMBER EATING THEM?
GUU
NO, I CAN'T.
A FORMER LIFE CAN'T BE CALLED UP JUST LIKE THAT.
IF YOU'RE LUCKY YOU CAN CATCH A FLASH OF IT, LIKE GLIMPSING SOMETHING THROUGH A TINY HOLE IN A WALL.
GURON
CAN YOU RECALL ANY OF YOUR FORMER LIVES?

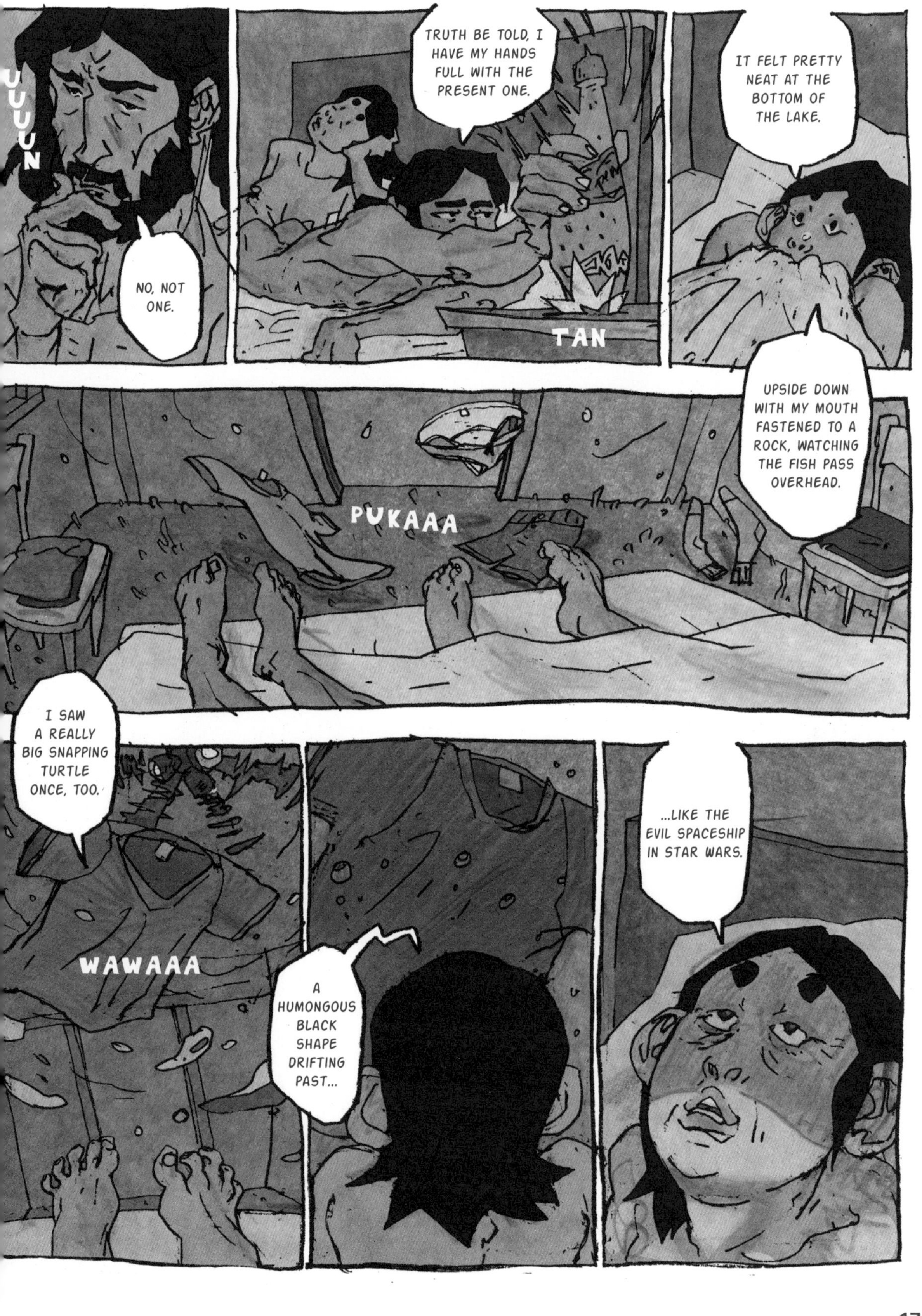
UUUUN
NO, NOT ONE.
TRUTH BE TOLD, I HAVE MY HANDS FULL WITH THE PRESENT ONE.
TAN
IT FELT PRETTY NEAT AT THE BOTTOM OF THE LAKE.
UPSIDE DOWN WITH MY MOUTH FASTENED TO A ROCK, WATCHING THE FISH PASS OVERHEAD.
PUKAAA
I SAW A REALLY BIG SNAPPING TURTLE ONCE, TOO.
WAWAAA
A HUMONGOUS BLACK SHAPE DRIFTING PAST...
...LIKE THE EVIL SPACESHIP IN STAR WARS.

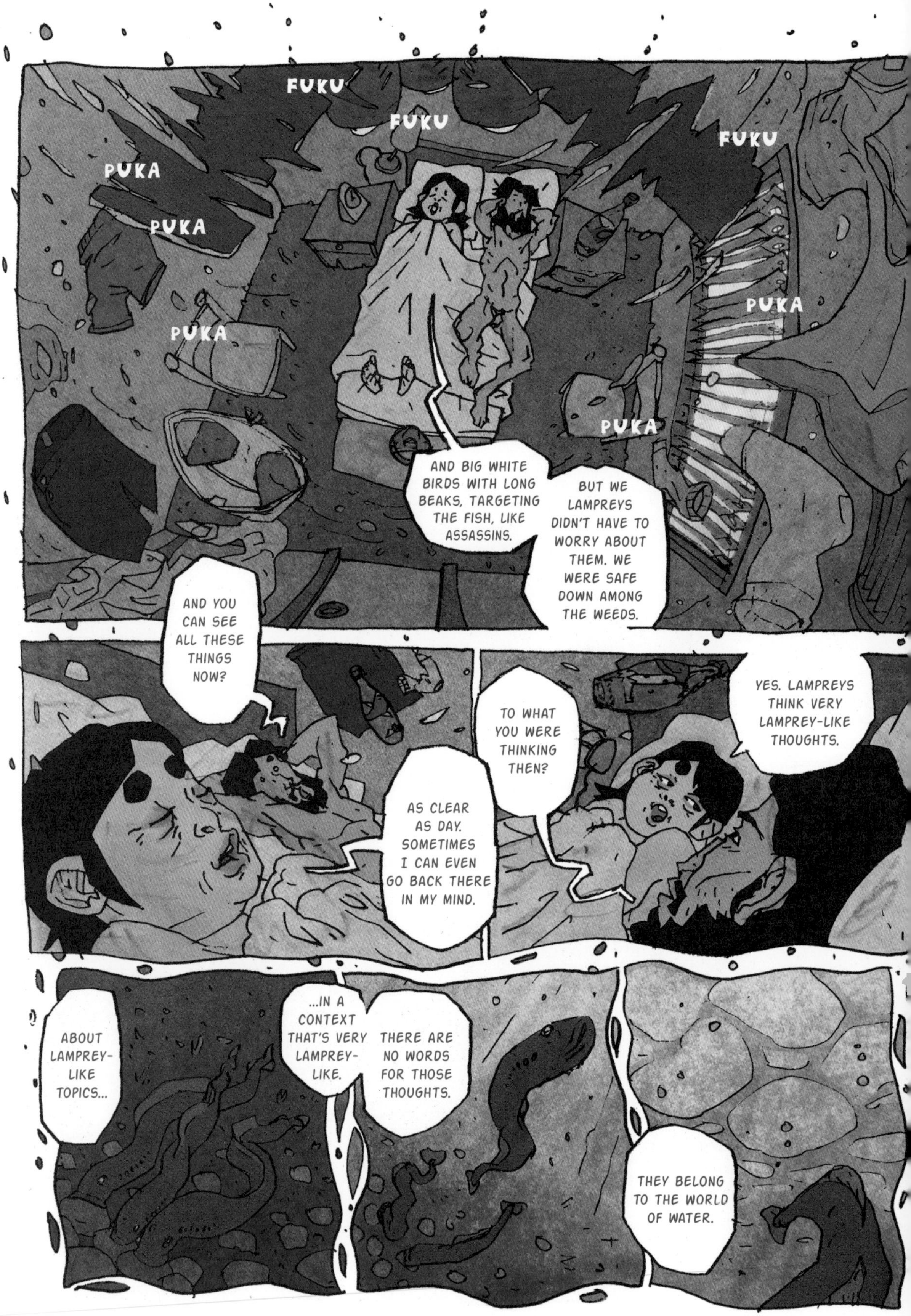
FUKU
FUKU
FUKU
PUKA
PUKA
PUKA
PUKA
PUKA
AND BIG WHITE BIRDS WITH LONG BEAKS, TARGETING THE FISH, LIKE ASSASSINS.
BUT WE LAMPREYS DIDN'T HAVE TO WORRY ABOUT THEM. WE WERE SAFE DOWN AMONG THE WEEDS.
AND YOU CAN SEE ALL THESE THINGS NOW?
AS CLEAR AS DAY. SOMETIMES I CAN EVEN GO BACK THERE IN MY MIND.
TO WHAT YOU WERE THINKING THEN?
YES. LAMPREYS THINK VERY LAMPREY-LIKE THOUGHTS.
ABOUT LAMPREY-LIKE TOPICS...
...IN A CONTEXT THAT'S VERY LAMPREY-LIKE.
THERE ARE NO WORDS FOR THOSE THOUGHTS.
THEY BELONG TO THE WORLD OF WATER.

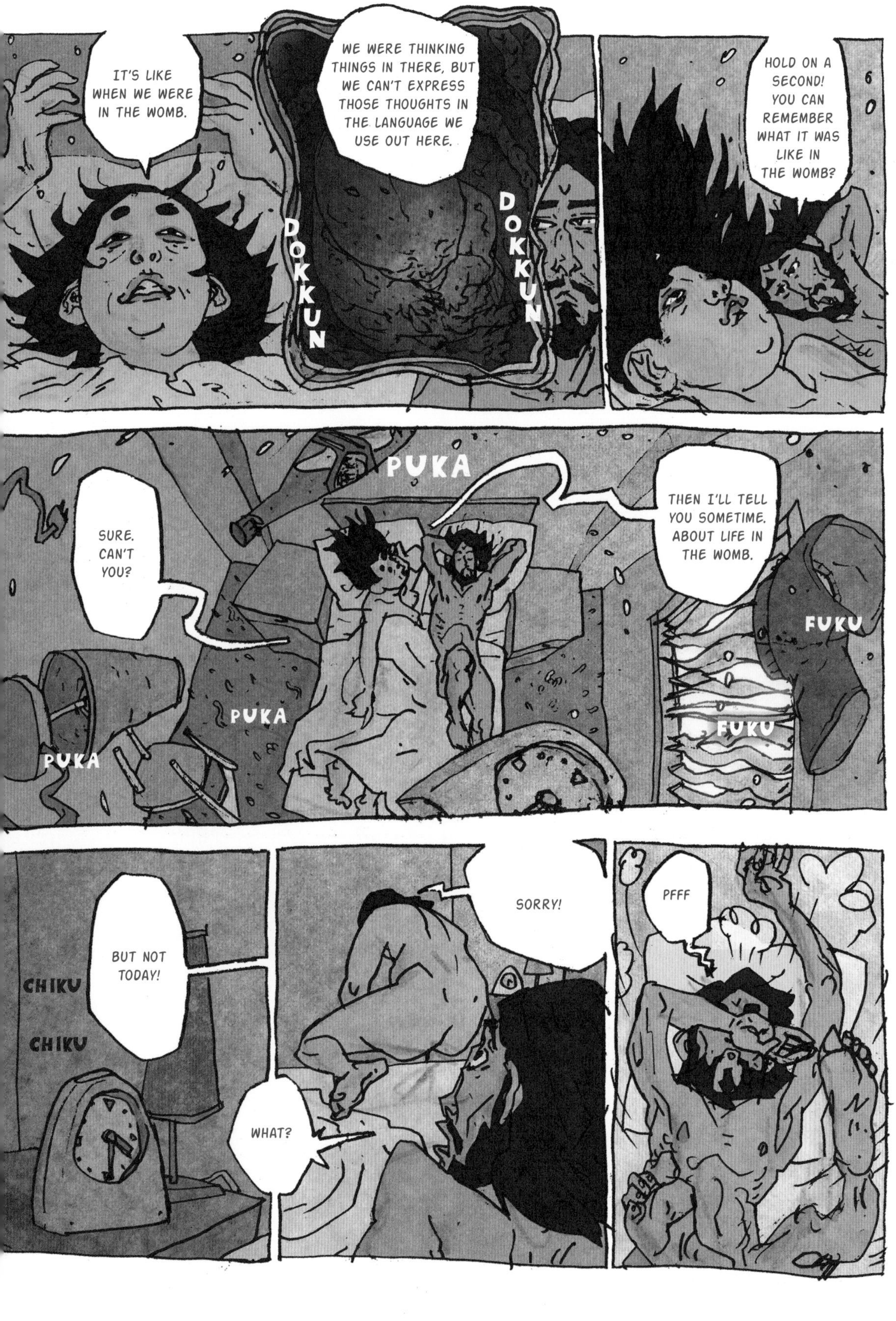
IT'S LIKE WHEN WE WERE IN THE WOMB.
WE WERE THINKING THINGS IN THERE, BUT WE CAN'T EXPRESS THOSE THOUGHTS IN THE LANGUAGE WE USE OUT HERE.
DOKKUN
DOKKUN
HOLD ON A SECOND! YOU CAN REMEMBER WHAT IT WAS LIKE IN THE WOMB?
PUKA
SURE. CAN'T YOU?
THEN I'LL TELL YOU SOMETIME. ABOUT LIFE IN THE WOMB.
FUKU
PUKA
PUKA
FUKU
CHIKU
CHIKU
BUT NOT TODAY!
SORRY!
WHAT?
PFFF

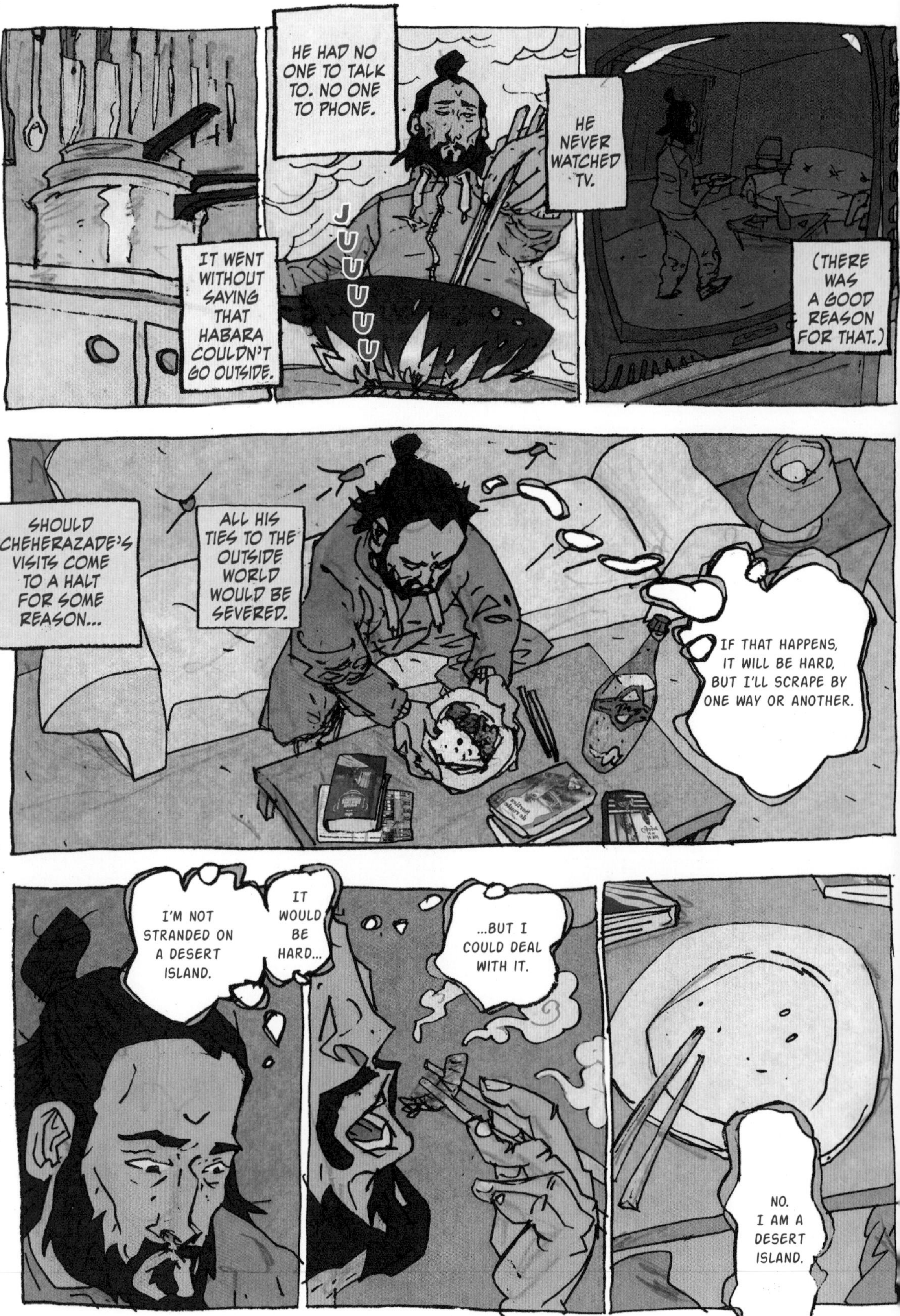
HE HAD NO ONE TO TALK TO. NO ONE TO PHONE.
IT WENT WITHOUT SAYING THAT HABARA COULDN'T GO OUTSIDE.
JUUUUU
HE NEVER WATCHED TV.
(THERE WAS A GOOD REASON FOR THAT.)
SHOULD SCHEHERAZADE'S VISITS COME TO A HALT FOR SOME REASON...
ALL HIS TIES TO THE OUTSIDE WORLD WOULD BE SEVERED.
IF THAT HAPPENS, IT WILL BE HARD, BUT I'LL SCRAPE BY ONE WAY OR ANOTHER.
I'M NOT STRANDED ON A DESERT ISLAND.
IT WOULD BE HARD...
...BUT I COULD DEAL WITH IT.
NO. I AM A DESERT ISLAND.

HE'D MET CHEHERAZADE OR THE FIRST TIME FOUR MONTHS EARLIER.

HE'D BEEN TAKEN TO THIS HOUSE NORTH OF TOKYO, AND SHE'D BEEN ASSIGNED AS HIS "SUPPORT LIAISON."

BURORORORORORO

SINCE HE COULDN'T GO OUTSIDE, HER ROLE WAS TO BUY FOOD AND OTHER ITEMS HE REQUIRED AND BRING THEM TO THE HOUSE.

SUSU SUSU

SHE ALSO TRACKED DOWN THE BOOKS AND MAGAZINES HE WISHED TO READ AND THE CDS HE WANTED TO LISTEN TO.

ART BLAKEY & THE JAZZ MESSENGERS A NIGHT IN TUNISIA

SHE ALSO CHOSE AN ASSORTMENT OF DVDS, THOUGH HE HAD A HARD TIME ACCEPTING HER CRITERIA FOR SELECTION.

MONKEY

NUMBER 5

HABARA COULDN'T TELL IF THE EVERYDAY SERVICES SHE PERFORMED FOR HIM STEMMED FROM AFFECTION, OR IF THEY WERE JUST PART OF HER ASSIGNMENT.

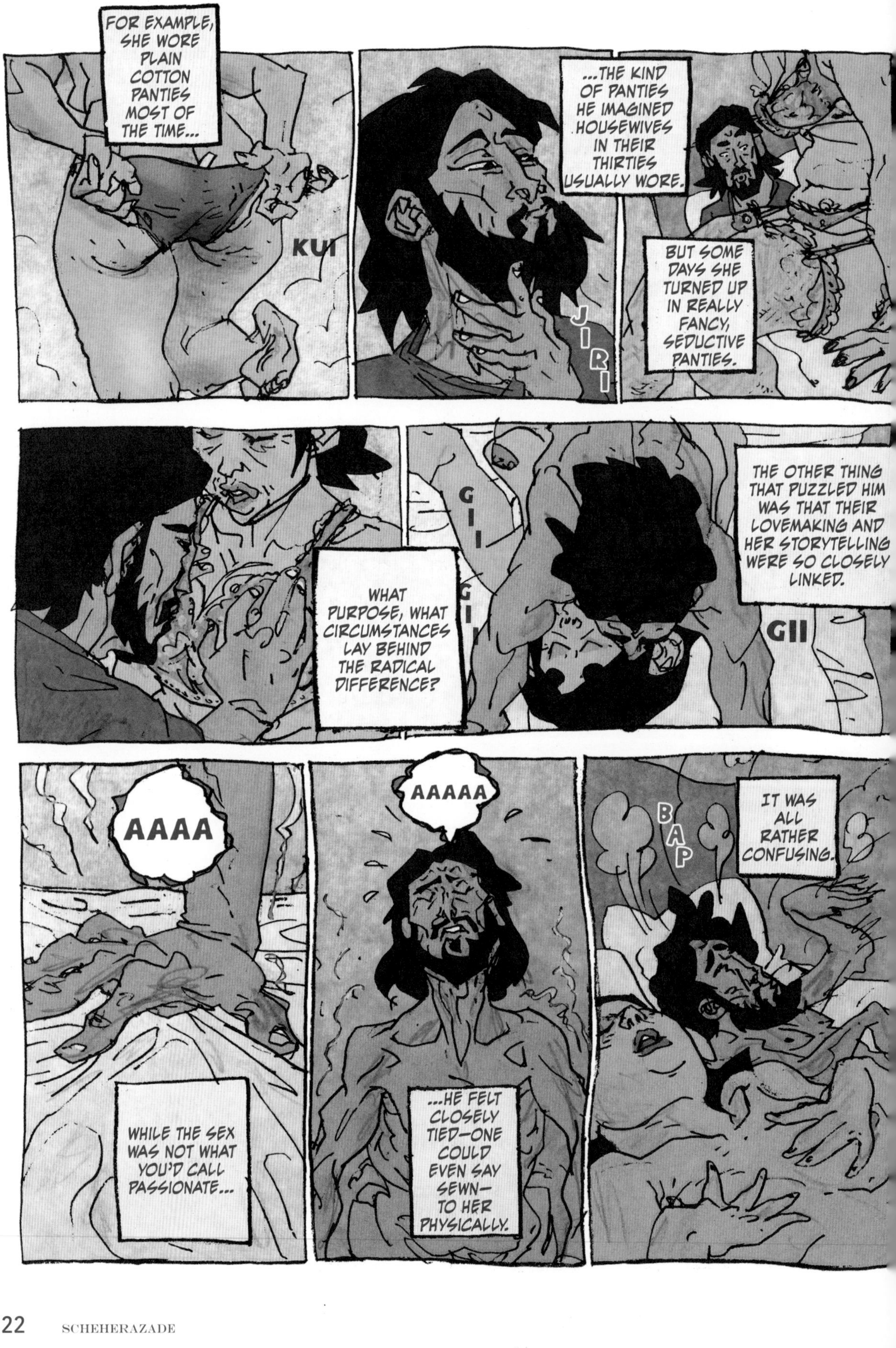

FOR EXAMPLE, SHE WORE PLAIN COTTON PANTIES MOST OF THE TIME...
KUI
...THE KIND OF PANTIES HE IMAGINED HOUSEWIVES IN THEIR THIRTIES USUALLY WORE.
JIRI
BUT SOME DAYS SHE TURNED UP IN REALLY FANCY, SEDUCTIVE PANTIES.
WHAT PURPOSE, WHAT CIRCUMSTANCES LAY BEHIND THE RADICAL DIFFERENCE?
GII
GII
THE OTHER THING THAT PUZZLED HIM WAS THAT THEIR LOVEMAKING AND HER STORYTELLING WERE SO CLOSELY LINKED.
GII
AAAA
WHILE THE SEX WAS NOT WHAT YOU'D CALL PASSIONATE...
AAAAA
...HE FELT CLOSELY TIED—ONE COULD EVEN SAY SEWN—TO HER PHYSICALLY.
BAP
IT WAS ALL RATHER CONFUSING.

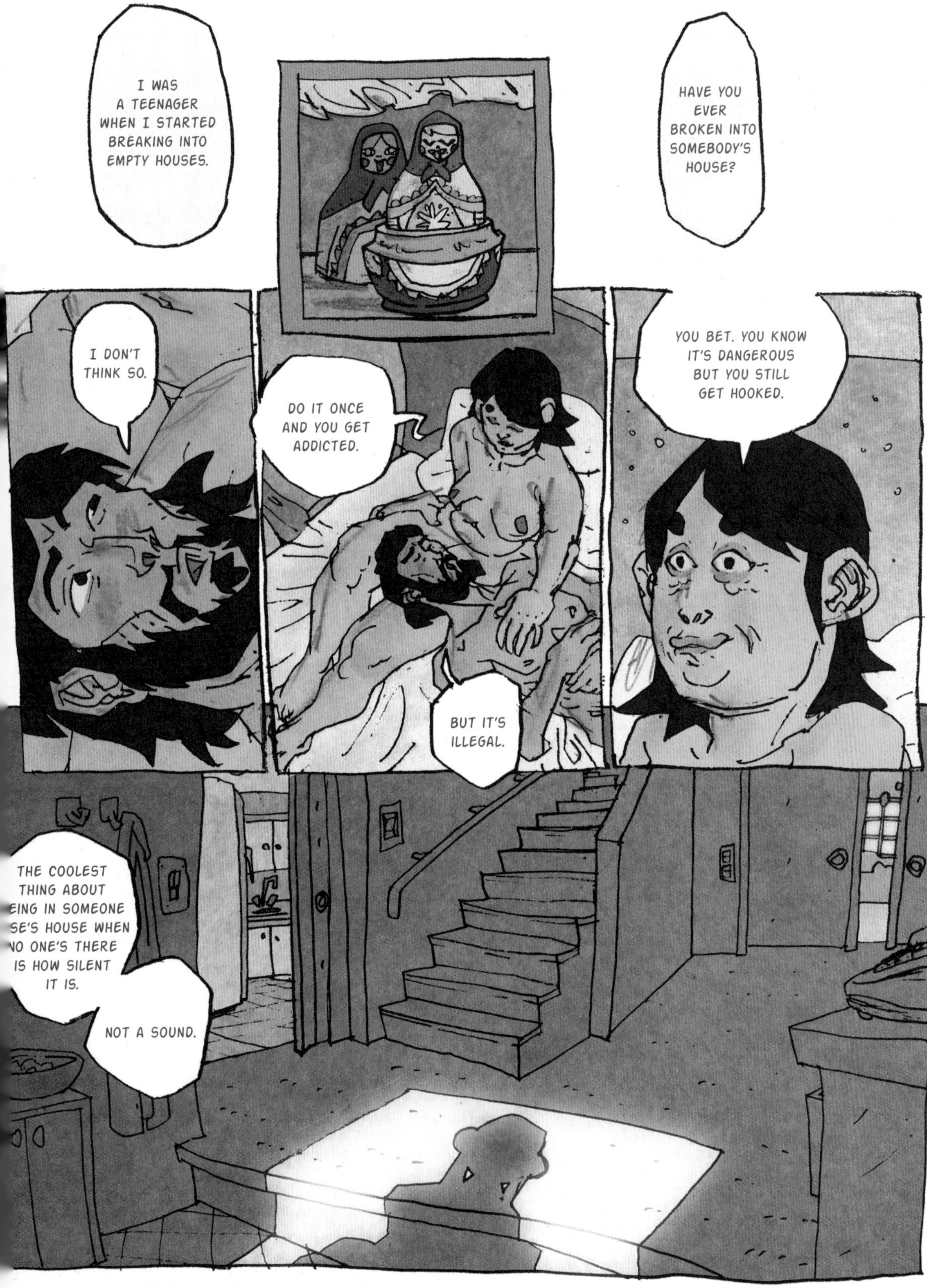
I WAS A TEENAGER WHEN I STARTED BREAKING INTO EMPTY HOUSES.
HAVE YOU EVER BROKEN INTO SOMEBODY'S HOUSE?
I DON'T THINK SO.
DO IT ONCE AND YOU GET ADDICTED.
BUT IT'S ILLEGAL.
YOU BET. YOU KNOW IT'S DANGEROUS BUT YOU STILL GET HOOKED.
THE COOLEST THING ABOUT EING IN SOMEONE SE'S HOUSE WHEN NO ONE'S THERE IS HOW SILENT IT IS.
NOT A SOUND.

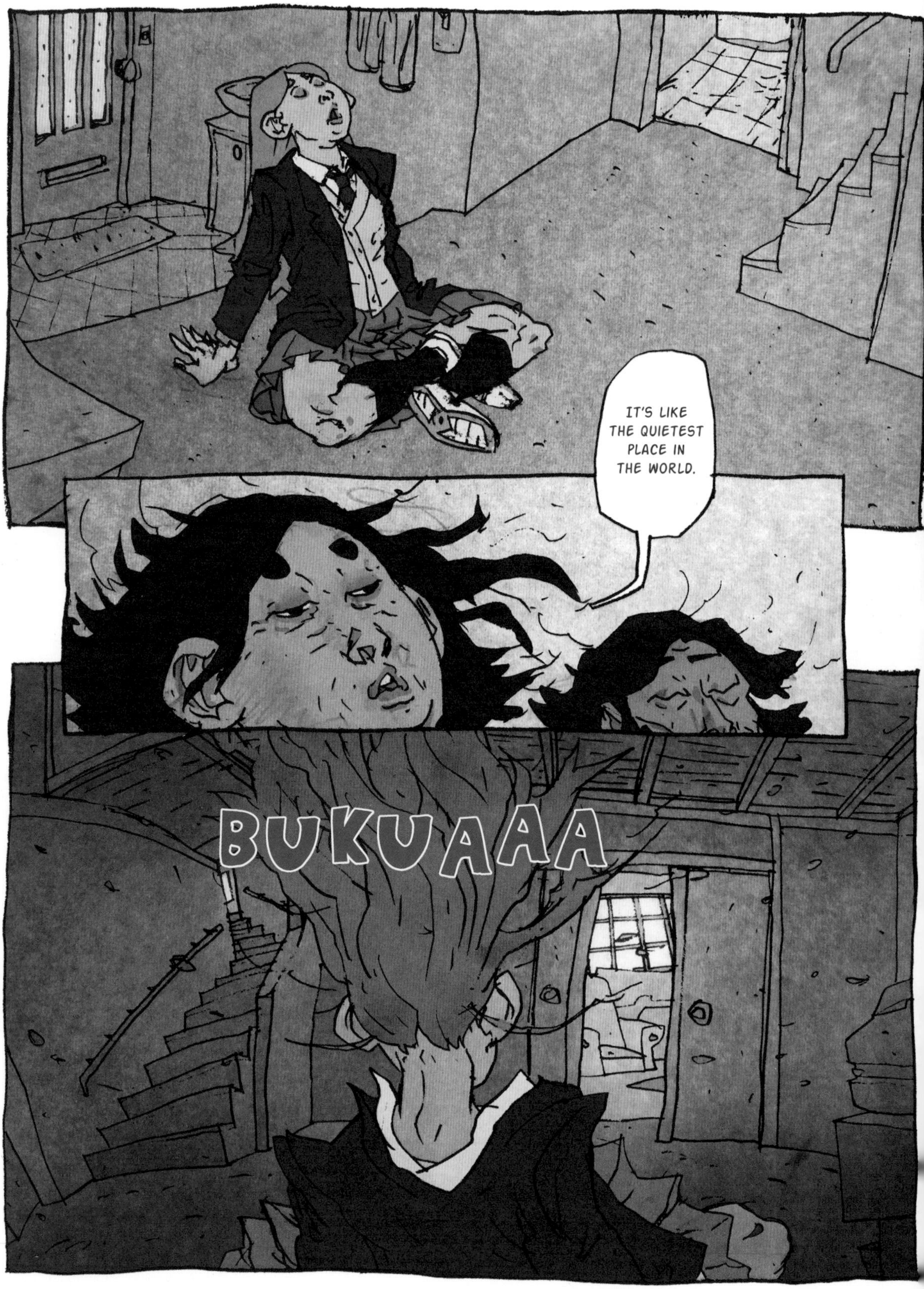
IT'S LIKE THE QUIETEST PLACE IN THE WORLD.
BUKUAAA

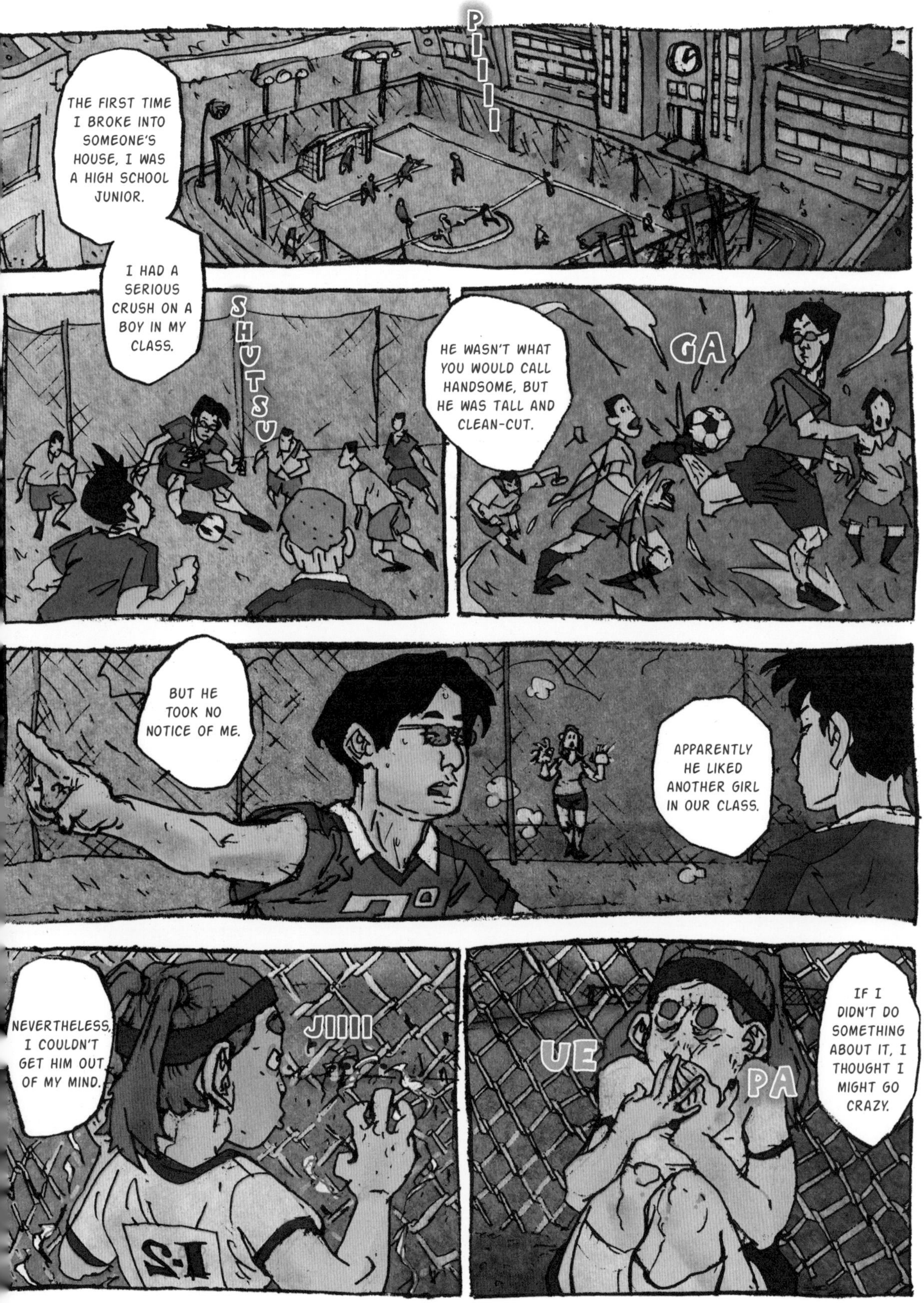
PIIIII
THE FIRST TIME I BROKE INTO SOMEONE'S HOUSE, I WAS A HIGH SCHOOL JUNIOR.
I HAD A SERIOUS CRUSH ON A BOY IN MY CLASS.
SHUTSU
HE WASN'T WHAT YOU WOULD CALL HANDSOME, BUT HE WAS TALL AND CLEAN-CUT.
GA
BUT HE TOOK NO NOTICE OF ME.
APPARENTLY HE LIKED ANOTHER GIRL IN OUR CLASS.
NEVERTHELESS, I COULDN'T GET HIM OUT OF MY MIND.
JIIII
UE
PA
IF I DIDN'T DO SOMETHING ABOUT IT, I THOUGHT I MIGHT GO CRAZY.

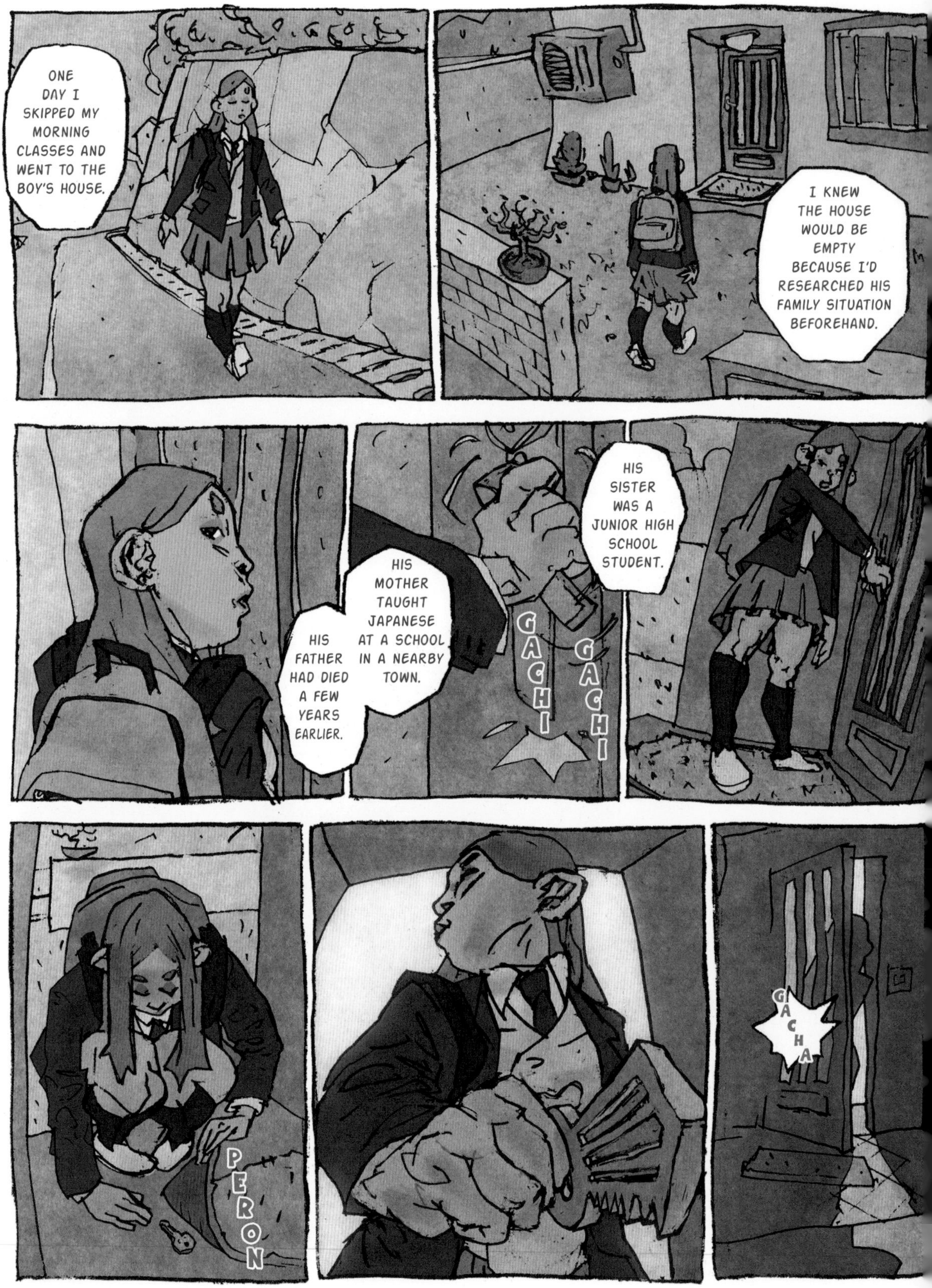
ONE DAY I SKIPPED MY MORNING CLASSES AND WENT TO THE BOY'S HOUSE.
I KNEW THE HOUSE WOULD BE EMPTY BECAUSE I'D RESEARCHED HIS FAMILY SITUATION BEFOREHAND.
HIS FATHER HAD DIED A FEW YEARS EARLIER.
HIS MOTHER TAUGHT JAPANESE AT A SCHOOL IN A NEARBY TOWN.
HIS SISTER WAS A JUNIOR HIGH SCHOOL STUDENT.
GACHI
GACHI
PERON
GACHA

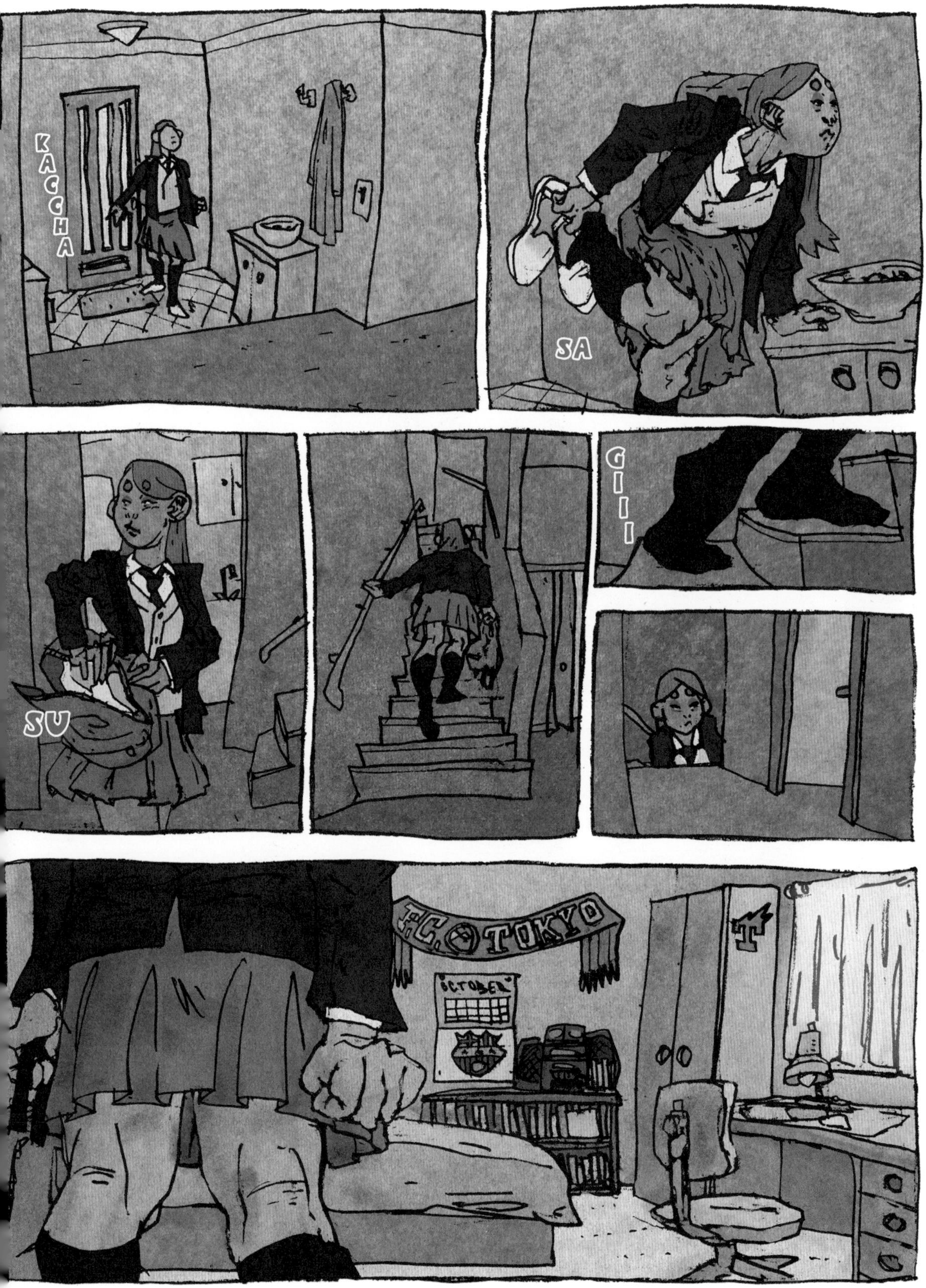
KACCHA
SA
SU
GIIII
F.C. TOKYO
OCTOBER

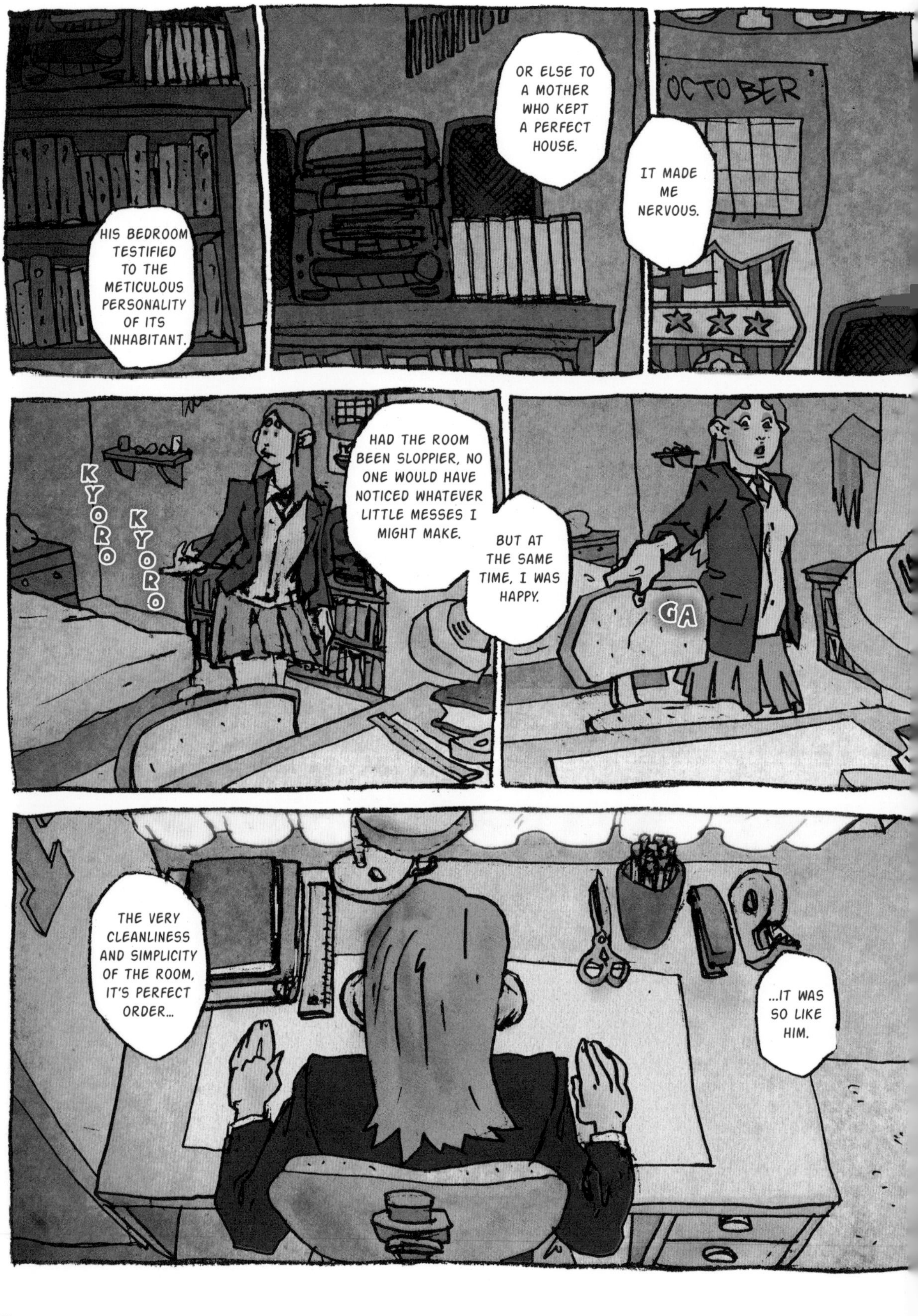
HIS BEDROOM TESTIFIED TO THE METICULOUS PERSONALITY OF ITS INHABITANT.
OR ELSE TO A MOTHER WHO KEPT A PERFECT HOUSE.
OCTOBER
IT MADE ME NERVOUS.
KYORO KYORO
HAD THE ROOM BEEN SLOPPIER, NO ONE WOULD HAVE NOTICED WHATEVER LITTLE MESSES I MIGHT MAKE.
BUT AT THE SAME TIME, I WAS HAPPY.
GA
THE VERY CLEANLINESS AND SIMPLICITY OF THE ROOM, IT'S PERFECT ORDER...
...IT WAS SO LIKE HIM.

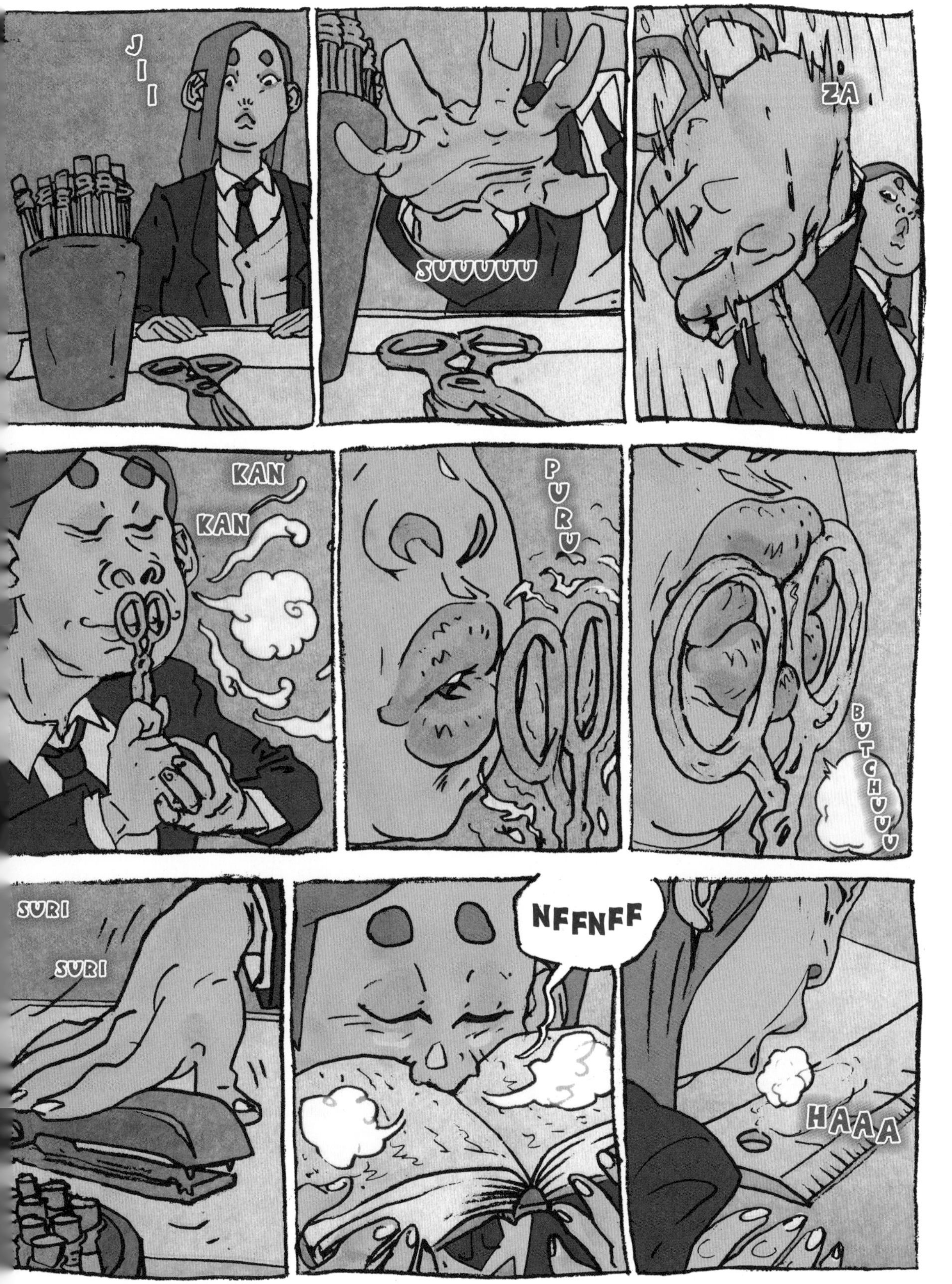
JIII
SUUUUU
ZA
KAN
KAN
PURU
BUTCHUUU
SURI
SURI
NFFNFF
HAAA

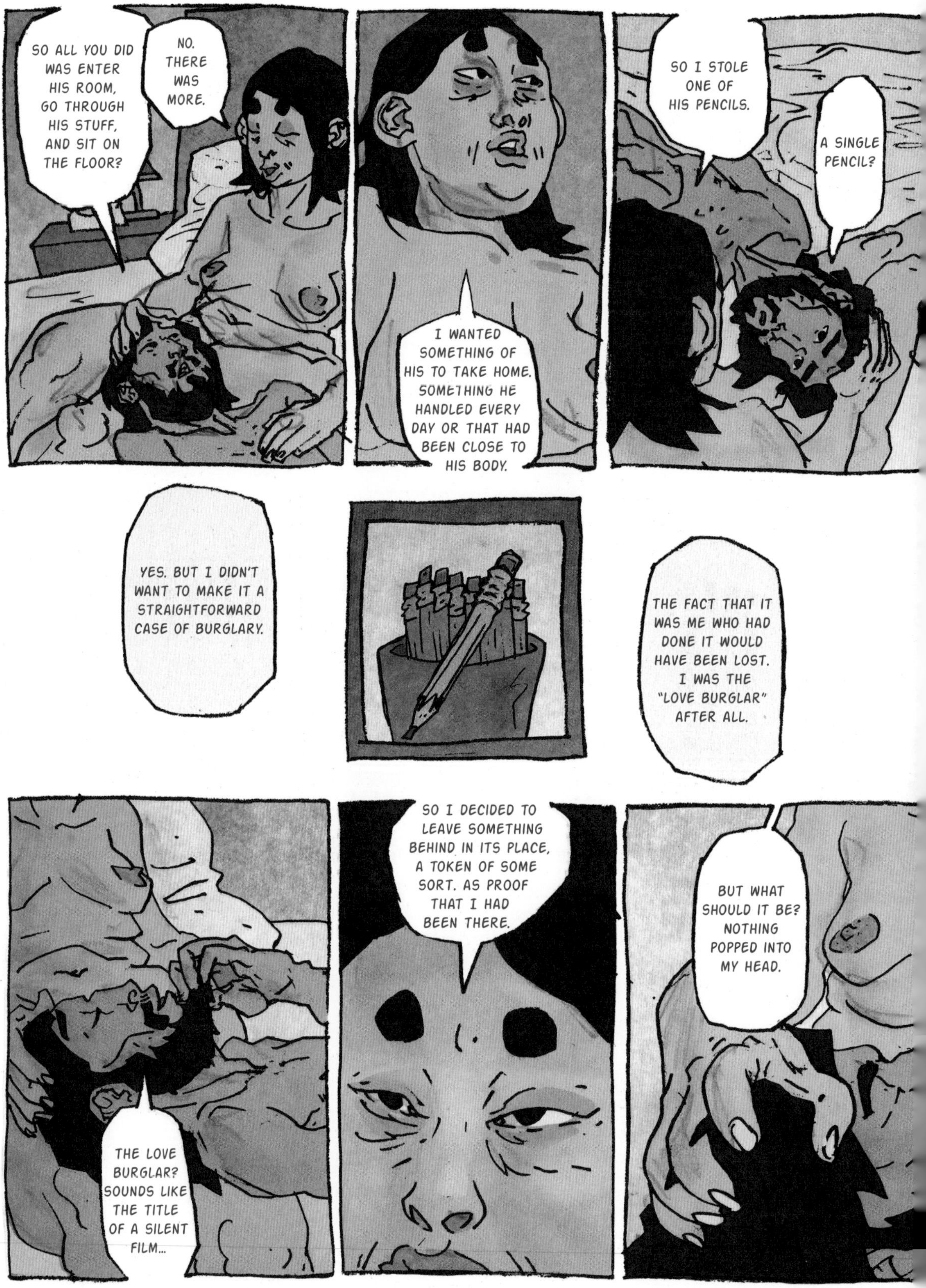
SO ALL YOU DID WAS ENTER HIS ROOM, GO THROUGH HIS STUFF, AND SIT ON THE FLOOR?
NO. THERE WAS MORE.
I WANTED SOMETHING OF HIS TO TAKE HOME. SOMETHING HE HANDLED EVERY DAY OR THAT HAD BEEN CLOSE TO HIS BODY.
SO I STOLE ONE OF HIS PENCILS.
A SINGLE PENCIL?
YES. BUT I DIDN'T WANT TO MAKE IT A STRAIGHTFORWARD CASE OF BURGLARY.
THE FACT THAT IT WAS ME WHO HAD DONE IT WOULD HAVE BEEN LOST. I WAS THE "LOVE BURGLAR" AFTER ALL.
THE LOVE BURGLAR? SOUNDS LIKE THE TITLE OF A SILENT FILM...
SO I DECIDED TO LEAVE SOMETHING BEHIND IN ITS PLACE, A TOKEN OF SOME SORT. AS PROOF THAT I HAD BEEN THERE.
BUT WHAT SHOULD IT BE? NOTHING POPPED INTO MY HEAD.

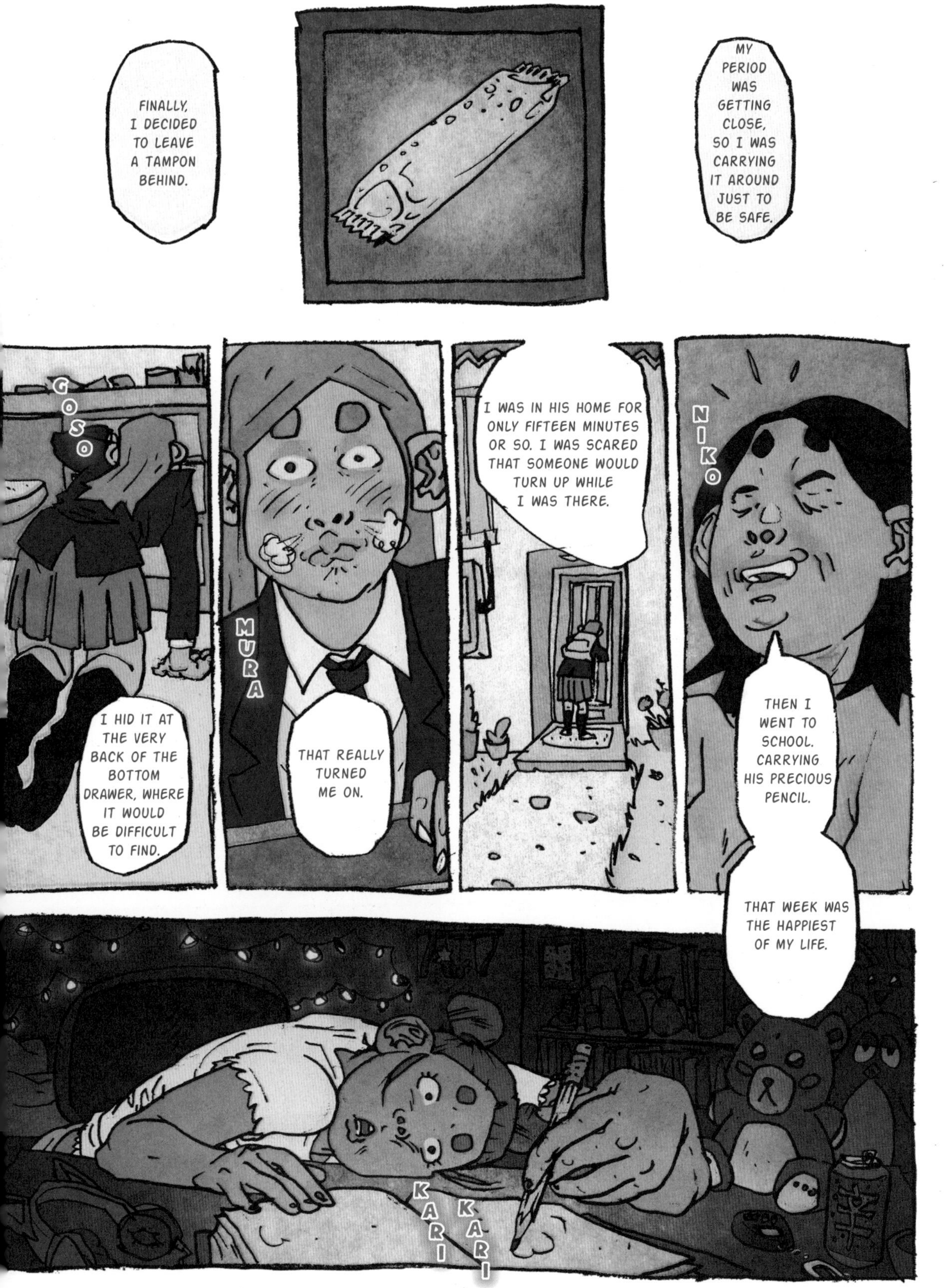
FINALLY, I DECIDED TO LEAVE A TAMPON BEHIND.
MY PERIOD WAS GETTING CLOSE, SO I WAS CARRYING IT AROUND JUST TO BE SAFE.
GOSO
I HID IT AT THE VERY BACK OF THE BOTTOM DRAWER, WHERE IT WOULD BE DIFFICULT TO FIND.
MURA
THAT REALLY TURNED ME ON.
I WAS IN HIS HOME FOR ONLY FIFTEEN MINUTES OR SO. I WAS SCARED THAT SOMEONE WOULD TURN UP WHILE I WAS THERE.
NIKO
THEN I WENT TO SCHOOL. CARRYING HIS PRECIOUS PENCIL.
THAT WEEK WAS THE HAPPIEST OF MY LIFE.
KARI KARI

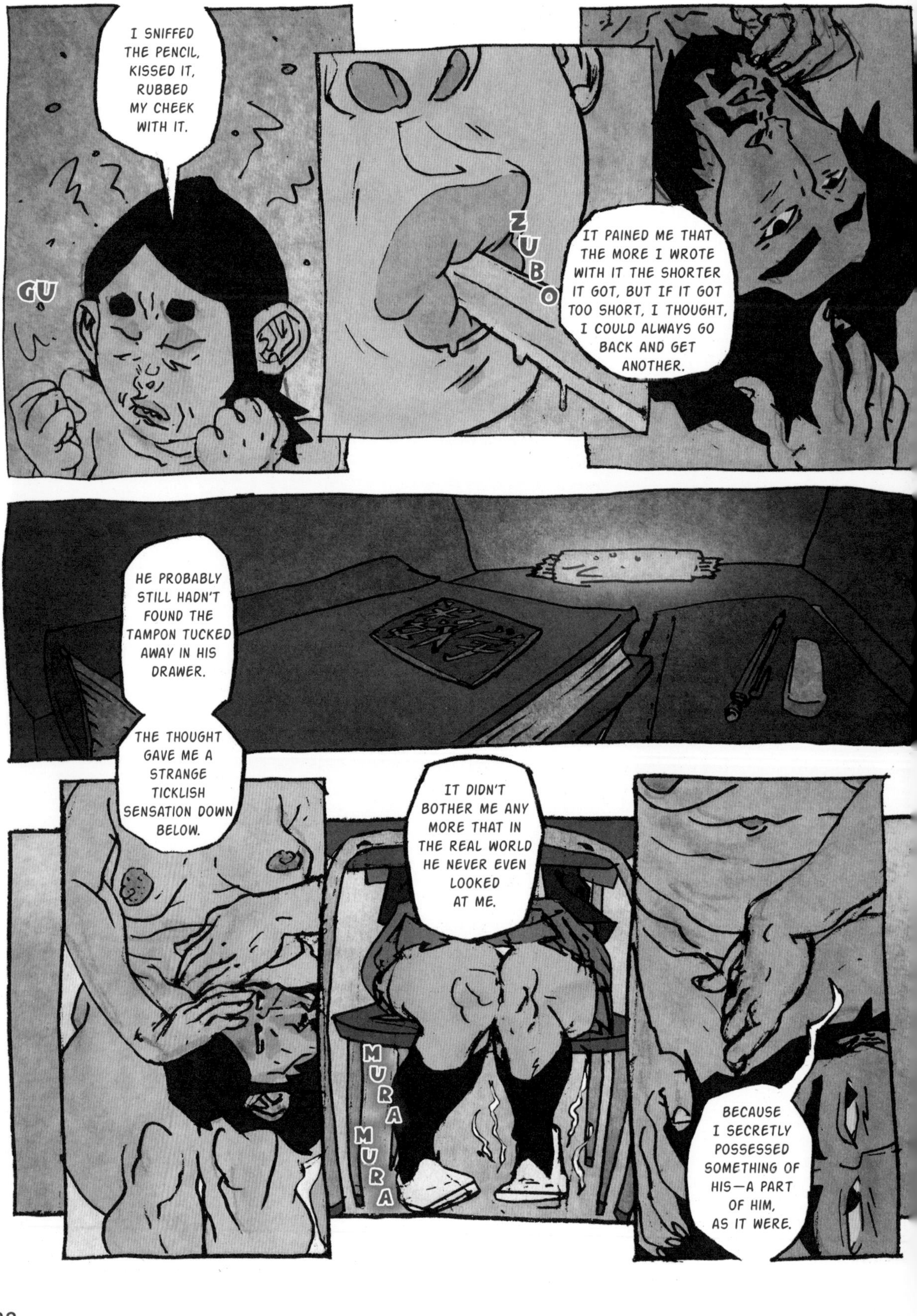
I SNIFFED THE PENCIL, KISSED IT, RUBBED MY CHEEK WITH IT.
GU
ZUBO
IT PAINED ME THAT THE MORE I WROTE WITH IT THE SHORTER IT GOT, BUT IF IT GOT TOO SHORT, I THOUGHT, I COULD ALWAYS GO BACK AND GET ANOTHER.
HE PROBABLY STILL HADN'T FOUND THE TAMPON TUCKED AWAY IN HIS DRAWER.
THE THOUGHT GAVE ME A STRANGE TICKLISH SENSATION DOWN BELOW.
IT DIDN'T BOTHER ME ANY MORE THAT IN THE REAL WORLD HE NEVER EVEN LOOKED AT ME.
MURA MURA
BECAUSE I SECRETLY POSSESSED SOMETHING OF HIS—A PART OF HIM, AS IT WERE.

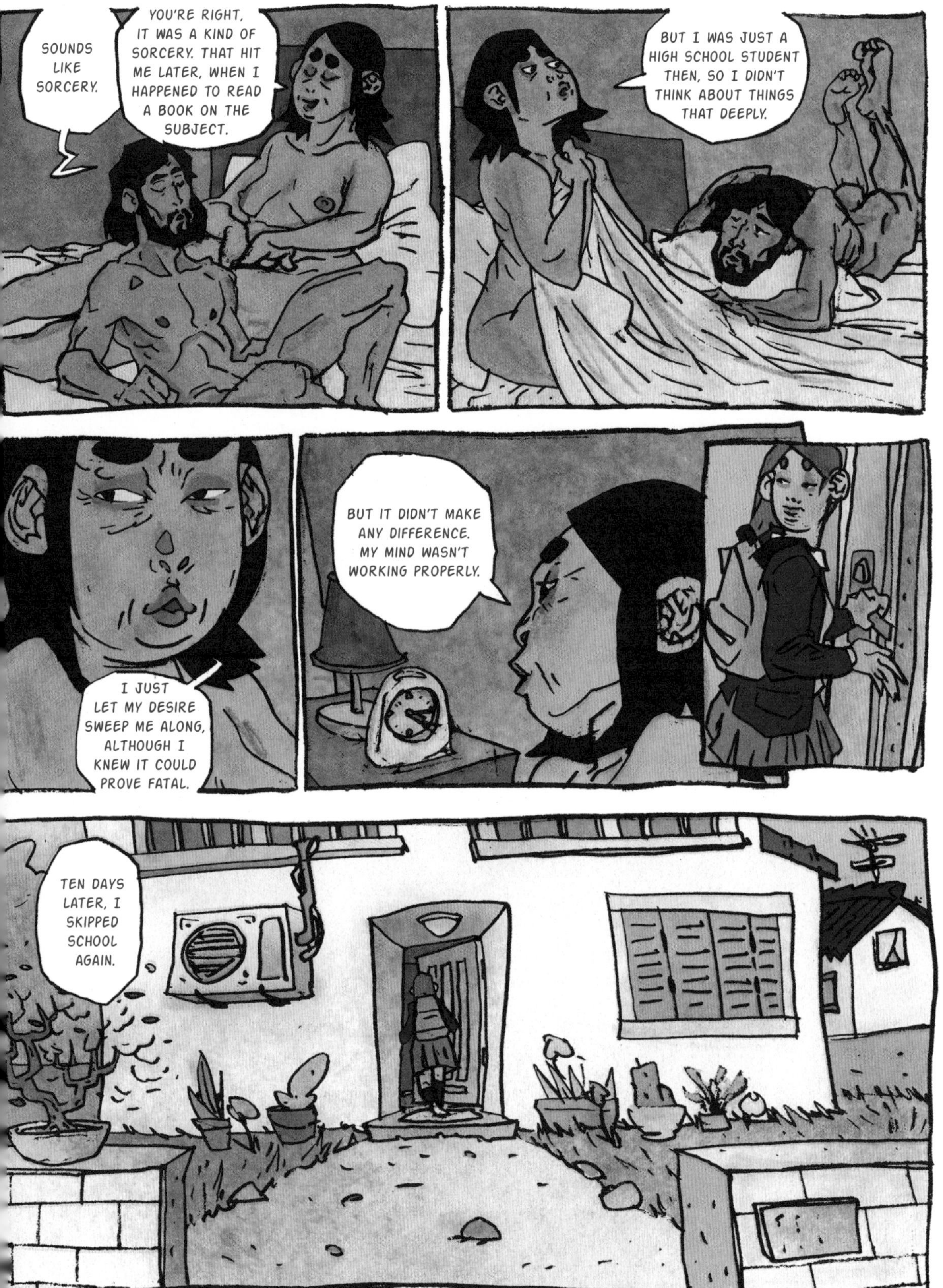
SOUNDS LIKE SORCERY.
YOU'RE RIGHT, IT WAS A KIND OF SORCERY. THAT HIT ME LATER, WHEN I HAPPENED TO READ A BOOK ON THE SUBJECT.
BUT I WAS JUST A HIGH SCHOOL STUDENT THEN, SO I DIDN'T THINK ABOUT THINGS THAT DEEPLY.
I JUST LET MY DESIRE SWEEP ME ALONG, ALTHOUGH I KNEW IT COULD PROVE FATAL.
BUT IT DIDN'T MAKE ANY DIFFERENCE. MY MIND WASN'T WORKING PROPERLY.
TEN DAYS LATER, I SKIPPED SCHOOL AGAIN.

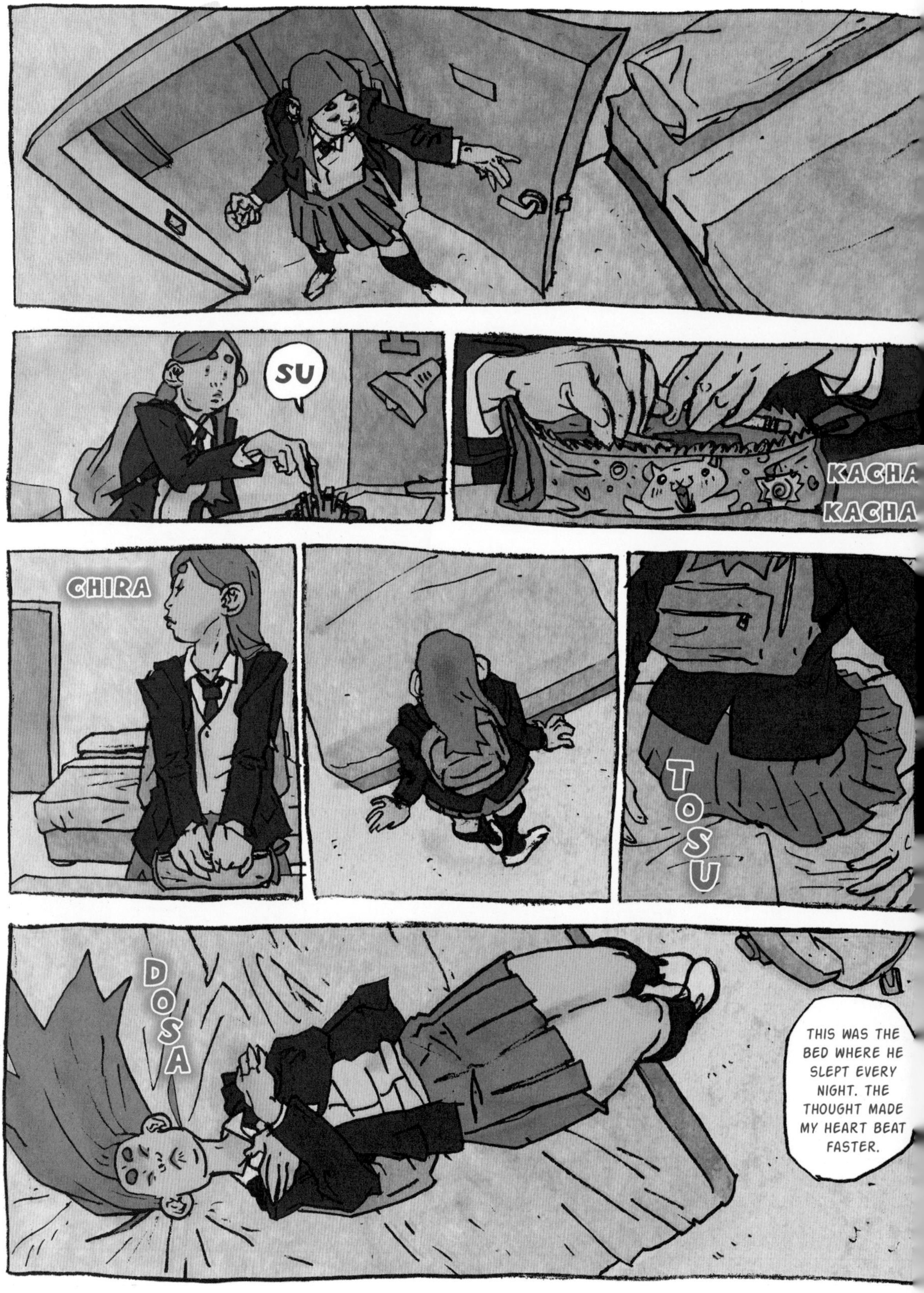
SU
KACHA
KACHA
CHIRA
TOSU
DOSA
THIS WAS THE BED WHERE HE SLEPT EVERY NIGHT. THE THOUGHT MADE MY HEART BEAT FASTER.

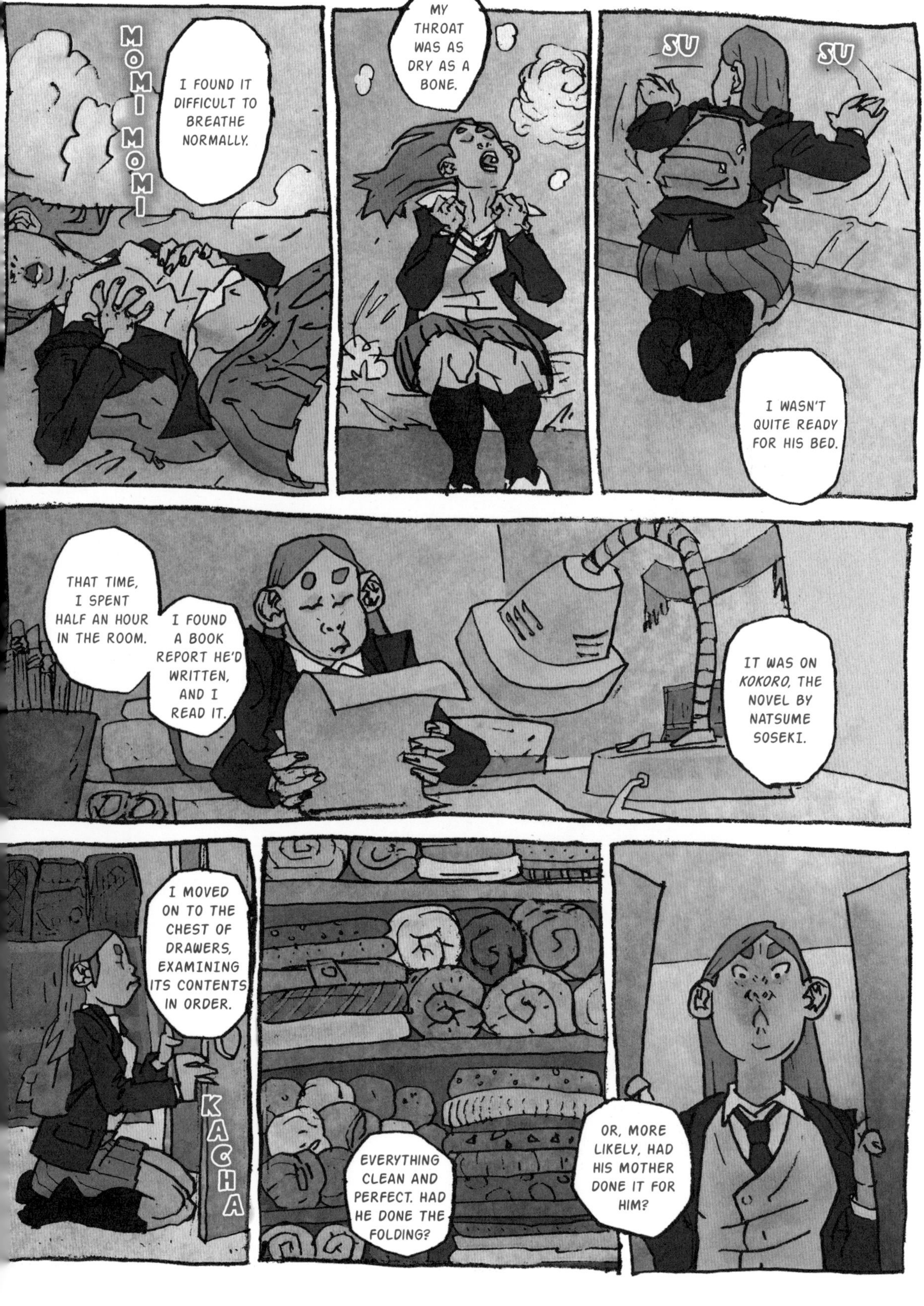
MOMI MOMI
I FOUND IT DIFFICULT TO BREATHE NORMALLY.
MY THROAT WAS AS DRY AS A BONE.
SU
SU
I WASN'T QUITE READY FOR HIS BED.
THAT TIME, I SPENT HALF AN HOUR IN THE ROOM.
I FOUND A BOOK REPORT HE'D WRITTEN, AND I READ IT.
IT WAS ON *KOKORO*, THE NOVEL BY NATSUME SOSEKI.
I MOVED ON TO THE CHEST OF DRAWERS, EXAMINING ITS CONTENTS IN ORDER.
KACHA
EVERYTHING CLEAN AND PERFECT. HAD HE DONE THE FOLDING?
OR, MORE LIKELY, HAD HIS MOTHER DONE IT FOR HIM?

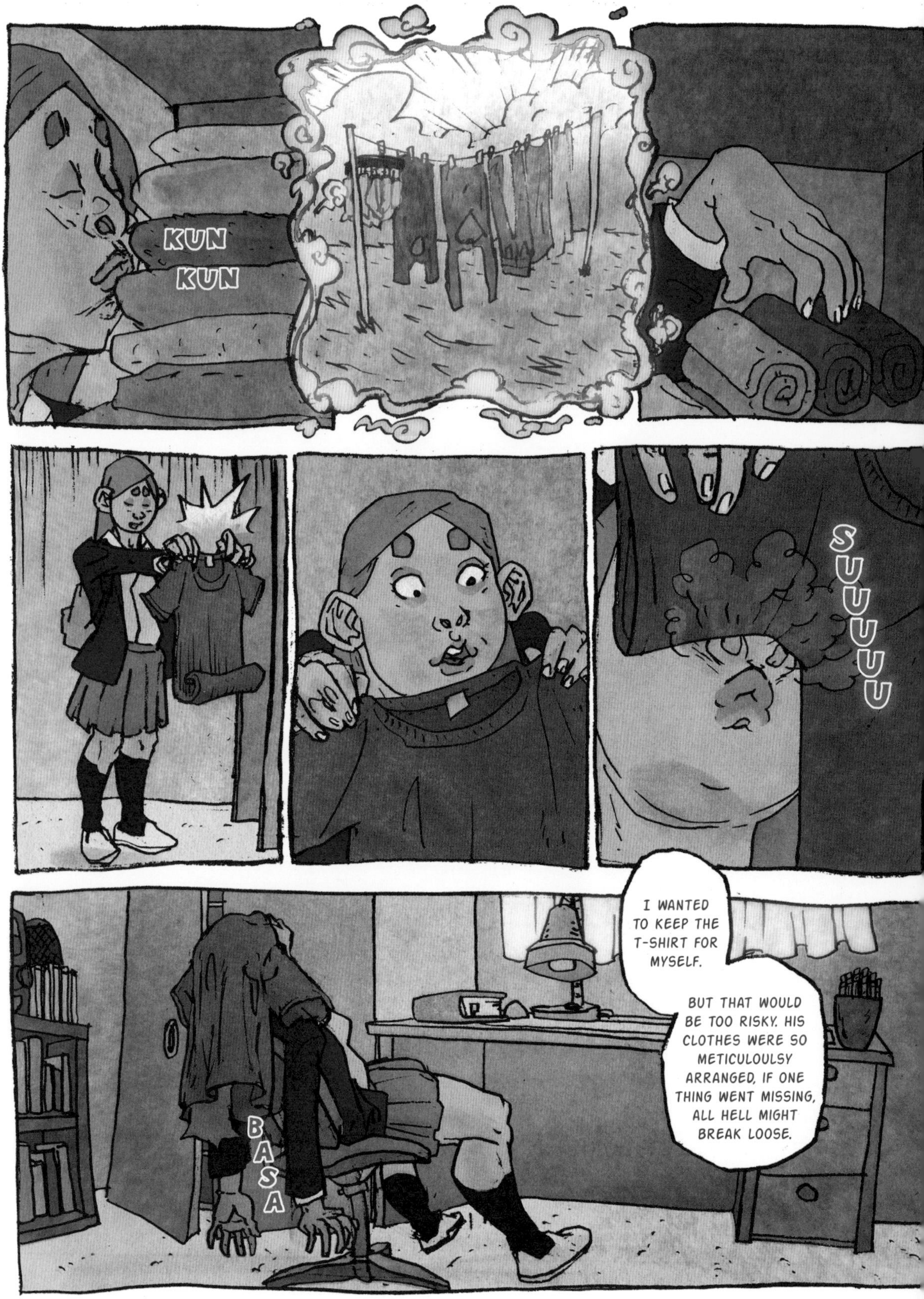
KUN
KUN
SUUUUU
I WANTED TO KEEP THE T-SHIRT FOR MYSELF.
BUT THAT WOULD BE TOO RISKY. HIS CLOTHES WERE SO METICULOULSY ARRANGED, IF ONE THING WENT MISSING, ALL HELL MIGHT BREAK LOOSE.
BASA

INSTEAD, I TOOK A SMALL BADGE, SHAPED LIKE A SOCCER BALL.

IT WAS OLD AND LIKELY OF NO PARTICULAR IMPORTANCE. I DOUBTED THAT HE WOULD MISS IT.

I TRIED TO IMAGINE WHAT WOULD HAPPEN IF HIS MOTHER DISCOVERED THE TAMPON.

I HAD NO IDEA.

BUT I DECIDED TO LEAVE THE TAMPON WHERE IT WAS.

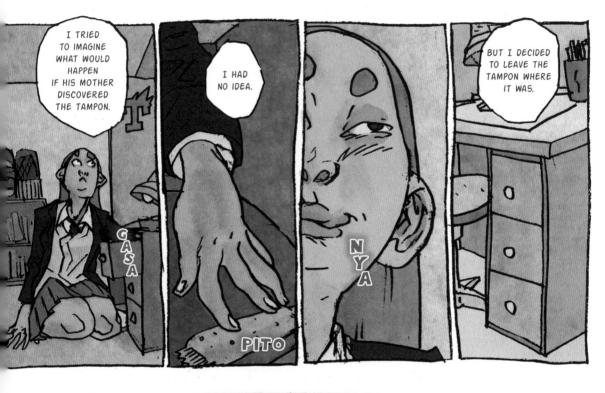

TO COMMEMORATE MY SECOND VISIT, I LEFT BEHIND THREE STRANDS OF MY HAIR.

THE NIGHT BEFORE, I'D PLUCKED THEM OUT AND SEALED THEM IN A TINY ENVELOPE.

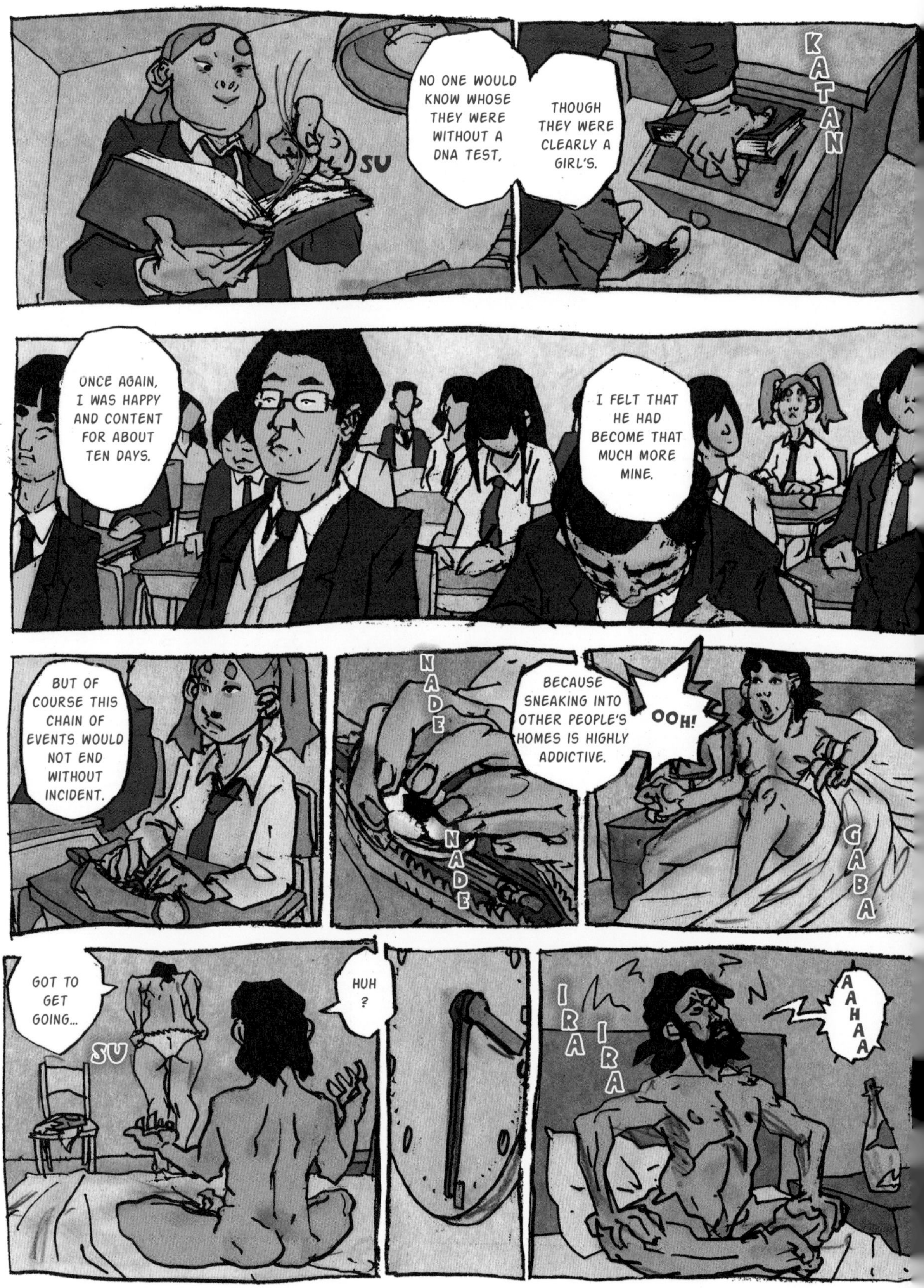
SU
NO ONE WOULD KNOW WHOSE THEY WERE WITHOUT A DNA TEST,
THOUGH THEY WERE CLEARLY A GIRL'S.
KATAN
ONCE AGAIN, I WAS HAPPY AND CONTENT FOR ABOUT TEN DAYS.
I FELT THAT HE HAD BECOME THAT MUCH MORE MINE.
BUT OF COURSE THIS CHAIN OF EVENTS WOULD NOT END WITHOUT INCIDENT.
NADE
NADE
BECAUSE SNEAKING INTO OTHER PEOPLE'S HOMES IS HIGHLY ADDICTIVE.
OOH!
GABA
GOT TO GET GOING...
SU
HUH ?
IRA IRA
AAHAA

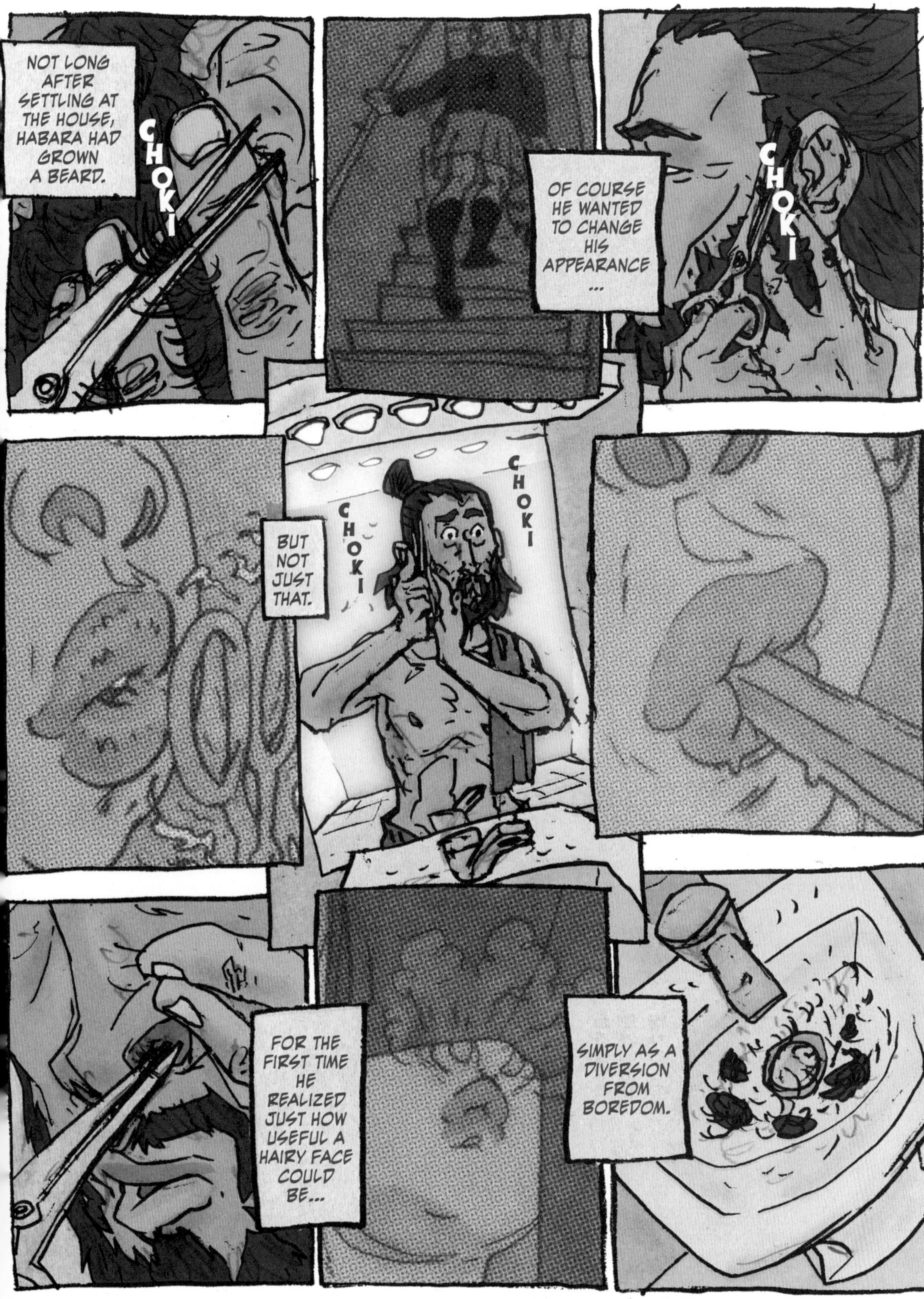
NOT LONG AFTER SETTLING AT THE HOUSE, HABARA HAD GROWN A BEARD.
CHOKI
OF COURSE HE WANTED TO CHANGE HIS APPEARANCE ...
CHOKI
BUT NOT JUST THAT.
CHOKI
CHOKI
FOR THE FIRST TIME HE REALIZED JUST HOW USEFUL A HAIRY FACE COULD BE...
SIMPLY AS A DIVERSION FROM BOREDOM.

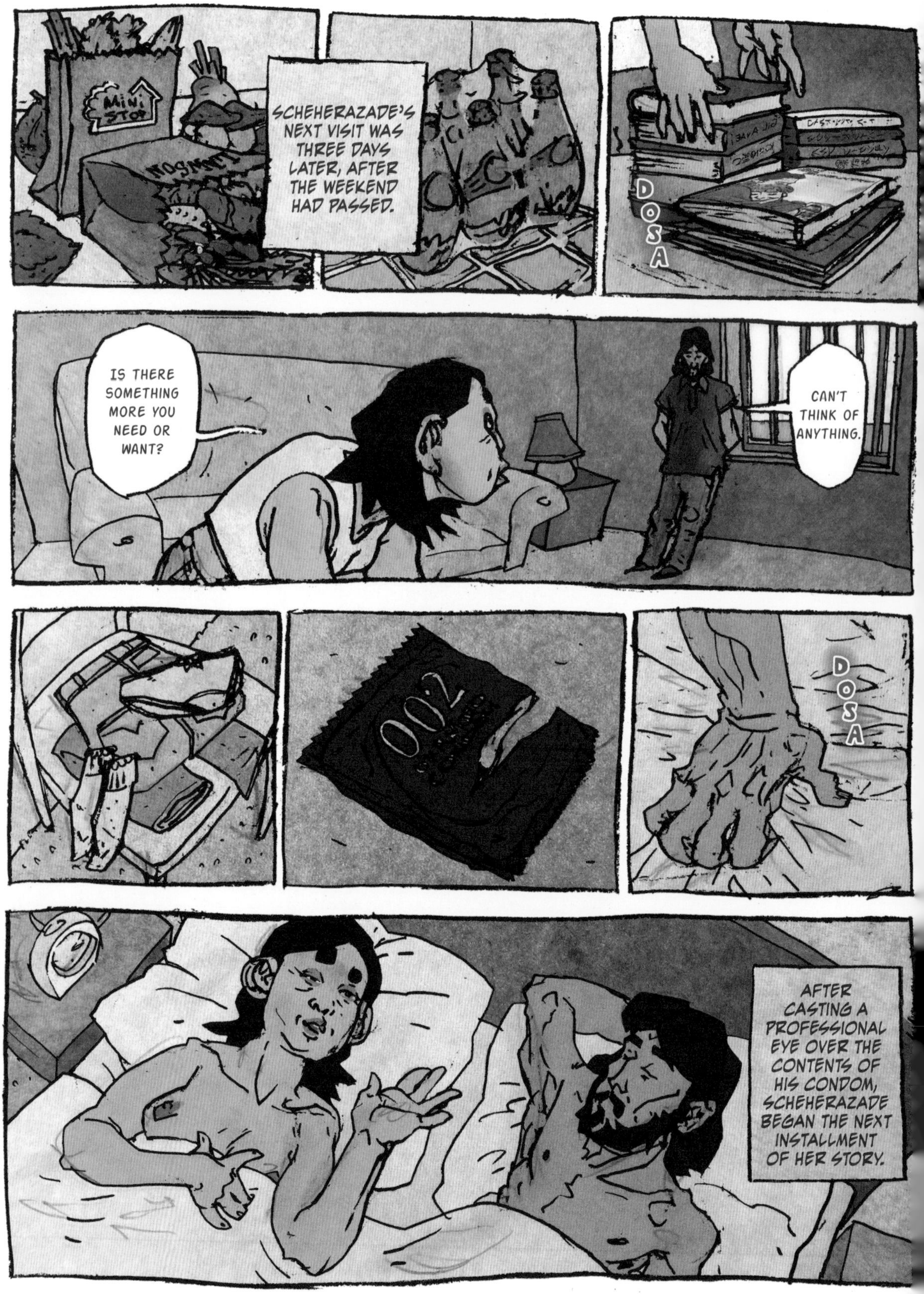
MINI STOP
SCHEHERAZADE'S NEXT VISIT WAS THREE DAYS LATER, AFTER THE WEEKEND HAD PASSED.
DOSA
IS THERE SOMETHING MORE YOU NEED OR WANT?
CAN'T THINK OF ANYTHING.
DOSA
AFTER CASTING A PROFESSIONAL EYE OVER THE CONTENTS OF HIS CONDOM, SCHEHERAZADE BEGAN THE NEXT INSTALLMENT OF HER STORY.

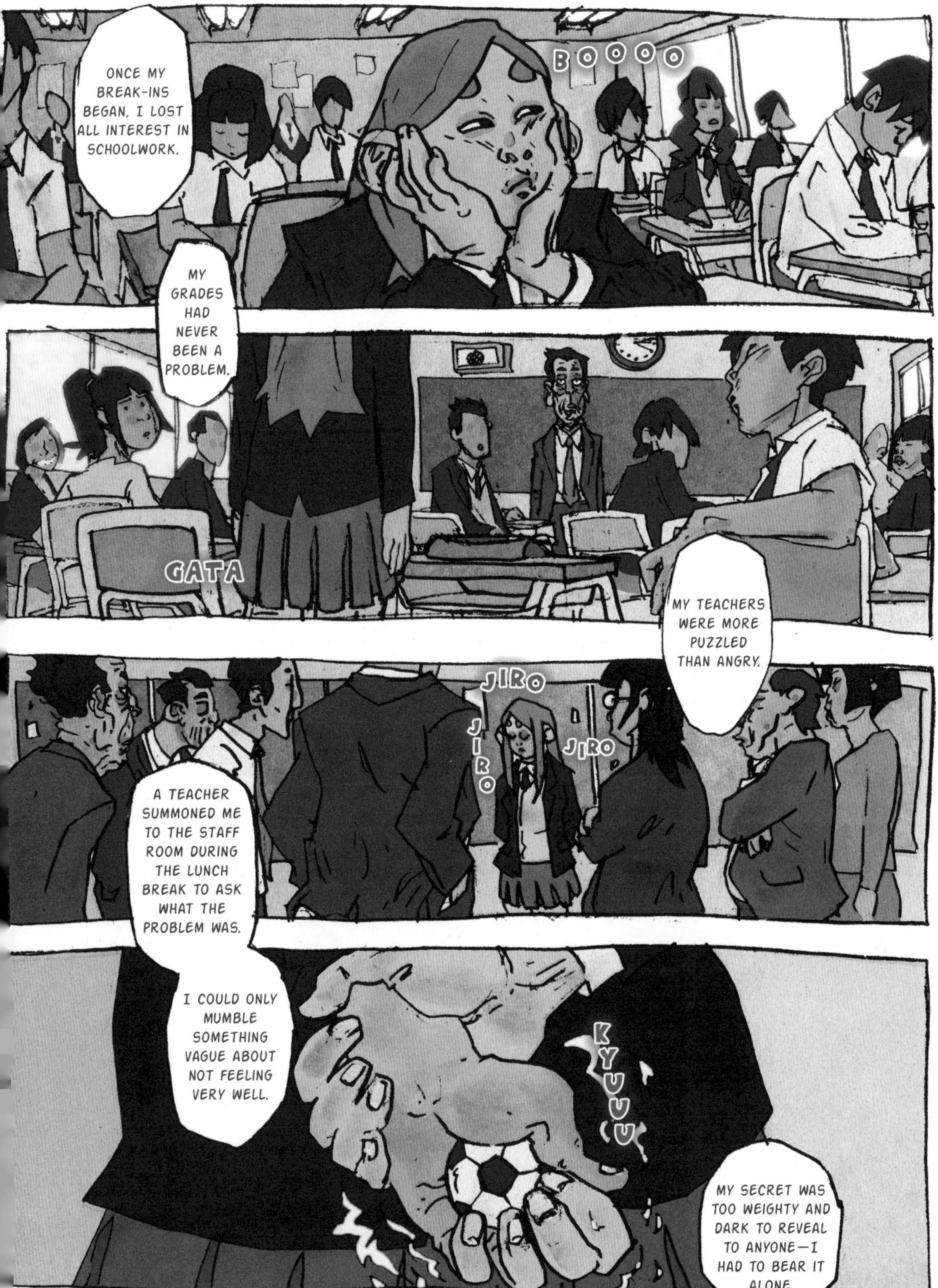
ONCE MY BREAK-INS BEGAN, I LOST ALL INTEREST IN SCHOOLWORK.
BOOOO
MY GRADES HAD NEVER BEEN A PROBLEM.
GATA
MY TEACHERS WERE MORE PUZZLED THAN ANGRY.
JIRO
JIRO
JIRO
A TEACHER SUMMONED ME TO THE STAFF ROOM DURING THE LUNCH BREAK TO ASK WHAT THE PROBLEM WAS.
I COULD ONLY MUMBLE SOMETHING VAGUE ABOUT NOT FEELING VERY WELL.
KYUUU
MY SECRET WAS TOO WEIGHTY AND DARK TO REVEAL TO ANYONE—I HAD TO BEAR IT ALONE.

TEN DAYS AFTER MY SECOND "VISIT," I WENT THERE AGAIN, AS IF MY FEET WERE MOVING ON THEIR OWN.

ONCE THE BALL WAS ROLLING, THERE WAS NO WAY I COULD STOP IT.

IT WAS AS QUIET AS BEFORE—

NO, EVEN QUIETER FOR SOME REASON.

BUNNNN

FURURURU

NO ONE PICKED UP, OF COURSE, AND IT STOPPED AFTER ABOUT TEN RINGS..

THE HOUSE FELT EVEN QUIETER THEN.

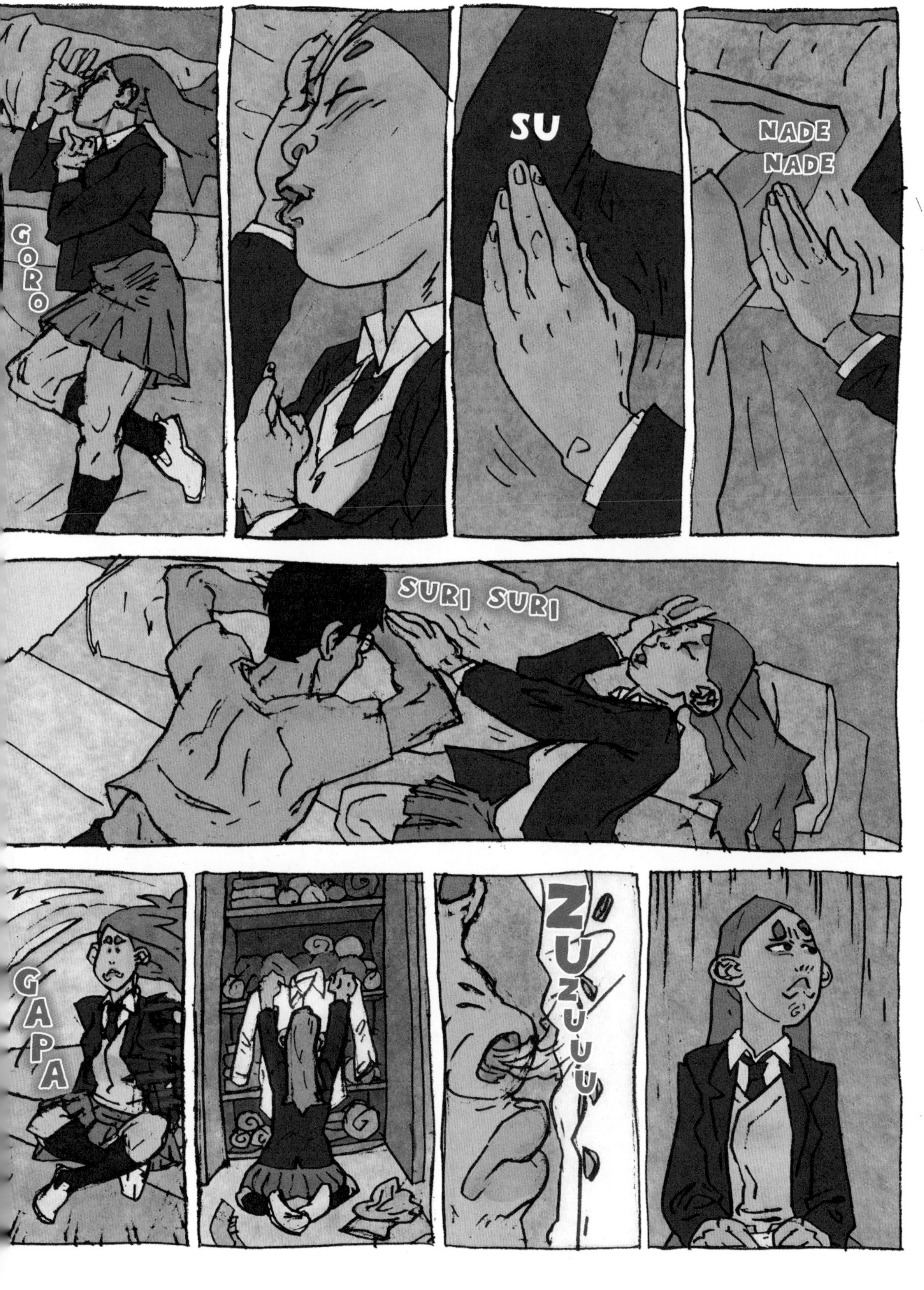
GORO
SU
NADE
NADE
SURI SURI
GAPA
ZUZUUU

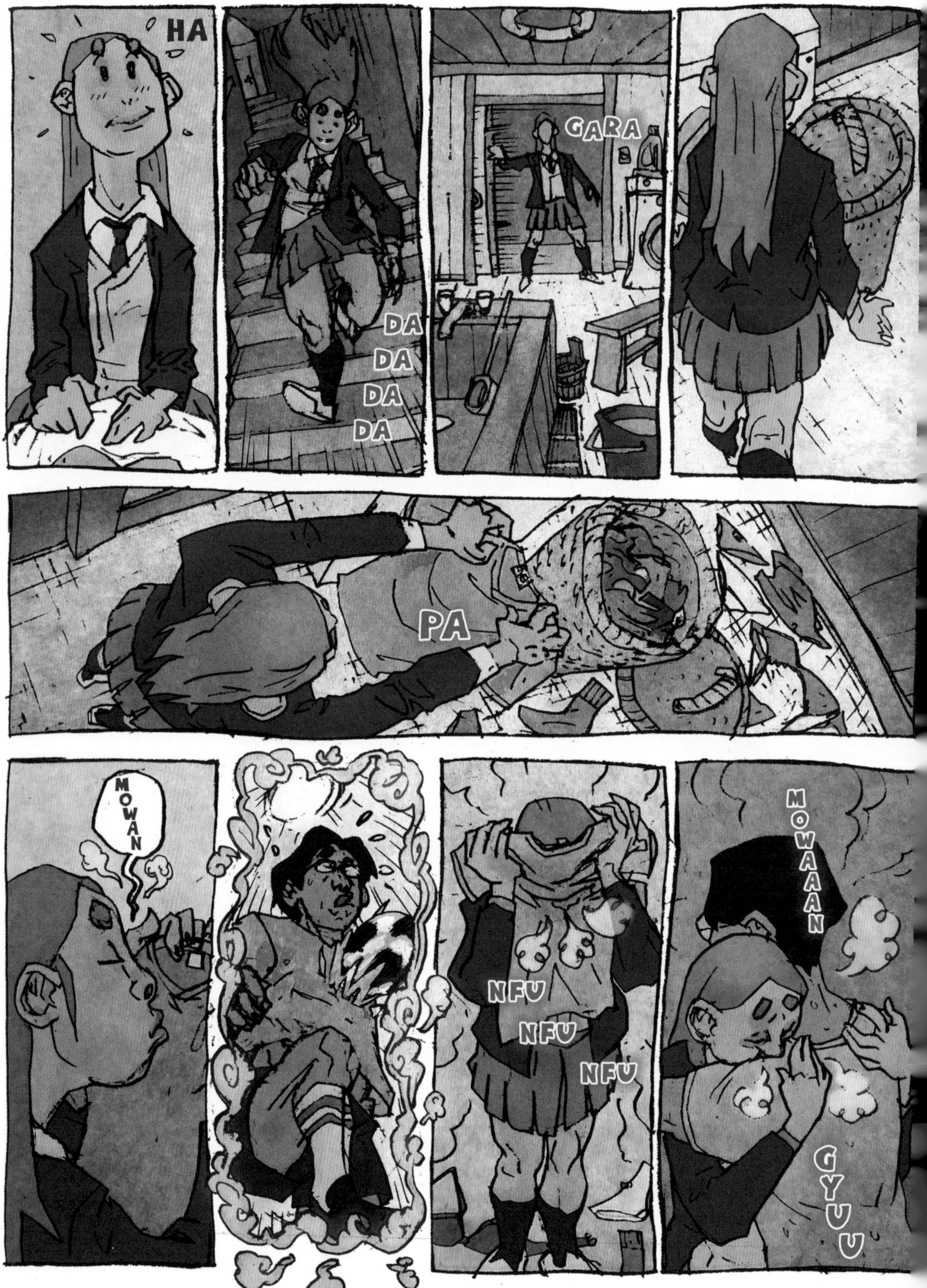
HA
DA
DA
DA
DA
GARA
PA
MOWAN
NFU
NFU
NFU
MOWAAAN
GYUU

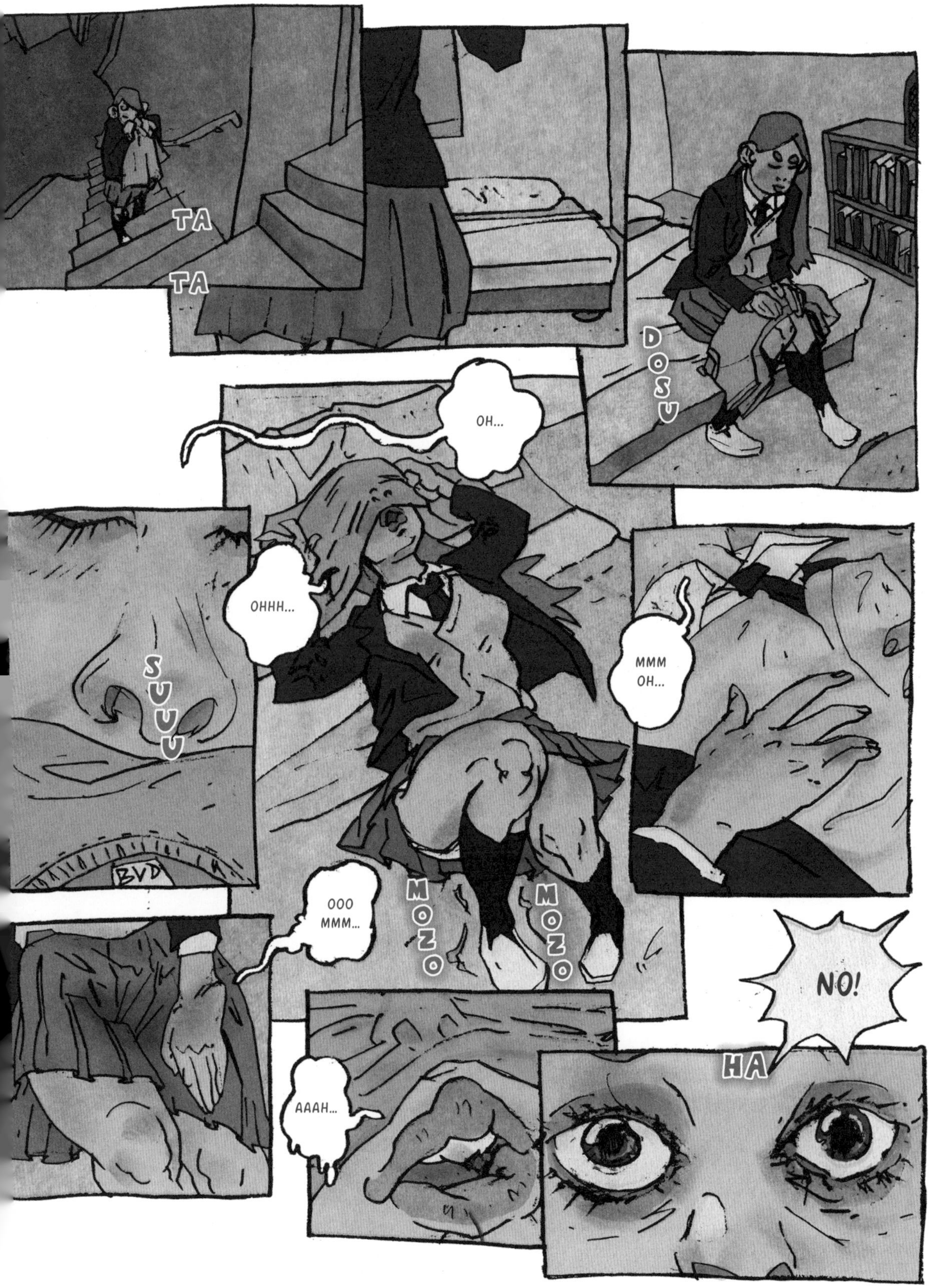
TA
TA
DOSU
OH...
OHHH...
SUUU
MMM
OH...
OOO
MMM...
MOZO
MOZO
AAAH...
HA
NO!

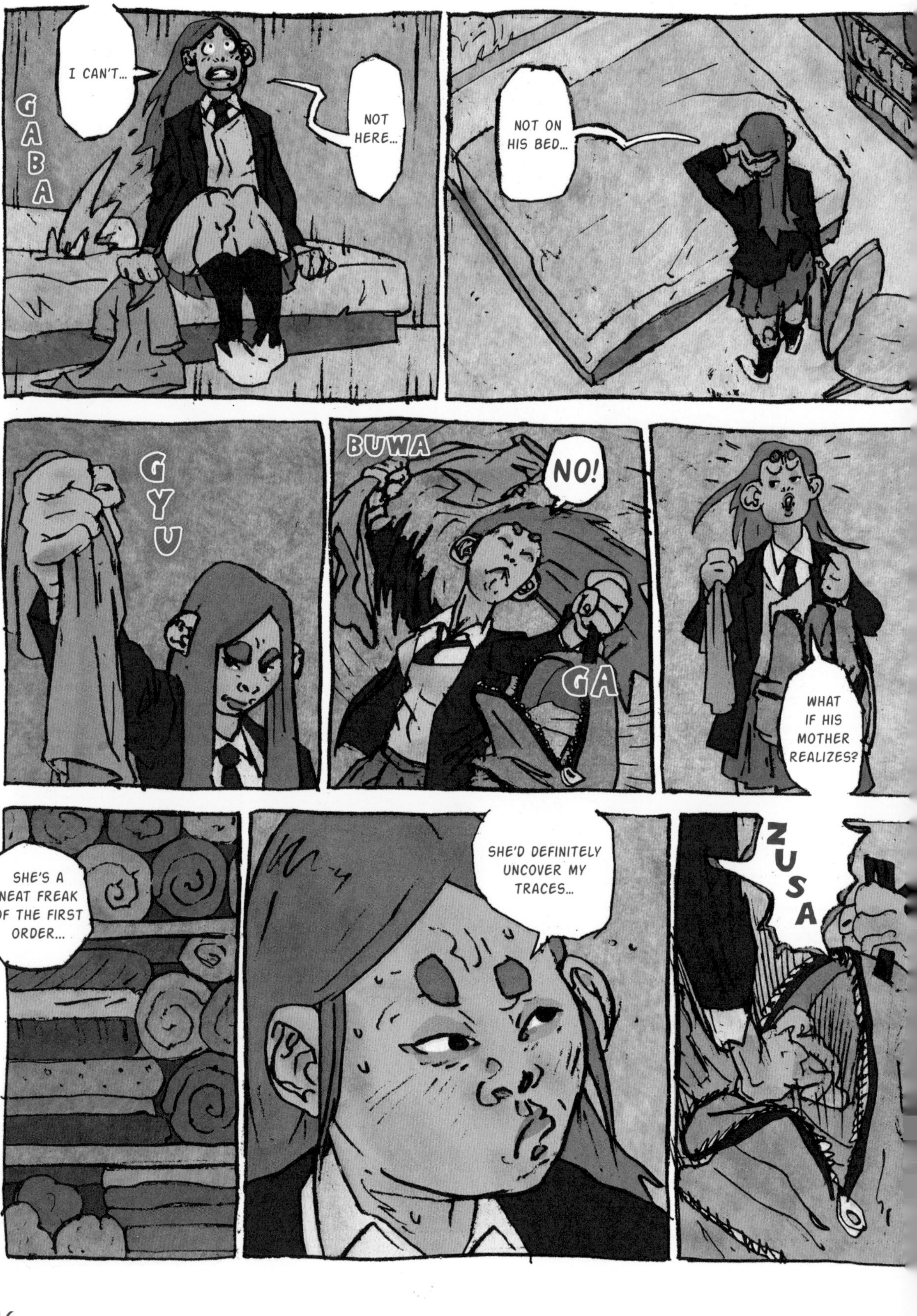
I CAN'T...
GABA
NOT HERE...
NOT ON HIS BED...
GYU
BUWA
NO!
GA
WHAT IF HIS MOTHER REALIZES?
SHE'S A NEAT FREAK OF THE FIRST ORDER...
SHE'D DEFINITELY UNCOVER MY TRACES...
ZUSA

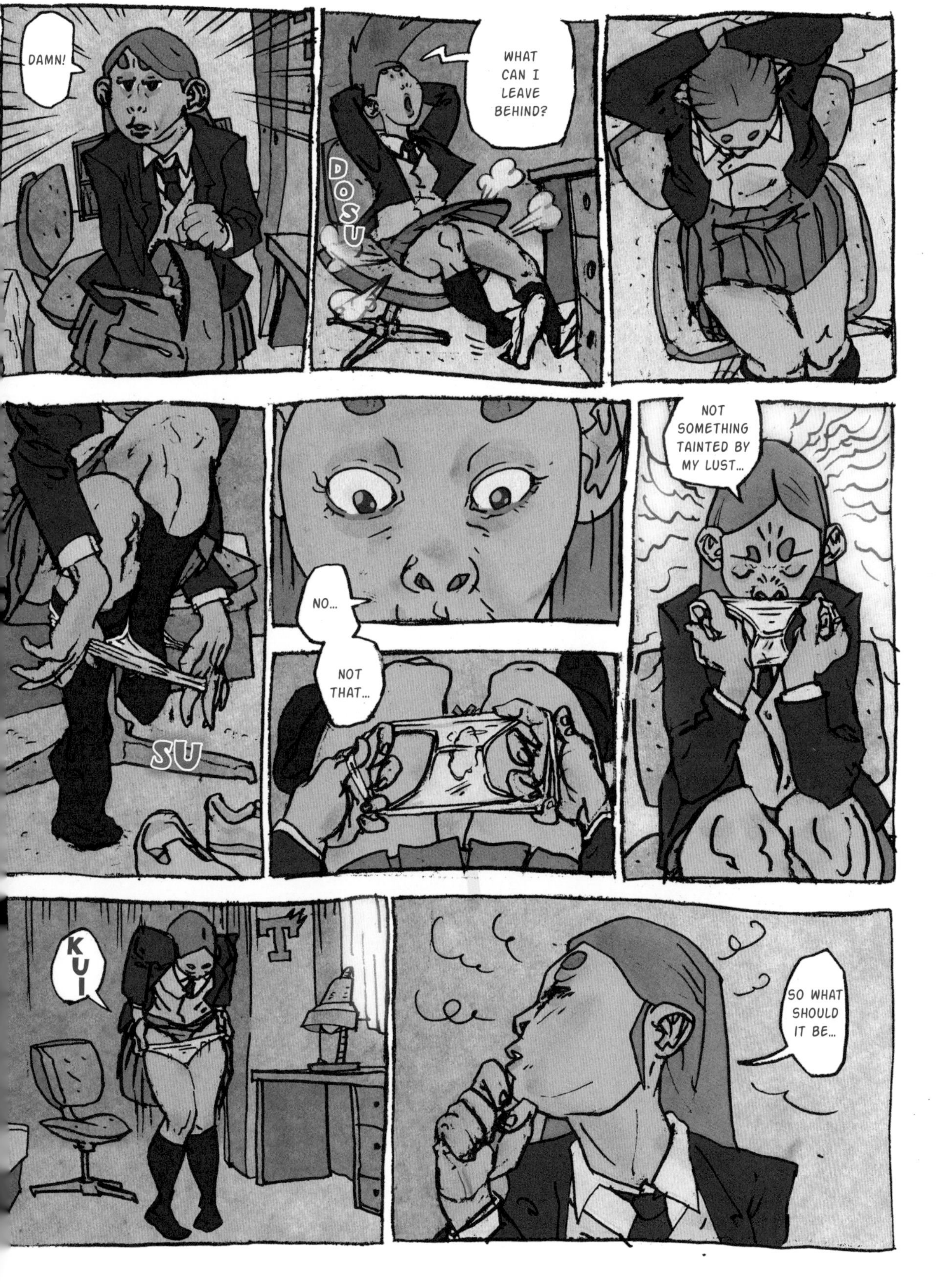
DAMN!
WHAT CAN I LEAVE BEHIND?
DOSU
SU
NO...
NOT THAT...
NOT SOMETHING TAINTED BY MY LUST...
KUI
SO WHAT SHOULD IT BE...

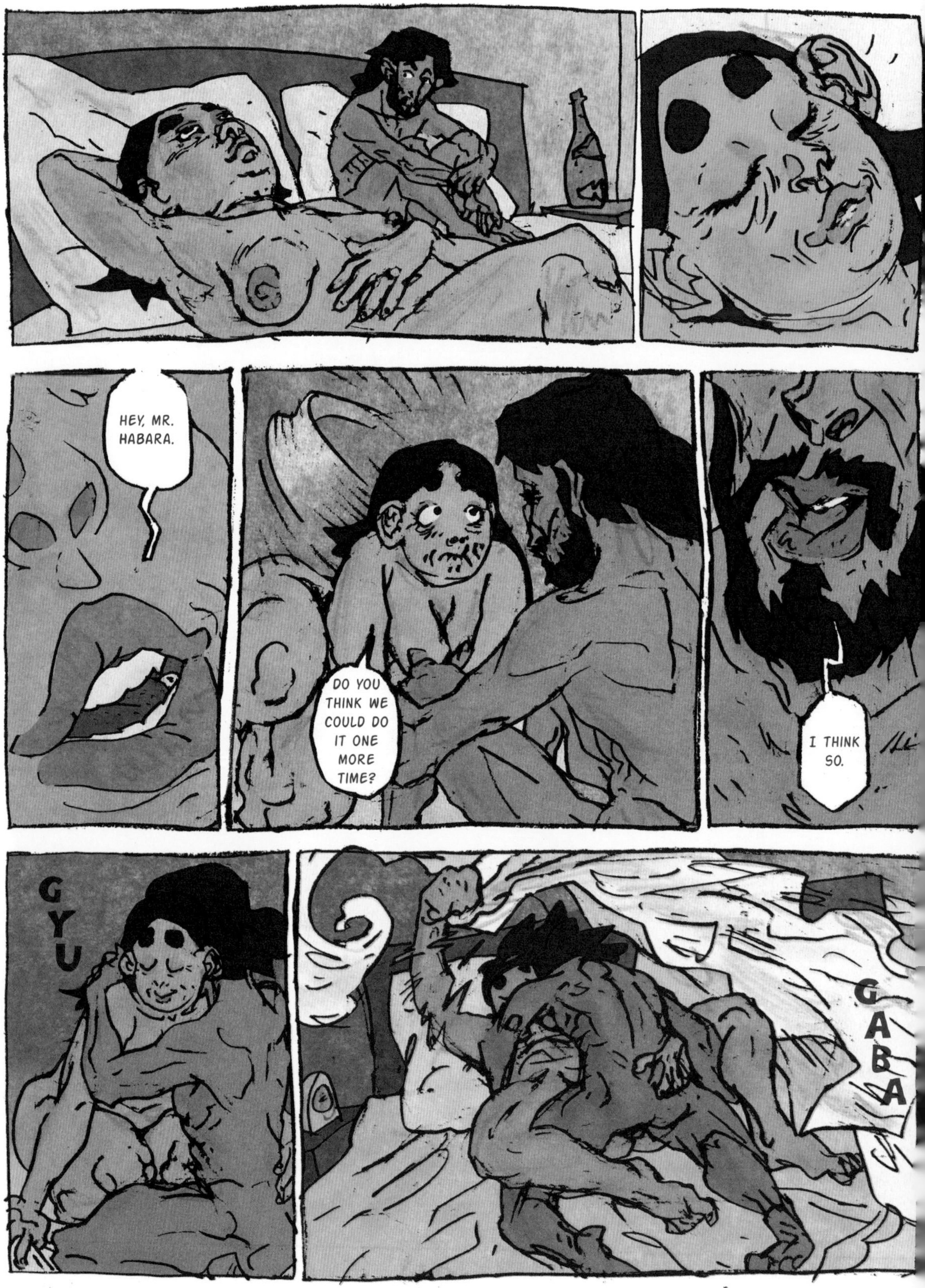
HEY, MR. HABARA.
DO YOU THINK WE COULD DO IT ONE MORE TIME?
I THINK SO.
GYU
GABA

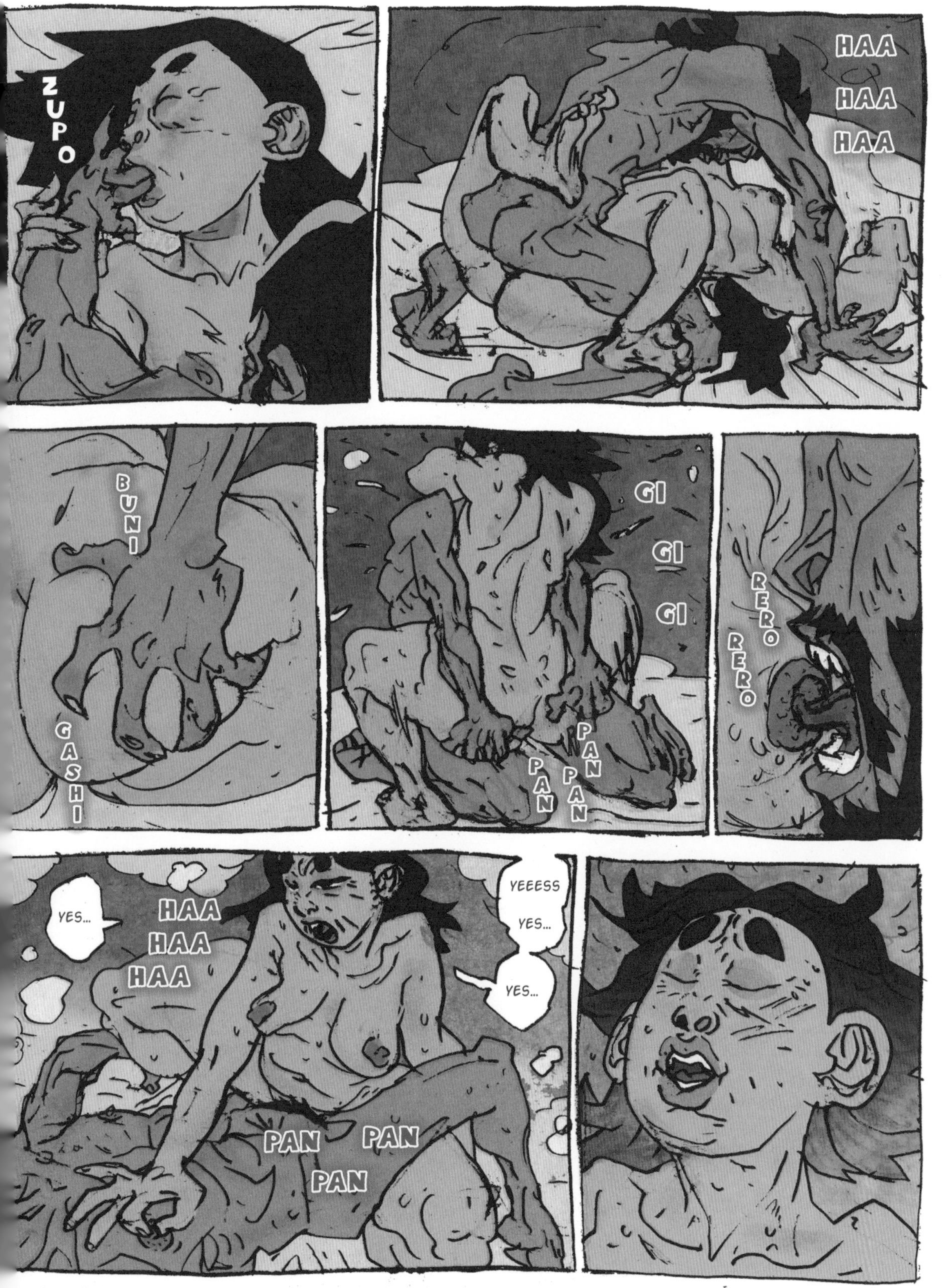
ZUPO
HAA
HAA
HAA
BUNI
GASHI
GI
GI
GI
PAN
PAN
PAN
PAN
RERO
RERO
YES...
HAA
HAA
HAA
YEEESS
YES...
YES...
PAN
PAN
PAN

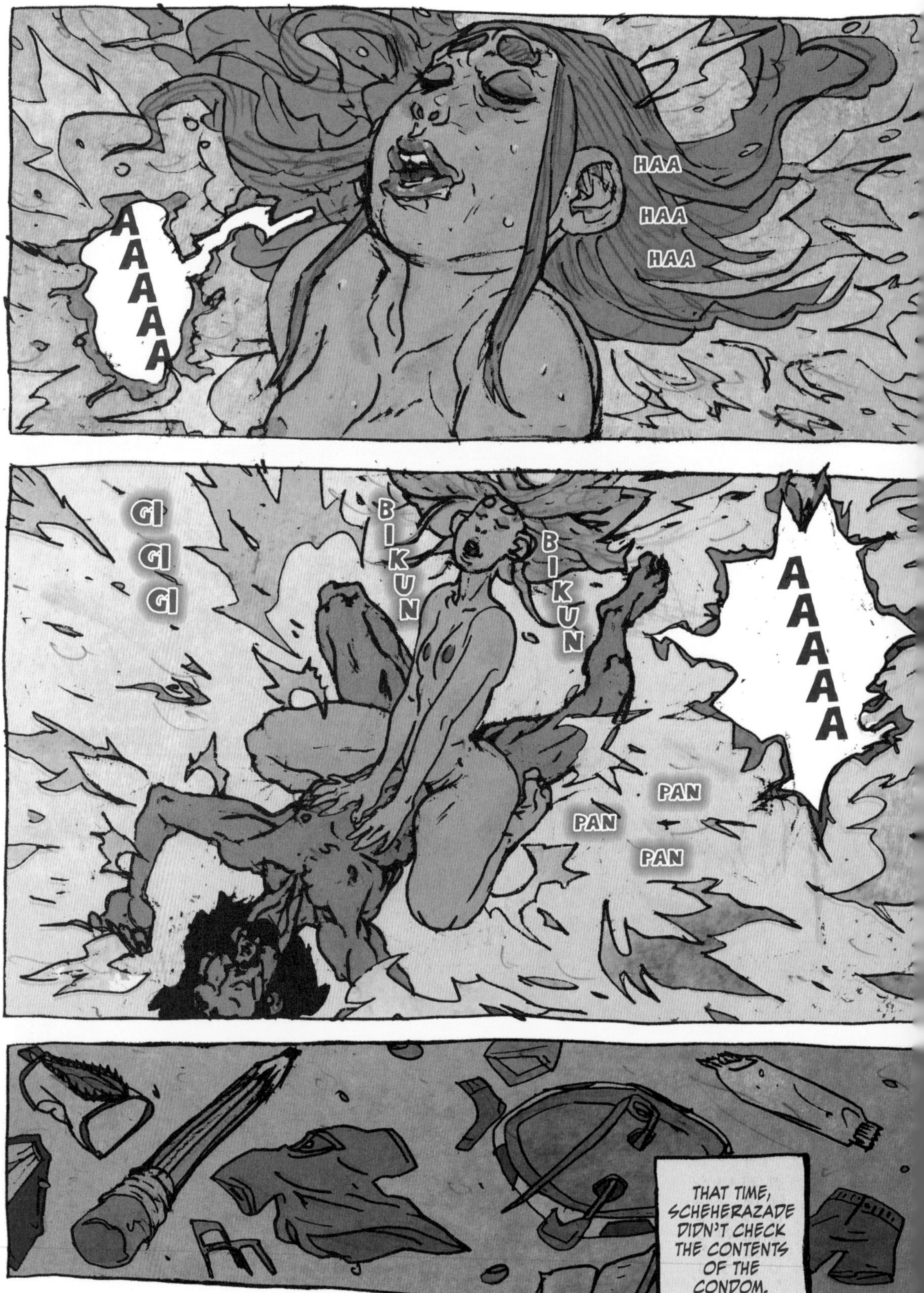
AAAAA
HAA
HAA
HAA
GI
GI
GI
BIKUN
BIKUN
AAAAA
PAN
PAN
PAN
THAT TIME, SCHEHERAZADE DIDN'T CHECK THE CONTENTS OF THE CONDOM.

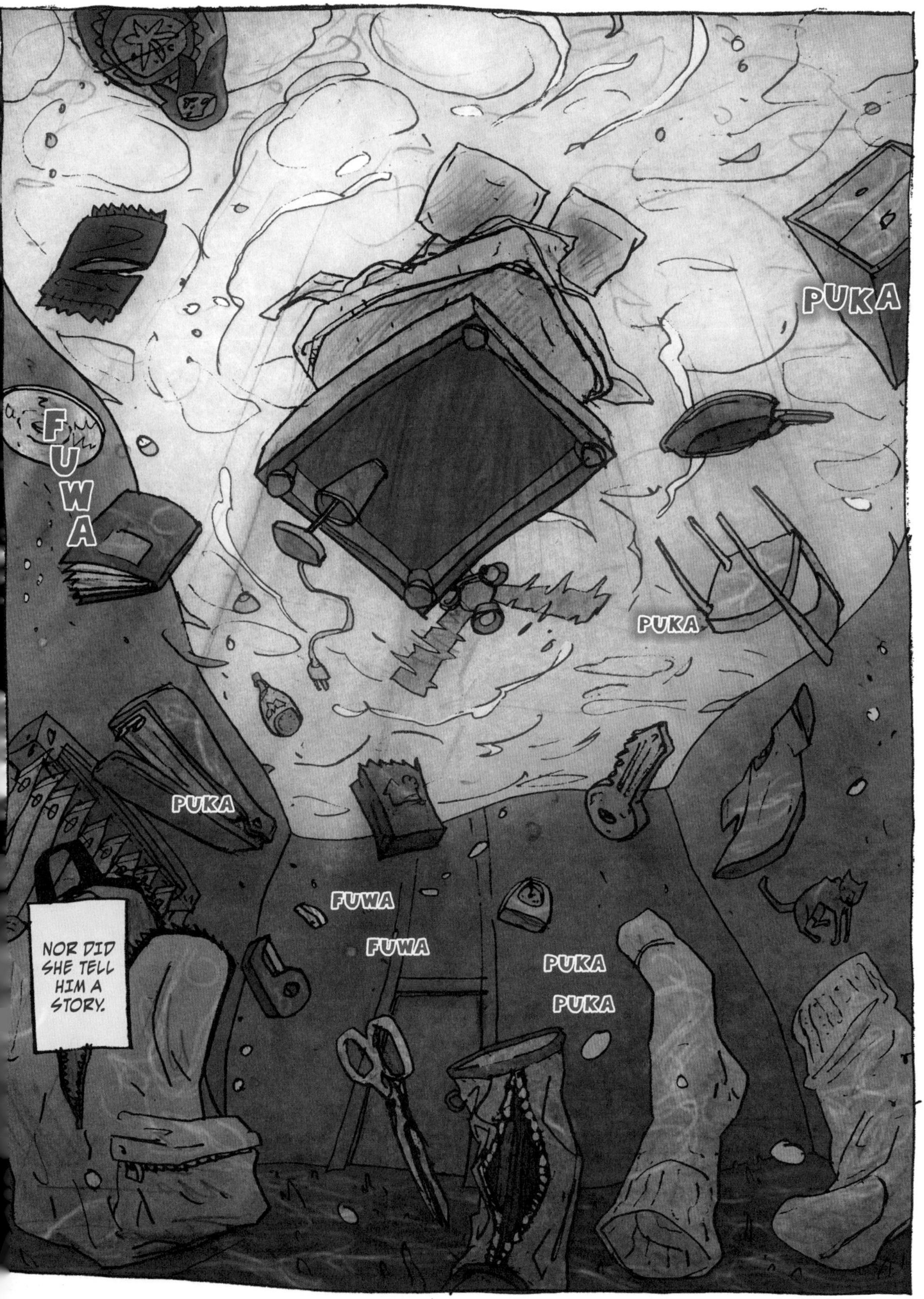
FUWA
PUKA
PUKA
PUKA
NOR DID SHE TELL HIM A STORY.
FUWA
FUWA
PUKA
PUKA

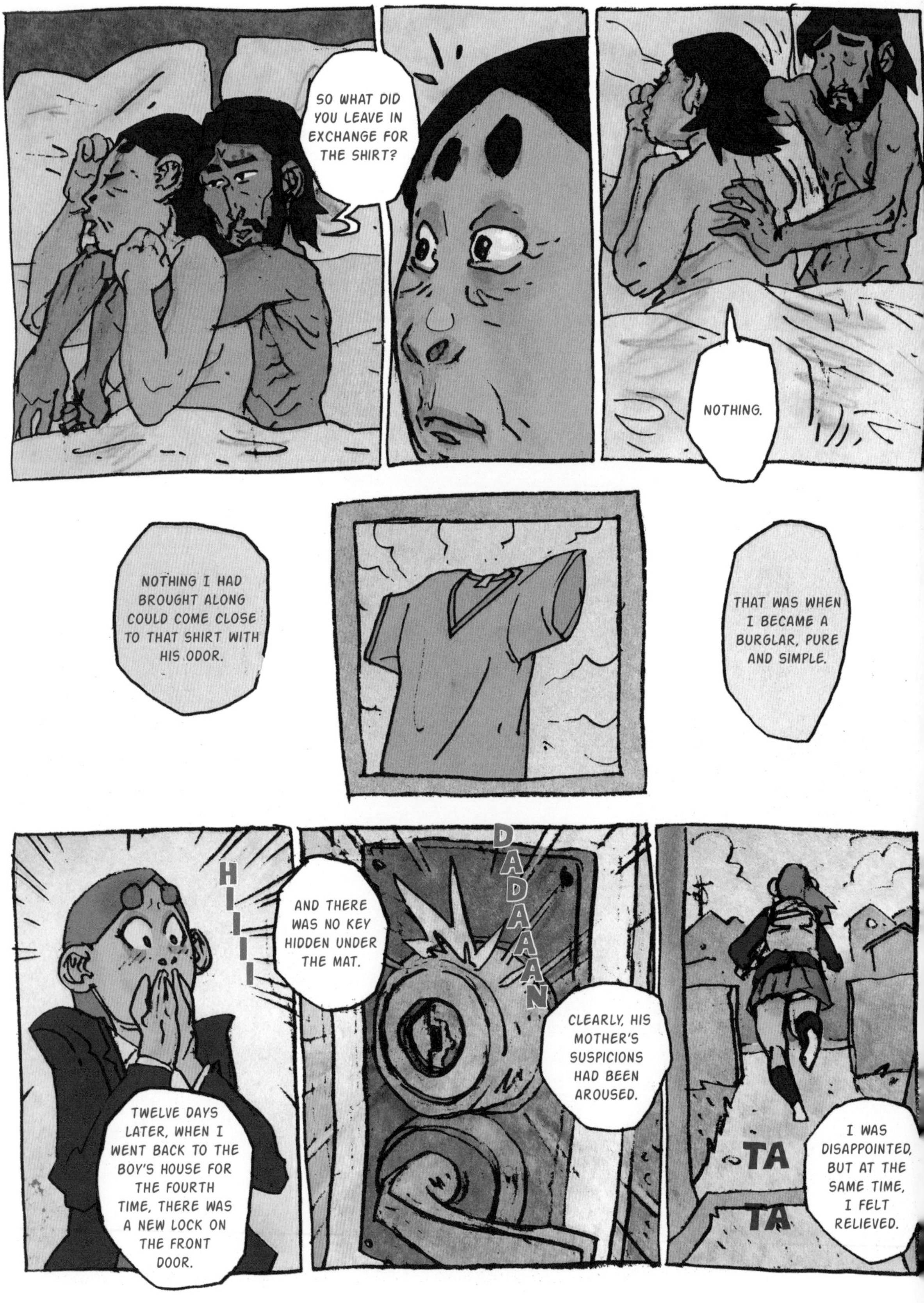
SO WHAT DID YOU LEAVE IN EXCHANGE FOR THE SHIRT?
NOTHING.
NOTHING I HAD BROUGHT ALONG COULD COME CLOSE TO THAT SHIRT WITH HIS ODOR.
THAT WAS WHEN I BECAME A BURGLAR, PURE AND SIMPLE.
HIIII
TWELVE DAYS LATER, WHEN I WENT BACK TO THE BOY'S HOUSE FOR THE FOURTH TIME, THERE WAS A NEW LOCK ON THE FRONT DOOR.
AND THERE WAS NO KEY HIDDEN UNDER THE MAT.
DADAAAN
CLEARLY, HIS MOTHER'S SUSPICIONS HAD BEEN AROUSED.
TA TA
I WAS DISAPPOINTED, BUT AT THE SAME TIME, I FELT RELIEVED.

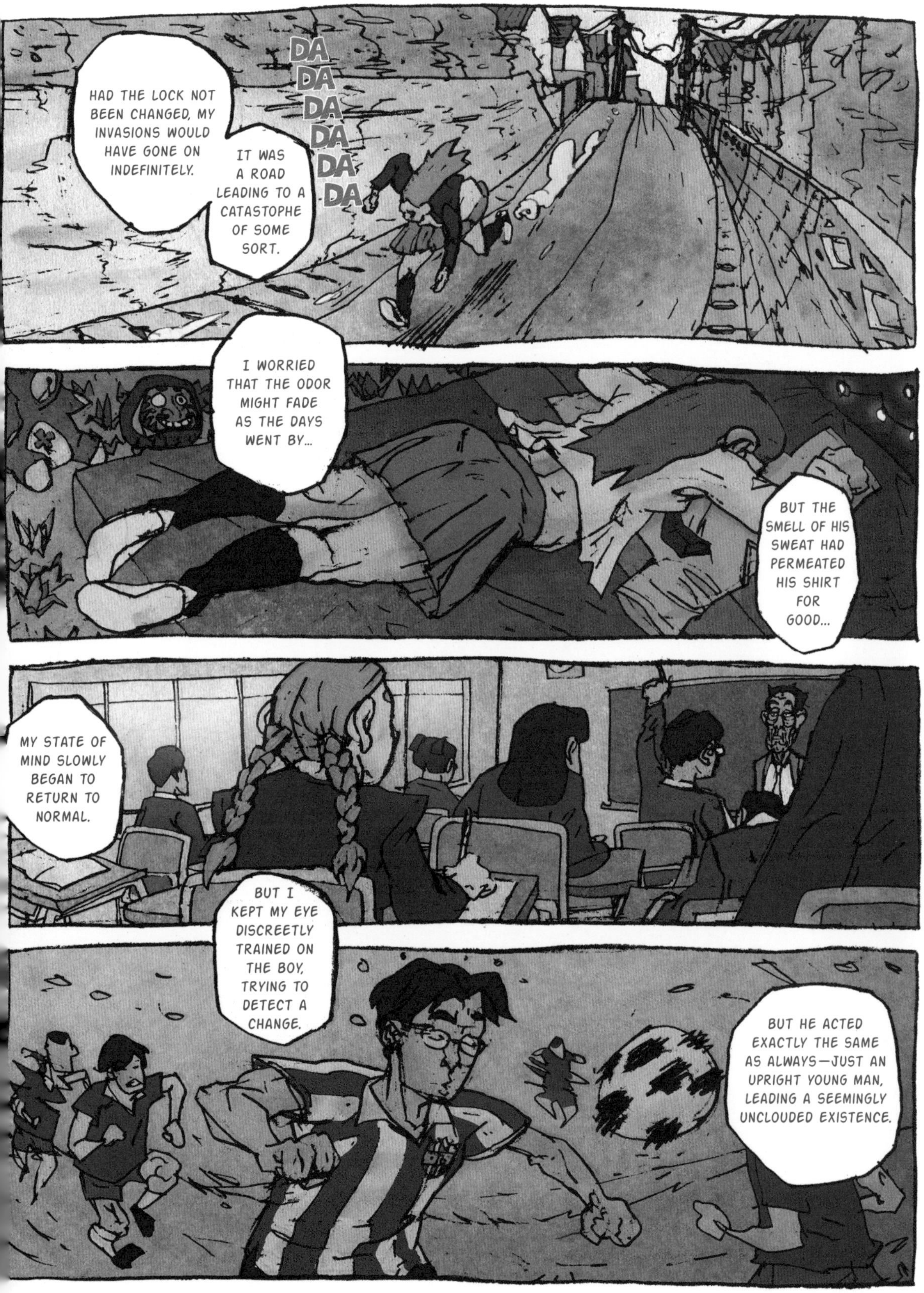
HAD THE LOCK NOT BEEN CHANGED, MY INVASIONS WOULD HAVE GONE ON INDEFINITELY.
IT WAS A ROAD LEADING TO A CATASTOPHE OF SOME SORT.
DA DA DA DA DA DA
I WORRIED THAT THE ODOR MIGHT FADE AS THE DAYS WENT BY...
BUT THE SMELL OF HIS SWEAT HAD PERMEATED HIS SHIRT FOR GOOD...
MY STATE OF MIND SLOWLY BEGAN TO RETURN TO NORMAL.
BUT I KEPT MY EYE DISCREETLY TRAINED ON THE BOY, TRYING TO DETECT A CHANGE.
BUT HE ACTED EXACTLY THE SAME AS ALWAYS—JUST AN UPRIGHT YOUNG MAN, LEADING A SEEMINGLY UNCLOUDED EXISTENCE.

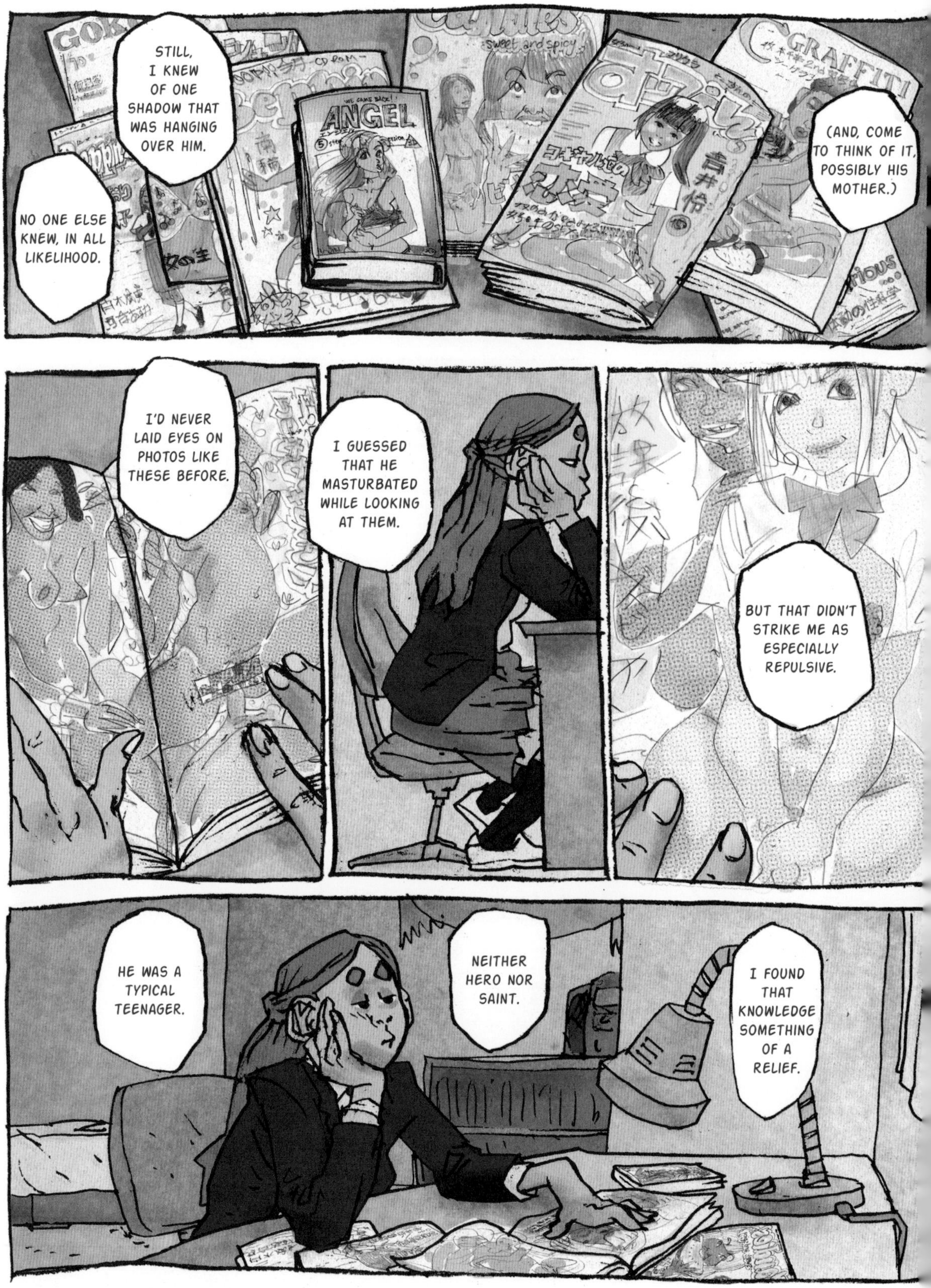
STILL, I KNEW OF ONE SHADOW THAT WAS HANGING OVER HIM.
NO ONE ELSE KNEW, IN ALL LIKELIHOOD.
ANGEL
GRAFFITI
sweet and spicy
(AND, COME TO THINK OF IT, POSSIBLY HIS MOTHER.)
I'D NEVER LAID EYES ON PHOTOS LIKE THESE BEFORE.
I GUESSED THAT HE MASTURBATED WHILE LOOKING AT THEM.
BUT THAT DIDN'T STRIKE ME AS ESPECIALLY REPULSIVE.
HE WAS A TYPICAL TEENAGER.
NEITHER HERO NOR SAINT.
I FOUND THAT KNOWLEDGE SOMETHING OF A RELIEF.

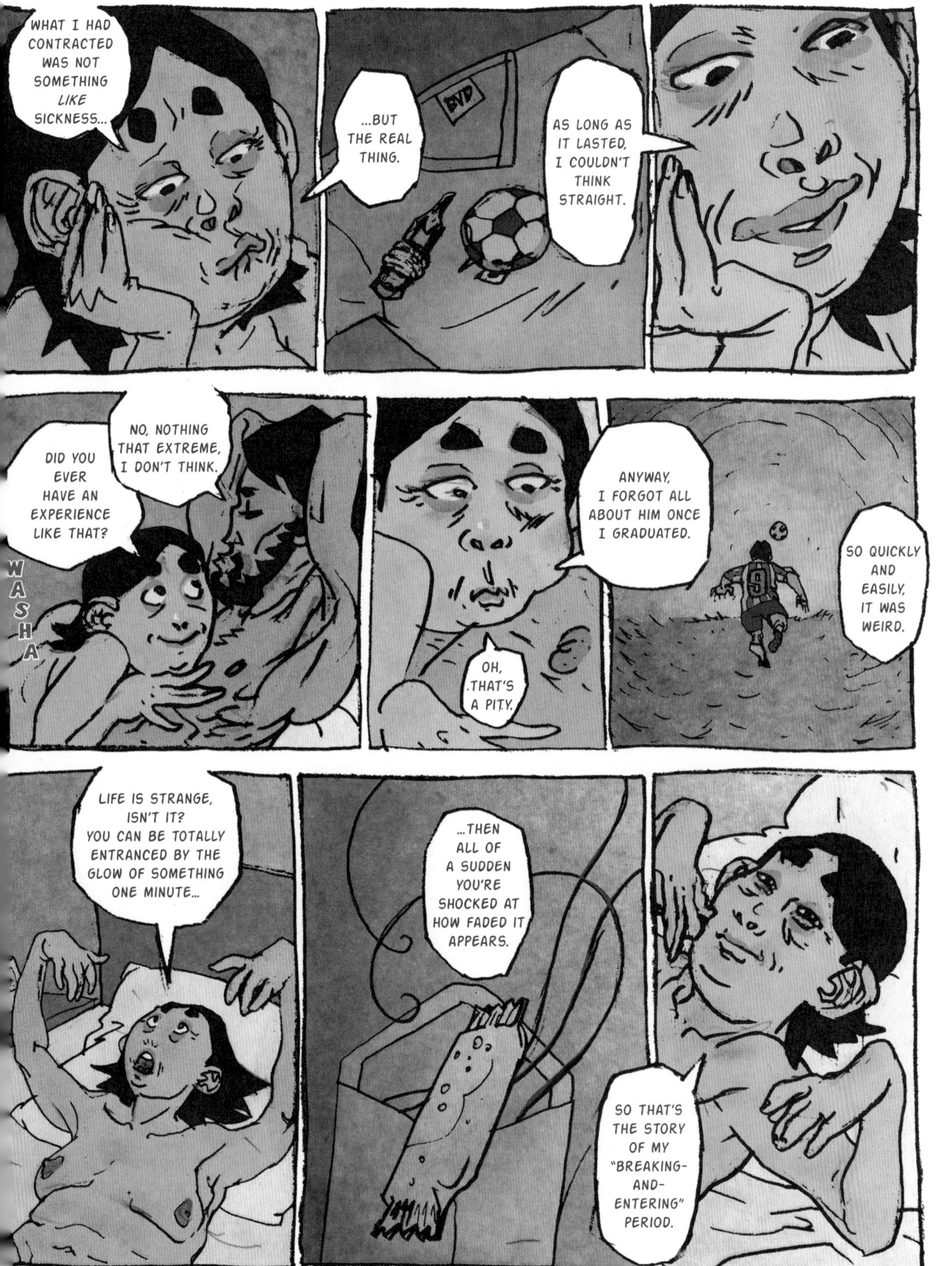
WHAT I HAD CONTRACTED WAS NOT SOMETHING *LIKE* SICKNESS...
...BUT THE REAL THING.
BVD
AS LONG AS IT LASTED, I COULDN'T THINK STRAIGHT.
DID YOU EVER HAVE AN EXPERIENCE LIKE THAT?
NO, NOTHING THAT EXTREME, I DON'T THINK.
WASHA
ANYWAY, I FORGOT ALL ABOUT HIM ONCE I GRADUATED.
OH, THAT'S A PITY.
SO QUICKLY AND EASILY, IT WAS WEIRD.
LIFE IS STRANGE, ISN'T IT? YOU CAN BE TOTALLY ENTRANCED BY THE GLOW OF SOMETHING ONE MINUTE...
...THEN ALL OF A SUDDEN YOU'RE SHOCKED AT HOW FADED IT APPEARS.
SO THAT'S THE STORY OF MY "BREAKING-AND-ENTERING" PERIOD.

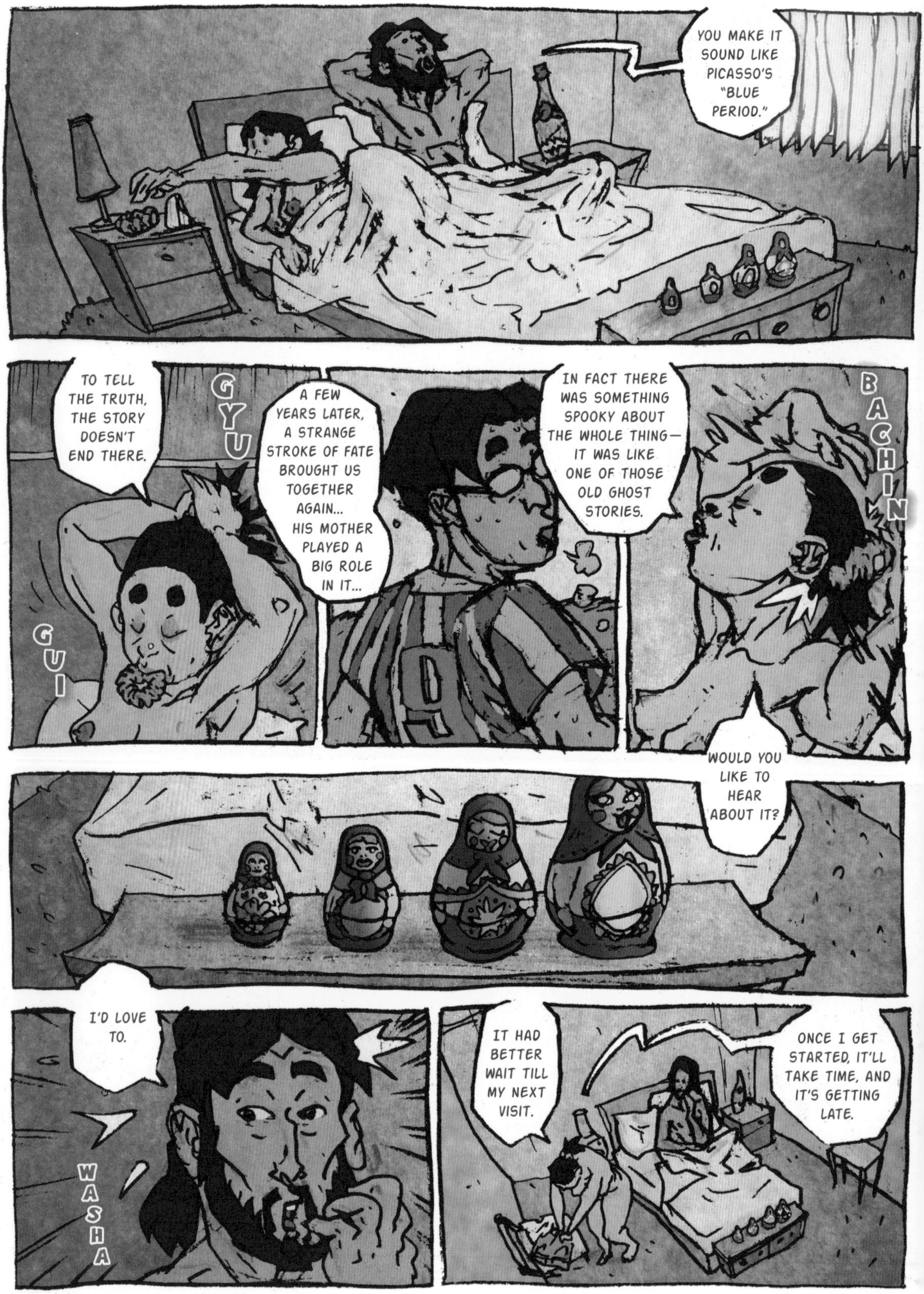
YOU MAKE IT SOUND LIKE PICASSO'S "BLUE PERIOD."
TO TELL THE TRUTH, THE STORY DOESN'T END THERE.
GYU
GUI
A FEW YEARS LATER, A STRANGE STROKE OF FATE BROUGHT US TOGETHER AGAIN... HIS MOTHER PLAYED A BIG ROLE IN IT...
IN FACT THERE WAS SOMETHING SPOOKY ABOUT THE WHOLE THING— IT WAS LIKE ONE OF THOSE OLD GHOST STORIES.
BACHIN
WOULD YOU LIKE TO HEAR ABOUT IT?
I'D LOVE TO.
WASHA
IT HAD BETTER WAIT TILL MY NEXT VISIT.
ONCE I GET STARTED, IT'LL TAKE TIME, AND IT'S GETTING LATE.

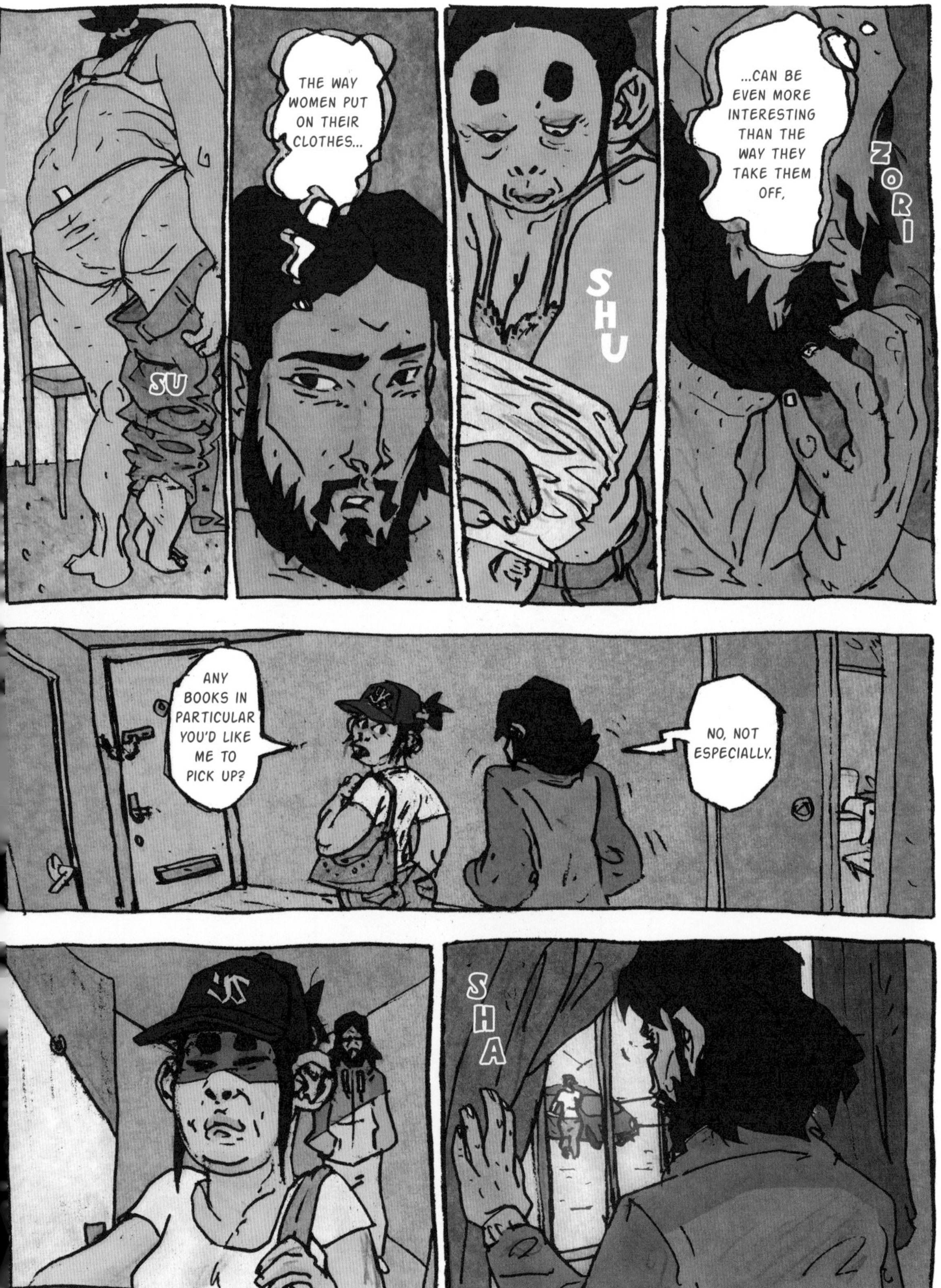
SU
THE WAY WOMEN PUT ON THEIR CLOTHES...
SHU
...CAN BE EVEN MORE INTERESTING THAN THE WAY THEY TAKE THEM OFF.
ZORI
ANY BOOKS IN PARTICULAR YOU'D LIKE ME TO PICK UP?
NO, NOT ESPECIALLY.
SHA

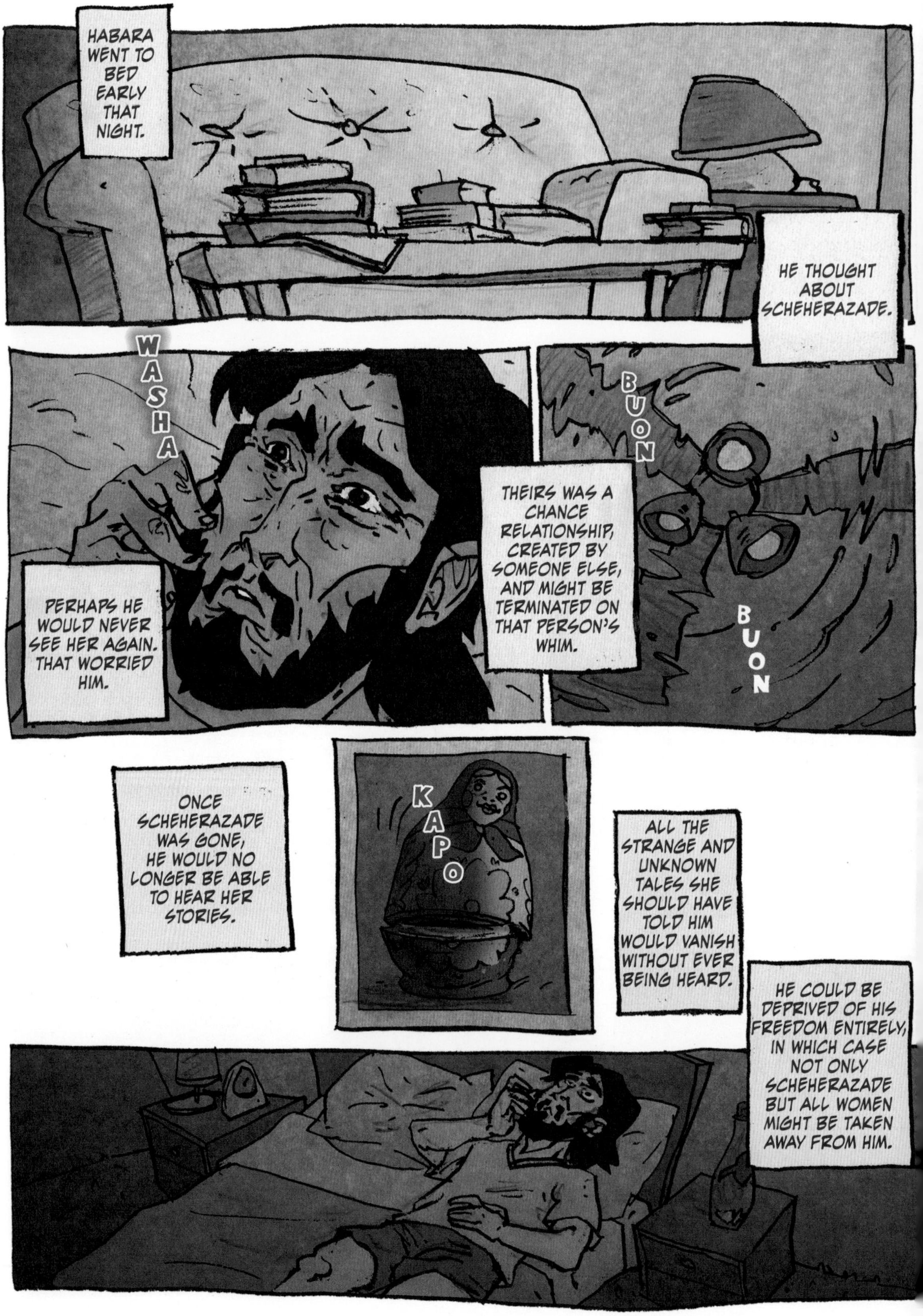
HABARA WENT TO BED EARLY THAT NIGHT.
HE THOUGHT ABOUT SCHEHERAZADE.
WASHA
PERHAPS HE WOULD NEVER SEE HER AGAIN. THAT WORRIED HIM.
THEIRS WAS A CHANCE RELATIONSHIP, CREATED BY SOMEONE ELSE, AND MIGHT BE TERMINATED ON THAT PERSON'S WHIM.
BUON
BUON
ONCE SCHEHERAZADE WAS GONE, HE WOULD NO LONGER BE ABLE TO HEAR HER STORIES.
KAPO
ALL THE STRANGE AND UNKNOWN TALES SHE SHOULD HAVE TOLD HIM WOULD VANISH WITHOUT EVER BEING HEARD.
HE COULD BE DEPRIVED OF HIS FREEDOM ENTIRELY, IN WHICH CASE NOT ONLY SCHEHERAZADE BUT ALL WOMEN MIGHT BE TAKEN AWAY FROM HIM.

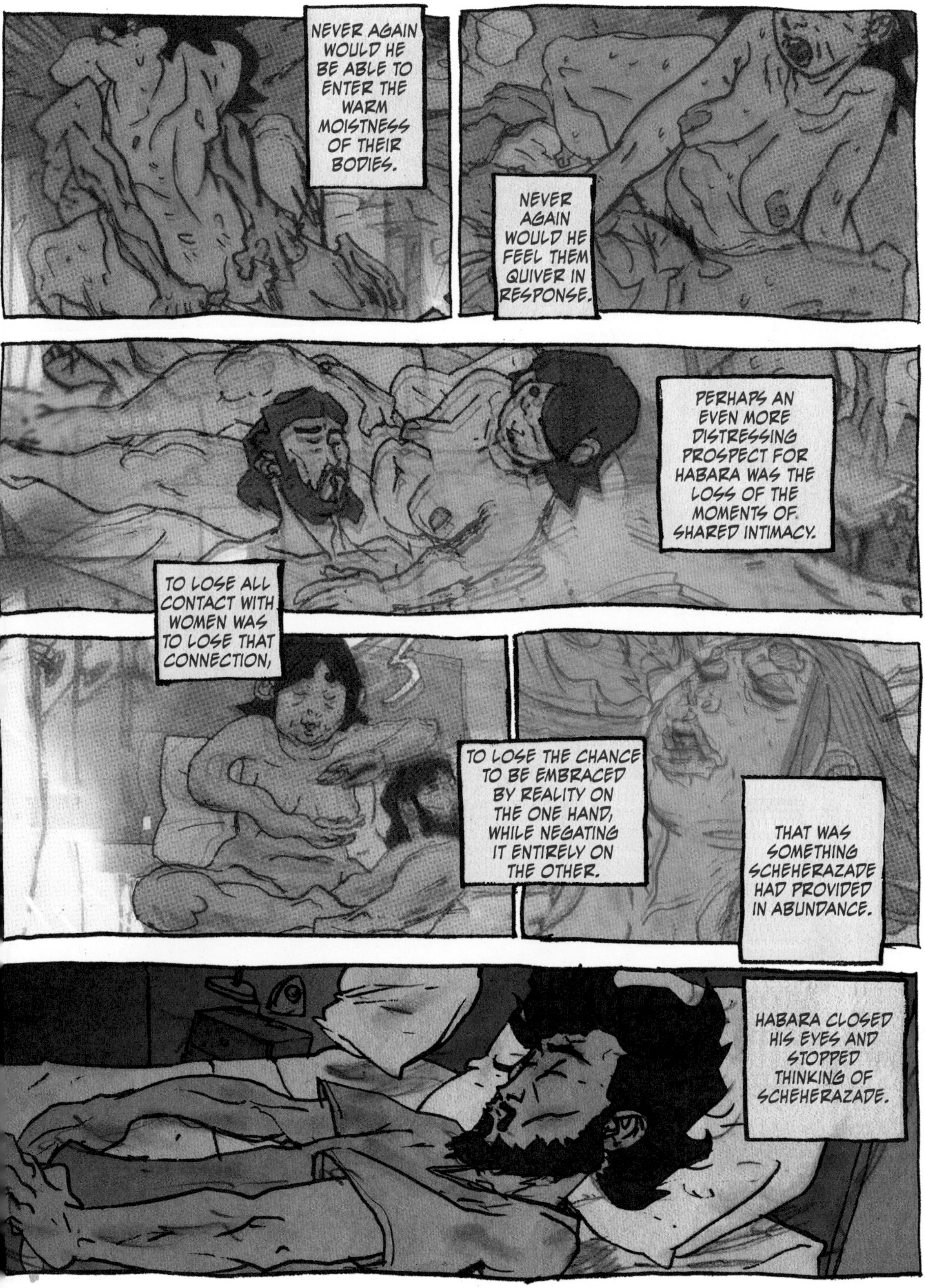
NEVER AGAIN WOULD HE BE ABLE TO ENTER THE WARM MOISTNESS OF THEIR BODIES.
NEVER AGAIN WOULD HE FEEL THEM QUIVER IN RESPONSE.
PERHAPS AN EVEN MORE DISTRESSING PROSPECT FOR HABARA WAS THE LOSS OF THE MOMENTS OF SHARED INTIMACY.
TO LOSE ALL CONTACT WITH WOMEN WAS TO LOSE THAT CONNECTION,
TO LOSE THE CHANCE TO BE EMBRACED BY REALITY ON THE ONE HAND, WHILE NEGATING IT ENTIRELY ON THE OTHER.
THAT WAS SOMETHING SCHEHERAZADE HAD PROVIDED IN ABUNDANCE.
HABARA CLOSED HIS EYES AND STOPPED THINKING OF SCHEHERAZADE.

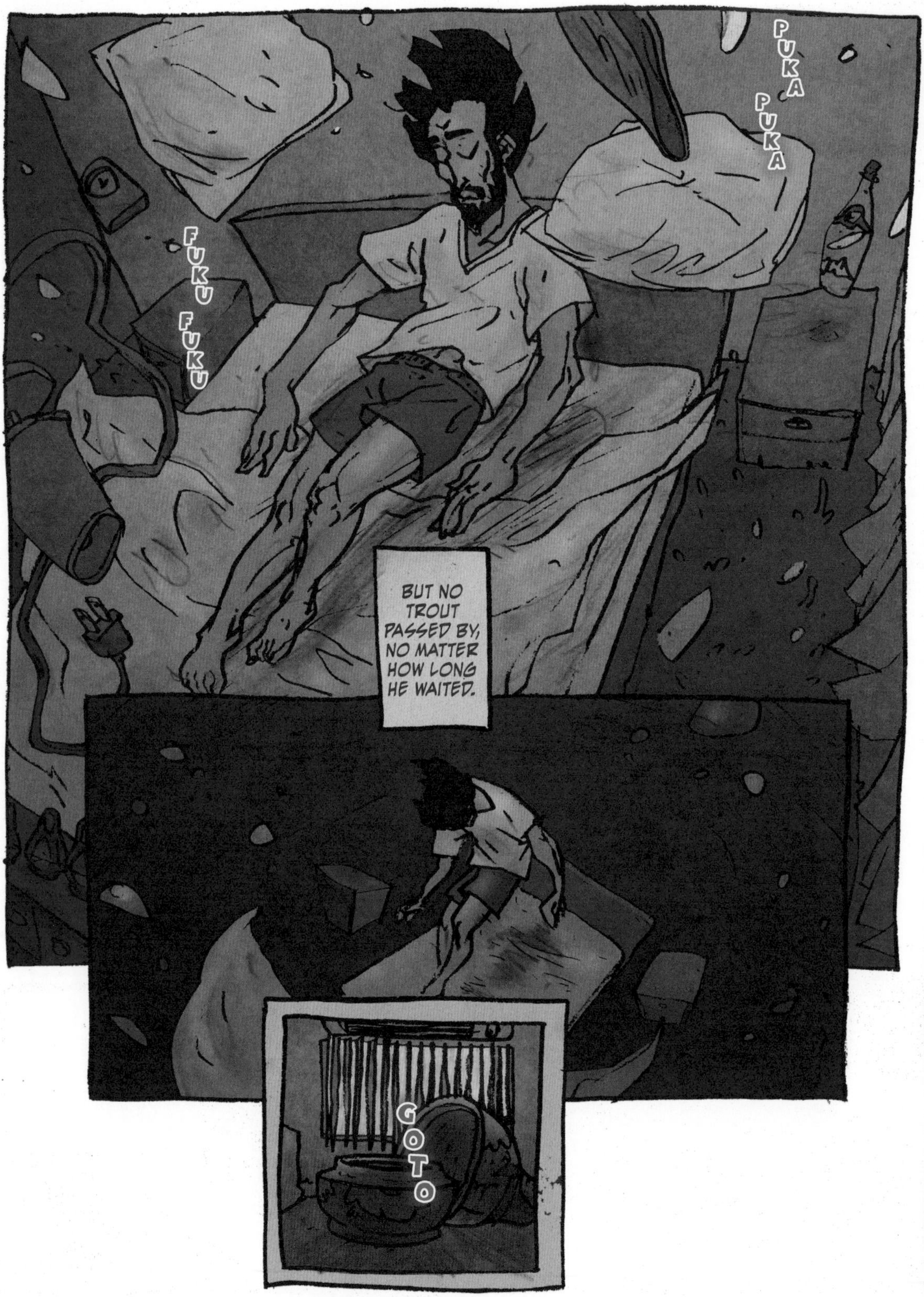
PUKA PUKA
FUKU FUKU
BUT NO TROUT PASSED BY, NO MATTER HOW LONG HE WAITED.
GOTO

SLEEP

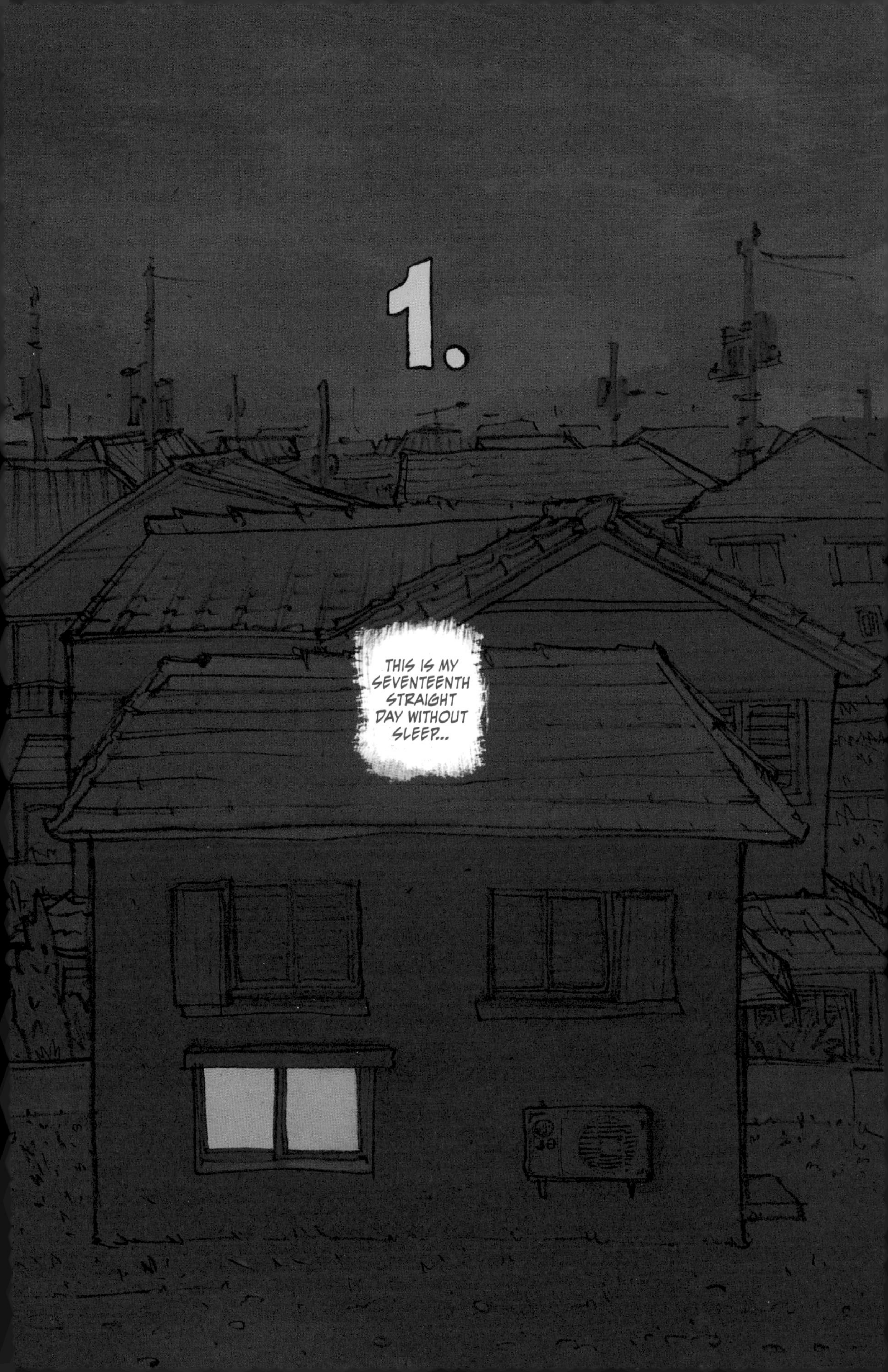
1.
THIS IS MY SEVENTEENTH STRAIGHT DAY WITHOUT SLEEP...

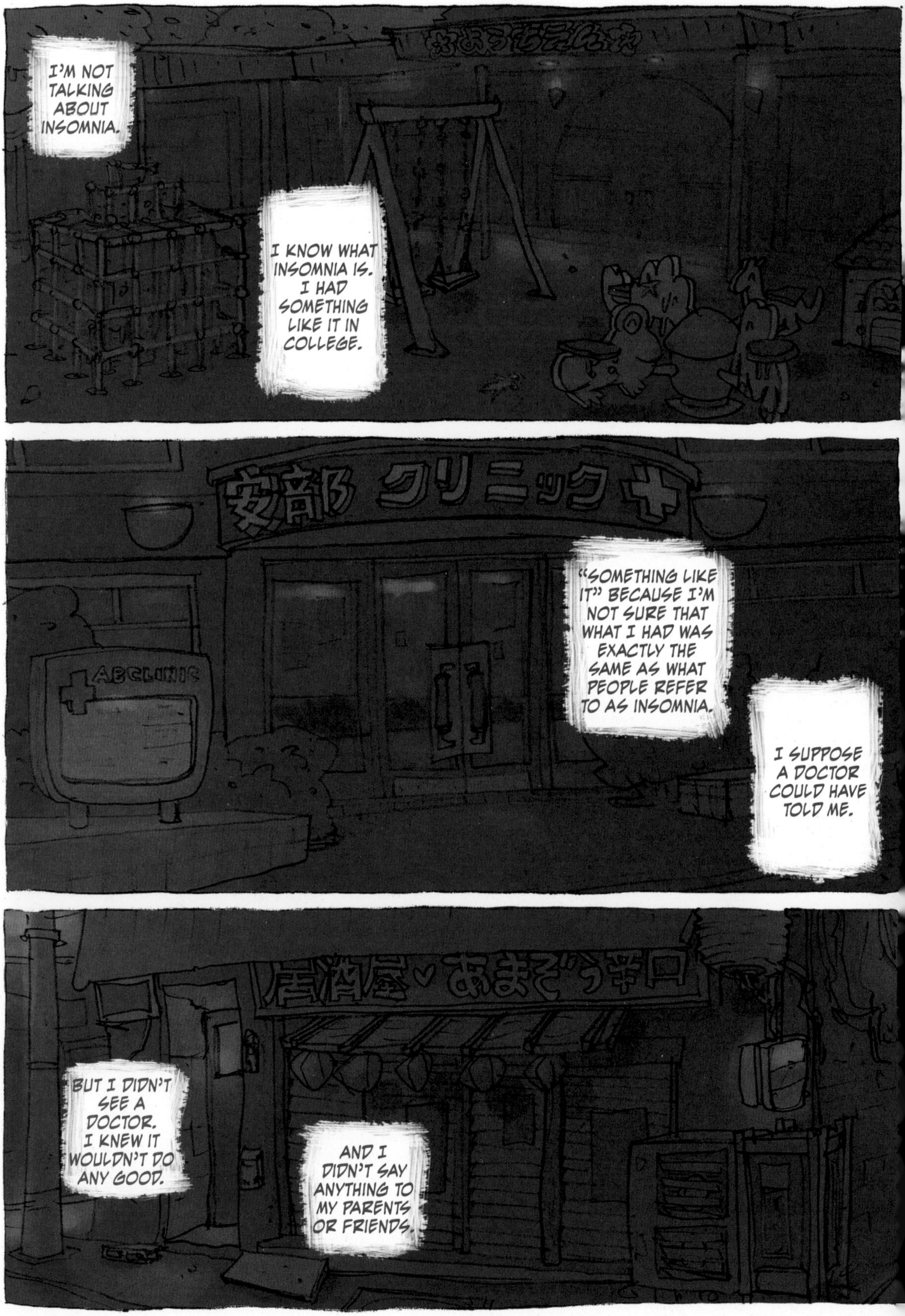
I'M NOT TALKING ABOUT INSOMNIA.
I KNOW WHAT INSOMNIA IS. I HAD SOMETHING LIKE IT IN COLLEGE.
安部 クリニック
ABCLINIC
"SOMETHING LIKE IT" BECAUSE I'M NOT SURE THAT WHAT I HAD WAS EXACTLY THE SAME AS WHAT PEOPLE REFER TO AS INSOMNIA.
I SUPPOSE A DOCTOR COULD HAVE TOLD ME.
BUT I DIDN'T SEE A DOCTOR. I KNEW IT WOULDN'T DO ANY GOOD.
AND I DIDN'T SAY ANYTHING TO MY PARENTS OR FRIENDS.

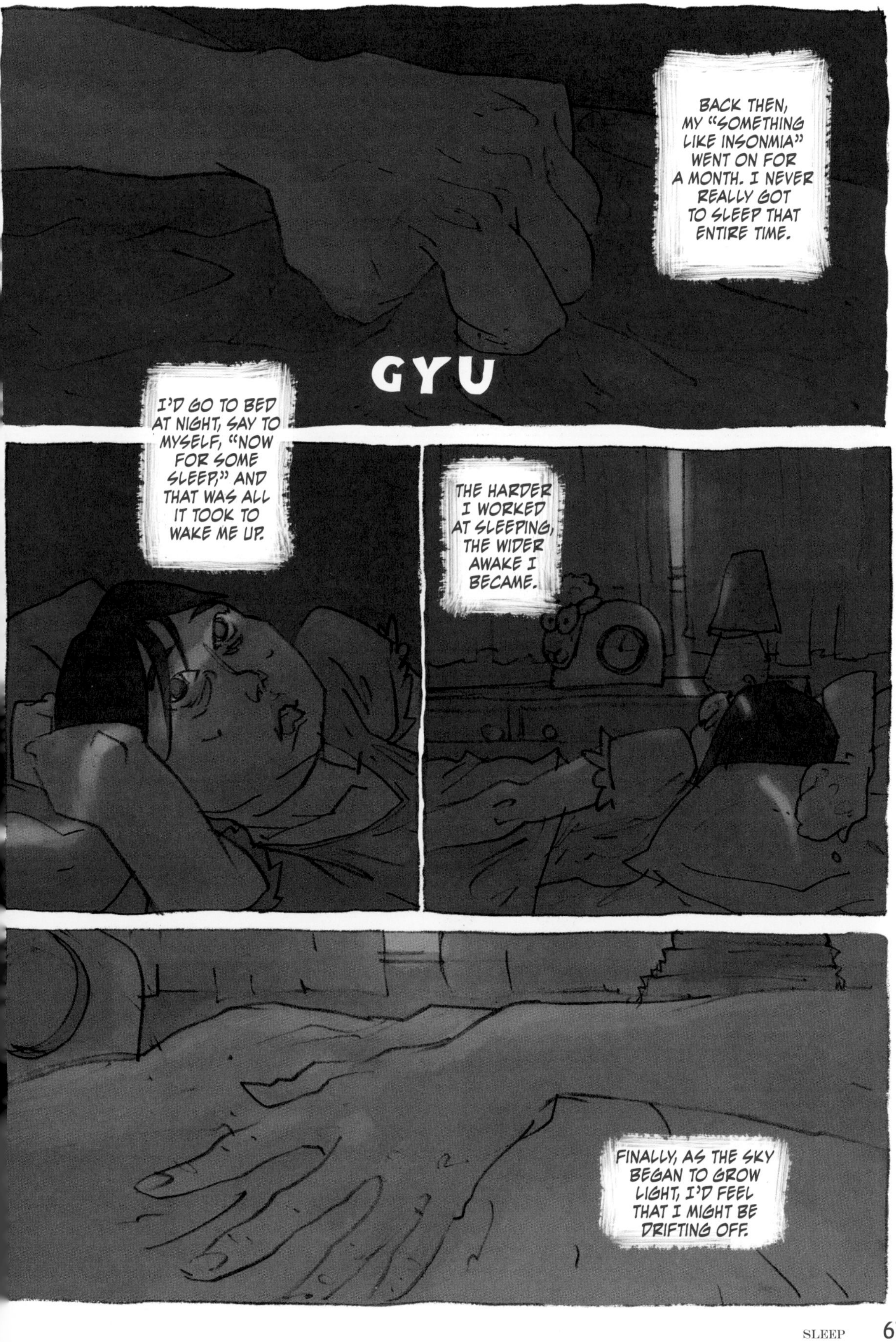
BACK THEN, MY "SOMETHING LIKE INSONMIA" WENT ON FOR A MONTH. I NEVER REALLY GOT TO SLEEP THAT ENTIRE TIME.
GYU
I'D GO TO BED AT NIGHT, SAY TO MYSELF, "NOW FOR SOME SLEEP," AND THAT WAS ALL IT TOOK TO WAKE ME UP.
THE HARDER I WORKED AT SLEEPING, THE WIDER AWAKE I BECAME.
FINALLY, AS THE SKY BEGAN TO GROW LIGHT, I'D FEEL THAT I MIGHT BE DRIFTING OFF.

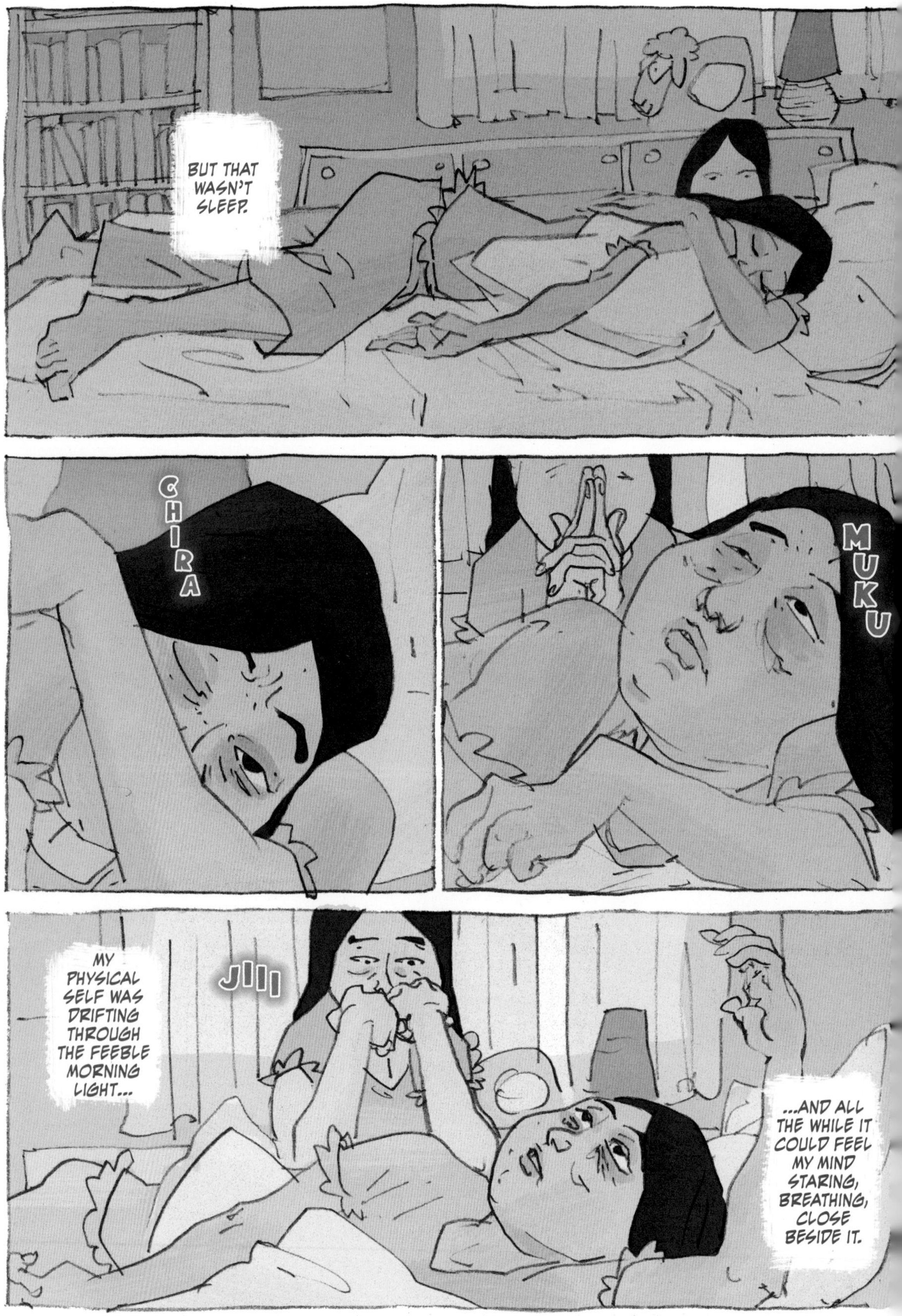
BUT THAT WASN'T SLEEP.
CHIRA
MUKU
MY PHYSICAL SELF WAS DRIFTING THROUGH THE FEEBLE MORNING LIGHT...
JIII
...AND ALL THE WHILE IT COULD FEEL MY MIND STARING, BREATHING, CLOSE BESIDE IT.

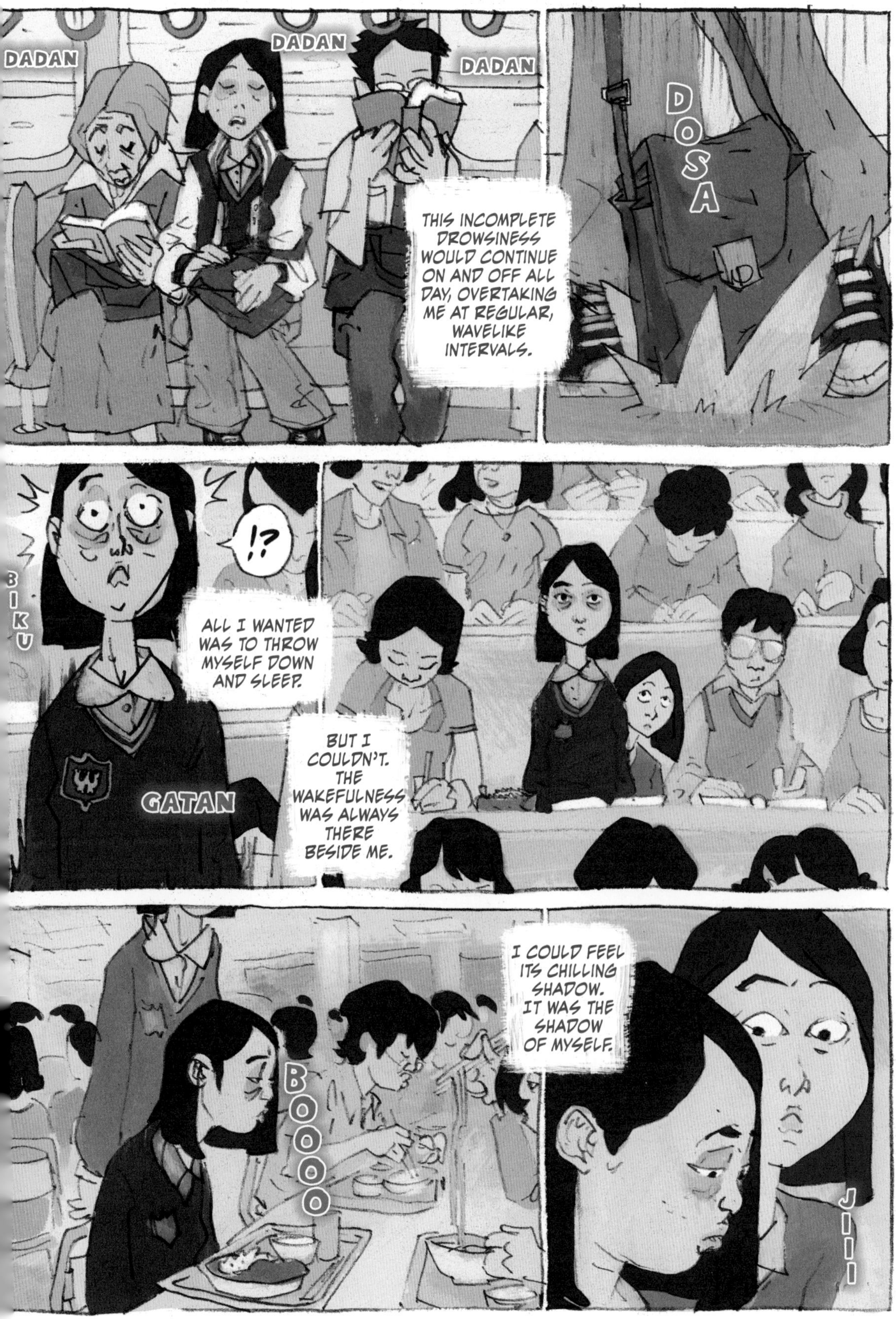

DADAN
DADAN
DADAN
THIS INCOMPLETE DROWSINESS WOULD CONTINUE ON AND OFF ALL DAY, OVERTAKING ME AT REGULAR, WAVELIKE INTERVALS.
DOSA
BIKU
!?
ALL I WANTED WAS TO THROW MYSELF DOWN AND SLEEP.
GATAN
BUT I COULDN'T. THE WAKEFULNESS WAS ALWAYS THERE BESIDE ME.
I COULD FEEL ITS CHILLING SHADOW. IT WAS THE SHADOW OF MYSELF.
BOOOO
JIII

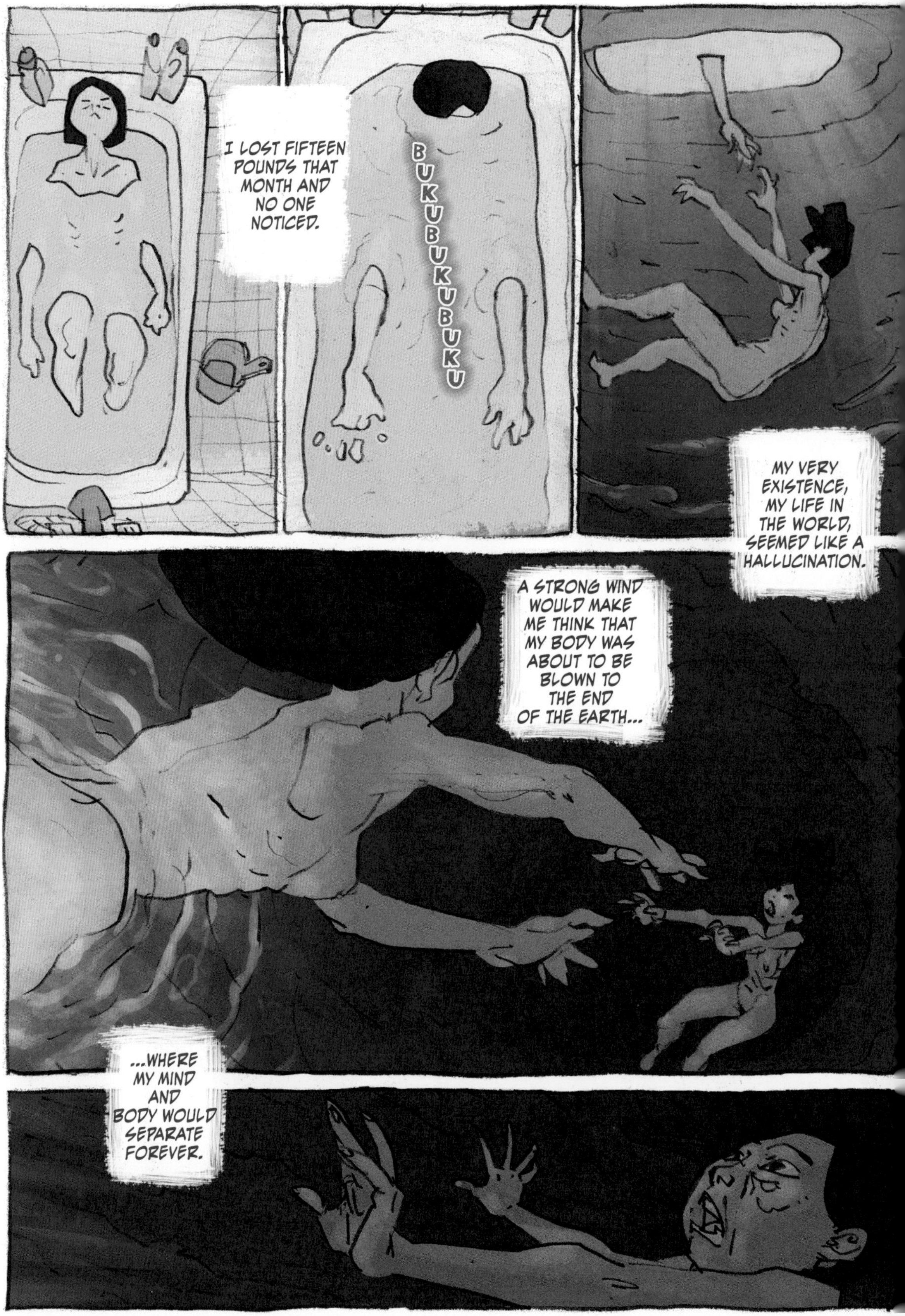
I LOST FIFTEEN POUNDS THAT MONTH AND NO ONE NOTICED.
BUKUBUKUBUKU
MY VERY EXISTENCE, MY LIFE IN THE WORLD, SEEMED LIKE A HALLUCINATION.
A STRONG WIND WOULD MAKE ME THINK THAT MY BODY WAS ABOUT TO BE BLOWN TO THE END OF THE EARTH...
...WHERE MY MIND AND BODY WOULD SEPARATE FOREVER.

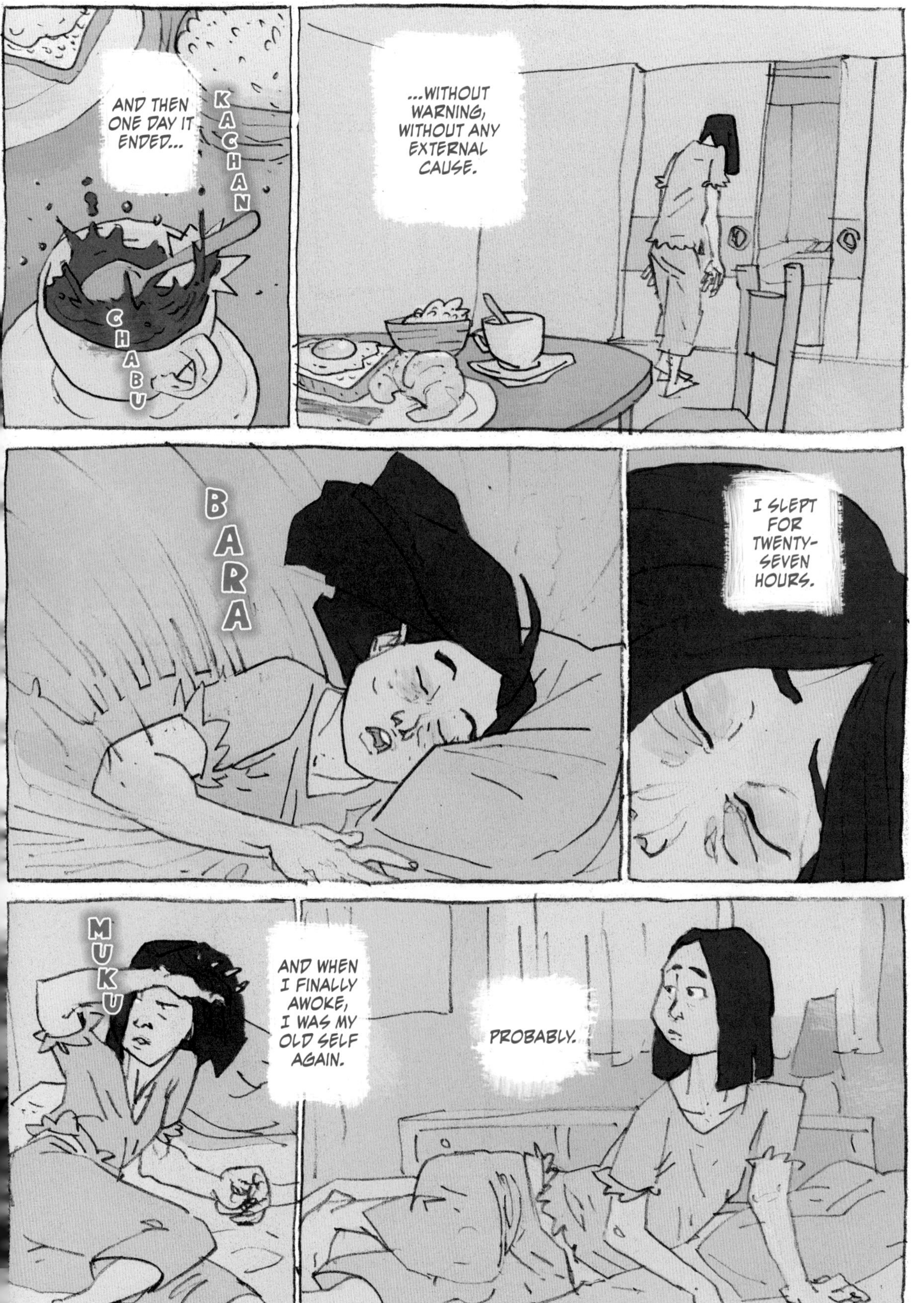
AND THEN ONE DAY IT ENDED...
KACHAN
CHABU
...WITHOUT WARNING, WITHOUT ANY EXTERNAL CAUSE.
BARA
I SLEPT FOR TWENTY-SEVEN HOURS.
MUKU
AND WHEN I FINALLY AWOKE, I WAS MY OLD SELF AGAIN.
PROBABLY.

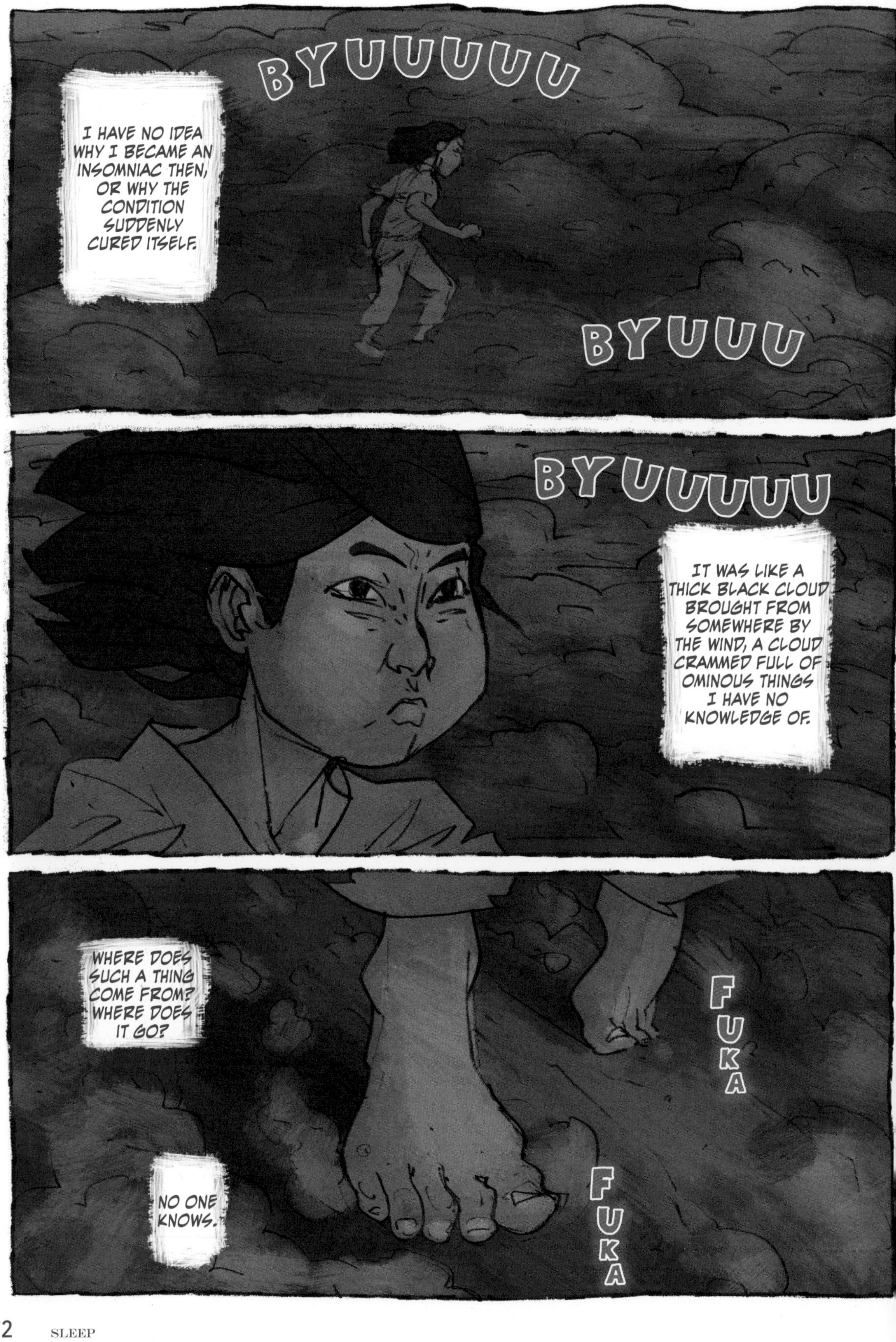
BYUUUUU
I HAVE NO IDEA WHY I BECAME AN INSOMNIAC THEN, OR WHY THE CONDITION SUDDENLY CURED ITSELF.
BYUUU
BYUUUUU
IT WAS LIKE A THICK BLACK CLOUD BROUGHT FROM SOMEWHERE BY THE WIND, A CLOUD CRAMMED FULL OF OMINOUS THINGS I HAVE NO KNOWLEDGE OF.
WHERE DOES SUCH A THING COME FROM? WHERE DOES IT GO?
FUKA
NO ONE KNOWS.
FUKA

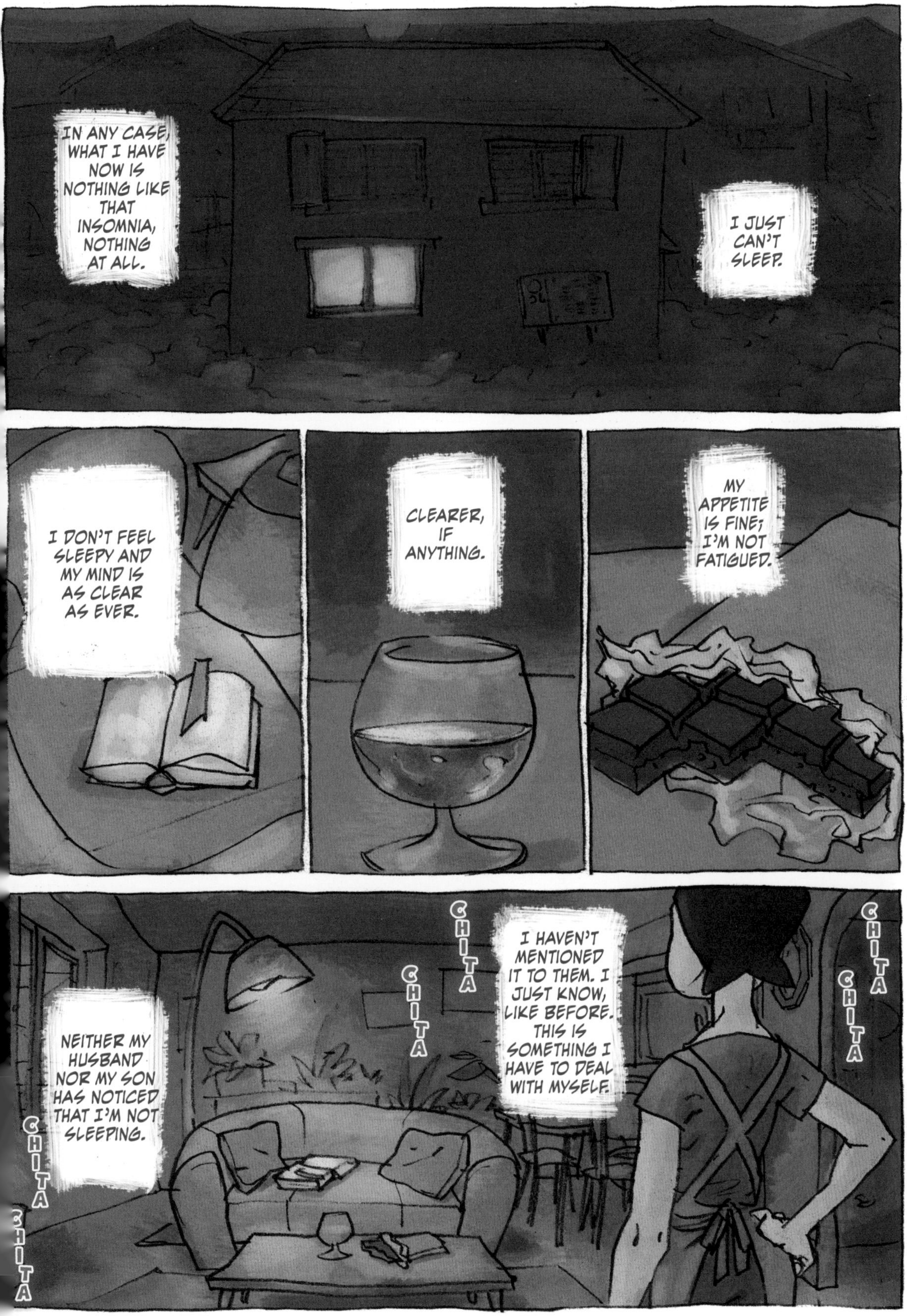
IN ANY CASE, WHAT I HAVE NOW IS NOTHING LIKE THAT INSOMNIA, NOTHING AT ALL.
I JUST CAN'T SLEEP.
I DON'T FEEL SLEEPY AND MY MIND IS AS CLEAR AS EVER.
CLEARER, IF ANYTHING.
MY APPETITE IS FINE; I'M NOT FATIGUED.
NEITHER MY HUSBAND NOR MY SON HAS NOTICED THAT I'M NOT SLEEPING.
CHITA
CHITA
CHITA
CHITA
I HAVEN'T MENTIONED IT TO THEM. I JUST KNOW, LIKE BEFORE. THIS IS SOMETHING I HAVE TO DEAL WITH MYSELF.
CHITA
CHITA

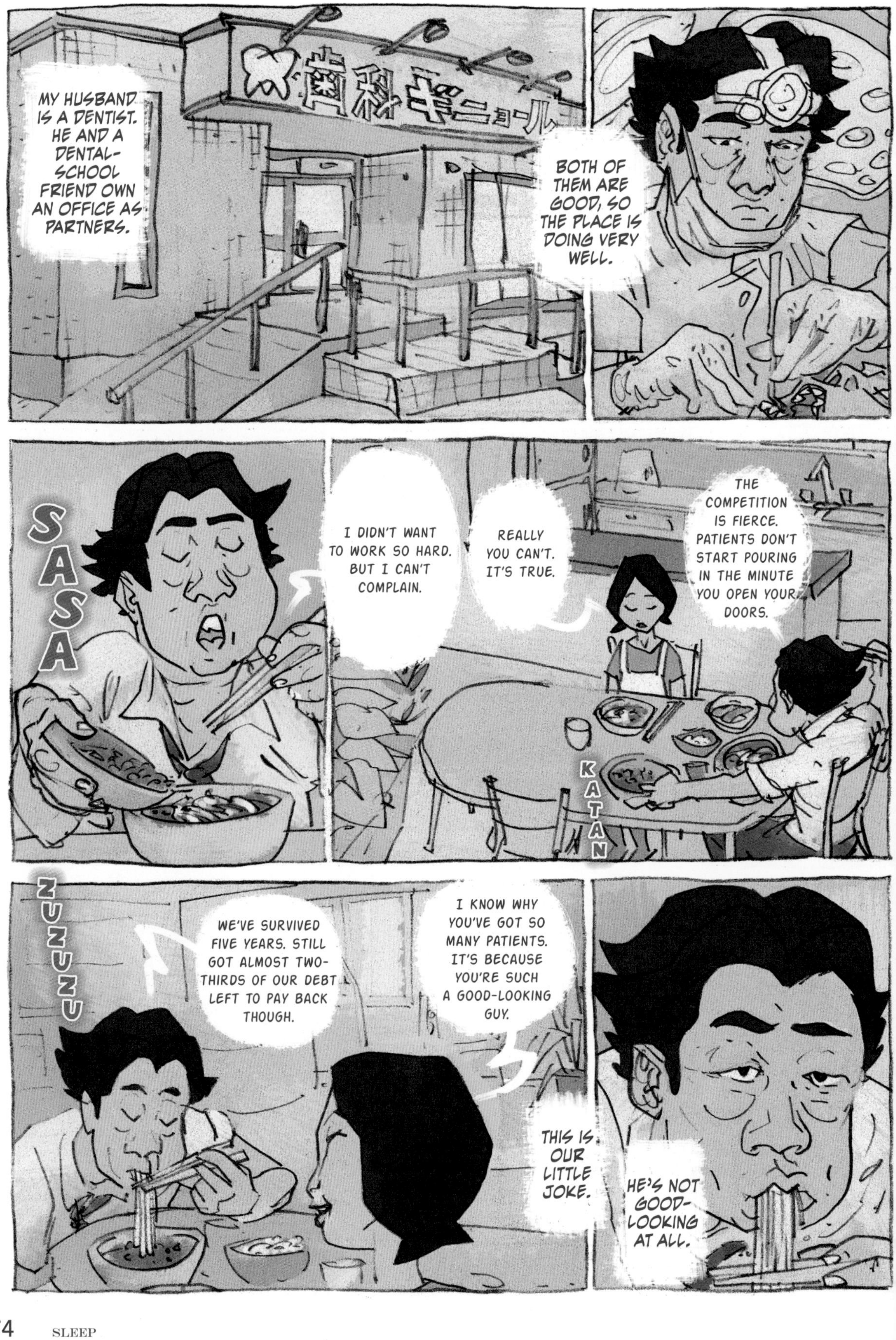
MY HUSBAND IS A DENTIST. HE AND A DENTAL-SCHOOL FRIEND OWN AN OFFICE AS PARTNERS.
BOTH OF THEM ARE GOOD, SO THE PLACE IS DOING VERY WELL.
SASA
I DIDN'T WANT TO WORK SO HARD. BUT I CAN'T COMPLAIN.
REALLY YOU CAN'T. IT'S TRUE.
THE COMPETITION IS FIERCE. PATIENTS DON'T START POURING IN THE MINUTE YOU OPEN YOUR DOORS.
KATAN
ZUZUZU
WE'VE SURVIVED FIVE YEARS. STILL GOT ALMOST TWO-THIRDS OF OUR DEBT LEFT TO PAY BACK THOUGH.
I KNOW WHY YOU'VE GOT SO MANY PATIENTS. IT'S BECAUSE YOU'RE SUCH A GOOD-LOOKING GUY.
THIS IS OUR LITTLE JOKE.
HE'S NOT GOOD-LOOKING AT ALL.

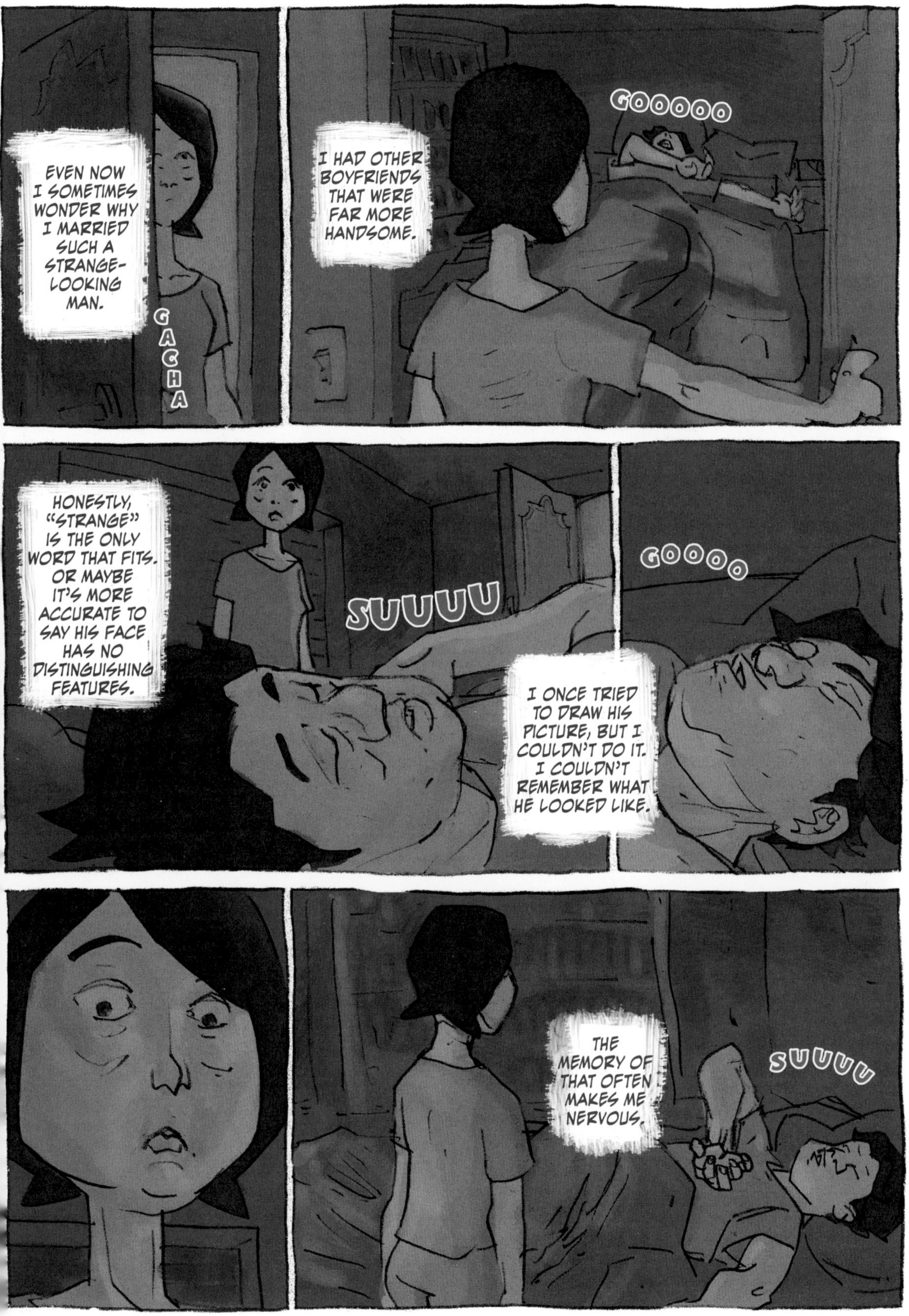

EVEN NOW I SOMETIMES WONDER WHY I MARRIED SUCH A STRANGE-LOOKING MAN.
GACHA
I HAD OTHER BOYFRIENDS THAT WERE FAR MORE HANDSOME.
GOOOOO
HONESTLY, "STRANGE" IS THE ONLY WORD THAT FITS. OR MAYBE IT'S MORE ACCURATE TO SAY HIS FACE HAS NO DISTINGUISHING FEATURES.
SUUUU
GOOOO
I ONCE TRIED TO DRAW HIS PICTURE, BUT I COULDN'T DO IT. I COULDN'T REMEMBER WHAT HE LOOKED LIKE.
THE MEMORY OF THAT OFTEN MAKES ME NERVOUS.
SUUUU

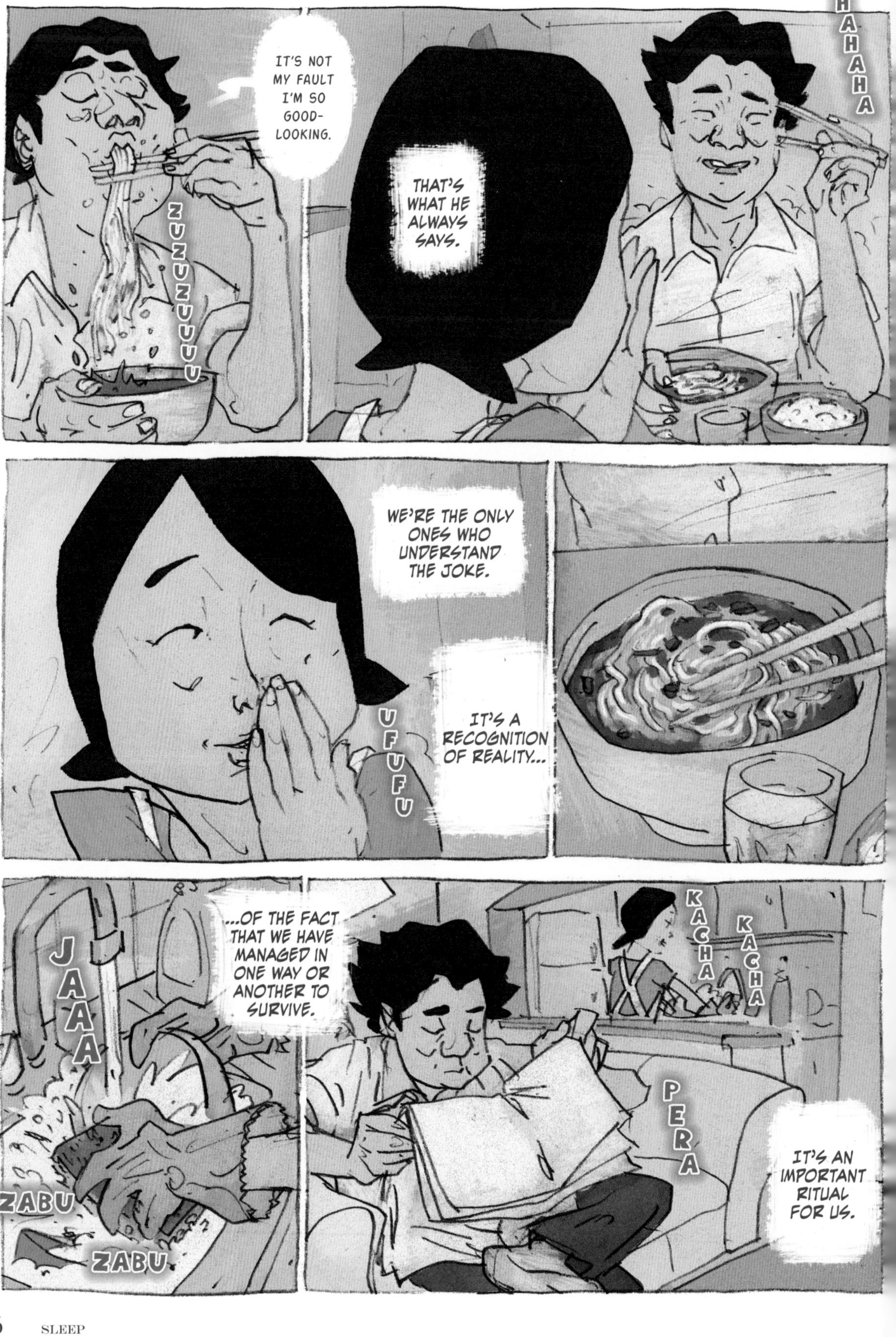
IT'S NOT MY FAULT I'M SO GOOD-LOOKING.
ZUZUZUUUU
HAHAHA
THAT'S WHAT HE ALWAYS SAYS.
WE'RE THE ONLY ONES WHO UNDERSTAND THE JOKE.
UFUFU
IT'S A RECOGNITION OF REALITY...
...OF THE FACT THAT WE HAVE MANAGED IN ONE WAY OR ANOTHER TO SURVIVE.
JAAAA
ZABU
ZABU
KACHA
KACHA
PERA
IT'S AN IMPORTANT RITUAL FOR US.

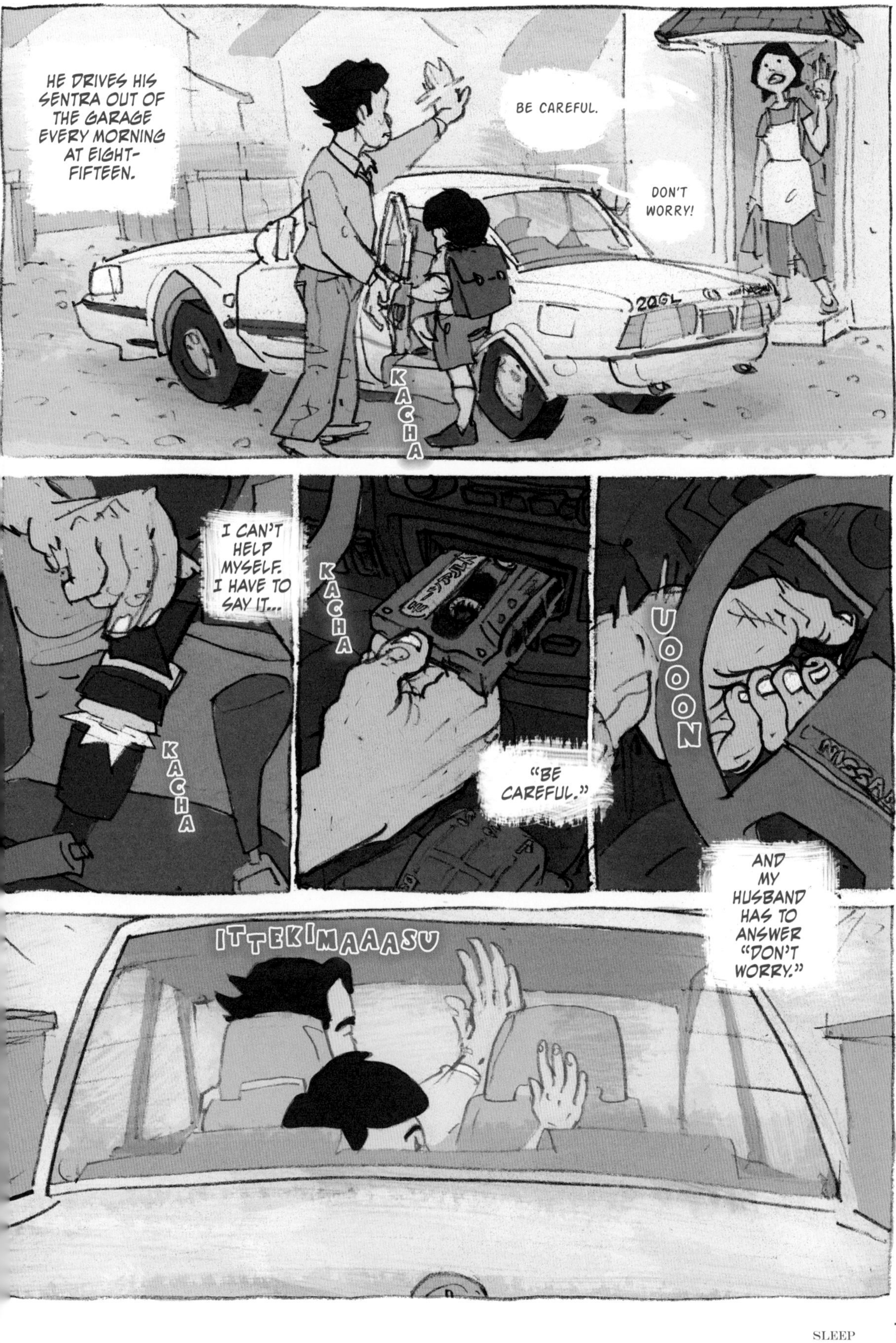
HE DRIVES HIS SENTRA OUT OF THE GARAGE EVERY MORNING AT EIGHT-FIFTEEN.
BE CAREFUL.
DON'T WORRY!
KACHA
I CAN'T HELP MYSELF. I HAVE TO SAY IT...
KACHA
KACHA
"BE CAREFUL."
UOOON
AND MY HUSBAND HAS TO ANSWER "DON'T WORRY."
ITTEKIMAAASU

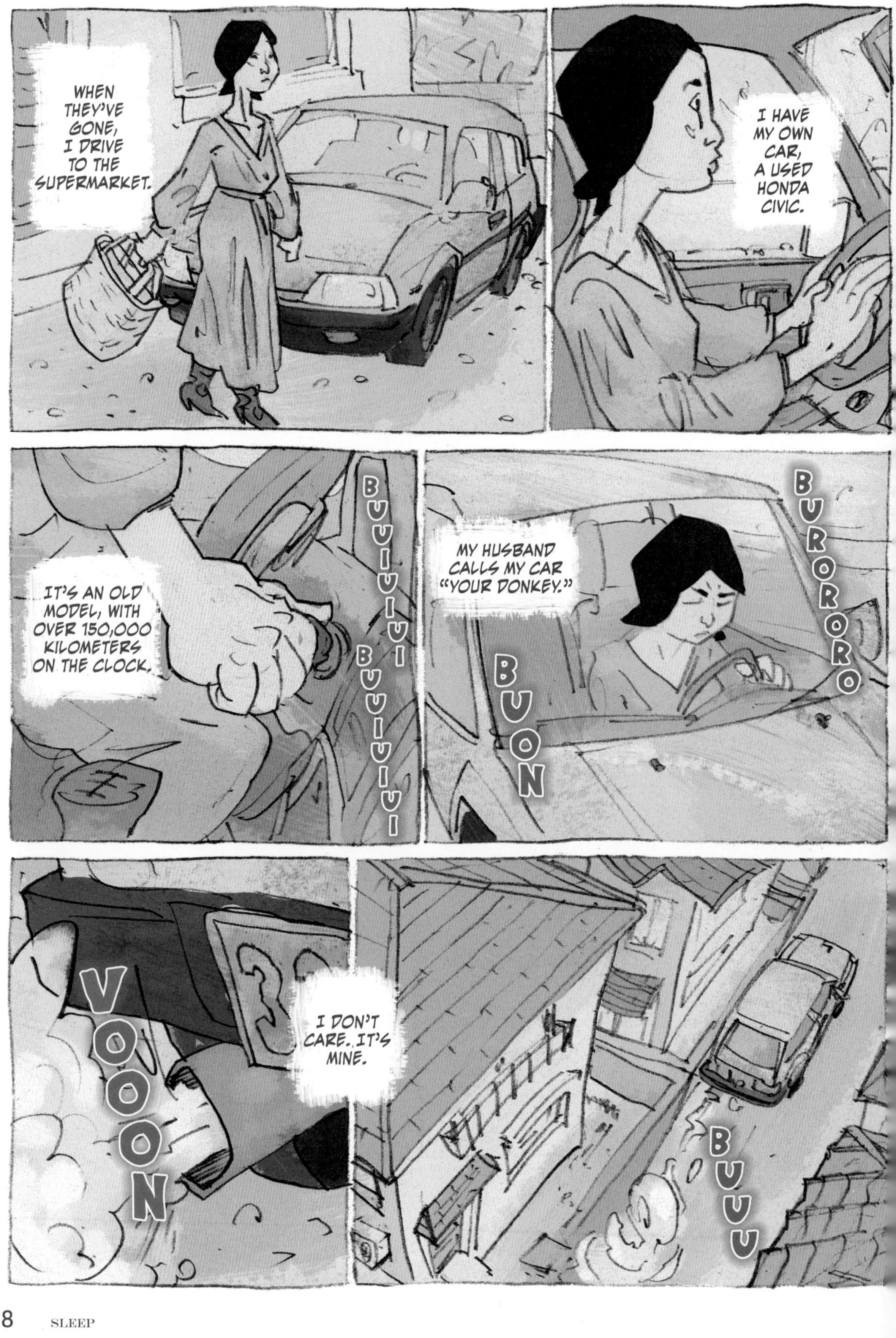

WHEN THEY'VE GONE, I DRIVE TO THE SUPERMARKET.
I HAVE MY OWN CAR, A USED HONDA CIVIC.
IT'S AN OLD MODEL, WITH OVER 150,000 KILOMETERS ON THE CLOCK.
BUUIUIUI
BUUIUIUI
MY HUSBAND CALLS MY CAR "YOUR DONKEY."
BURORORO
BUON
VOOOON
I DON'T CARE. IT'S MINE.
BUUU

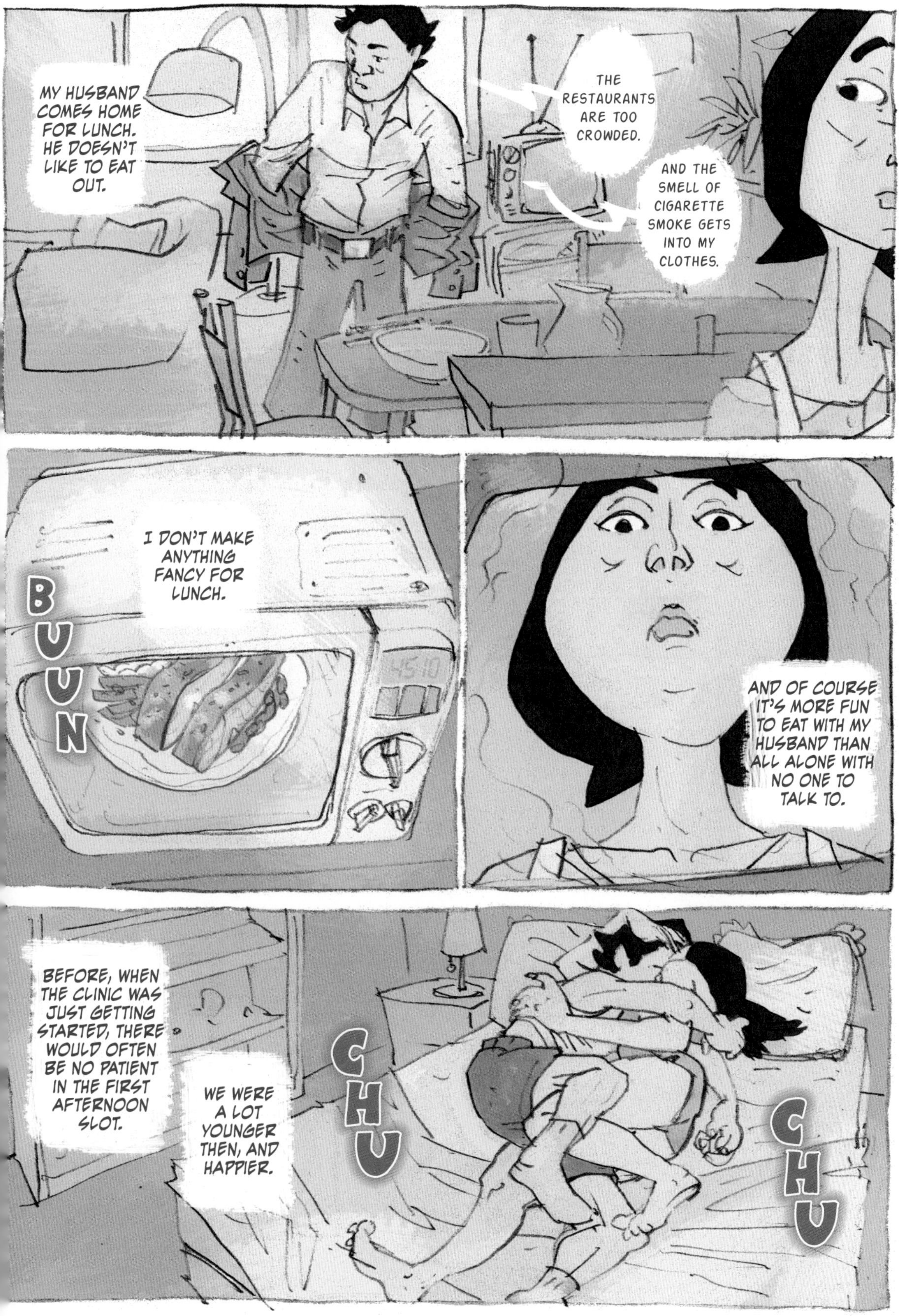
MY HUSBAND COMES HOME FOR LUNCH. HE DOESN'T LIKE TO EAT OUT.
THE RESTAURANTS ARE TOO CROWDED.
AND THE SMELL OF CIGARETTE SMOKE GETS INTO MY CLOTHES.
I DON'T MAKE ANYTHING FANCY FOR LUNCH.
BUUN
AND OF COURSE IT'S MORE FUN TO EAT WITH MY HUSBAND THAN ALL ALONE WITH NO ONE TO TALK TO.
BEFORE, WHEN THE CLINIC WAS JUST GETTING STARTED, THERE WOULD OFTEN BE NO PATIENT IN THE FIRST AFTERNOON SLOT.
WE WERE A LOT YOUNGER THEN, AND HAPPIER.
CHU
CHU

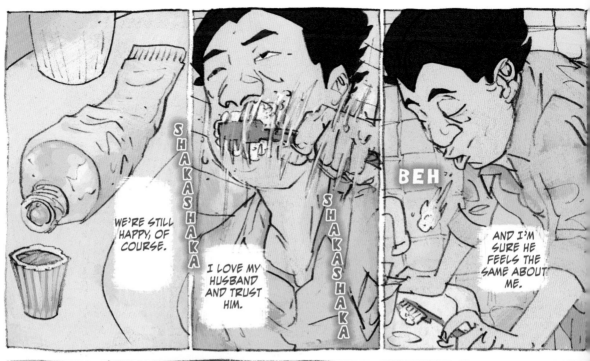

SHAKA SHAKA

SHAKA SHAKA

BEH

WE'RE STILL HAPPY, OF COURSE.

I LOVE MY HUSBAND AND TRUST HIM.

AND I'M SURE HE FEELS THE SAME ABOUT ME.

BE CAREFUL.

DON'T WORRY.

BUT LITTLE BY LITTLE, AS THE MONTHS AND YEARS GO BY, YOUR LIFE CHANGES. THAT'S JUST HOW IT IS.

BUUU

BUT THAT'S ALL RIGHT. WE BOTH KNOW YOU CAN'T HAVE EVERYTHING YOUR OWN WAY.

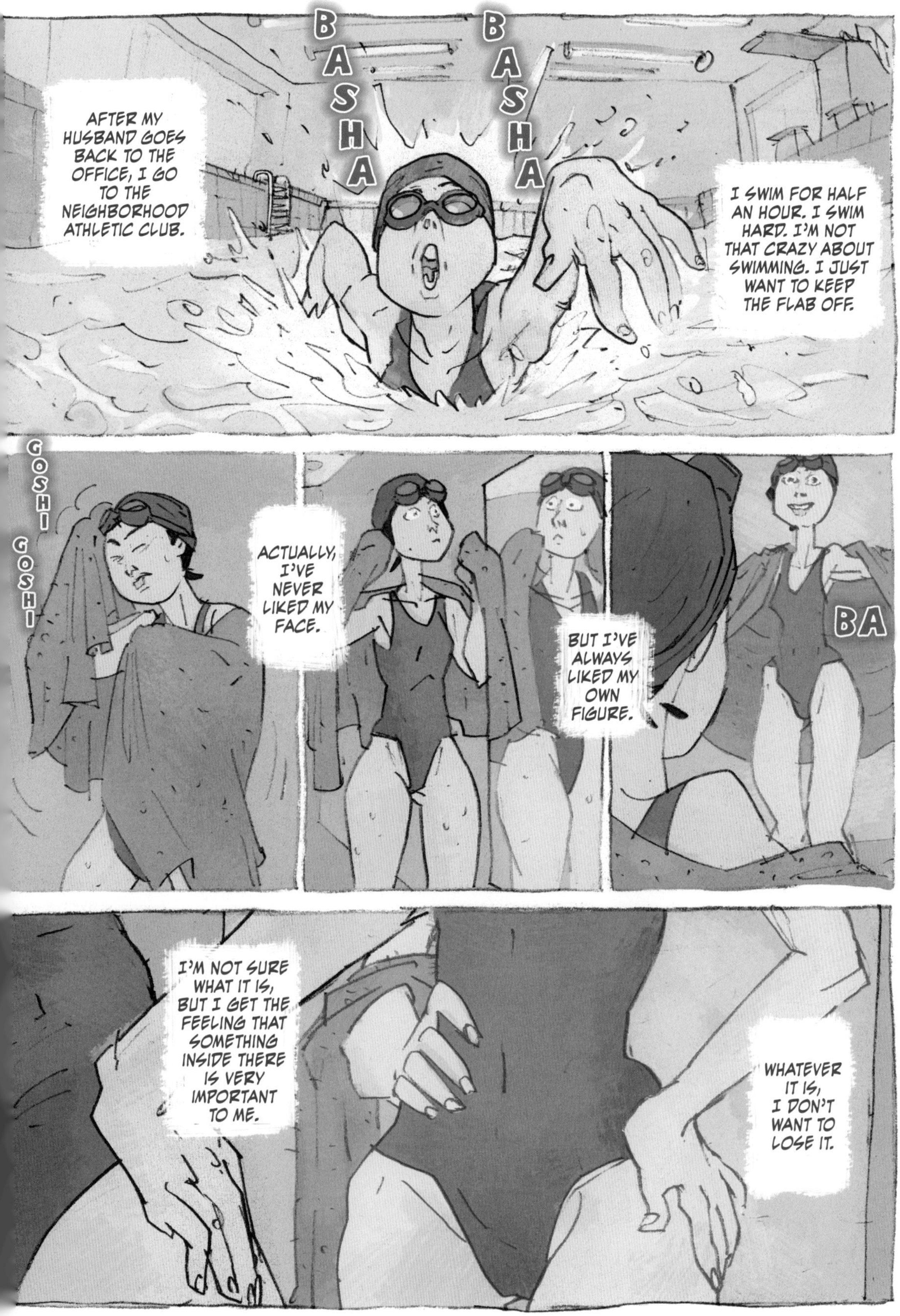
BASHA
BASHA
AFTER MY HUSBAND GOES BACK TO THE OFFICE, I GO TO THE NEIGHBORHOOD ATHLETIC CLUB.
I SWIM FOR HALF AN HOUR. I SWIM HARD. I'M NOT THAT CRAZY ABOUT SWIMMING. I JUST WANT TO KEEP THE FLAB OFF.
GOSHI GOSHI
ACTUALLY, I'VE NEVER LIKED MY FACE.
BUT I'VE ALWAYS LIKED MY OWN FIGURE.
BA
I'M NOT SURE WHAT IT IS, BUT I GET THE FEELING THAT SOMETHING INSIDE THERE IS VERY IMPORTANT TO ME.
WHATEVER IT IS, I DON'T WANT TO LOSE IT.

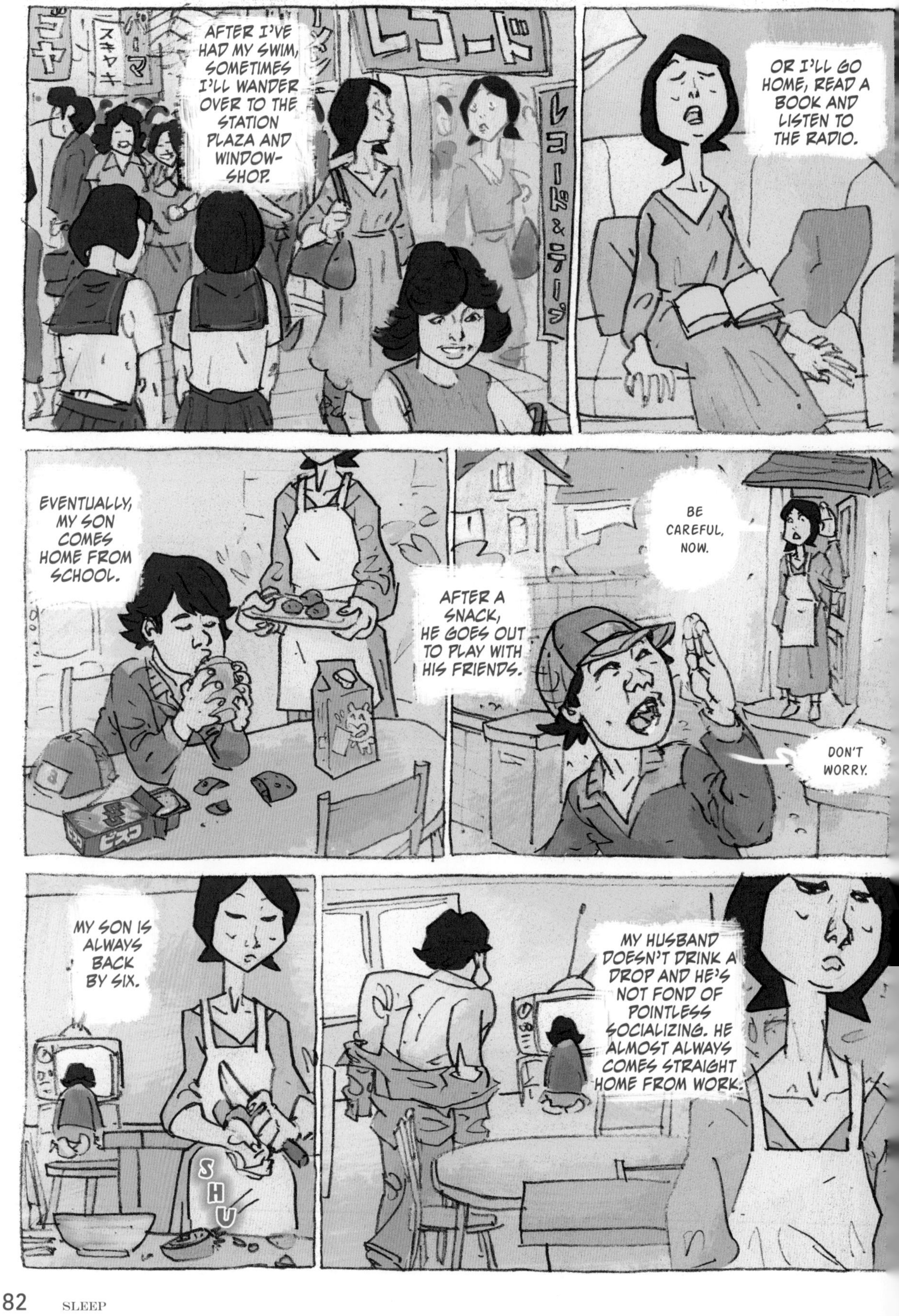
スキヤキ
パーマ
レコード
レコード&テープ
AFTER I'VE HAD MY SWIM, SOMETIMES I'LL WANDER OVER TO THE STATION PLAZA AND WINDOW-SHOP.
OR I'LL GO HOME, READ A BOOK AND LISTEN TO THE RADIO.
EVENTUALLY, MY SON COMES HOME FROM SCHOOL.
ビスコ
AFTER A SNACK, HE GOES OUT TO PLAY WITH HIS FRIENDS.
BE CAREFUL, NOW.
DON'T WORRY.
MY SON IS ALWAYS BACK BY SIX.
SHU
MY HUSBAND DOESN'T DRINK A DROP AND HE'S NOT FOND OF POINTLESS SOCIALIZING. HE ALMOST ALWAYS COMES STRAIGHT HOME FROM WORK.

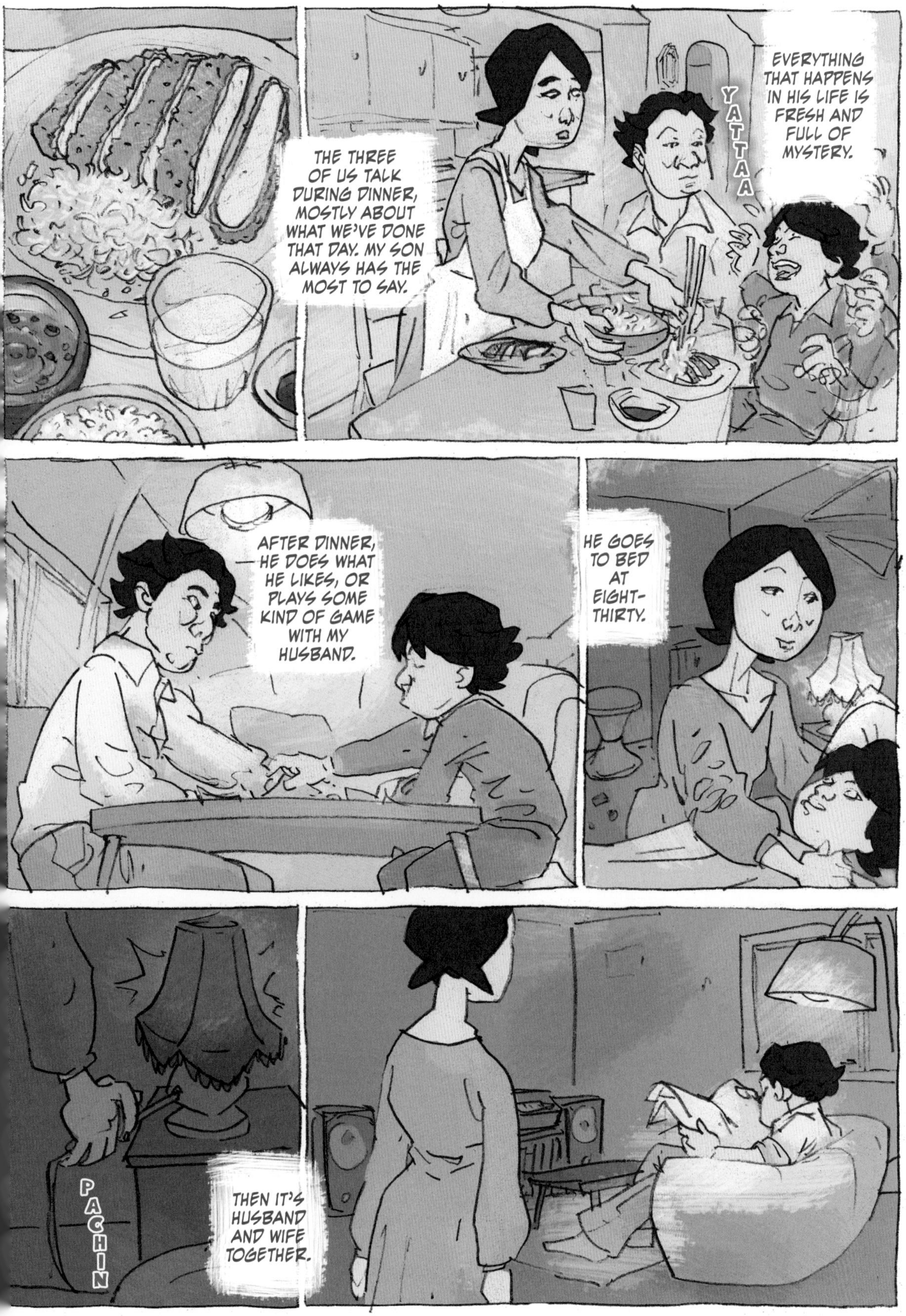
THE THREE OF US TALK DURING DINNER, MOSTLY ABOUT WHAT WE'VE DONE THAT DAY. MY SON ALWAYS HAS THE MOST TO SAY.
YATTAA
EVERYTHING THAT HAPPENS IN HIS LIFE IS FRESH AND FULL OF MYSTERY.
AFTER DINNER, HE DOES WHAT HE LIKES, OR PLAYS SOME KIND OF GAME WITH MY HUSBAND.
HE GOES TO BED AT EIGHT-THIRTY.
PACHIN
THEN IT'S HUSBAND AND WIFE TOGETHER.

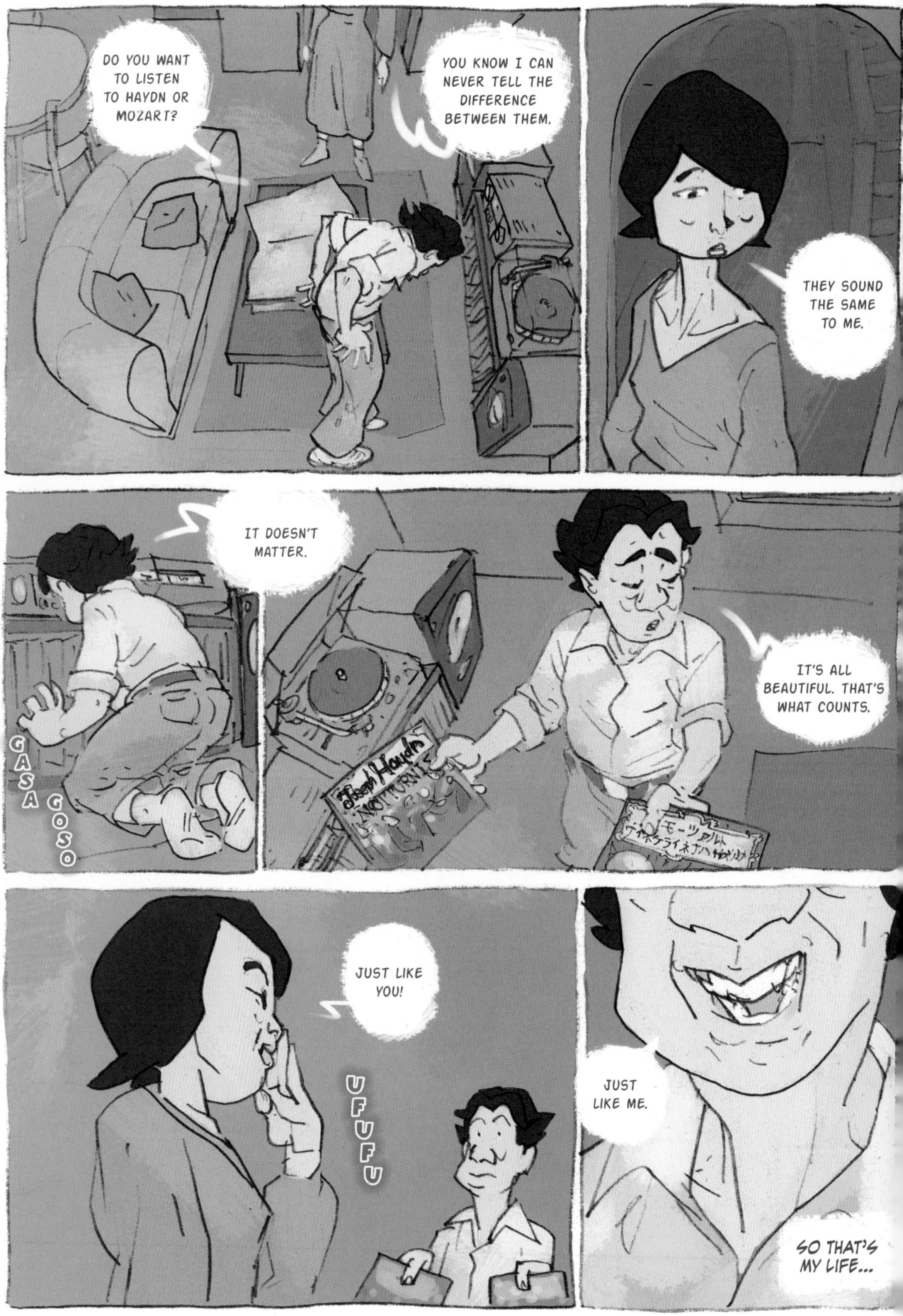
DO YOU WANT TO LISTEN TO HAYDN OR MOZART?
YOU KNOW I CAN NEVER TELL THE DIFFERENCE BETWEEN THEM.
THEY SOUND THE SAME TO ME.
IT DOESN'T MATTER.
GASA GOSO
IT'S ALL BEAUTIFUL. THAT'S WHAT COUNTS.
Joseph Haydn
NOTTURNI
JUST LIKE YOU!
UFUFU
JUST LIKE ME.
SO THAT'S MY LIFE...

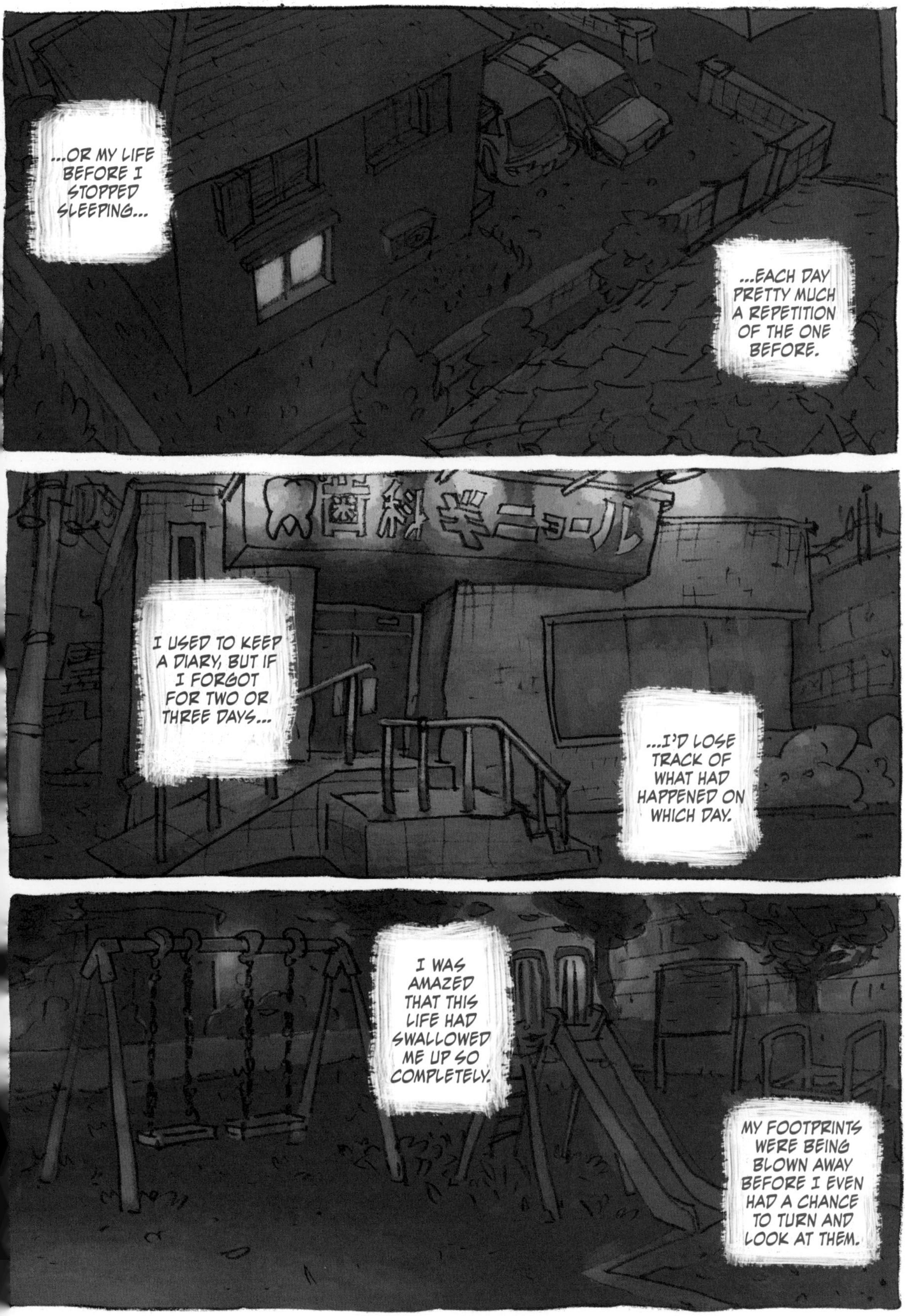
...OR MY LIFE BEFORE I STOPPED SLEEPING...
...EACH DAY PRETTY MUCH A REPETITION OF THE ONE BEFORE.
I USED TO KEEP A DIARY, BUT IF I FORGOT FOR TWO OR THREE DAYS...
...I'D LOSE TRACK OF WHAT HAD HAPPENED ON WHICH DAY.
I WAS AMAZED THAT THIS LIFE HAD SWALLOWED ME UP SO COMPLETELY.
MY FOOTPRINTS WERE BEING BLOWN AWAY BEFORE I EVEN HAD A CHANCE TO TURN AND LOOK AT THEM.

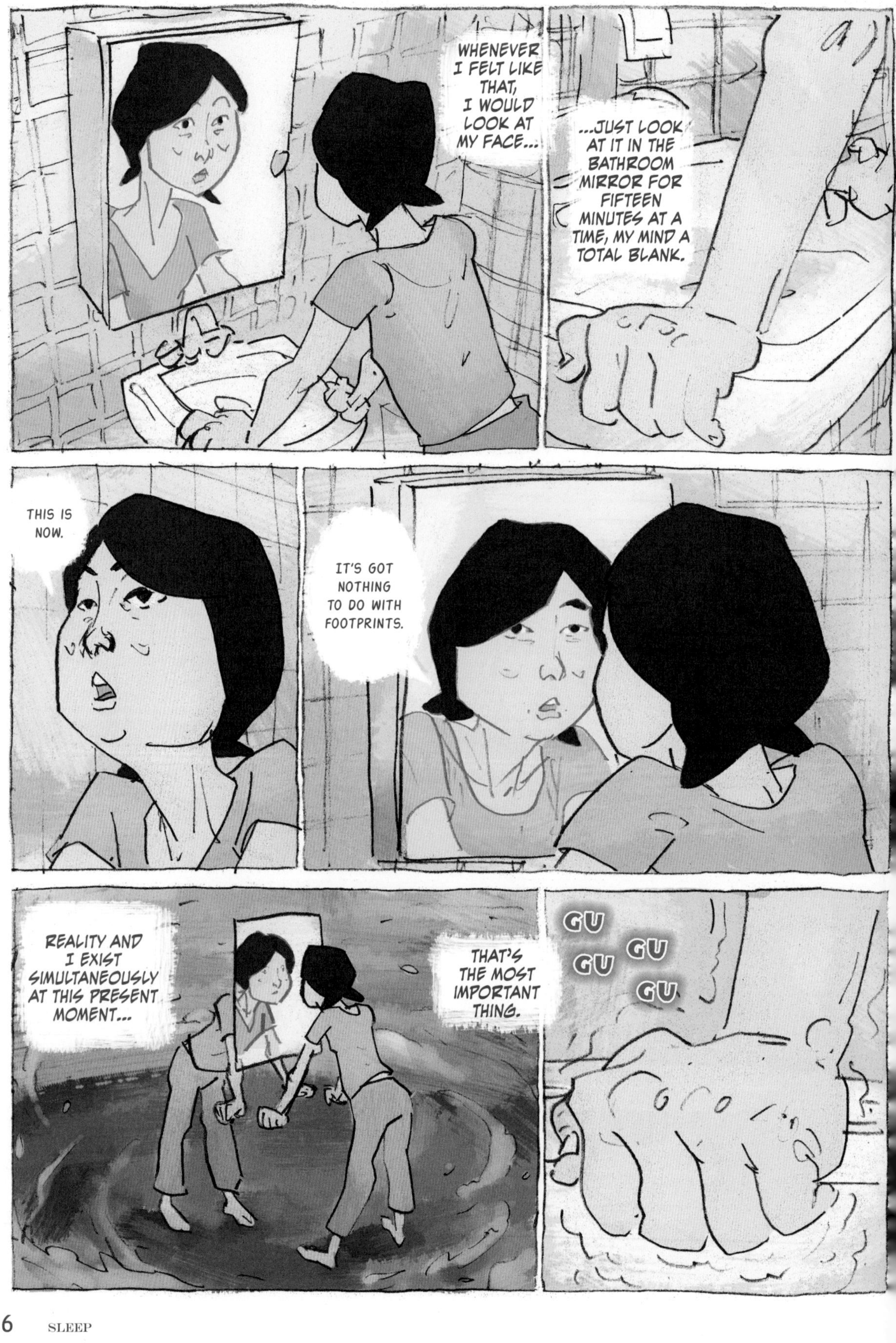
WHENEVER I FELT LIKE THAT, I WOULD LOOK AT MY FACE...
...JUST LOOK AT IT IN THE BATHROOM MIRROR FOR FIFTEEN MINUTES AT A TIME, MY MIND A TOTAL BLANK.
THIS IS NOW.
IT'S GOT NOTHING TO DO WITH FOOTPRINTS.
REALITY AND I EXIST SIMULTANEOUSLY AT THIS PRESENT MOMENT...
THAT'S THE MOST IMPORTANT THING.
GU GU GU GU

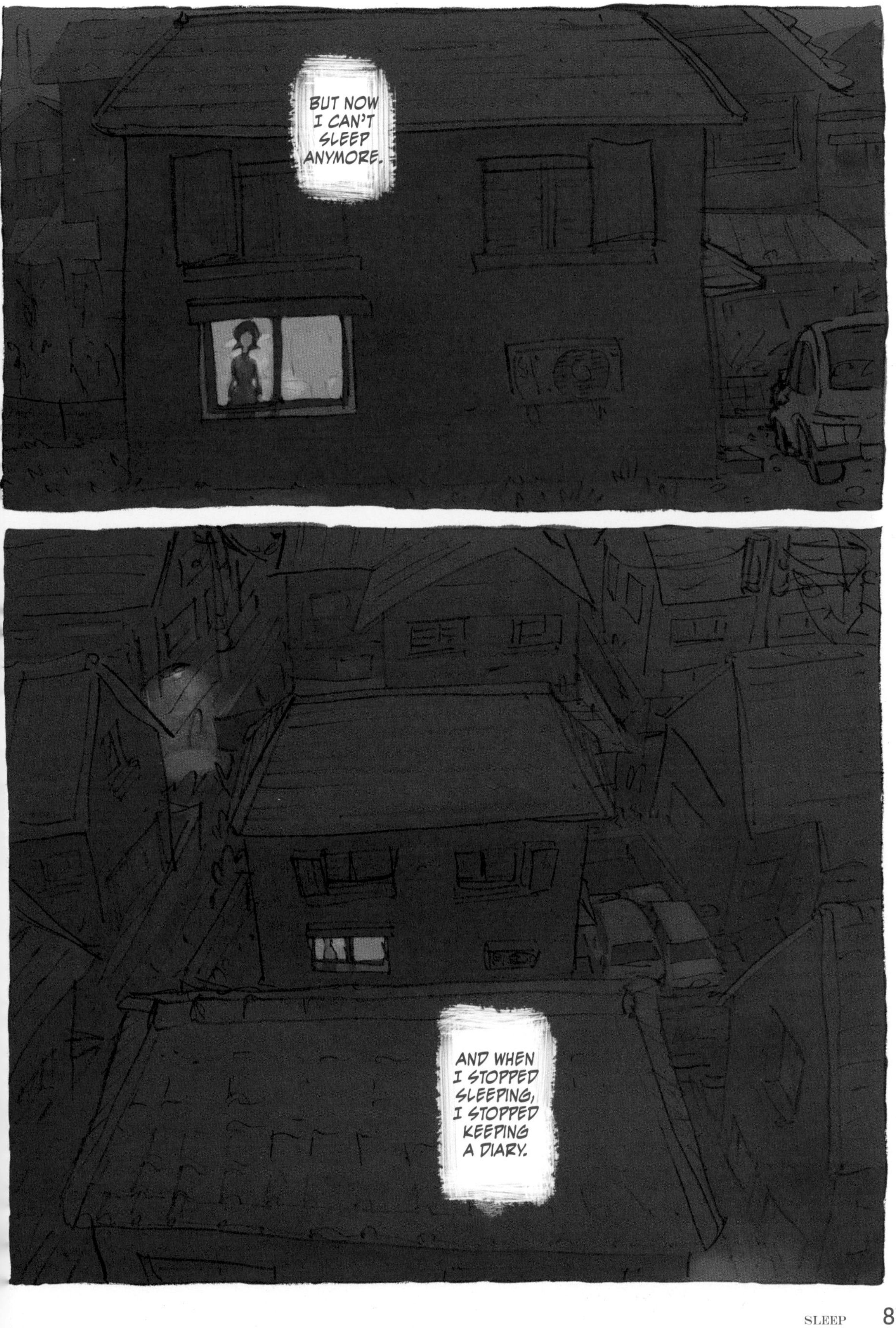
BUT NOW I CAN'T SLEEP ANYMORE.
AND WHEN I STOPPED SLEEPING, I STOPPED KEEPING A DIARY.

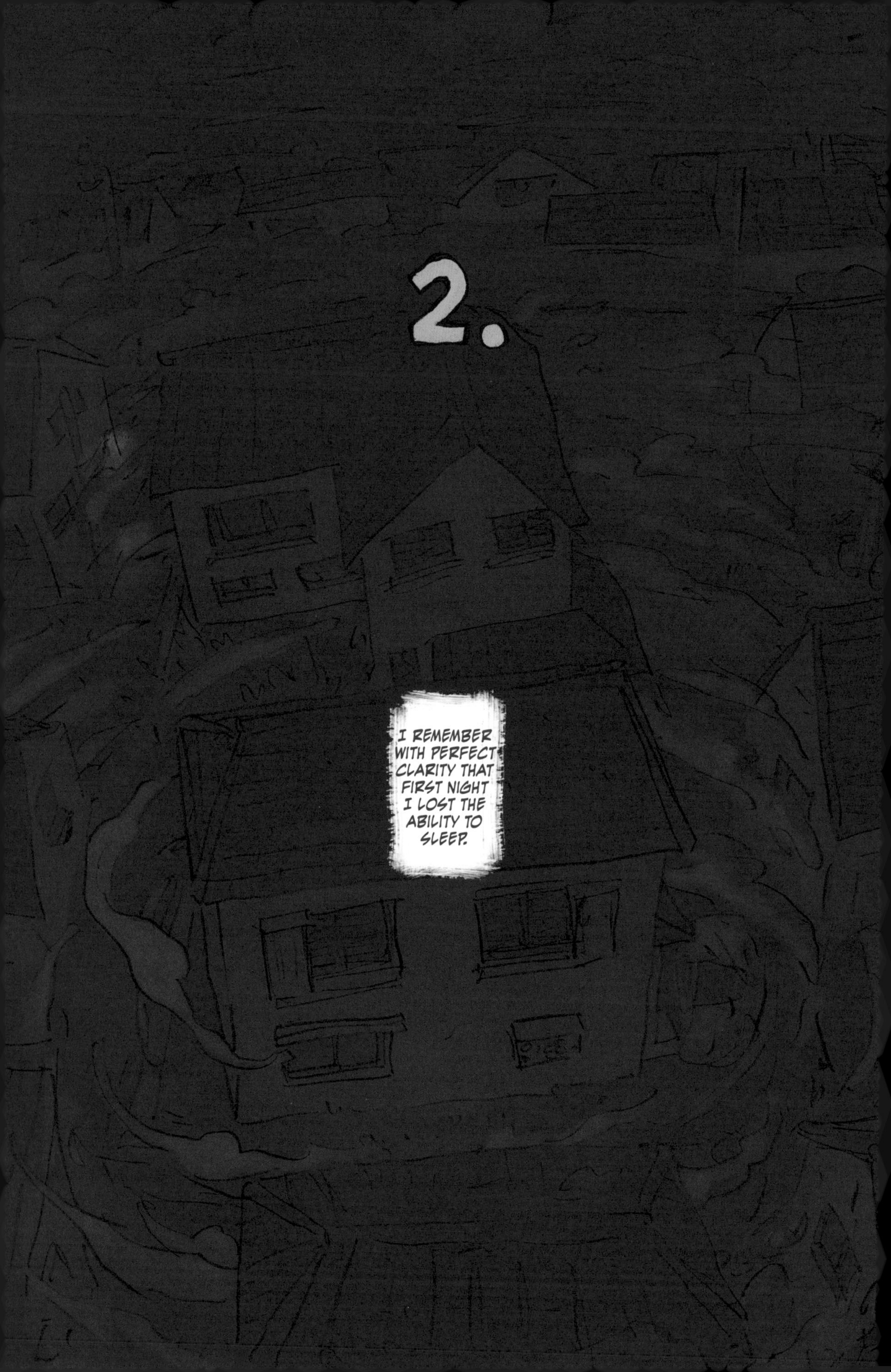
2.
I REMEMBER WITH PERFECT CLARITY THAT FIRST NIGHT I LOST THE ABILITY TO SLEEP.

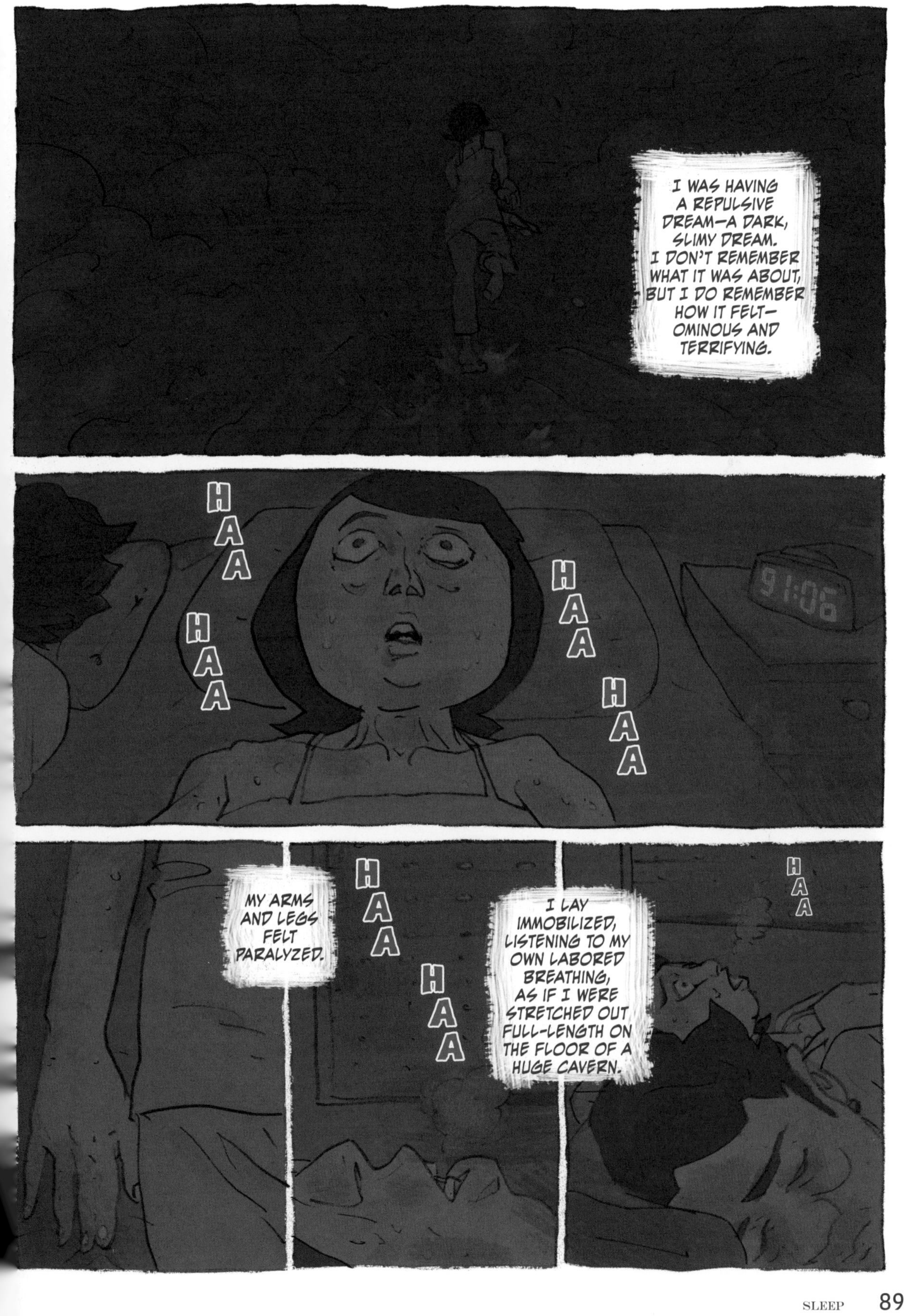
I WAS HAVING A REPULSIVE DREAM—A DARK, SLIMY DREAM. I DON'T REMEMBER WHAT IT WAS ABOUT, BUT I DO REMEMBER HOW IT FELT—OMINOUS AND TERRIFYING.
HAA
HAA
HAA
HAA
MY ARMS AND LEGS FELT PARALYZED.
HAA
HAA
I LAY IMMOBILIZED, LISTENING TO MY OWN LABORED BREATHING, AS IF I WERE STRETCHED OUT FULL-LENGTH ON THE FLOOR OF A HUGE CAVERN.
HAA

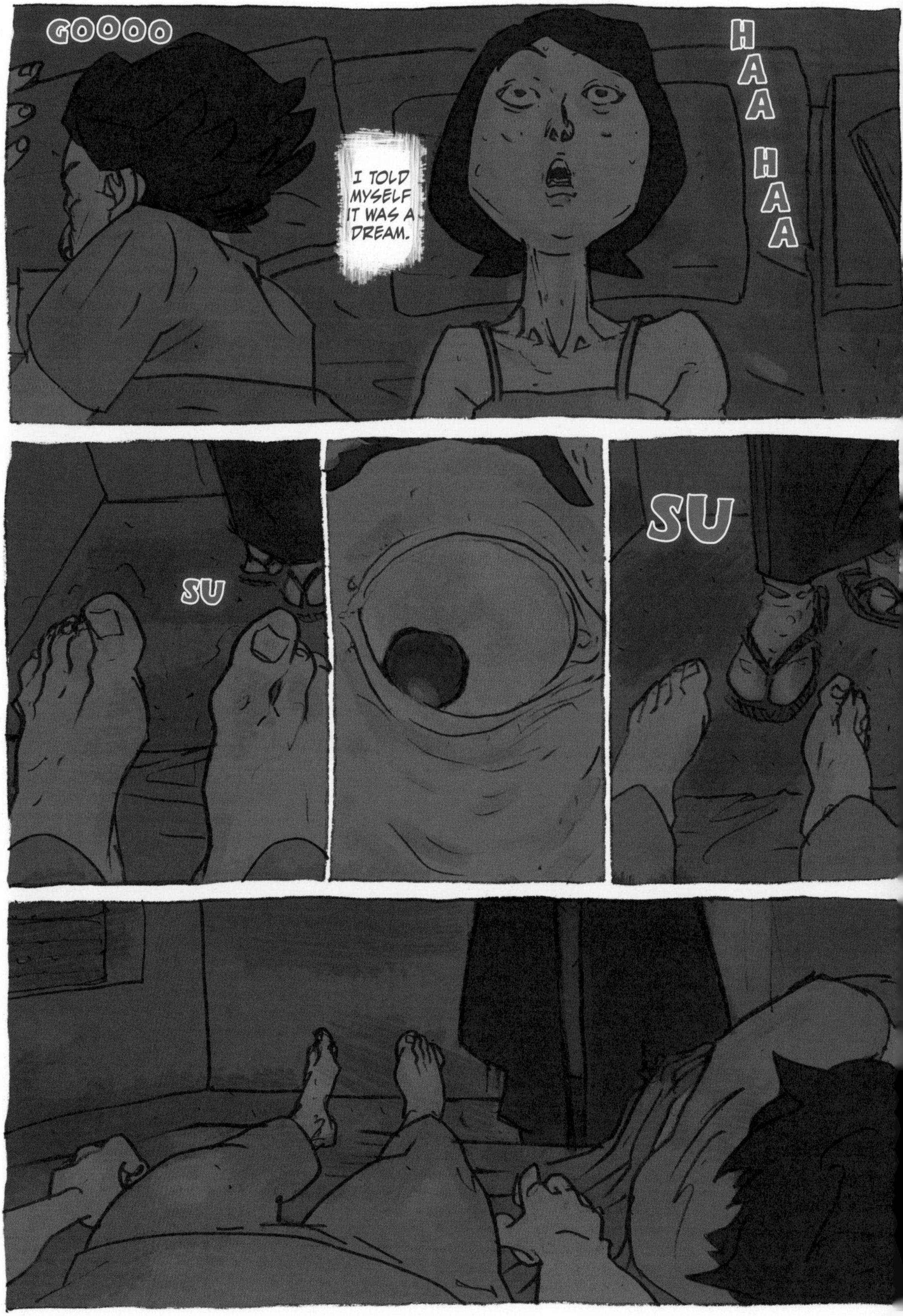
GOOOO
I TOLD MYSELF IT WAS A DREAM.
HAA HAA
SU
SU

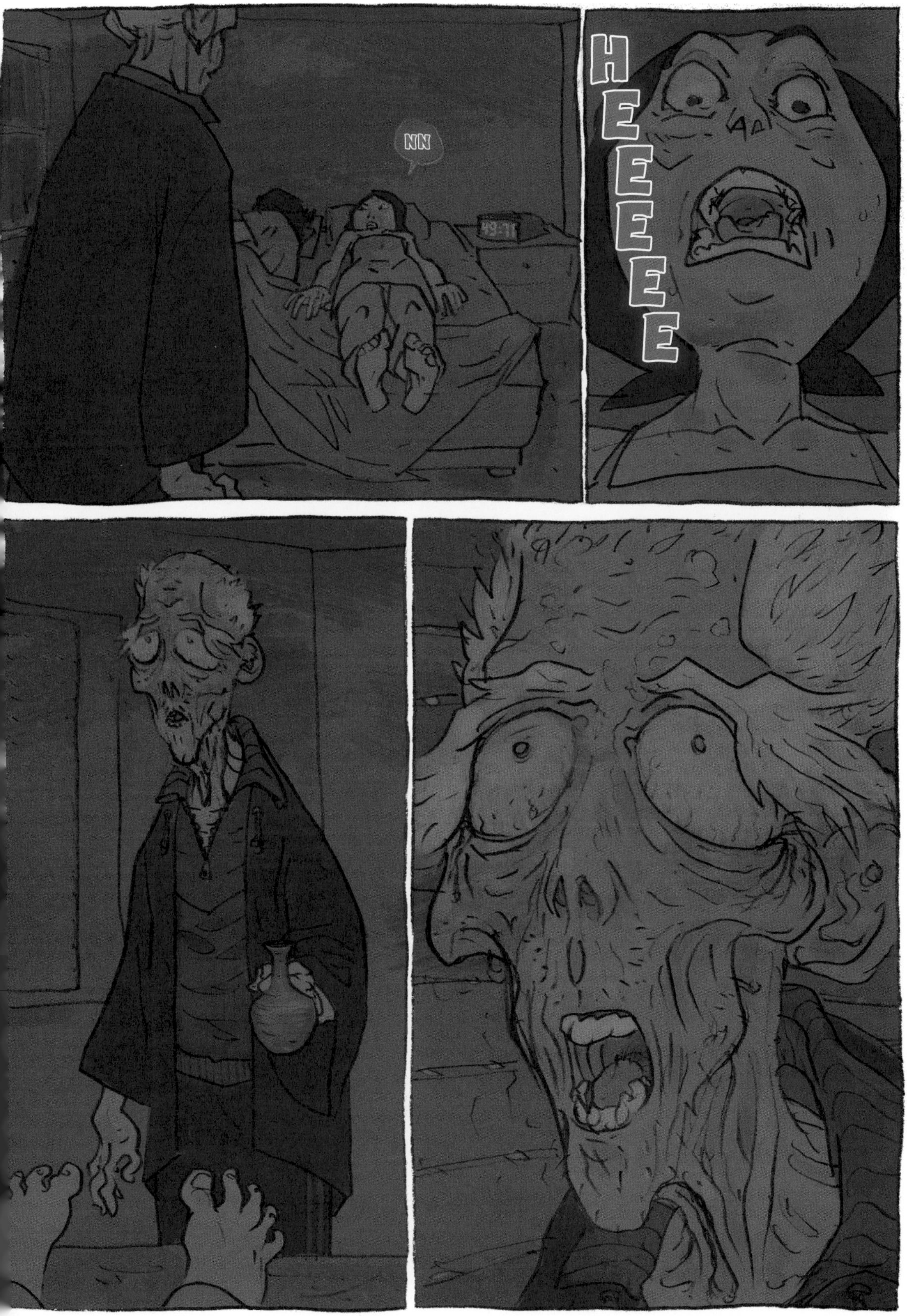
NN
HEEEEE

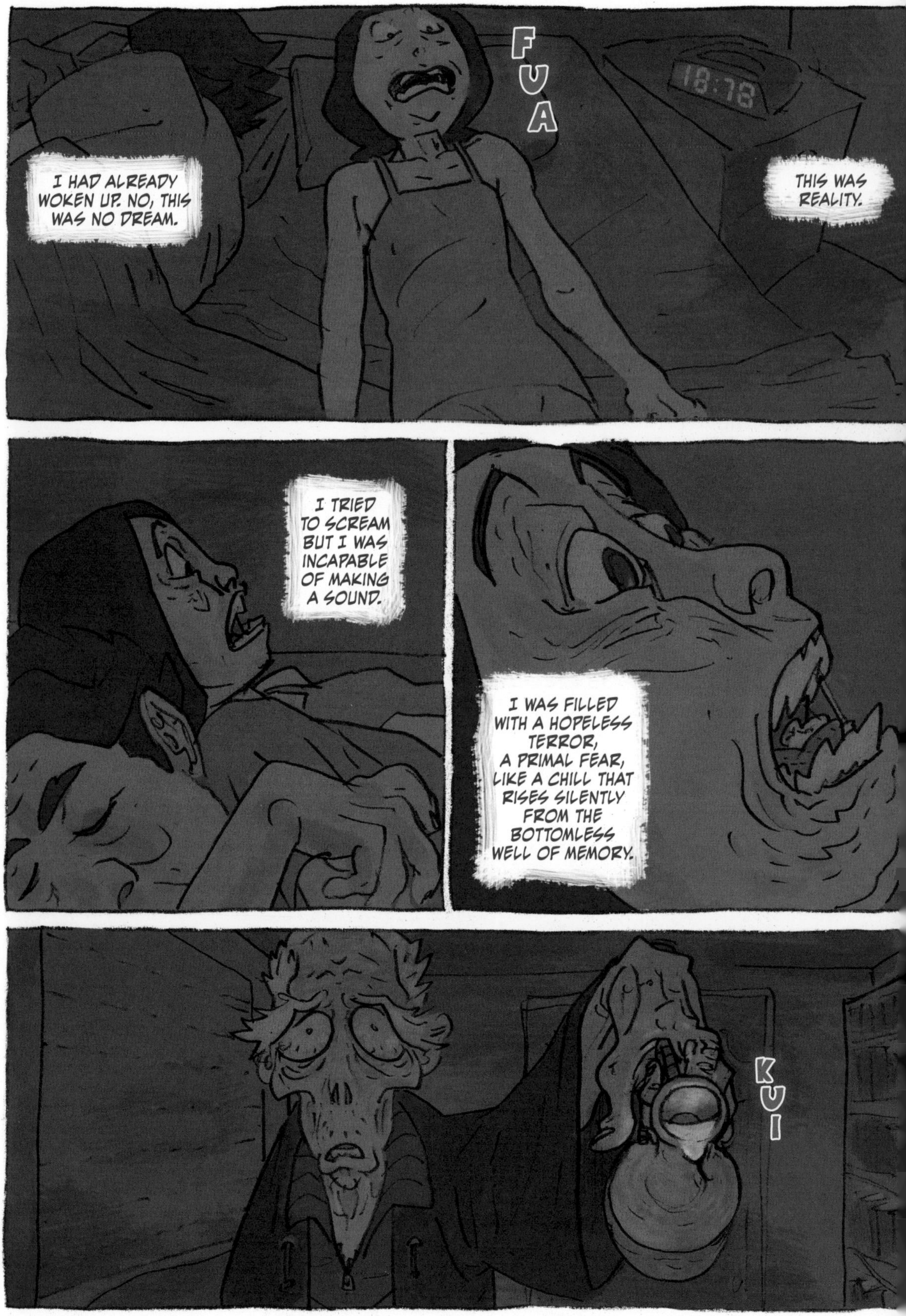
FUA
18:78
I HAD ALREADY WOKEN UP. NO, THIS WAS NO DREAM.
THIS WAS REALITY.
I TRIED TO SCREAM BUT I WAS INCAPABLE OF MAKING A SOUND.
I WAS FILLED WITH A HOPELESS TERROR, A PRIMAL FEAR, LIKE A CHILL THAT RISES SILENTLY FROM THE BOTTOMLESS WELL OF MEMORY.
KUI

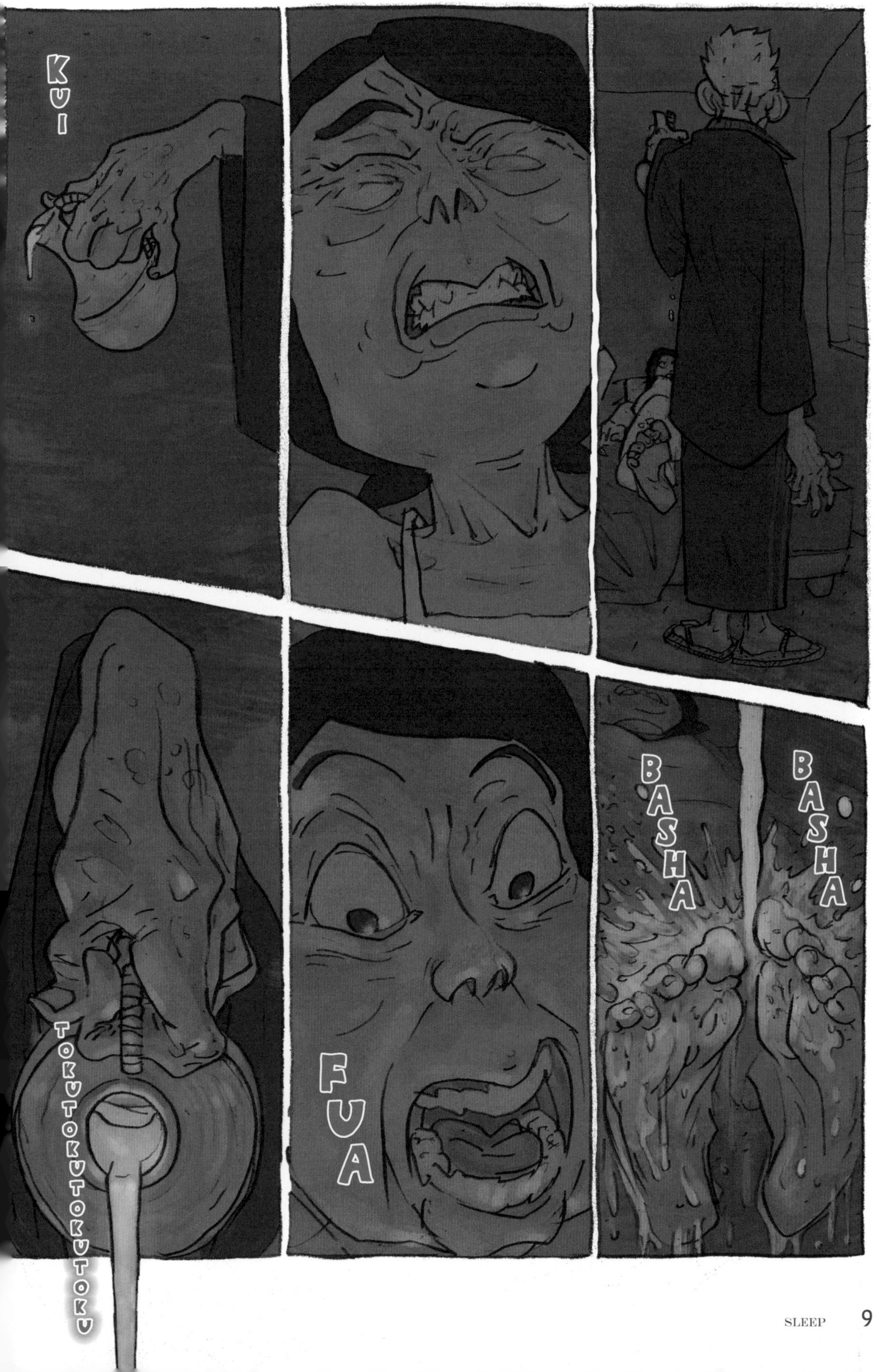
KUI
FUA
BASHA
BASHA
TOKUTOKUTOKUTOKU

BASHA BASHA

BASHA

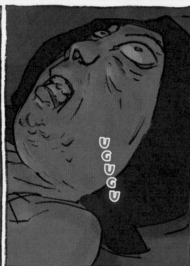

UGUGU

SHUUUUU

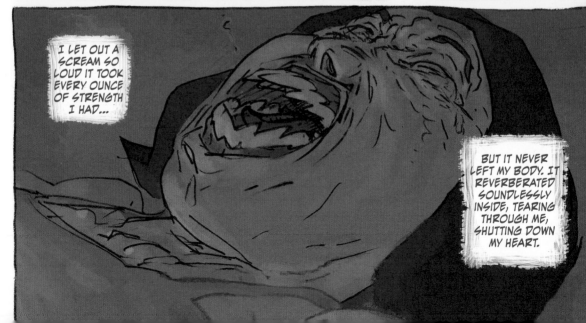

I LET OUT A SCREAM SO LOUD IT TOOK EVERY OUNCE OF STRENGTH I HAD...

BUT IT NEVER LEFT MY BODY. IT REVERBERATED SOUNDLESSLY INSIDE, TEARING THROUGH ME, SHUTTING DOWN MY HEART.

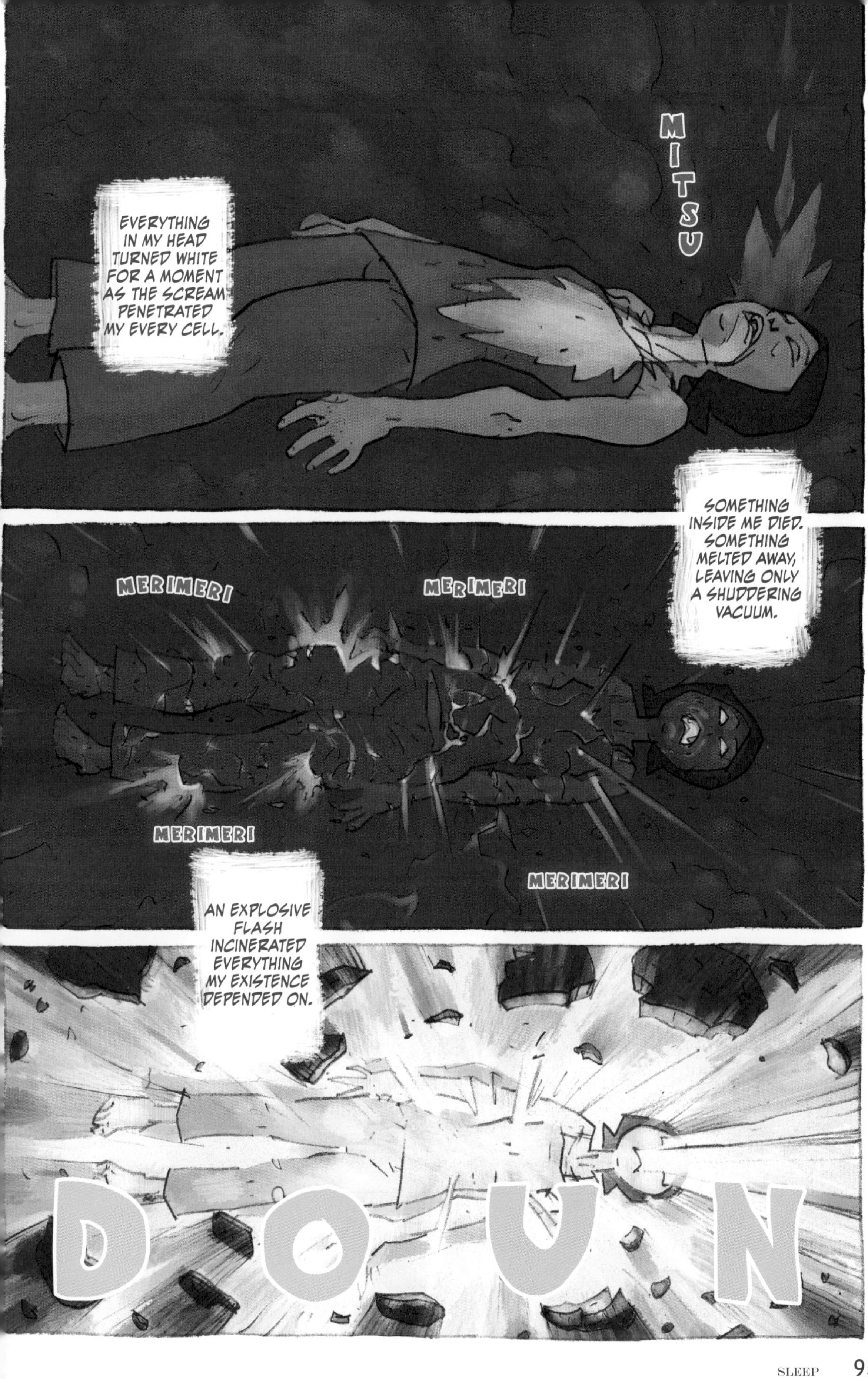
EVERYTHING IN MY HEAD TURNED WHITE FOR A MOMENT AS THE SCREAM PENETRATED MY EVERY CELL.
MITSU
SOMETHING INSIDE ME DIED. SOMETHING MELTED AWAY, LEAVING ONLY A SHUDDERING VACUUM.
MERIMERI
MERIMERI
MERIMERI
MERIMERI
AN EXPLOSIVE FLASH INCINERATED EVERYTHING MY EXISTENCE DEPENDED ON.
DOUN

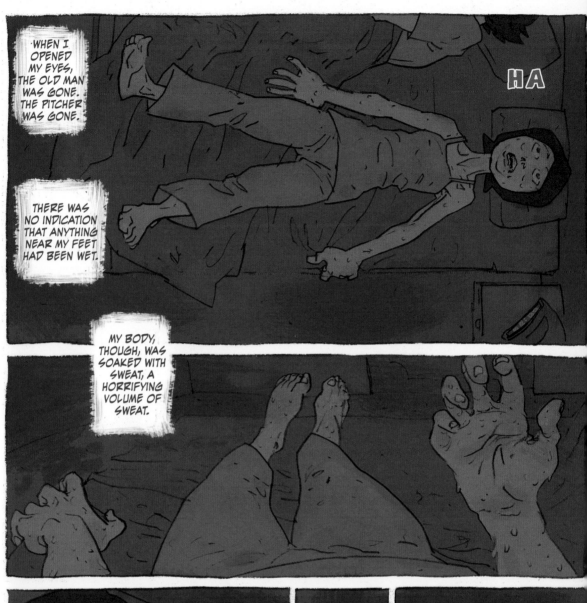

·WHEN I OPENED MY EYES, THE OLD MAN WAS GONE. THE PITCHER WAS GONE.

THERE WAS NO INDICATION THAT ANYTHING NEAR MY FEET HAD BEEN WET.

MY BODY, THOUGH, WAS SOAKED WITH SWEAT, A HORRIFYING VOLUME OF SWEAT.

HA

I MUST HAVE BEEN IN A TRANCE.

GUOOOO

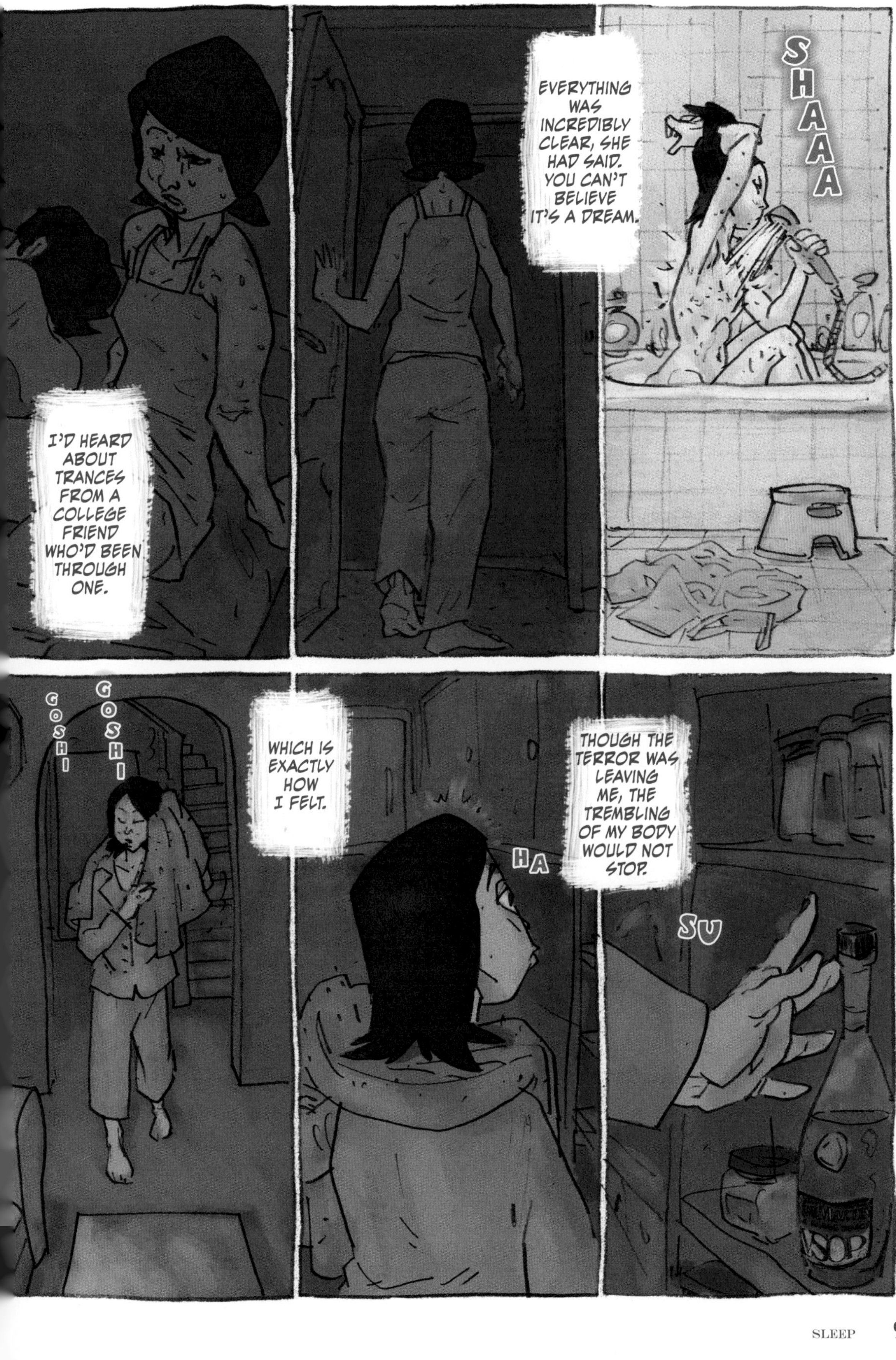
I'D HEARD ABOUT TRANCES FROM A COLLEGE FRIEND WHO'D BEEN THROUGH ONE.
EVERYTHING WAS INCREDIBLY CLEAR, SHE HAD SAID. YOU CAN'T BELIEVE IT'S A DREAM.
SHAAA
GOSHI GOSHI
WHICH IS EXACTLY HOW I FELT.
HA
THOUGH THE TERROR WAS LEAVING ME, THE TREMBLING OF MY BODY WOULD NOT STOP.
SU
VSOP

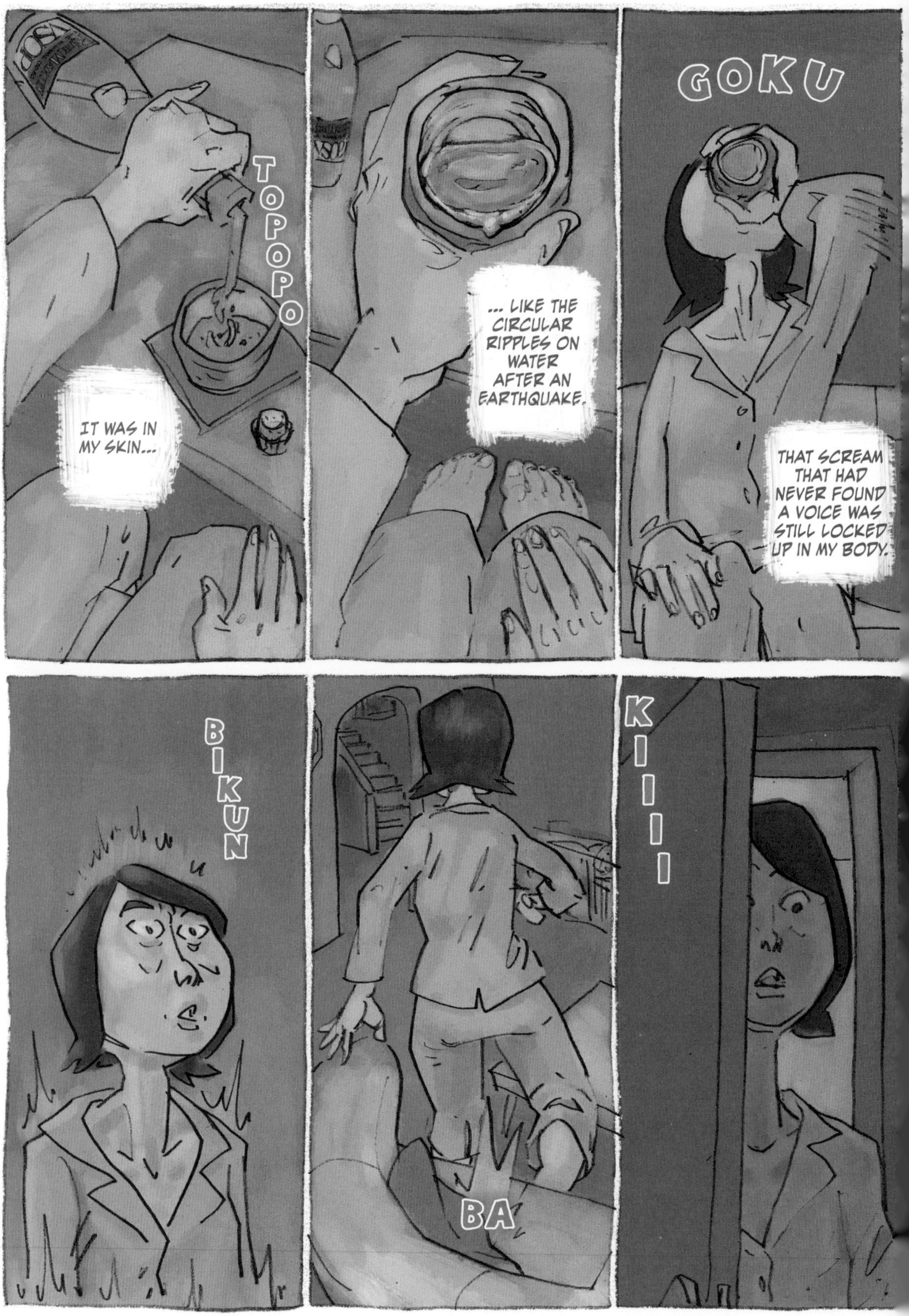
TOPOPO
IT WAS IN MY SKIN...
... LIKE THE CIRCULAR RIPPLES ON WATER AFTER AN EARTHQUAKE.
GOKU
THAT SCREAM THAT HAD NEVER FOUND A VOICE WAS STILL LOCKED UP IN MY BODY.
BIKUN
BA
KIIIII

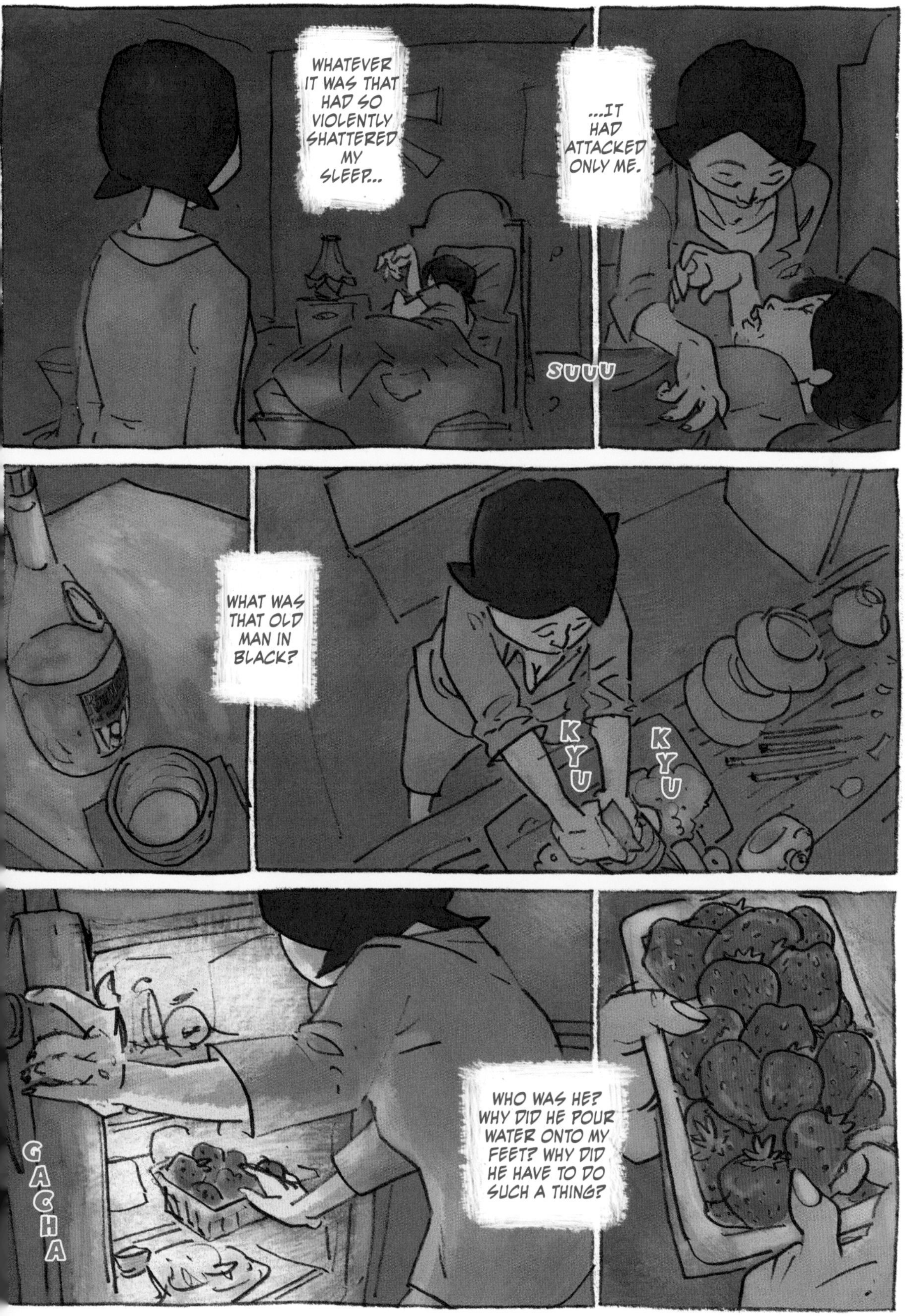
WHATEVER IT WAS THAT HAD SO VIOLENTLY SHATTERED MY SLEEP...
...IT HAD ATTACKED ONLY ME.
SUUU
WHAT WAS THAT OLD MAN IN BLACK?
KYU
KYU
GACHA
WHO WAS HE? WHY DID HE POUR WATER ONTO MY FEET? WHY DID HE HAVE TO DO SUCH A THING?

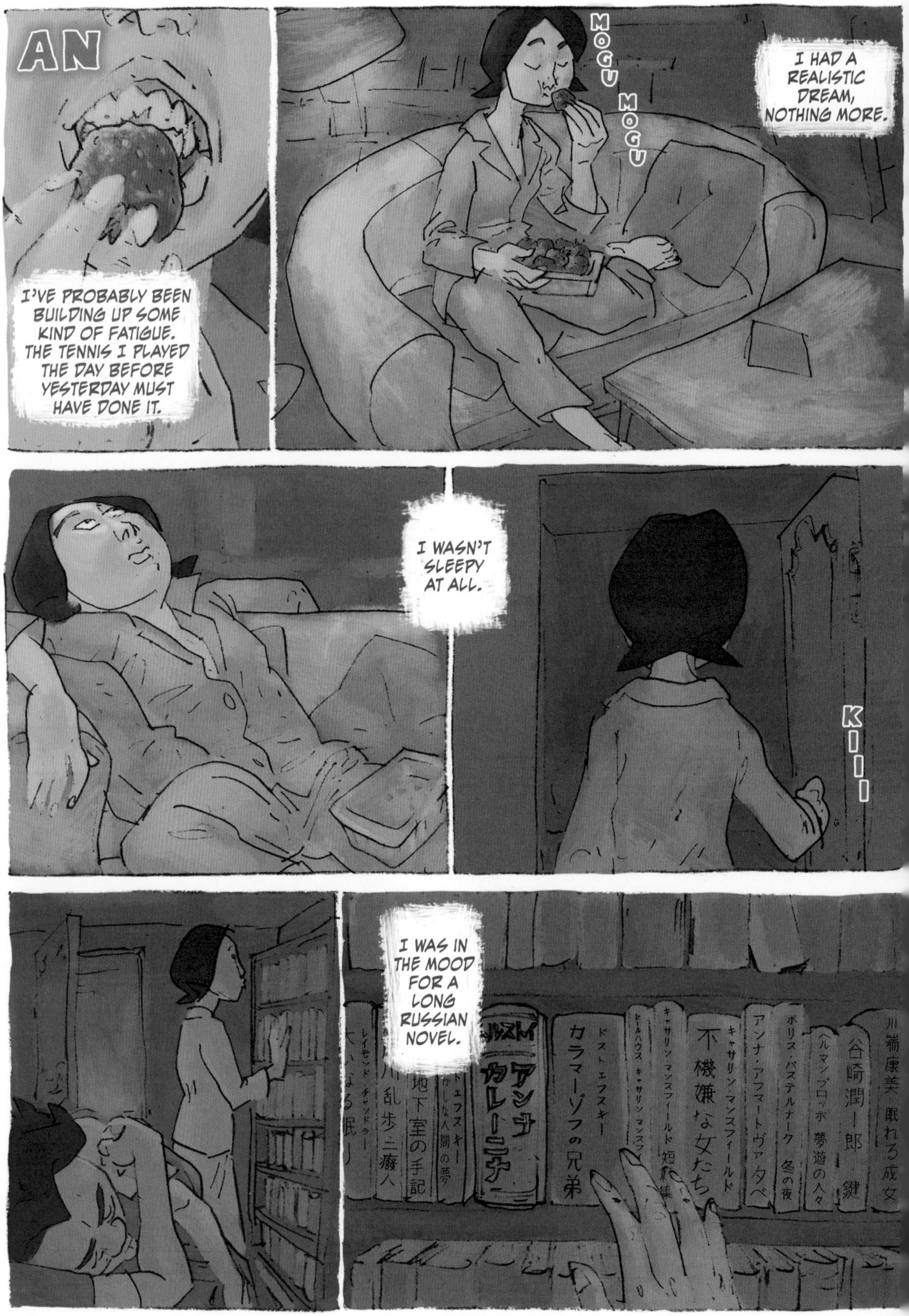

AN
I'VE PROBABLY BEEN BUILDING UP SOME KIND OF FATIGUE. THE TENNIS I PLAYED THE DAY BEFORE YESTERDAY MUST HAVE DONE IT.
MOGU MOGU
I HAD A REALISTIC DREAM, NOTHING MORE.
I WASN'T SLEEPY AT ALL.
KIII
I WAS IN THE MOOD FOR A LONG RUSSIAN NOVEL.
地下室の手記
アンナ カレーニナ
ドストエフスキー
カラマーゾフの兄弟
不機嫌な女たち
谷崎潤一郎 鍵

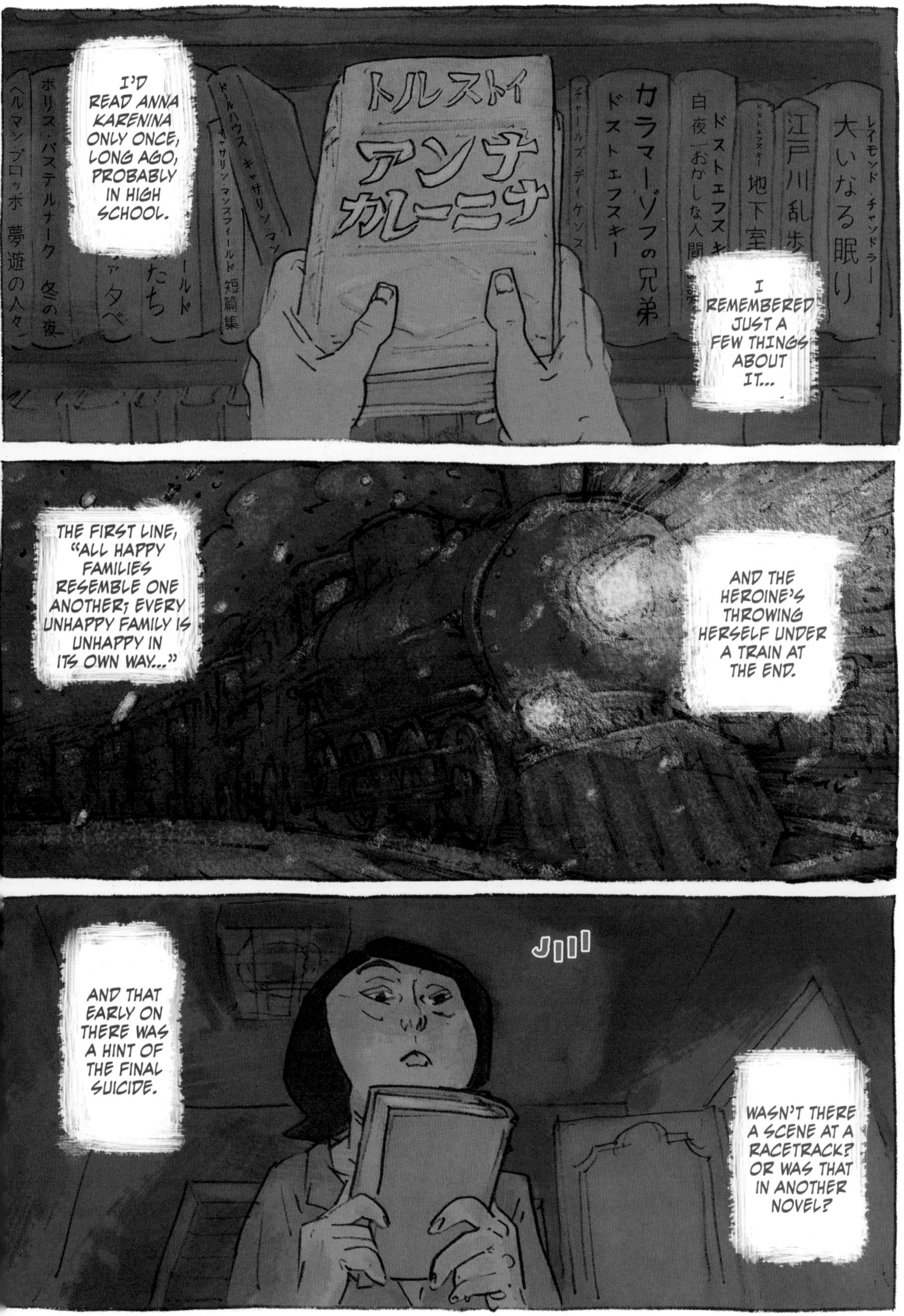
I'D READ ANNA KARENINA ONLY ONCE, LONG AGO, PROBABLY IN HIGH SCHOOL.
トルストイ
アンナ カレーニナ
ヘルマン・ブロッホ 夢遊の人々
ボリス・パステルナーク 冬の夜
カラマーゾフの兄弟
ドストエフスキー
白夜 おかしな人間の夢
江戸川乱歩
レイモンド・チャンドラー
大いなる眠り
I REMEMBERED JUST A FEW THINGS ABOUT IT...
THE FIRST LINE, "ALL HAPPY FAMILIES RESEMBLE ONE ANOTHER; EVERY UNHAPPY FAMILY IS UNHAPPY IN ITS OWN WAY..."
AND THE HEROINE'S THROWING HERSELF UNDER A TRAIN AT THE END.
AND THAT EARLY ON THERE WAS A HINT OF THE FINAL SUICIDE.
JIII
WASN'T THERE A SCENE AT A RACETRACK? OR WAS THAT IN ANOTHER NOVEL?

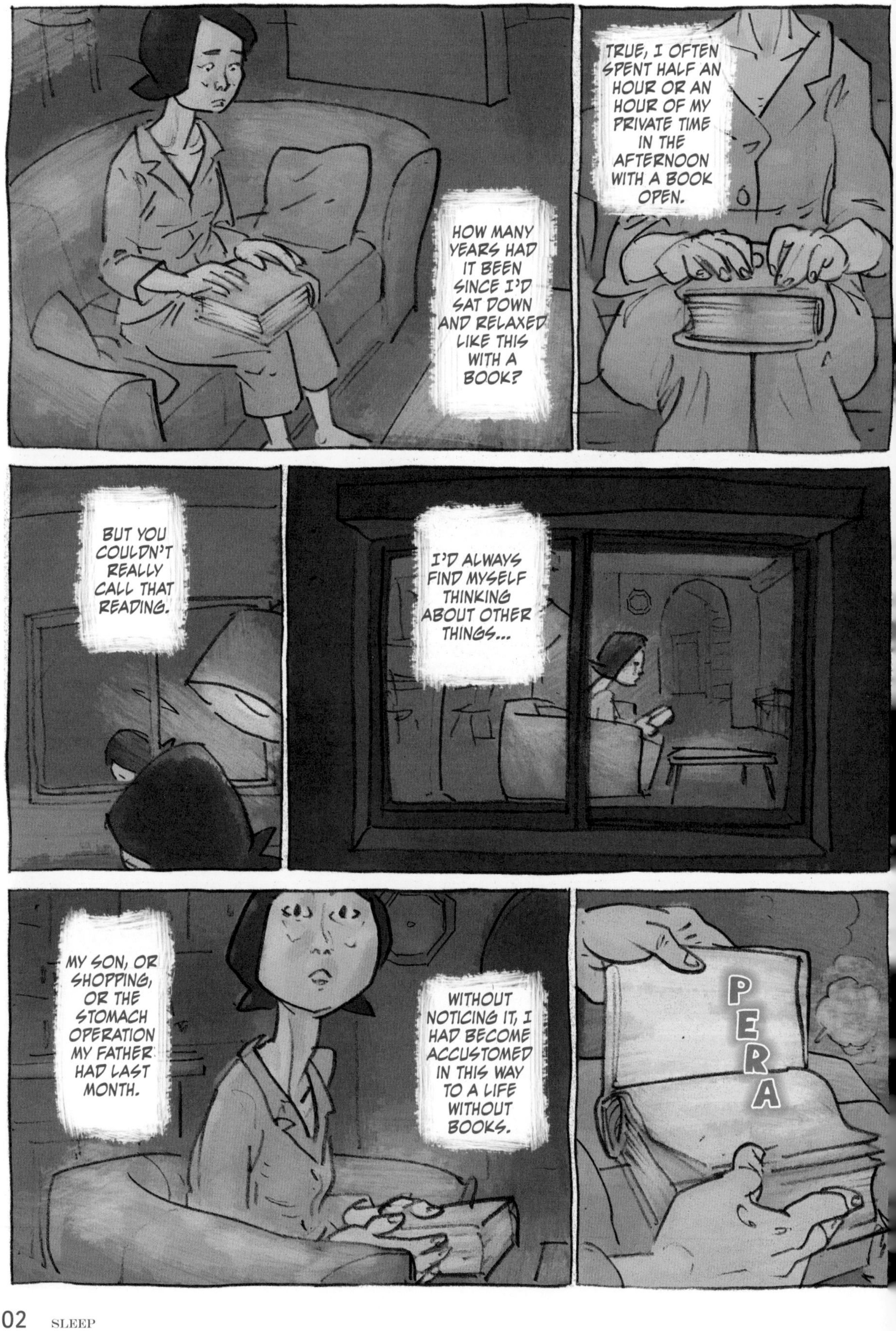
HOW MANY YEARS HAD IT BEEN SINCE I'D SAT DOWN AND RELAXED LIKE THIS WITH A BOOK?
TRUE, I OFTEN SPENT HALF AN HOUR OR AN HOUR OF MY PRIVATE TIME IN THE AFTERNOON WITH A BOOK OPEN.
BUT YOU COULDN'T REALLY CALL THAT READING.
I'D ALWAYS FIND MYSELF THINKING ABOUT OTHER THINGS...
MY SON, OR SHOPPING, OR THE STOMACH OPERATION MY FATHER HAD LAST MONTH.
WITHOUT NOTICING IT, I HAD BECOME ACCUSTOMED IN THIS WAY TO A LIFE WITHOUT BOOKS.
PERA

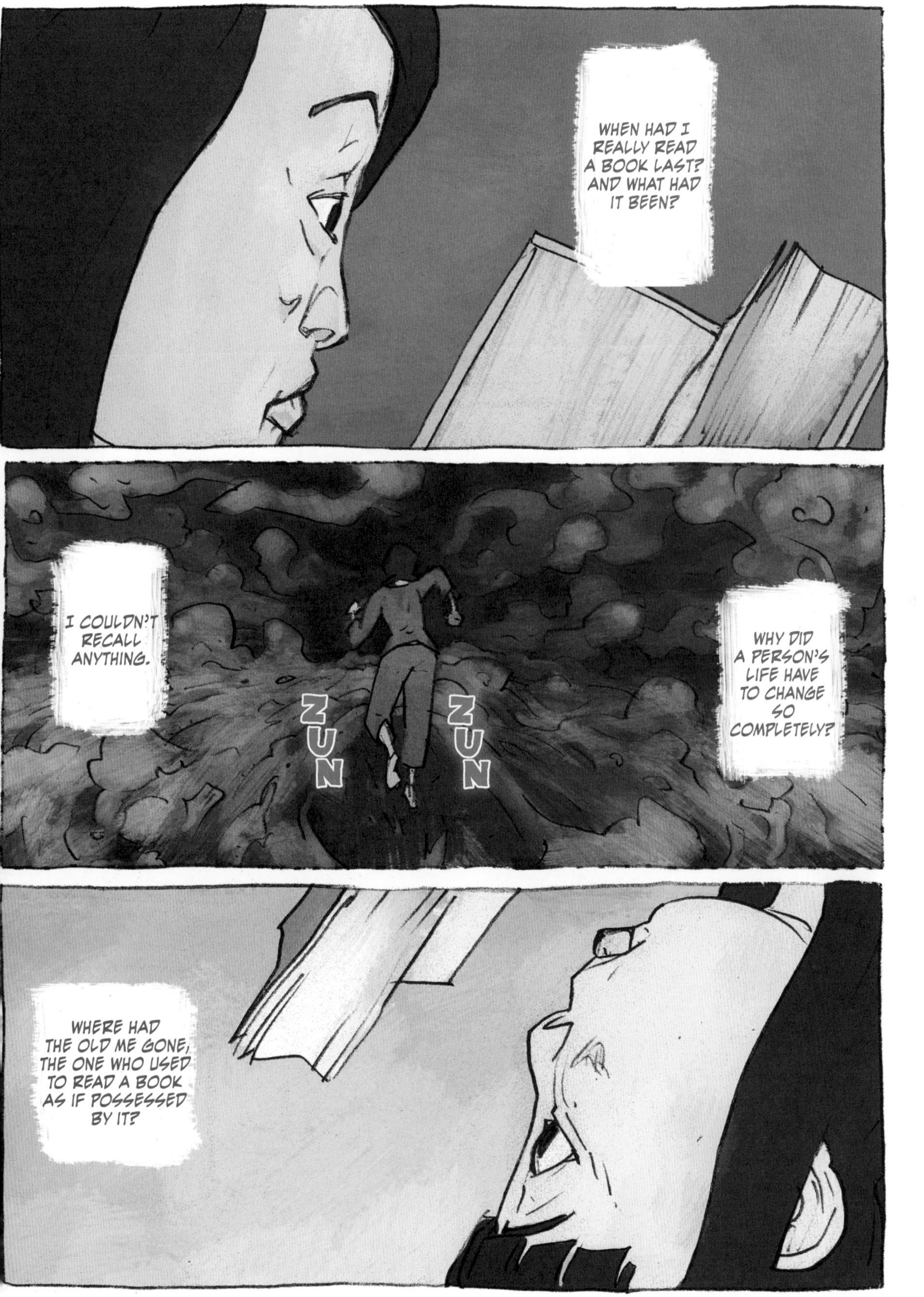
WHEN HAD I REALLY READ A BOOK LAST? AND WHAT HAD IT BEEN?
I COULDN'T RECALL ANYTHING.
ZUN
ZUN
WHY DID A PERSON'S LIFE HAVE TO CHANGE SO COMPLETELY?
WHERE HAD THE OLD ME GONE, THE ONE WHO USED TO READ A BOOK AS IF POSSESSED BY IT?

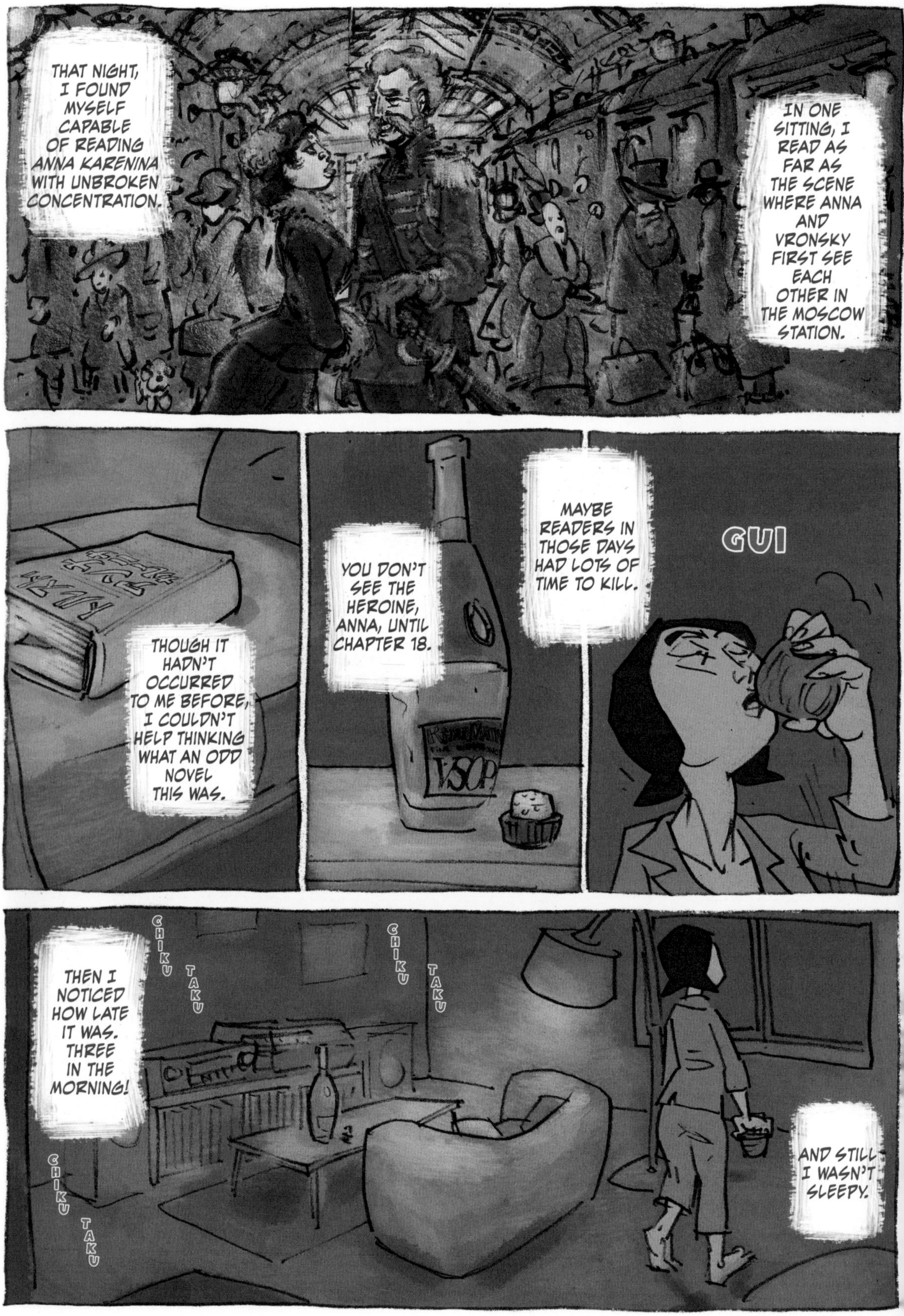
THAT NIGHT, I FOUND MYSELF CAPABLE OF READING ANNA KARENINA WITH UNBROKEN CONCENTRATION.
IN ONE SITTING, I READ AS FAR AS THE SCENE WHERE ANNA AND VRONSKY FIRST SEE EACH OTHER IN THE MOSCOW STATION.
THOUGH IT HADN'T OCCURRED TO ME BEFORE, I COULDN'T HELP THINKING WHAT AN ODD NOVEL THIS WAS.
YOU DON'T SEE THE HEROINE, ANNA, UNTIL CHAPTER 18.
VSOP
MAYBE READERS IN THOSE DAYS HAD LOTS OF TIME TO KILL.
GUI
THEN I NOTICED HOW LATE IT WAS. THREE IN THE MORNING!
CHIKU TAKU
CHIKU TAKU
CHIKU TAKU
AND STILL I WASN'T SLEEPY.

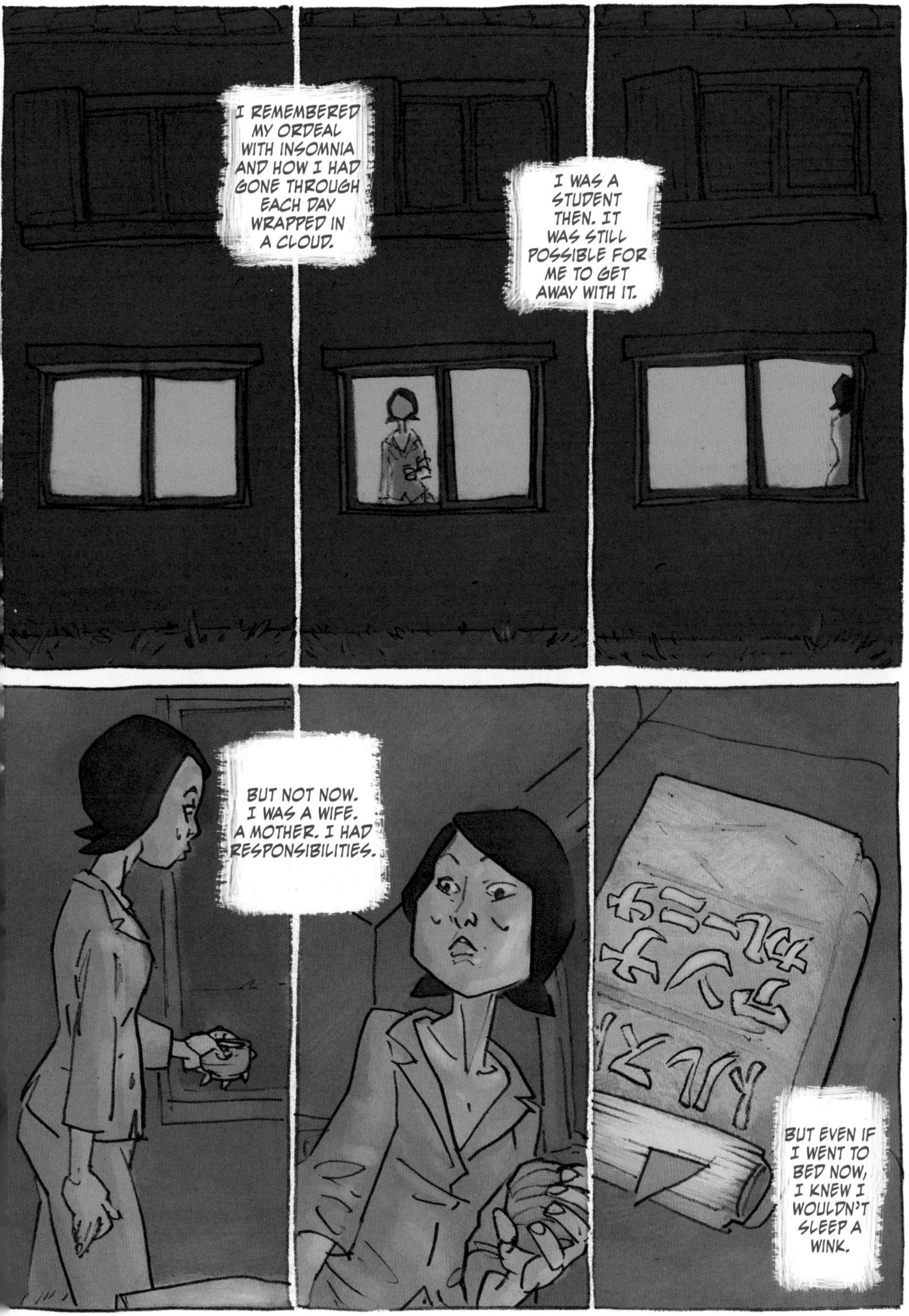
I REMEMBERED MY ORDEAL WITH INSOMNIA AND HOW I HAD GONE THROUGH EACH DAY WRAPPED IN A CLOUD.
I WAS A STUDENT THEN. IT WAS STILL POSSIBLE FOR ME TO GET AWAY WITH IT.
BUT NOT NOW. I WAS A WIFE. A MOTHER. I HAD RESPONSIBILITIES.
BUT EVEN IF I WENT TO BED NOW, I KNEW I WOULDN'T SLEEP A WINK.

SO I PLUNGED INTO ANNA KARENINA AND KEPT READING UNTIL THE SUN CAME UP.

ANNA AND VRONSKI STARED AT EACH OTHER AT THE BALL AND FELL INTO THEIR DOOMED LOVE.

ANNA WENT TO PIECES WHEN VRONSKY'S HORSE FELL AT THE RACETRACK AND CONFESSED HER INFIDELITY TO HER HUSBAND.

(SO THERE WAS A RACETRACK SCENE, AFTER ALL!)

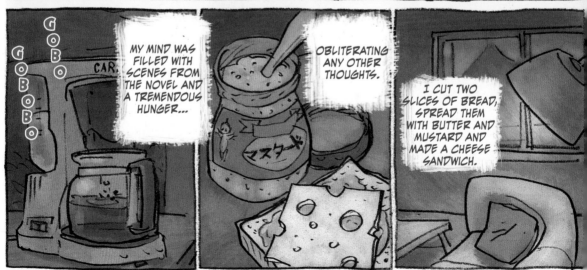

GOBOBOBO
GOBO
CAR...

MY MIND WAS FILLED WITH SCENES FROM THE NOVEL AND A TREMENDOUS HUNGER...

OBLITERATING ANY OTHER THOUGHTS.

I CUT TWO SLICES OF BREAD, SPREAD THEM WITH BUTTER AND MUSTARD AND MADE A CHEESE SANDWICH.

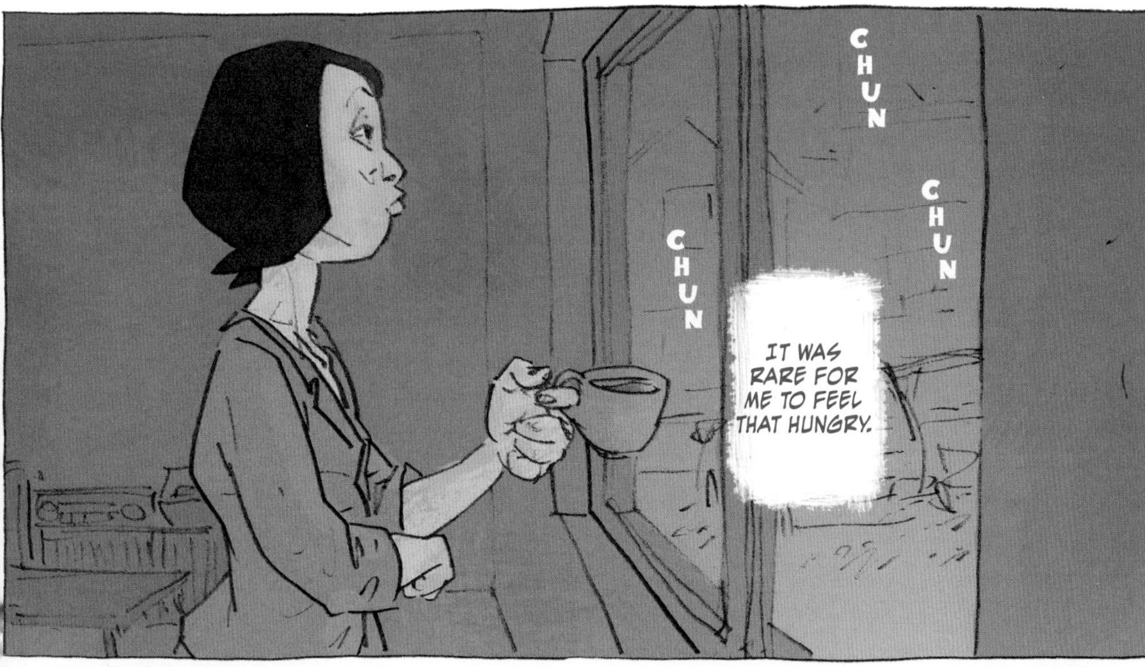
CHUN
CHUN
CHUN
IT WAS RARE FOR ME TO FEEL THAT HUNGRY.

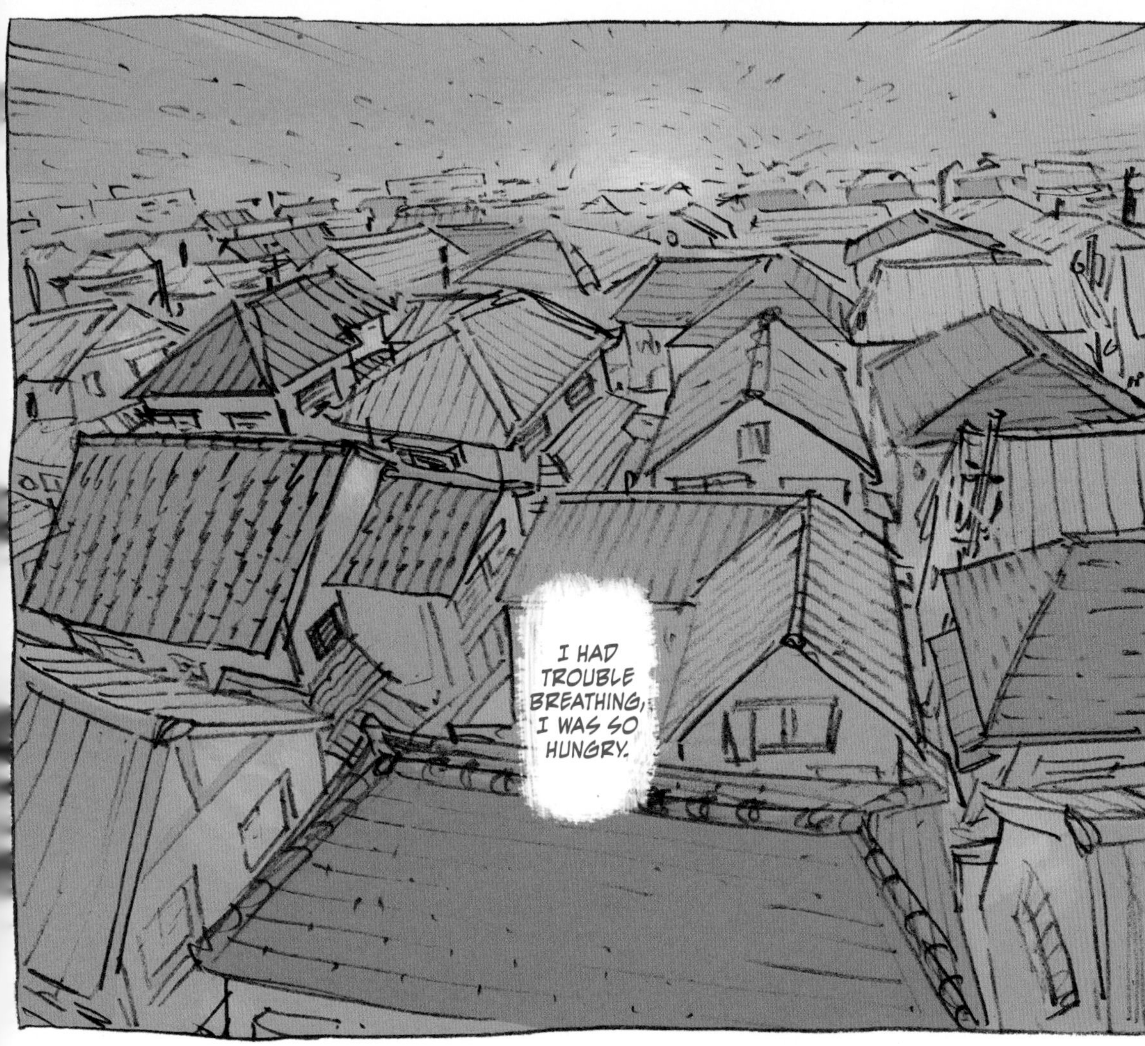
I HAD TROUBLE BREATHING, I WAS SO HUNGRY.

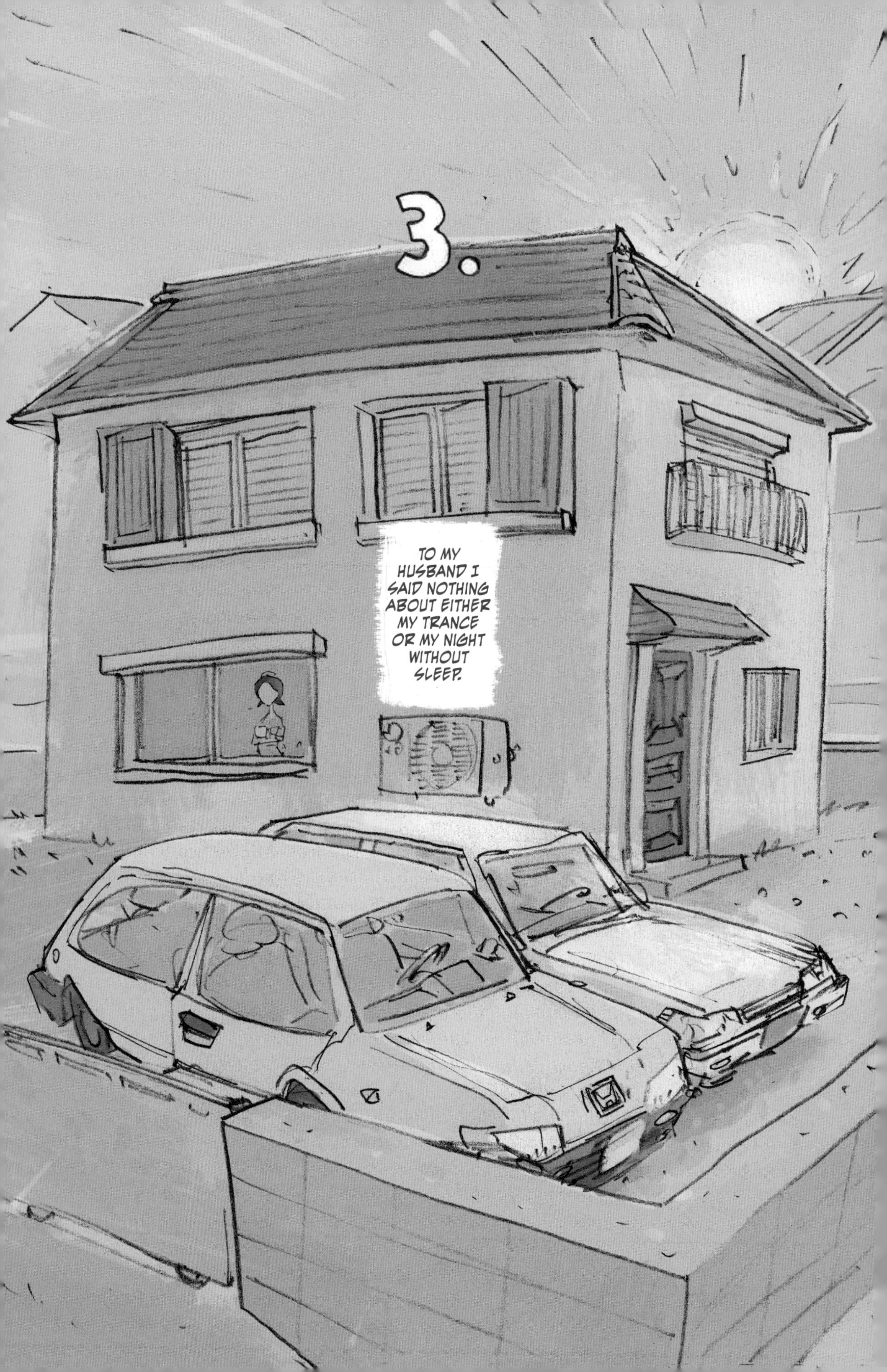
3.
TO MY HUSBAND I SAID NOTHING ABOUT EITHER MY TRANCE OR MY NIGHT WITHOUT SLEEP.

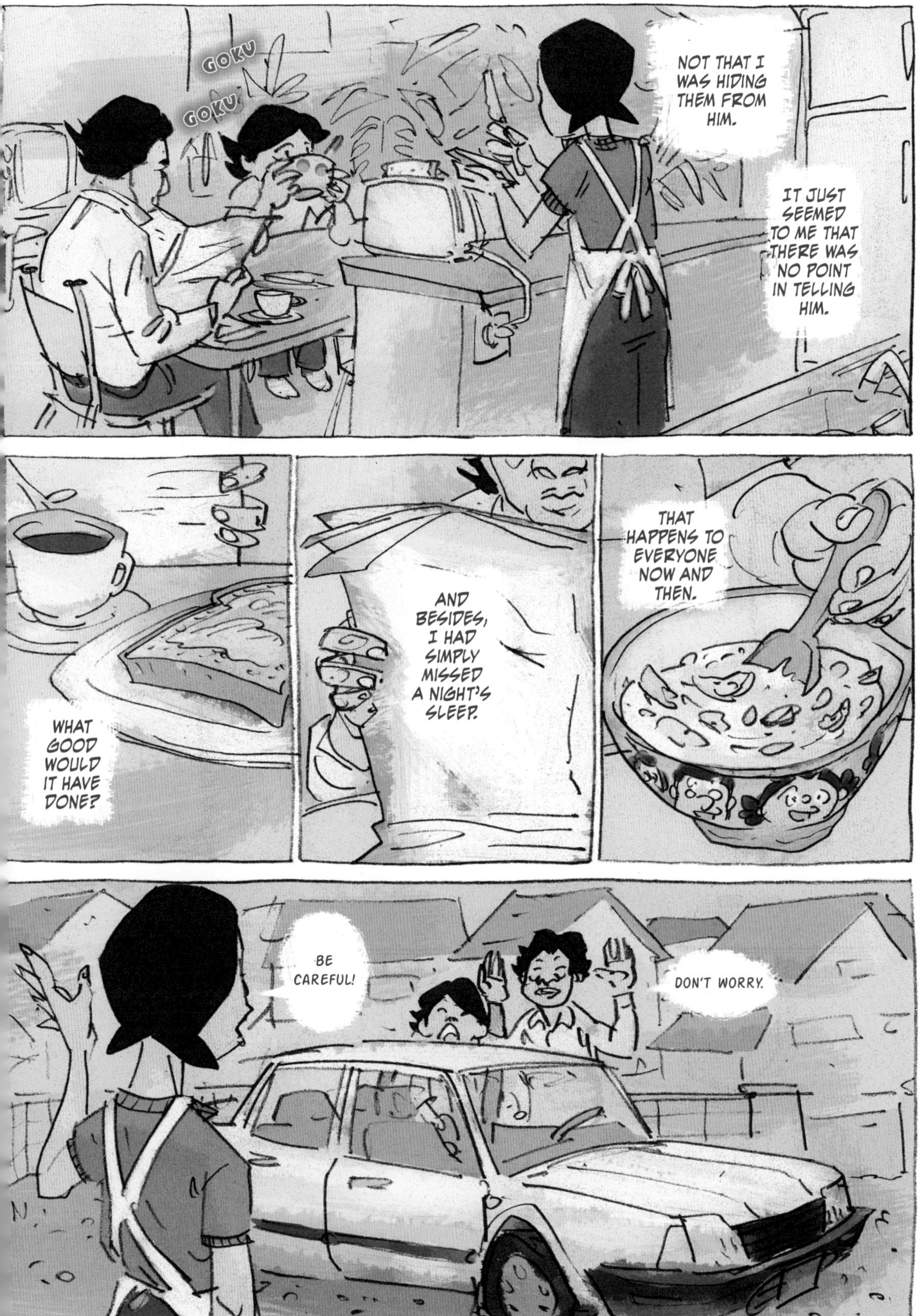
GOKU
GOKU
NOT THAT I WAS HIDING THEM FROM HIM.
IT JUST SEEMED TO ME THAT THERE WAS NO POINT IN TELLING HIM.
WHAT GOOD WOULD IT HAVE DONE?
AND BESIDES, I HAD SIMPLY MISSED A NIGHT'S SLEEP.
THAT HAPPENS TO EVERYONE NOW AND THEN.
BE CAREFUL!
DON'T WORRY.

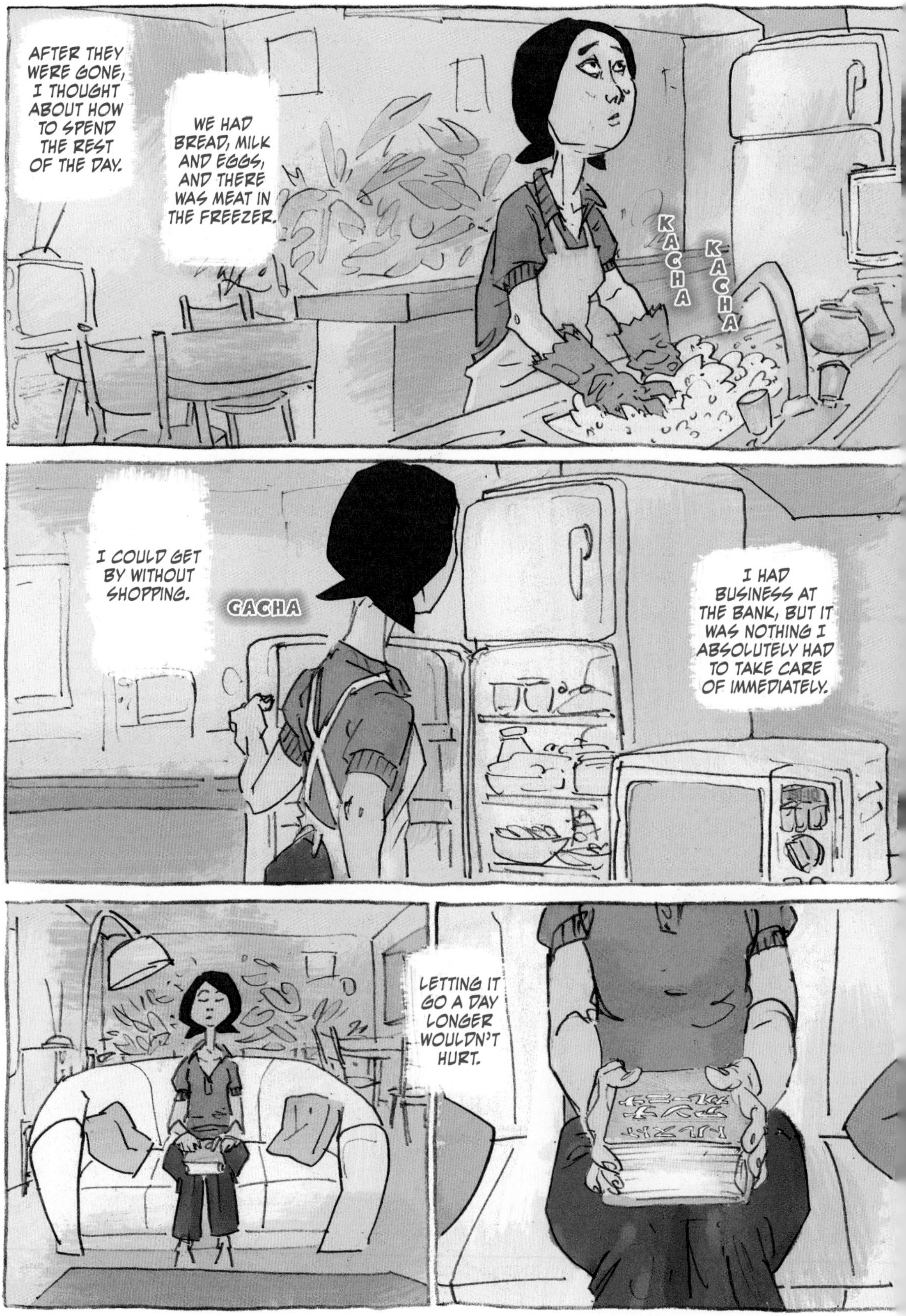

AFTER THEY WERE GONE, I THOUGHT ABOUT HOW TO SPEND THE REST OF THE DAY.
WE HAD BREAD, MILK AND EGGS, AND THERE WAS MEAT IN THE FREEZER.
KACHA
KACHA
I COULD GET BY WITHOUT SHOPPING.
GACHA
I HAD BUSINESS AT THE BANK, BUT IT WAS NOTHING I ABSOLUTELY HAD TO TAKE CARE OF IMMEDIATELY.
LETTING IT GO A DAY LONGER WOULDN'T HURT.

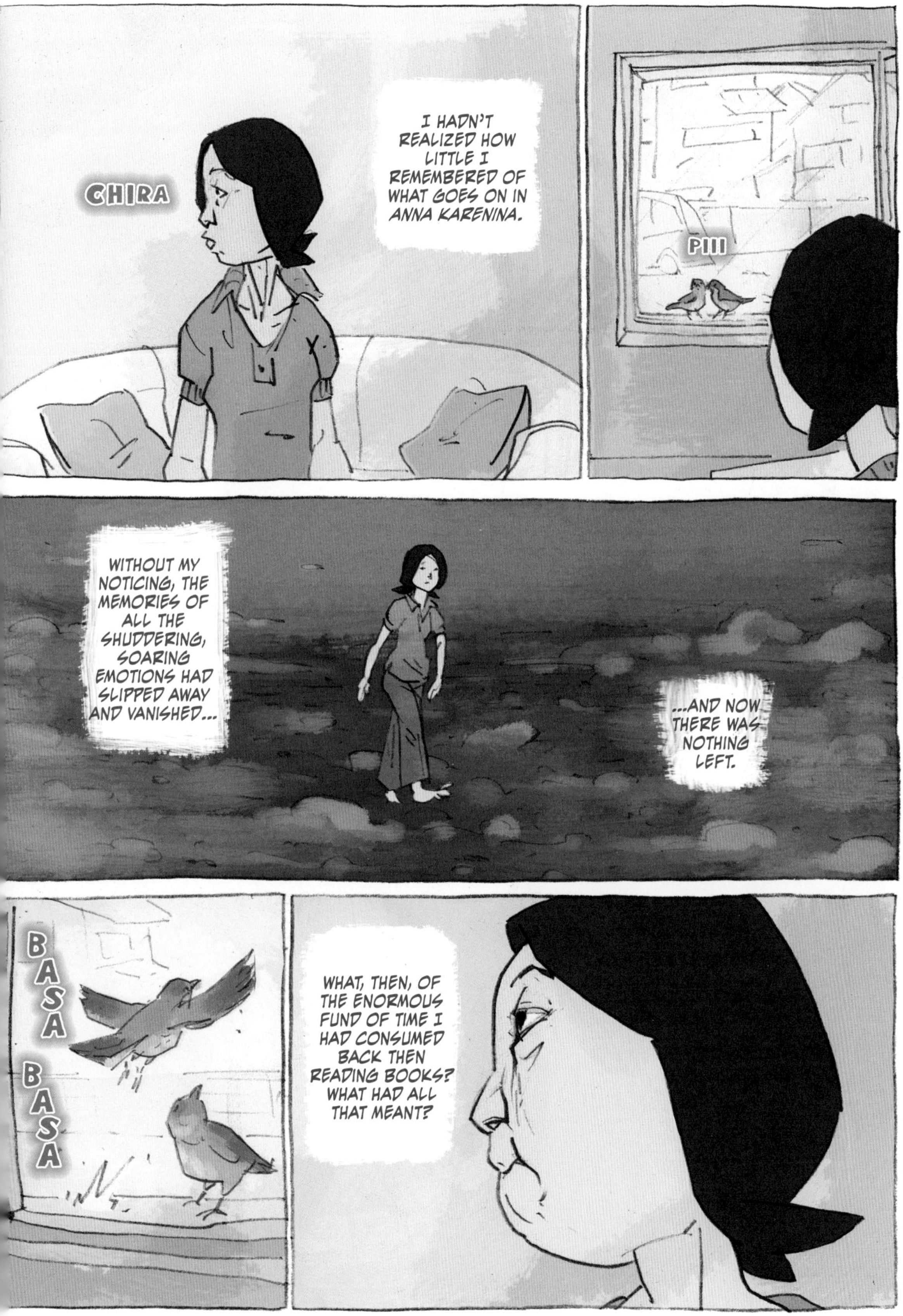
CHIRA
I HADN'T REALIZED HOW LITTLE I REMEMBERED OF WHAT GOES ON IN ANNA KARENINA.
PIII
WITHOUT MY NOTICING, THE MEMORIES OF ALL THE SHUDDERING, SOARING EMOTIONS HAD SLIPPED AWAY AND VANISHED...
...AND NOW THERE WAS NOTHING LEFT.
BASA BASA
WHAT, THEN, OF THE ENORMOUS FUND OF TIME I HAD CONSUMED BACK THEN READING BOOKS? WHAT HAD ALL THAT MEANT?

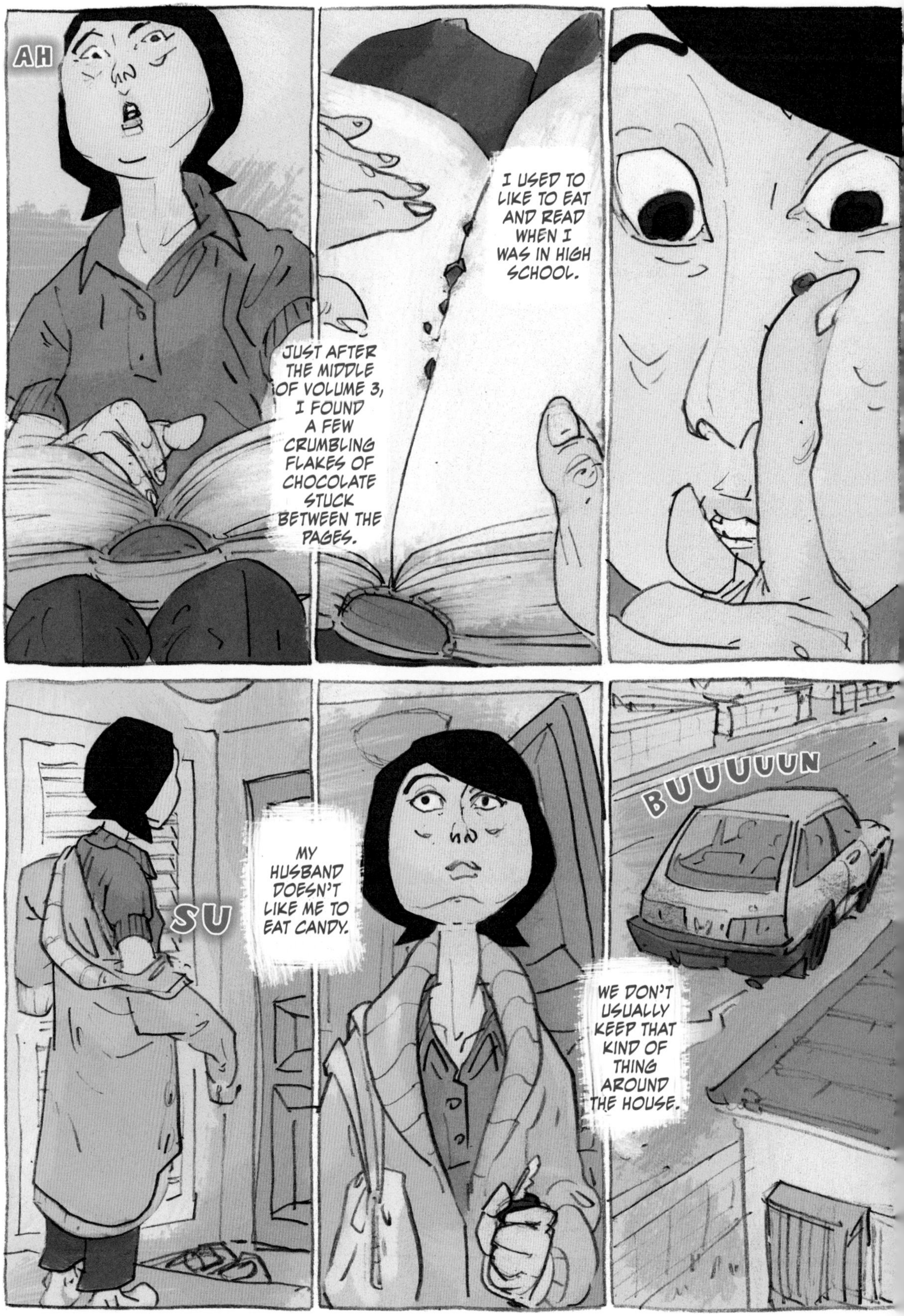
AH
I USED TO LIKE TO EAT AND READ WHEN I WAS IN HIGH SCHOOL.
JUST AFTER THE MIDDLE OF VOLUME 3, I FOUND A FEW CRUMBLING FLAKES OF CHOCOLATE STUCK BETWEEN THE PAGES.
SU
MY HUSBAND DOESN'T LIKE ME TO EAT CANDY.
BUUUUUN
WE DON'T USUALLY KEEP THAT KIND OF THING AROUND THE HOUSE.

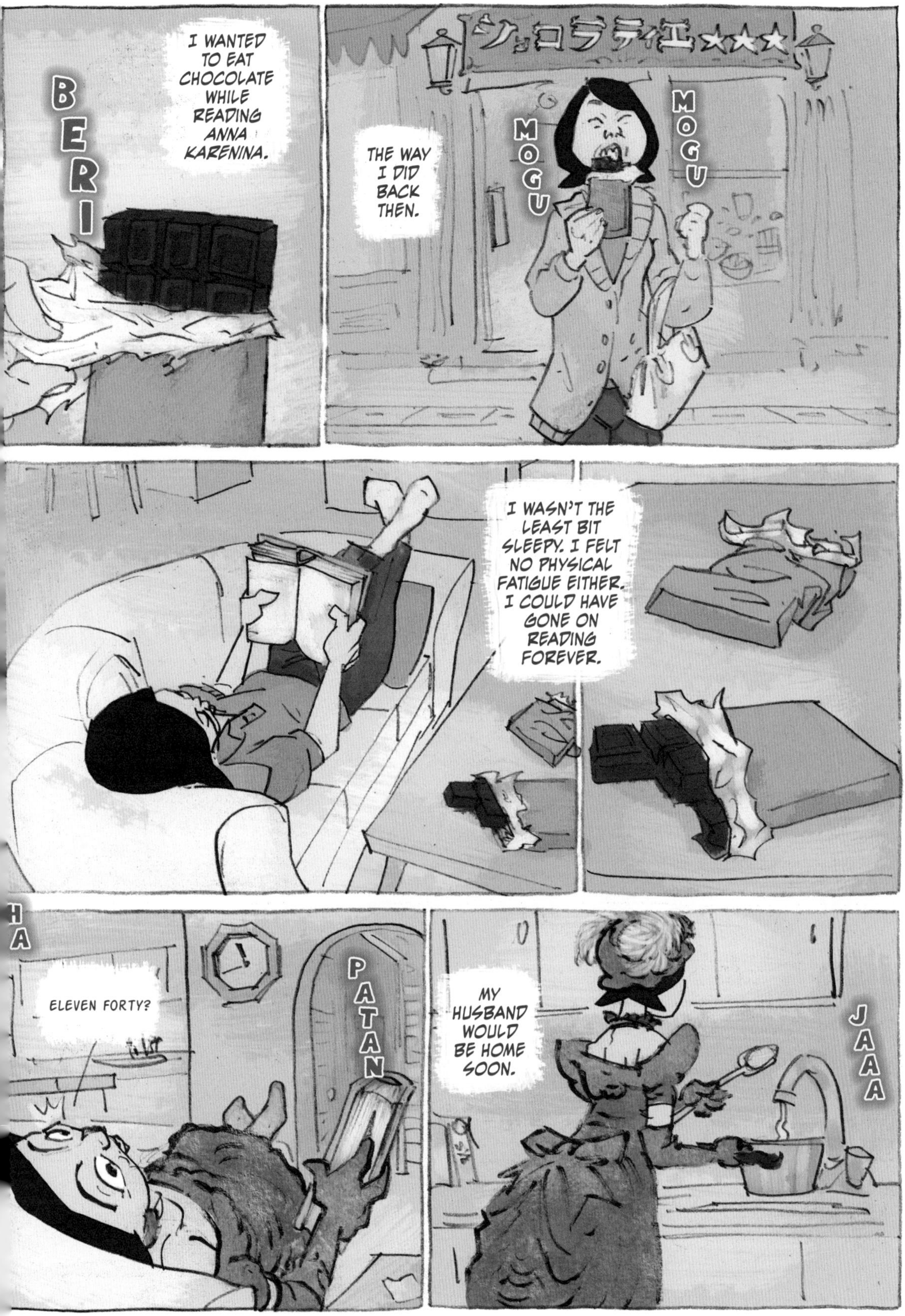
BERI
I WANTED TO EAT CHOCOLATE WHILE READING ANNA KARENINA.
ショコラティエ★★★
THE WAY I DID BACK THEN.
MOGU
MOGU
I WASN'T THE LEAST BIT SLEEPY. I FELT NO PHYSICAL FATIGUE EITHER. I COULD HAVE GONE ON READING FOREVER.
HA
ELEVEN FORTY?
PATAN
MY HUSBAND WOULD BE HOME SOON.
JAAA

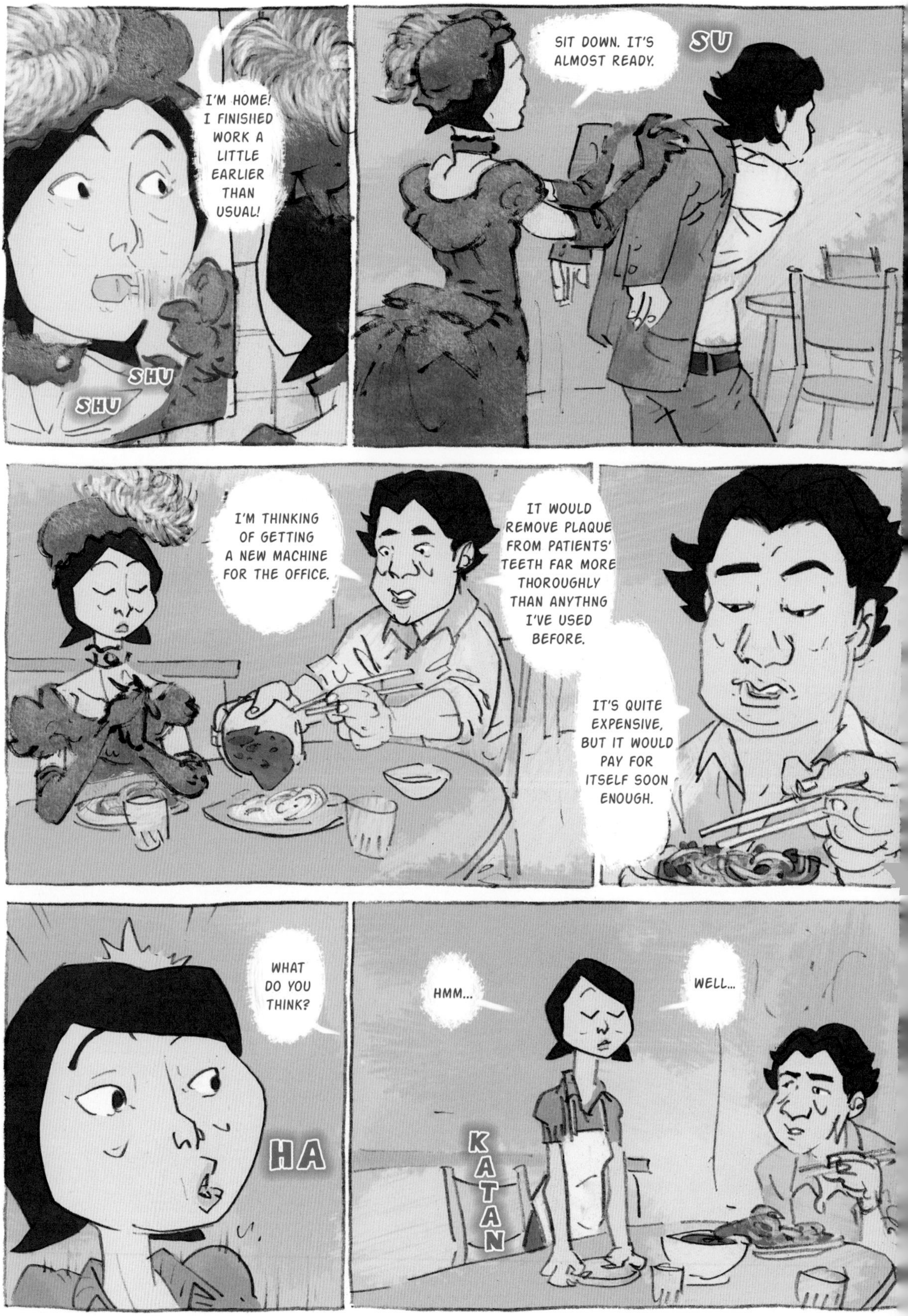
I'M HOME! I FINISHED WORK A LITTLE EARLIER THAN USUAL!
SHU
SHU
SIT DOWN. IT'S ALMOST READY.
SU
I'M THINKING OF GETTING A NEW MACHINE FOR THE OFFICE.
IT WOULD REMOVE PLAQUE FROM PATIENTS' TEETH FAR MORE THOROUGHLY THAN ANYTHNG I'VE USED BEFORE.
IT'S QUITE EXPENSIVE, BUT IT WOULD PAY FOR ITSELF SOON ENOUGH.
WHAT DO YOU THINK?
HA
HMM...
WELL...
KATAN

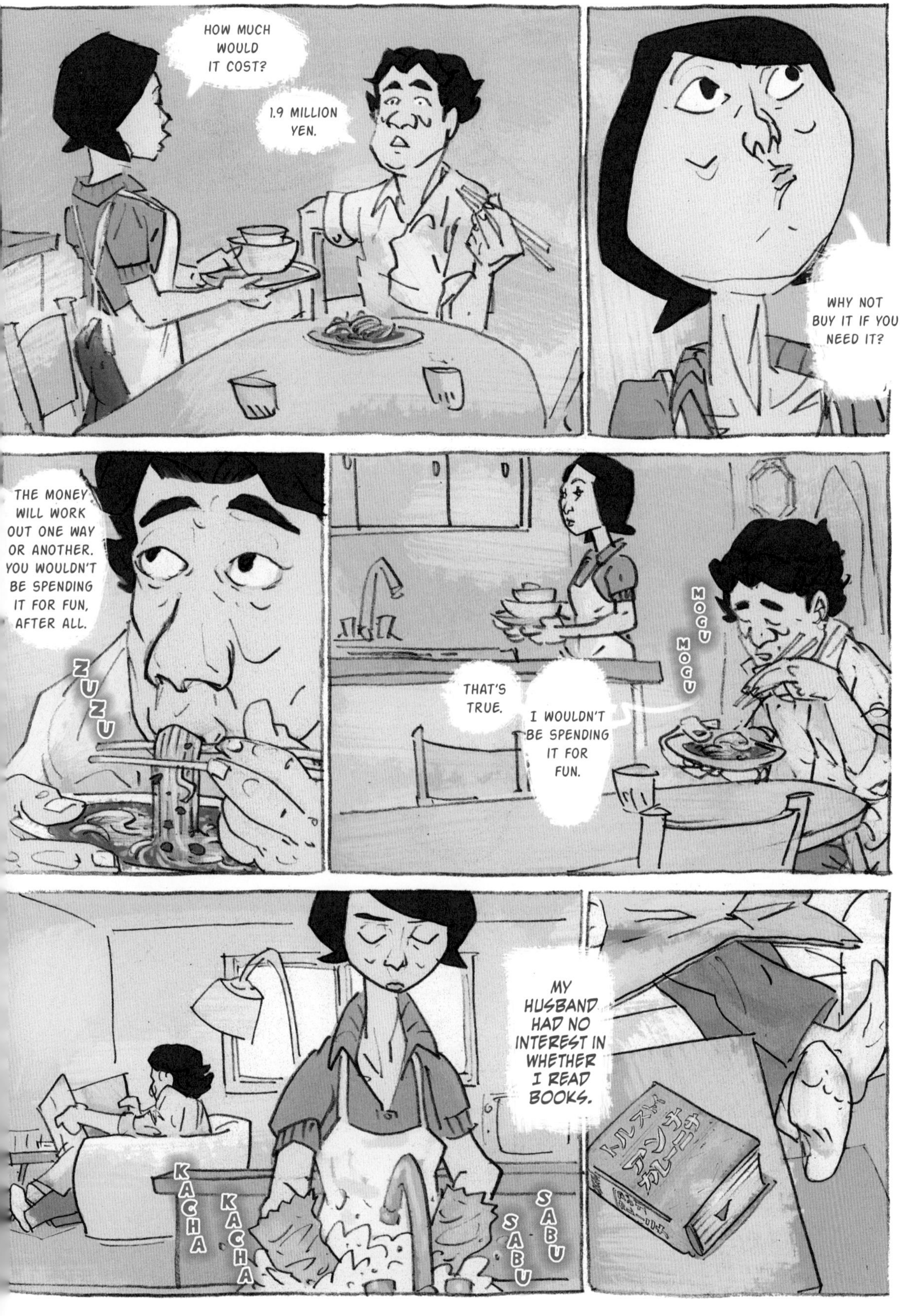
HOW MUCH WOULD IT COST?
1.9 MILLION YEN.
WHY NOT BUY IT IF YOU NEED IT?
THE MONEY WILL WORK OUT ONE WAY OR ANOTHER. YOU WOULDN'T BE SPENDING IT FOR FUN, AFTER ALL.
ZUZU
MOGU MOGU
THAT'S TRUE.
I WOULDN'T BE SPENDING IT FOR FUN.
KACHA KACHA
SABU SABU
MY HUSBAND HAD NO INTEREST IN WHETHER I READ BOOKS.

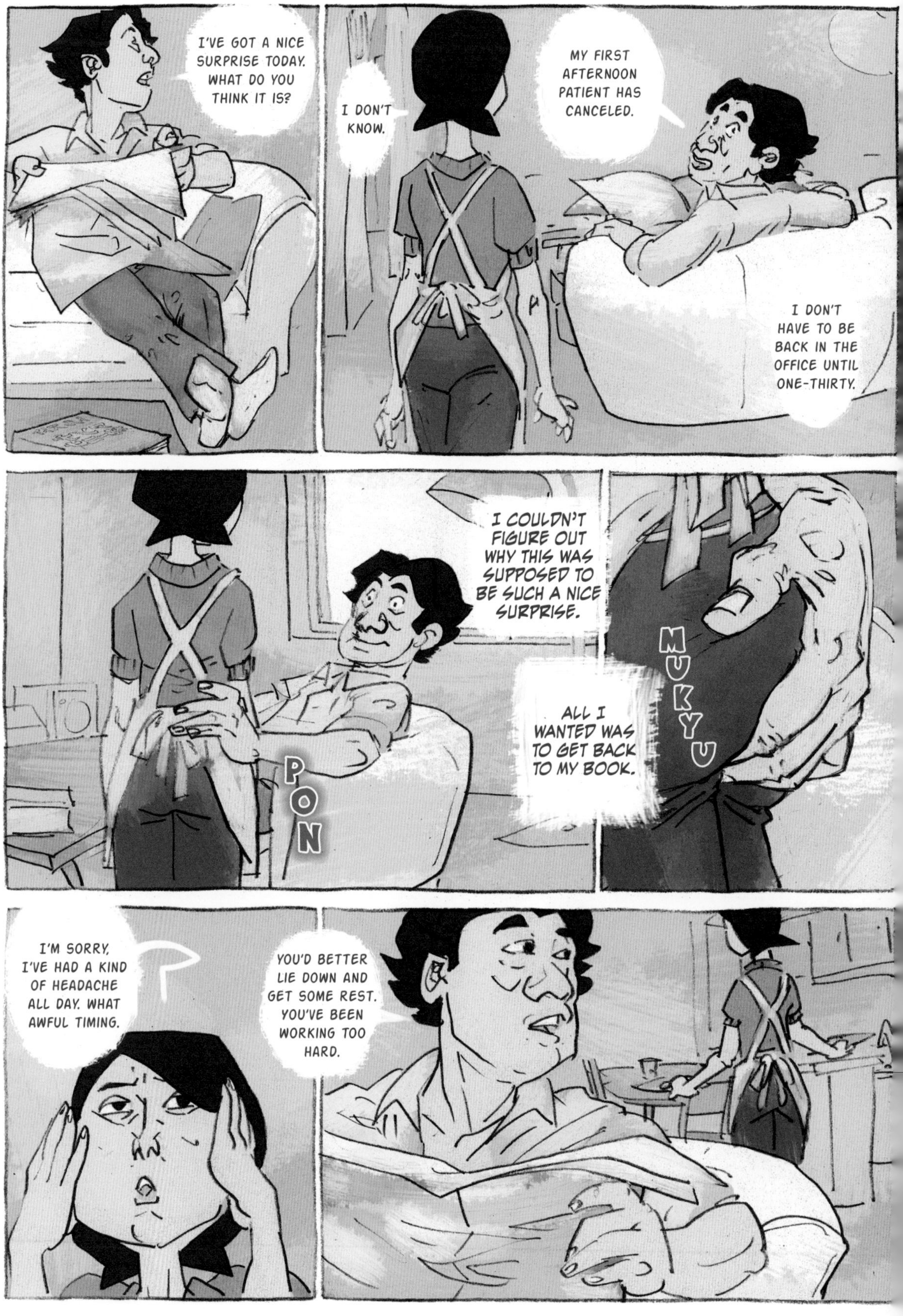
I'VE GOT A NICE SURPRISE TODAY. WHAT DO YOU THINK IT IS?
I DON'T KNOW.
MY FIRST AFTERNOON PATIENT HAS CANCELED.
I DON'T HAVE TO BE BACK IN THE OFFICE UNTIL ONE-THIRTY.
I COULDN'T FIGURE OUT WHY THIS WAS SUPPOSED TO BE SUCH A NICE SURPRISE.
PON
ALL I WANTED WAS TO GET BACK TO MY BOOK.
MUKYU
I'M SORRY, I'VE HAD A KIND OF HEADACHE ALL DAY. WHAT AWFUL TIMING.
YOU'D BETTER LIE DOWN AND GET SOME REST. YOU'VE BEEN WORKING TOO HARD.

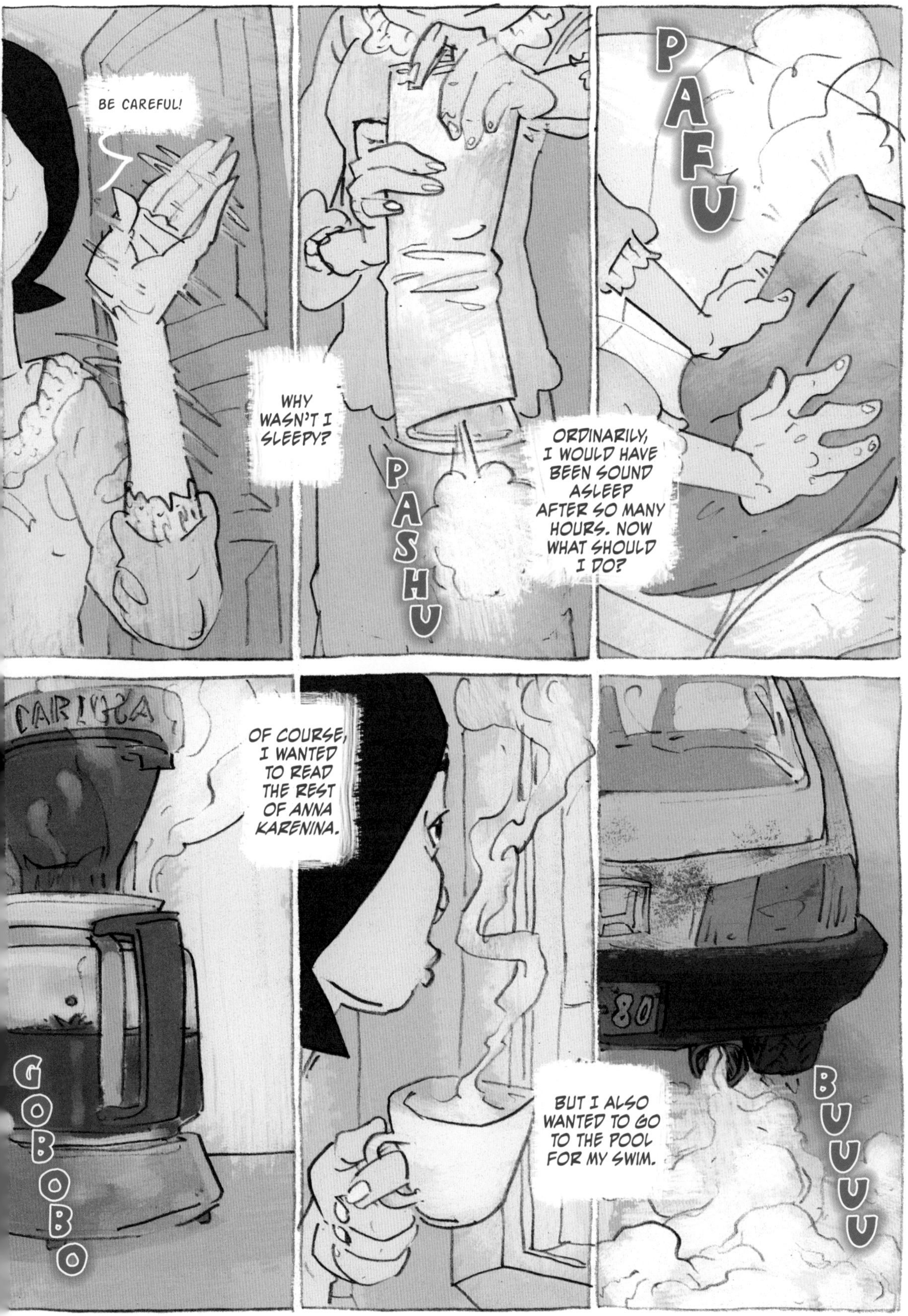
BE CAREFUL!
PASHU
WHY WASN'T I SLEEPY?
PAFU
ORDINARILY, I WOULD HAVE BEEN SOUND ASLEEP AFTER SO MANY HOURS. NOW WHAT SHOULD I DO?
CARIOCA
GOBOBO
OF COURSE, I WANTED TO READ THE REST OF ANNA KARENINA.
BUT I ALSO WANTED TO GO TO THE POOL FOR MY SWIM.
80
BUUUU

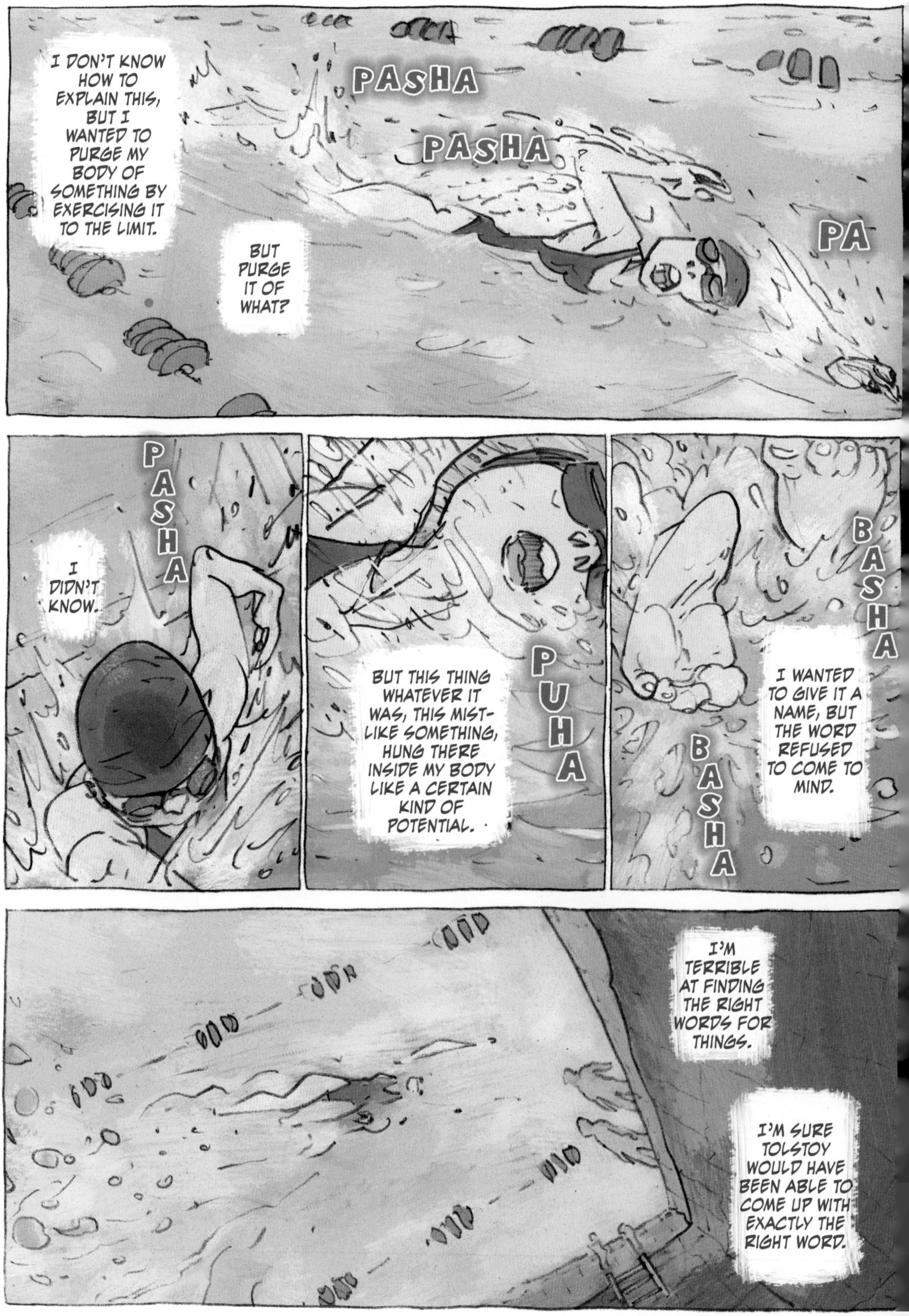
I DON'T KNOW HOW TO EXPLAIN THIS, BUT I WANTED TO PURGE MY BODY OF SOMETHING BY EXERCISING IT TO THE LIMIT.
PASHA
PASHA
BUT PURGE IT OF WHAT?
PA
PASHA
I DIDN'T KNOW.
BUT THIS THING WHATEVER IT WAS, THIS MIST-LIKE SOMETHING, HUNG THERE INSIDE MY BODY LIKE A CERTAIN KIND OF POTENTIAL.
PUHA
BASHA
I WANTED TO GIVE IT A NAME, BUT THE WORD REFUSED TO COME TO MIND.
BASHA
I'M TERRIBLE AT FINDING THE RIGHT WORDS FOR THINGS.
I'M SURE TOLSTOY WOULD HAVE BEEN ABLE TO COME UP WITH EXACTLY THE RIGHT WORD.

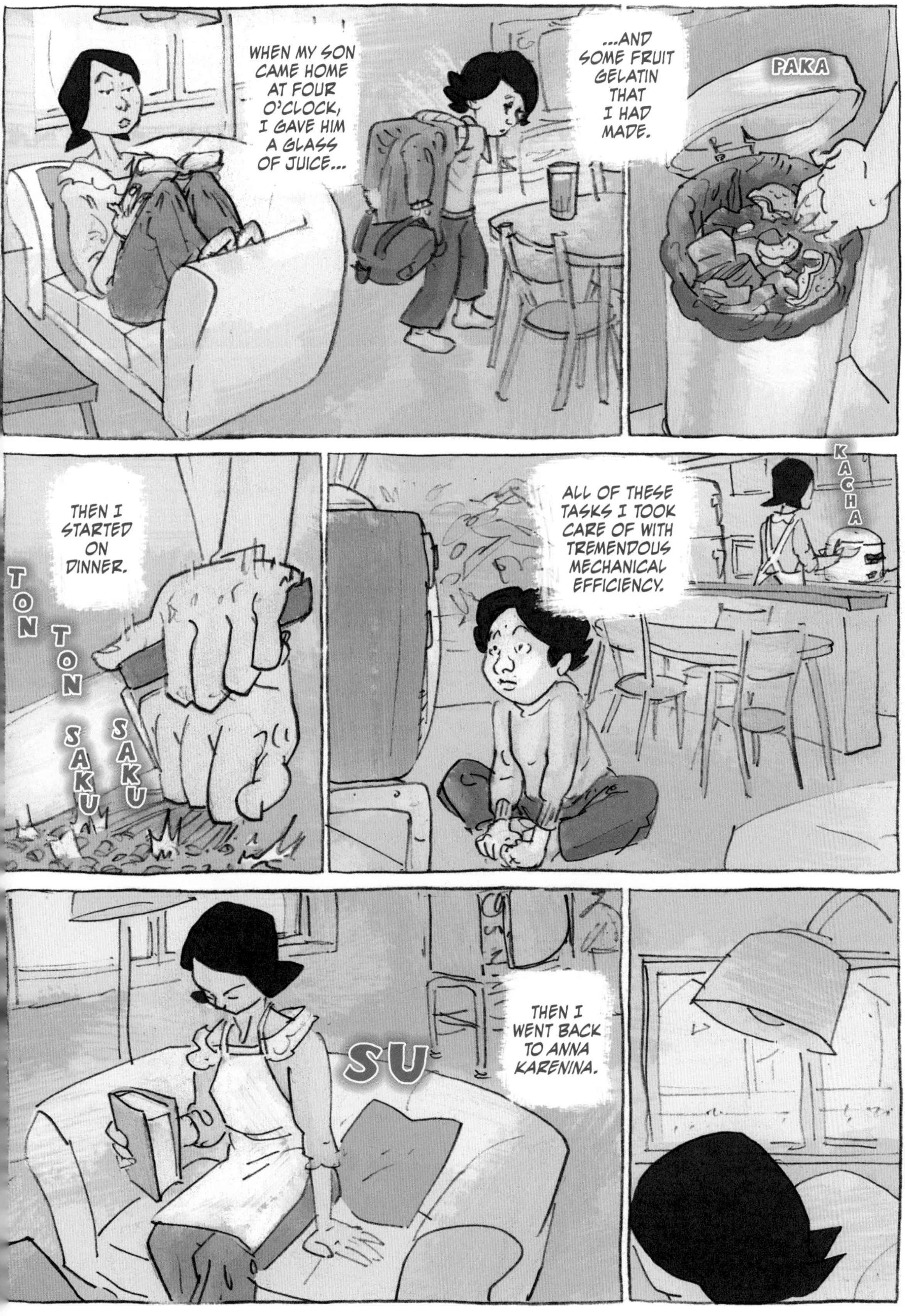
WHEN MY SON CAME HOME AT FOUR O'CLOCK, I GAVE HIM A GLASS OF JUICE...
...AND SOME FRUIT GELATIN THAT I HAD MADE.
PAKA
THEN I STARTED ON DINNER.
TON TON
SAKU SAKU
ALL OF THESE TASKS I TOOK CARE OF WITH TREMENDOUS MECHANICAL EFFICIENCY.
KACHA
SU
THEN I WENT BACK TO ANNA KARENINA.

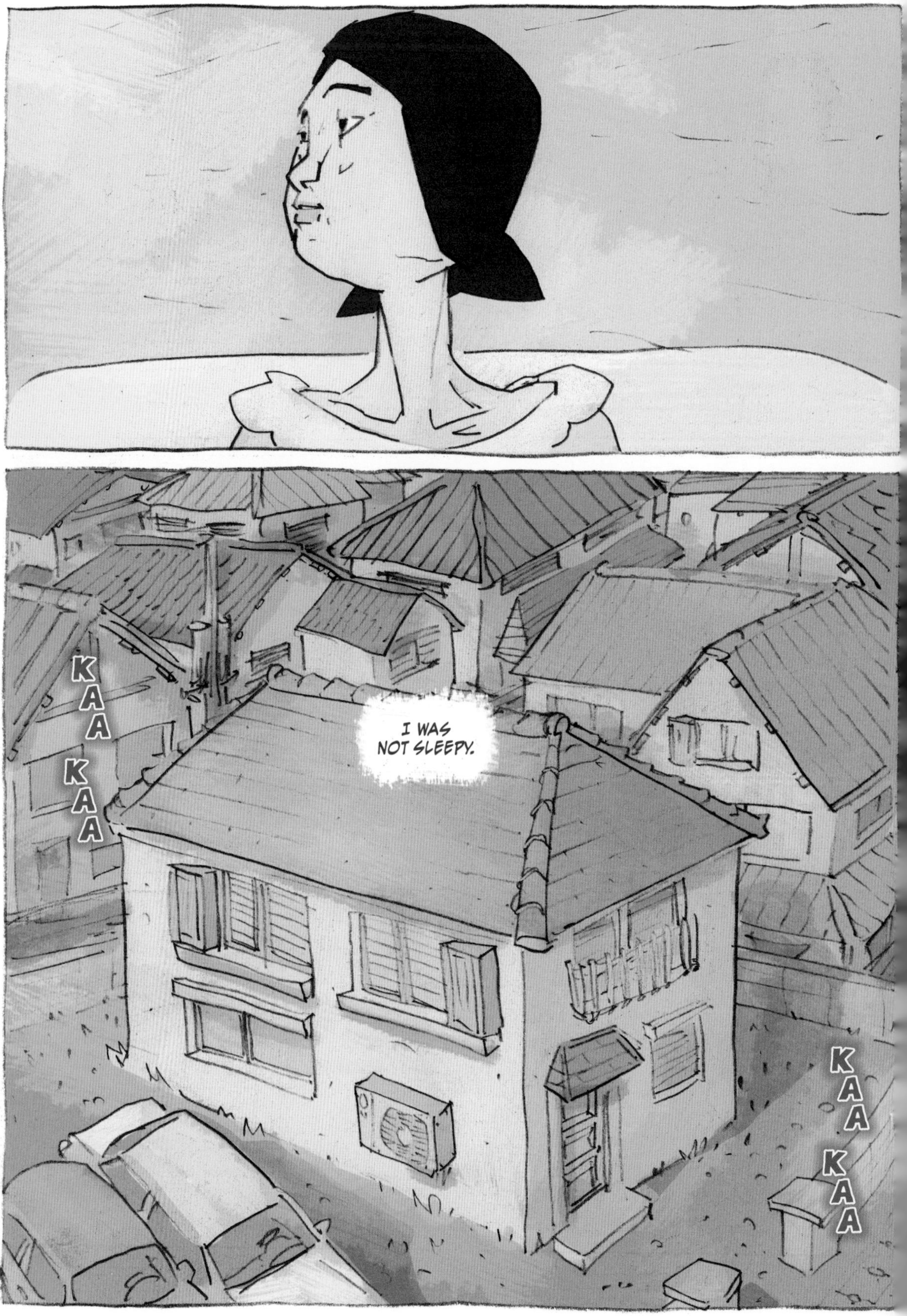
KAA KAA
I WAS NOT SLEEPY.
KAA KAA

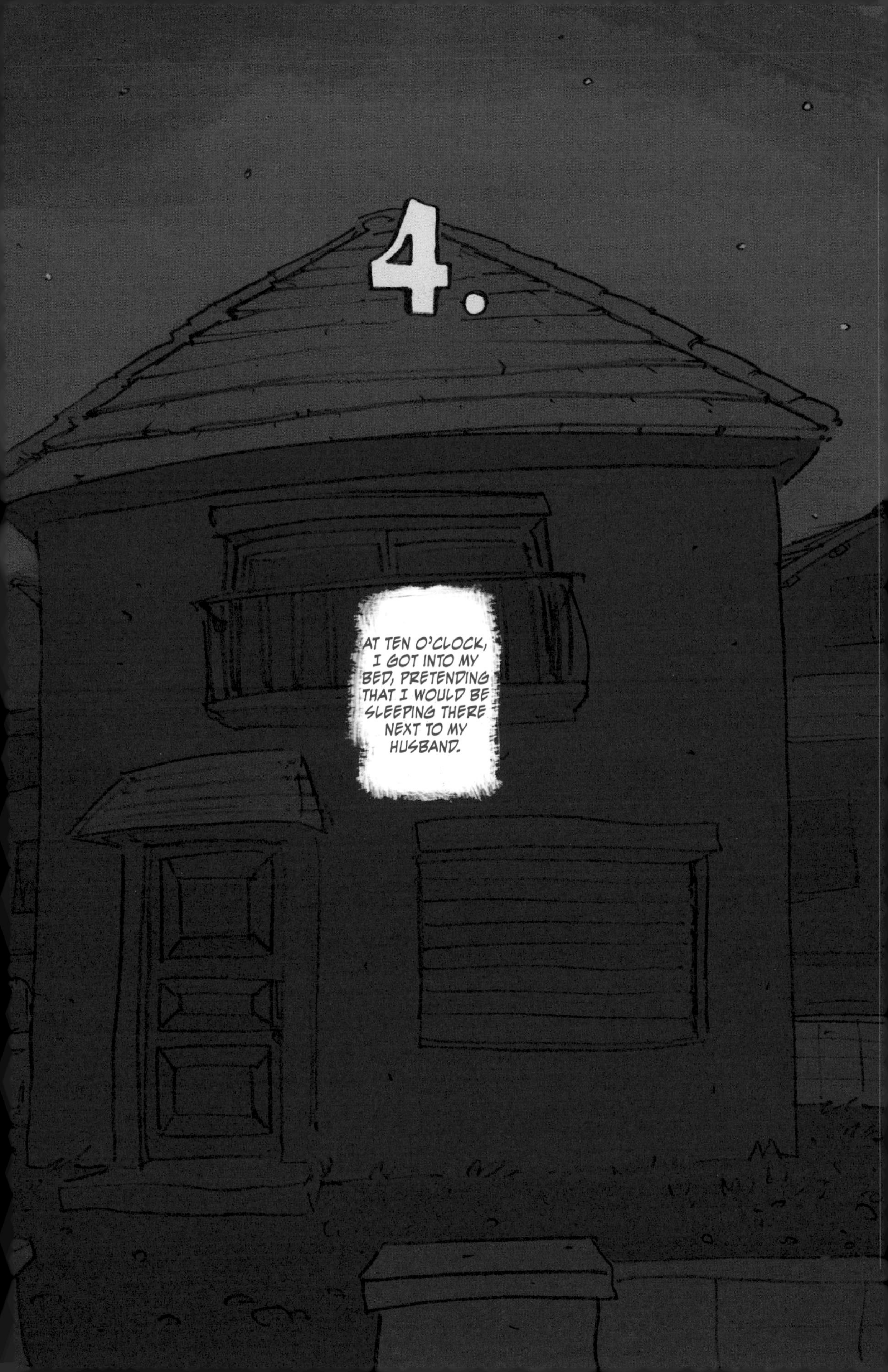
4.
AT TEN O'CLOCK, I GOT INTO MY BED, PRETENDING THAT I WOULD BE SLEEPING THERE NEXT TO MY HUSBAND.

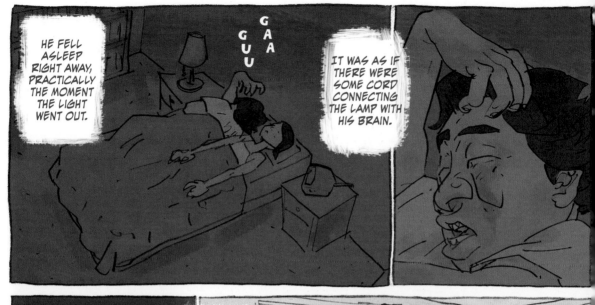

HE FELL ASLEEP RIGHT AWAY, PRACTICALLY THE MOMENT THE LIGHT WENT OUT.

GUU GAA

IT WAS AS IF THERE WERE SOME CORD CONNECTING THE LAMP WITH HIS BRAIN.

WHEN WE WERE NEWLYWEDS I EXPERIMENTED TO SEE WHAT IT WOULD TAKE TO WAKE HIM.

NOTHING WORKED.

GUOOO

HE SLEPT. HE SLEPT LIKE A TURTLE BURIED IN MUD.

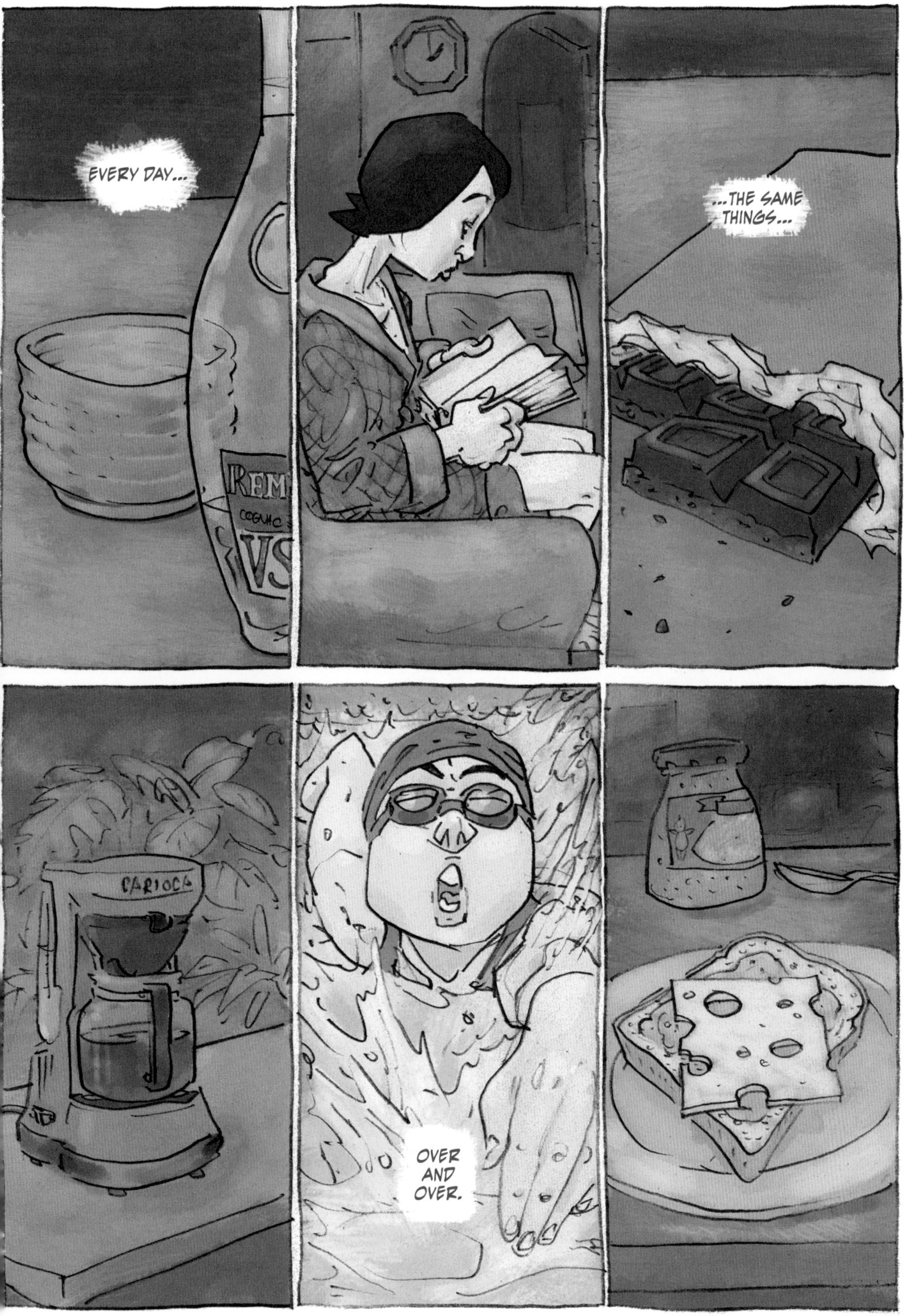
EVERY DAY...
...THE SAME THINGS...
CARIOCA
OVER AND OVER.

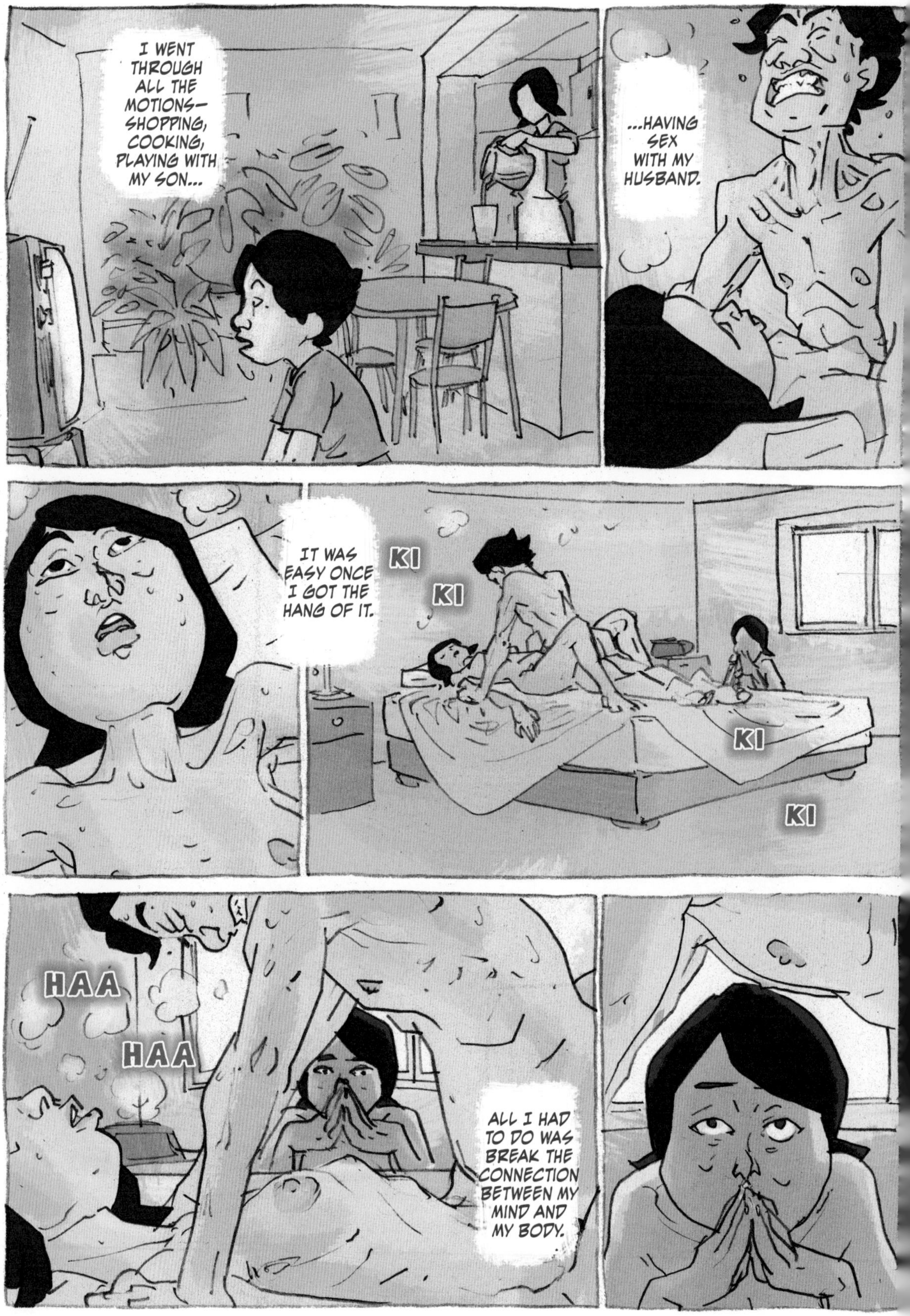
I WENT THROUGH ALL THE MOTIONS—SHOPPING, COOKING, PLAYING WITH MY SON...
...HAVING SEX WITH MY HUSBAND.
IT WAS EASY ONCE I GOT THE HANG OF IT.
KI
KI
KI
KI
HAA
HAA
ALL I HAD TO DO WAS BREAK THE CONNECTION BETWEEN MY MIND AND MY BODY.

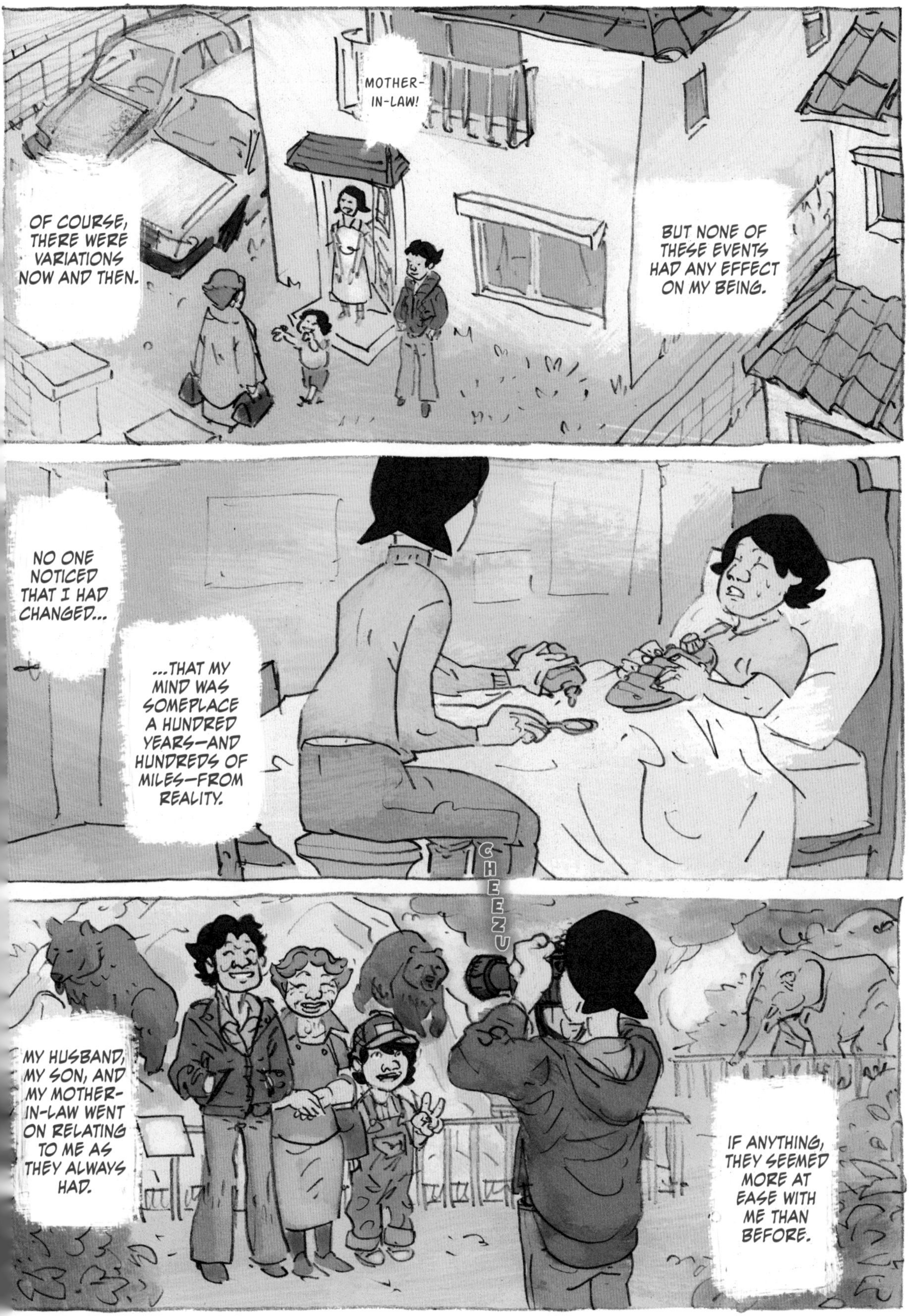
OF COURSE, THERE WERE VARIATIONS NOW AND THEN.
MOTHER-IN-LAW!
BUT NONE OF THESE EVENTS HAD ANY EFFECT ON MY BEING.
NO ONE NOTICED THAT I HAD CHANGED...
...THAT MY MIND WAS SOMEPLACE A HUNDRED YEARS—AND HUNDREDS OF MILES—FROM REALITY.
CHEEZU
MY HUSBAND, MY SON, AND MY MOTHER-IN-LAW WENT ON RELATING TO ME AS THEY ALWAYS HAD.
IF ANYTHING, THEY SEEMED MORE AT EASE WITH ME THAN BEFORE.

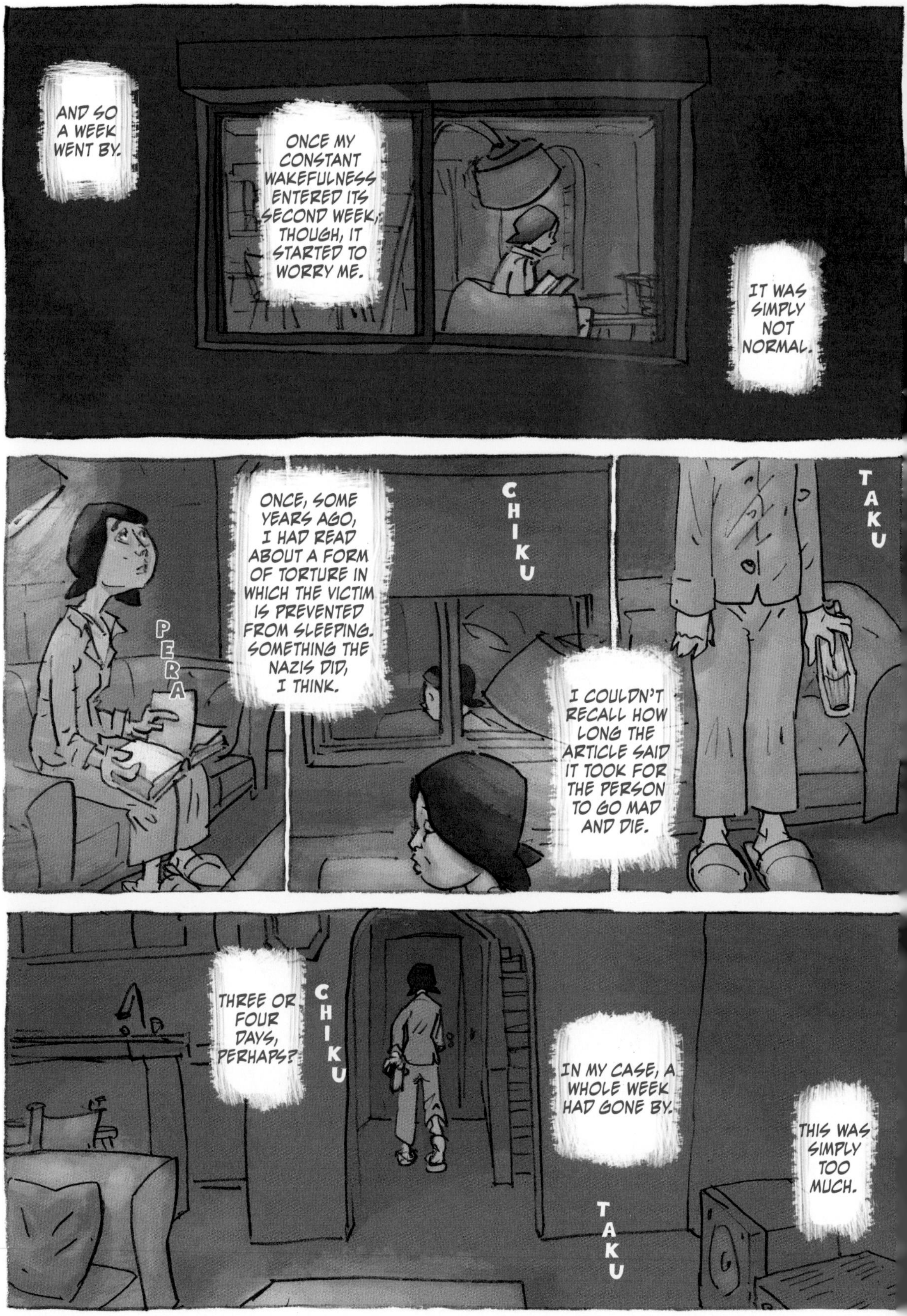
AND SO A WEEK WENT BY.
ONCE MY CONSTANT WAKEFULNESS ENTERED ITS SECOND WEEK, THOUGH, IT STARTED TO WORRY ME.
IT WAS SIMPLY NOT NORMAL.
PERA
ONCE, SOME YEARS AGO, I HAD READ ABOUT A FORM OF TORTURE IN WHICH THE VICTIM IS PREVENTED FROM SLEEPING. SOMETHING THE NAZIS DID, I THINK.
CHIKU
TAKU
I COULDN'T RECALL HOW LONG THE ARTICLE SAID IT TOOK FOR THE PERSON TO GO MAD AND DIE.
THREE OR FOUR DAYS, PERHAPS?
CHIKU
IN MY CASE, A WHOLE WEEK HAD GONE BY.
TAKU
THIS WAS SIMPLY TOO MUCH.

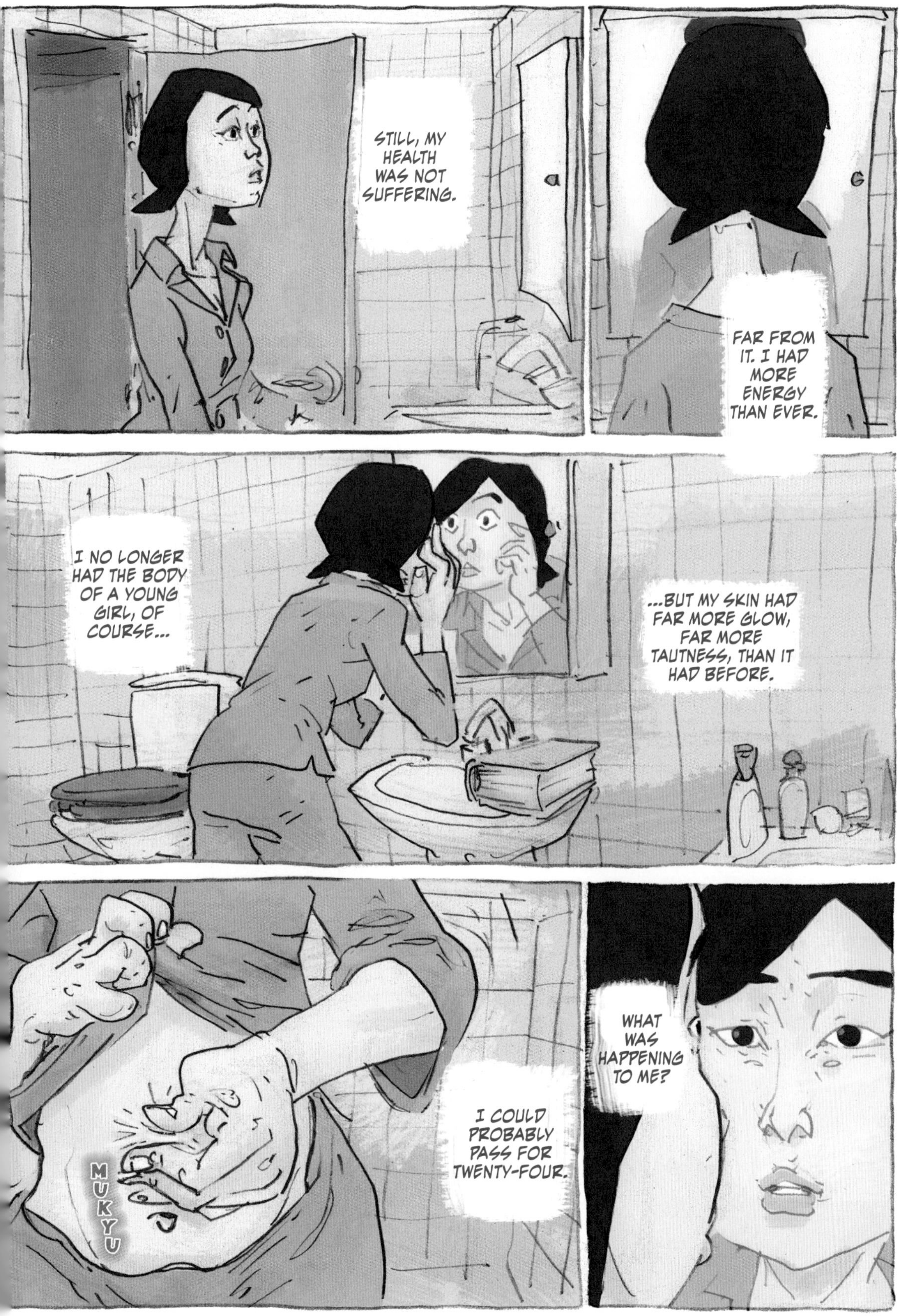
STILL, MY HEALTH WAS NOT SUFFERING.
FAR FROM IT. I HAD MORE ENERGY THAN EVER.
I NO LONGER HAD THE BODY OF A YOUNG GIRL, OF COURSE...
...BUT MY SKIN HAD FAR MORE GLOW, FAR MORE TAUTNESS, THAN IT HAD BEFORE.
MUKYU
I COULD PROBABLY PASS FOR TWENTY-FOUR.
WHAT WAS HAPPENING TO ME?

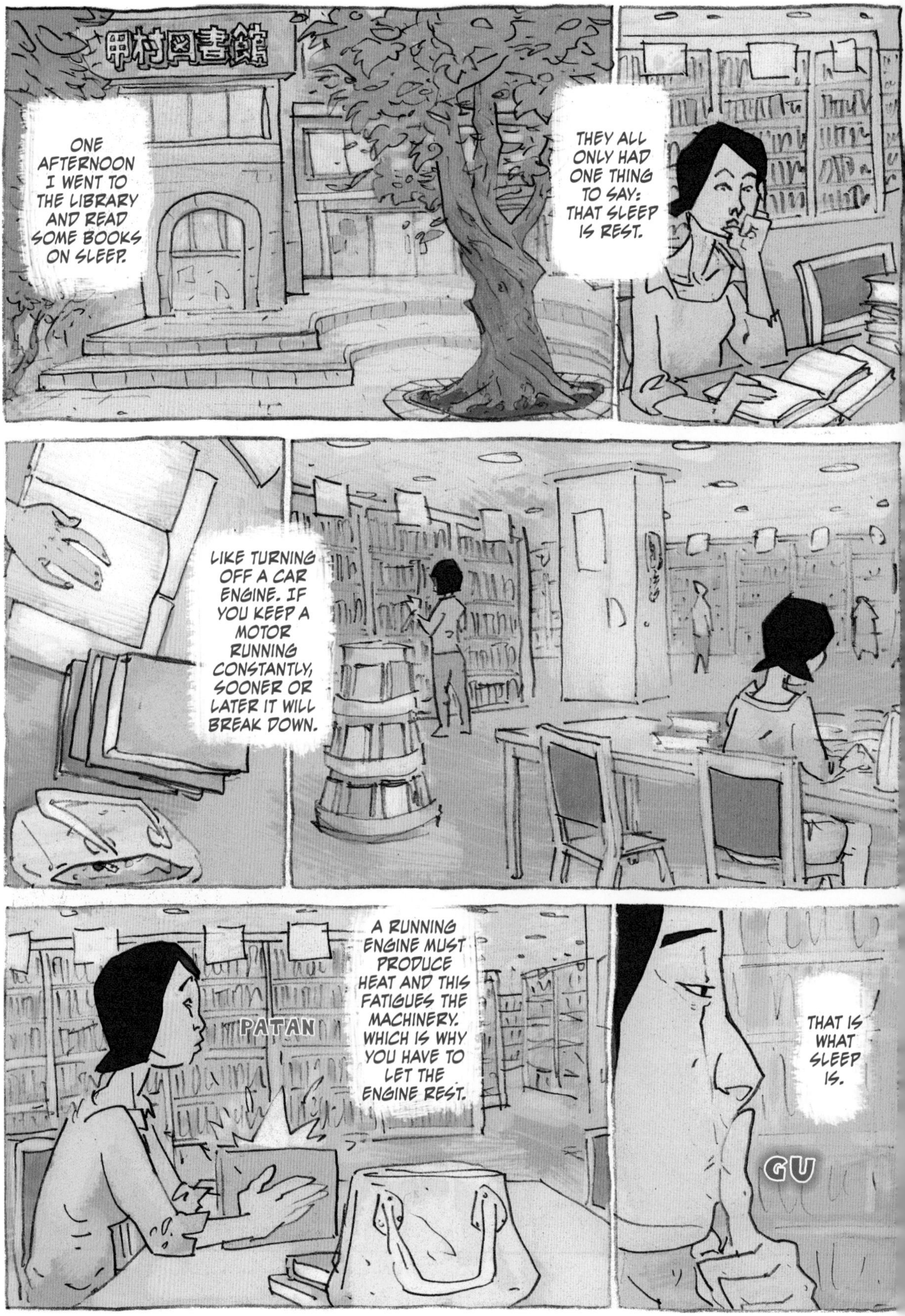
甲村図書館
ONE AFTERNOON I WENT TO THE LIBRARY AND READ SOME BOOKS ON SLEEP.
THEY ALL ONLY HAD ONE THING TO SAY: THAT SLEEP IS REST.
LIKE TURNING OFF A CAR ENGINE. IF YOU KEEP A MOTOR RUNNING CONSTANTLY, SOONER OR LATER IT WILL BREAK DOWN.
PATAN
A RUNNING ENGINE MUST PRODUCE HEAT AND THIS FATIGUES THE MACHINERY. WHICH IS WHY YOU HAVE TO LET THE ENGINE REST.
THAT IS WHAT SLEEP IS.
GU

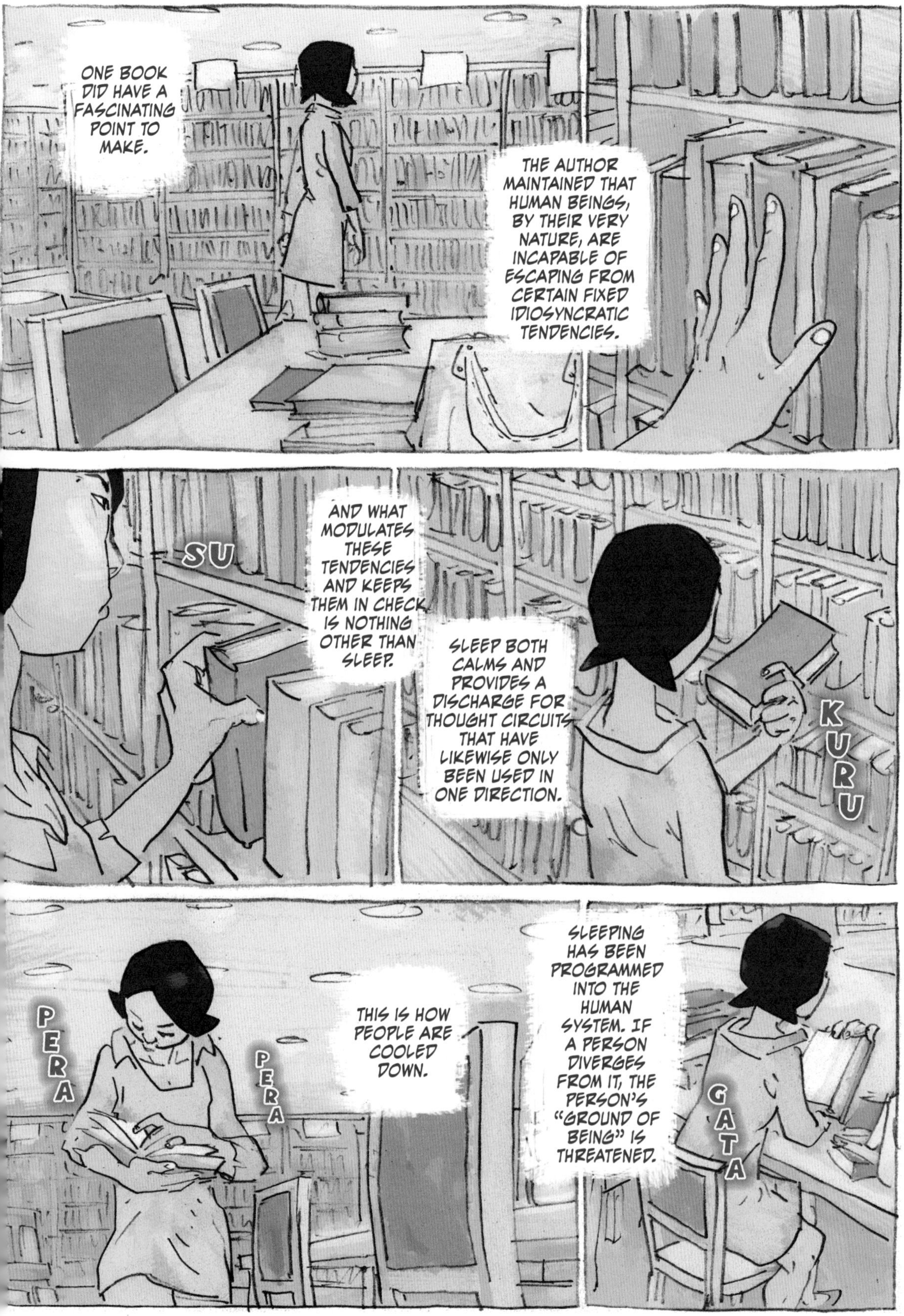
ONE BOOK DID HAVE A FASCINATING POINT TO MAKE.
THE AUTHOR MAINTAINED THAT HUMAN BEINGS, BY THEIR VERY NATURE, ARE INCAPABLE OF ESCAPING FROM CERTAIN FIXED IDIOSYNCRATIC TENDENCIES.
SU
AND WHAT MODULATES THESE TENDENCIES AND KEEPS THEM IN CHECK IS NOTHING OTHER THAN SLEEP.
SLEEP BOTH CALMS AND PROVIDES A DISCHARGE FOR THOUGHT CIRCUITS THAT HAVE LIKEWISE ONLY BEEN USED IN ONE DIRECTION.
KURU
PERA
PERA
THIS IS HOW PEOPLE ARE COOLED DOWN.
SLEEPING HAS BEEN PROGRAMMED INTO THE HUMAN SYSTEM. IF A PERSON DIVERGES FROM IT, THE PERSON'S "GROUND OF BEING" IS THREATENED.
GATA

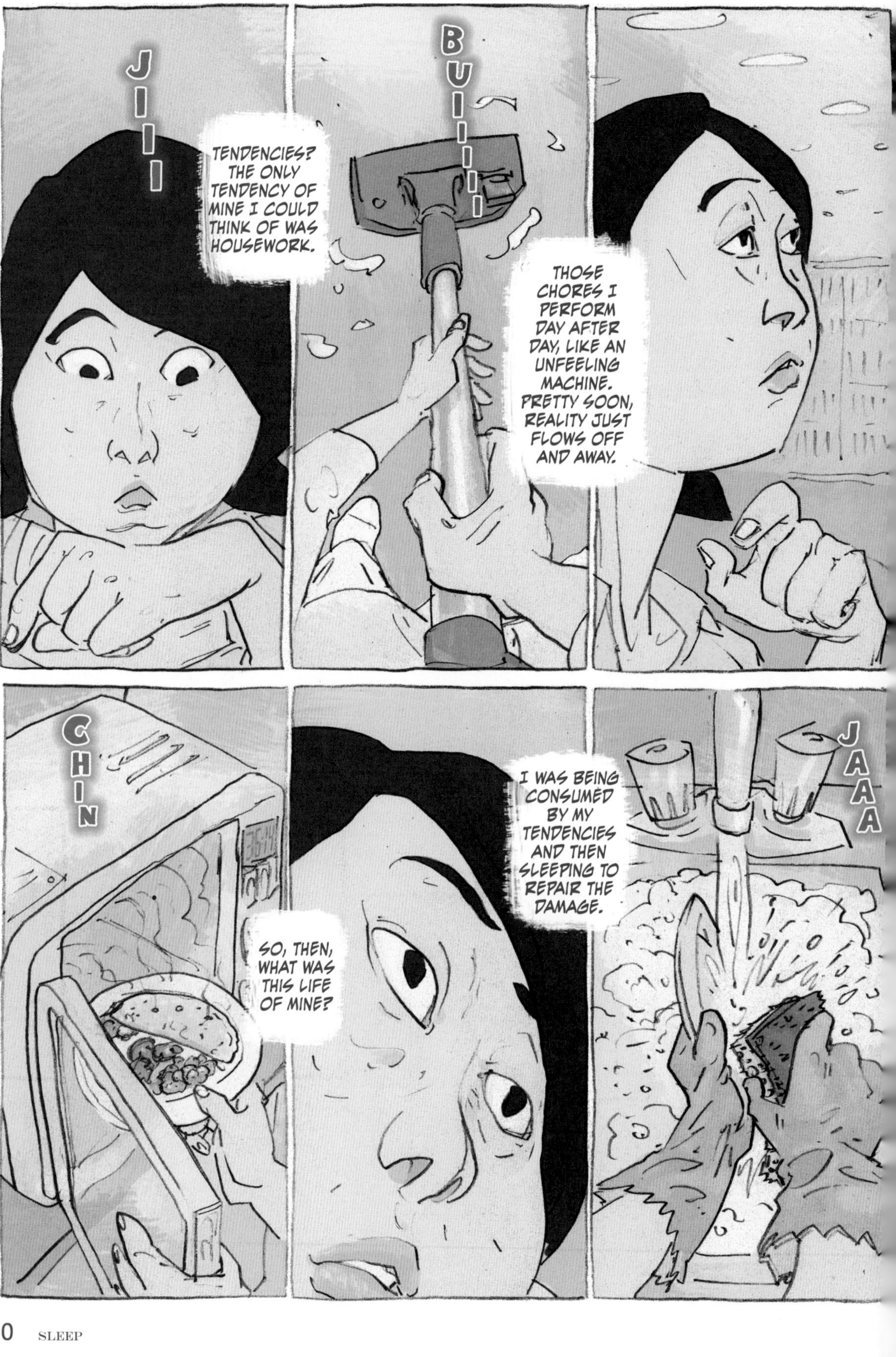
JIII
TENDENCIES? THE ONLY TENDENCY OF MINE I COULD THINK OF WAS HOUSEWORK.
BUIIIII
THOSE CHORES I PERFORM DAY AFTER DAY, LIKE AN UNFEELING MACHINE. PRETTY SOON, REALITY JUST FLOWS OFF AND AWAY.
CHIN
SO, THEN, WHAT WAS THIS LIFE OF MINE?
I WAS BEING CONSUMED BY MY TENDENCIES AND THEN SLEEPING TO REPAIR THE DAMAGE.
JAAA

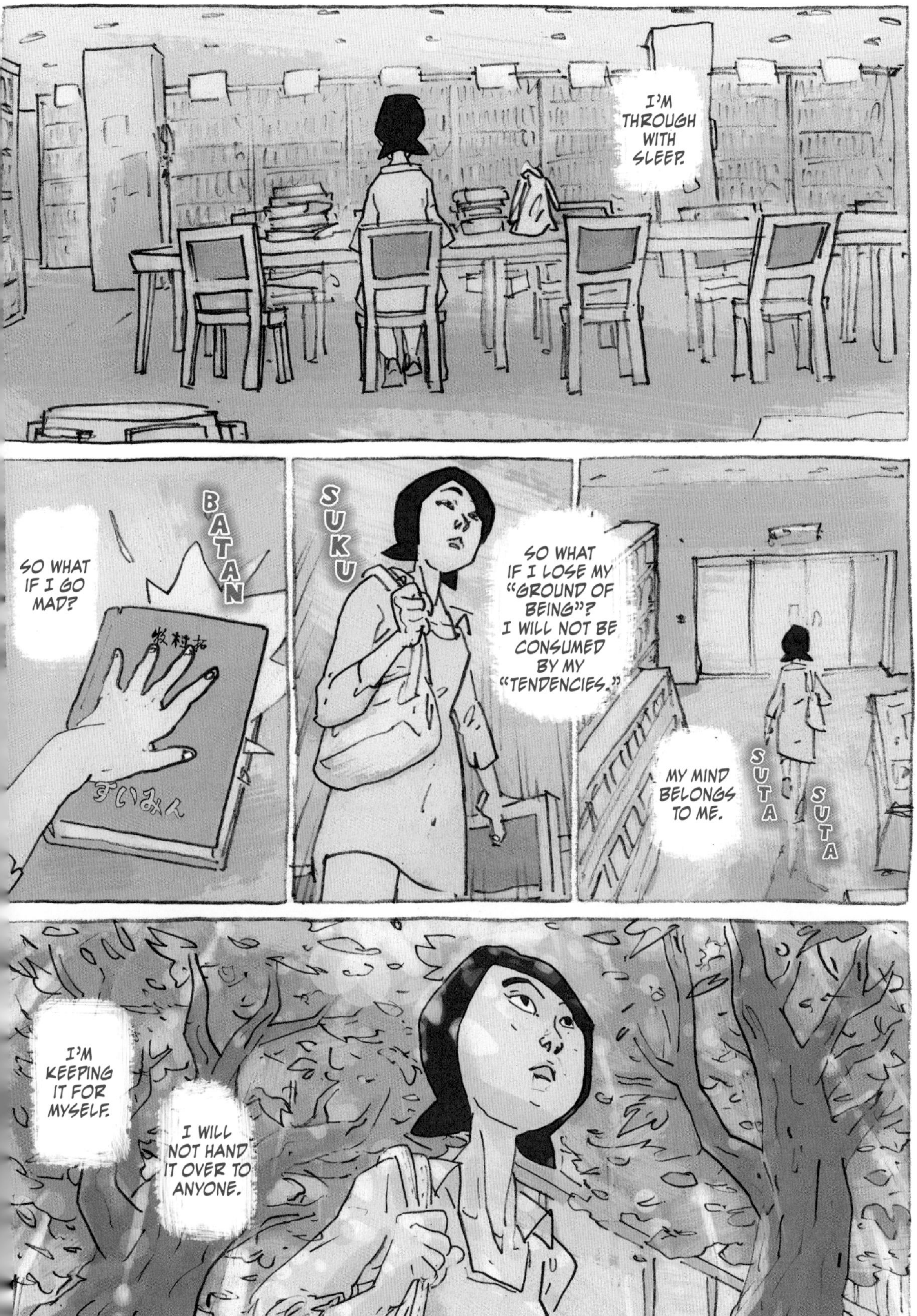
I'M THROUGH WITH SLEEP.
SO WHAT IF I GO MAD?
BATAN
牧村拓
すいみん
SUKU
SO WHAT IF I LOSE MY "GROUND OF BEING"? I WILL NOT BE CONSUMED BY MY "TENDENCIES."
MY MIND BELONGS TO ME.
SUTA
SUTA
I'M KEEPING IT FOR MYSELF.
I WILL NOT HAND IT OVER TO ANYONE.

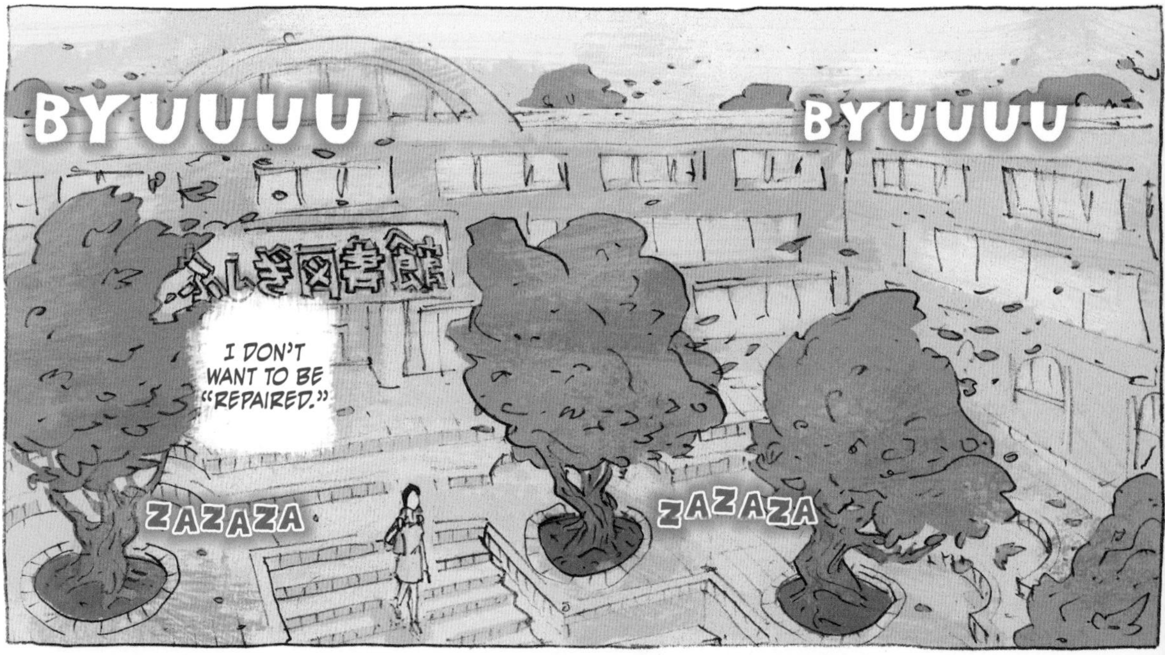
BYUUUU
BYUUUU
ふしぎ図書館
I DON'T WANT TO BE "REPAIRED."
ZAZAZA
ZAZAZA

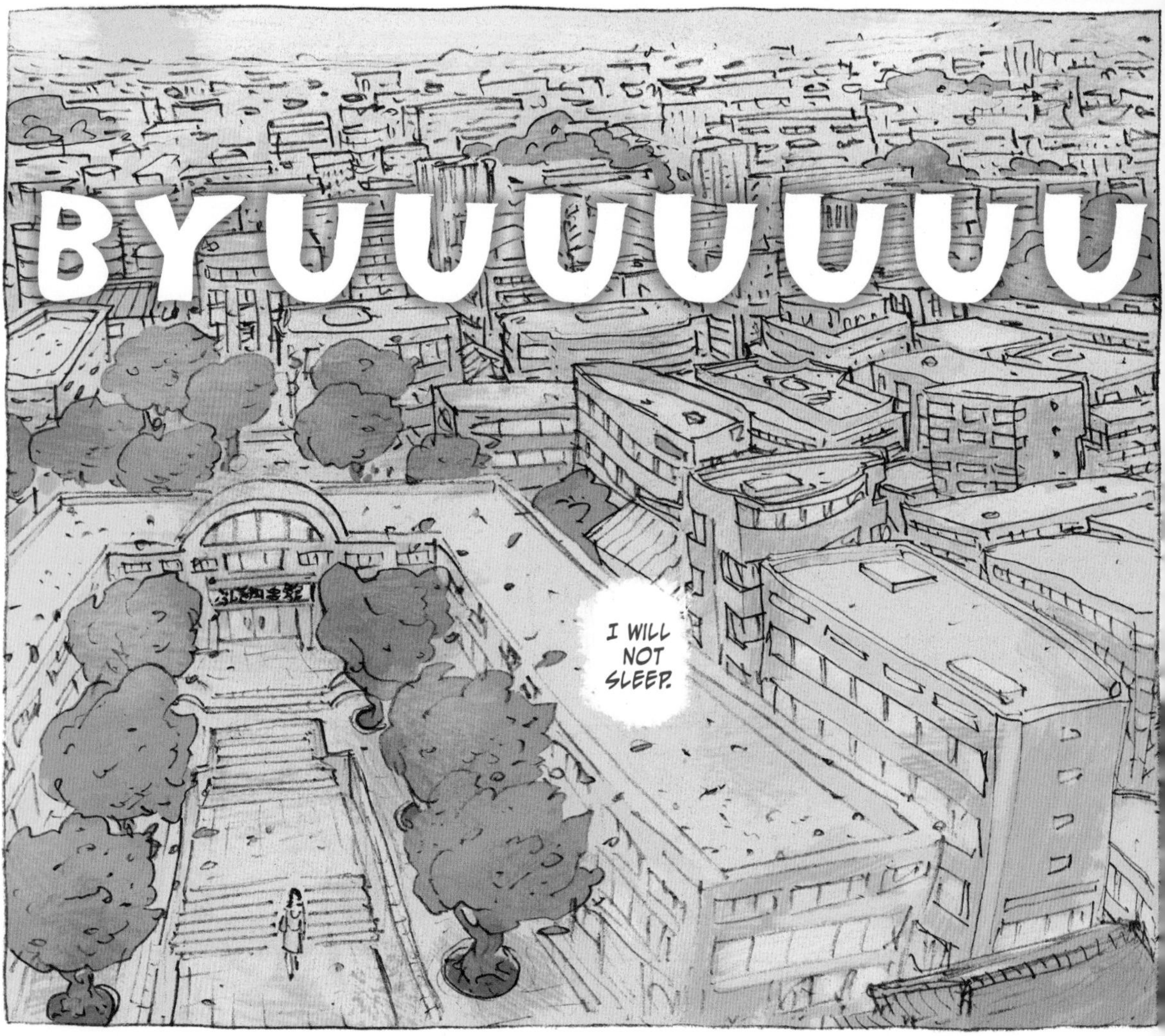
BYUUUUUUUU
I WILL NOT SLEEP.

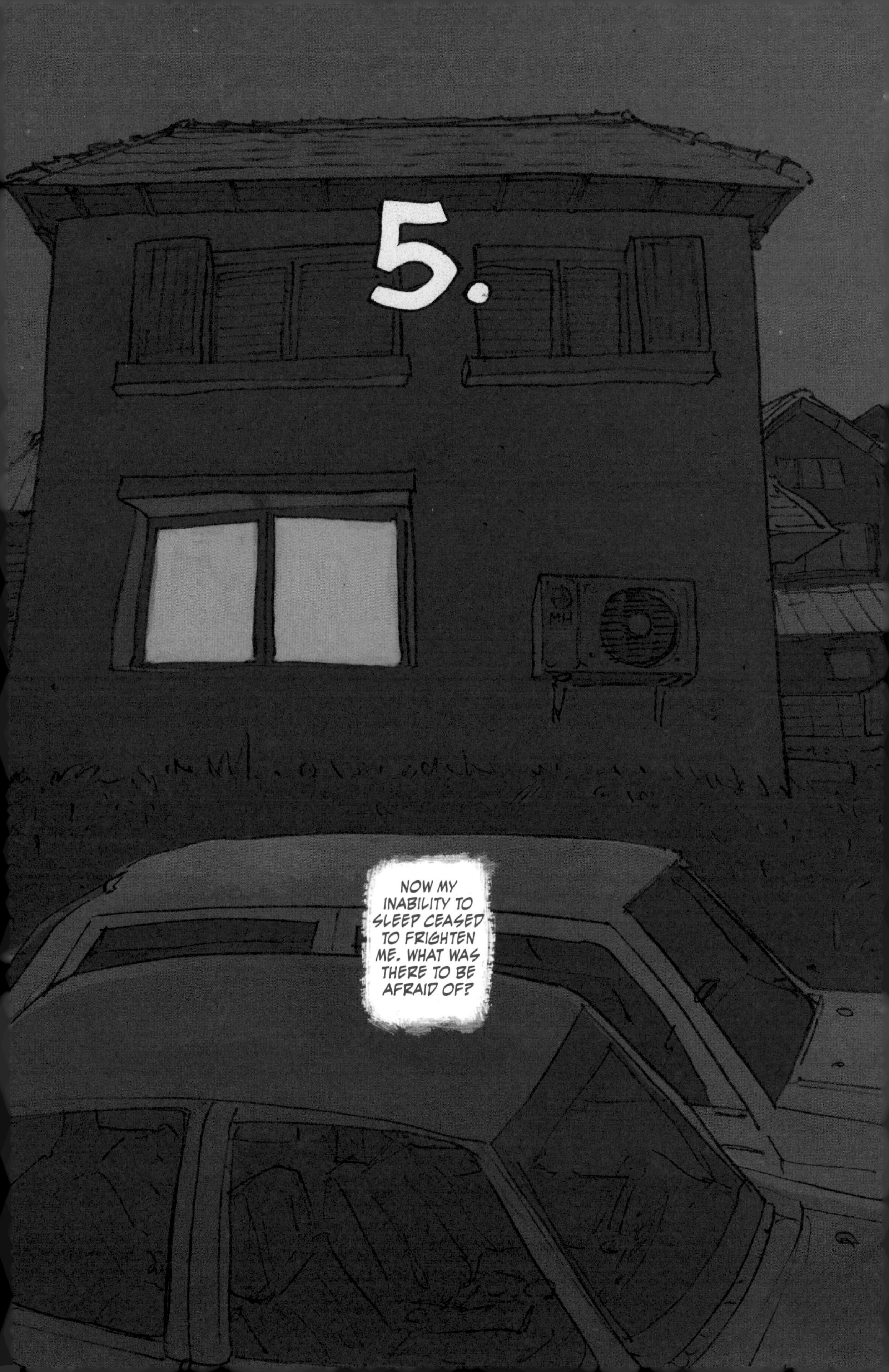
5.
NOW MY INABILITY TO SLEEP CEASED TO FRIGHTEN ME. WHAT WAS THERE TO BE AFRAID OF?

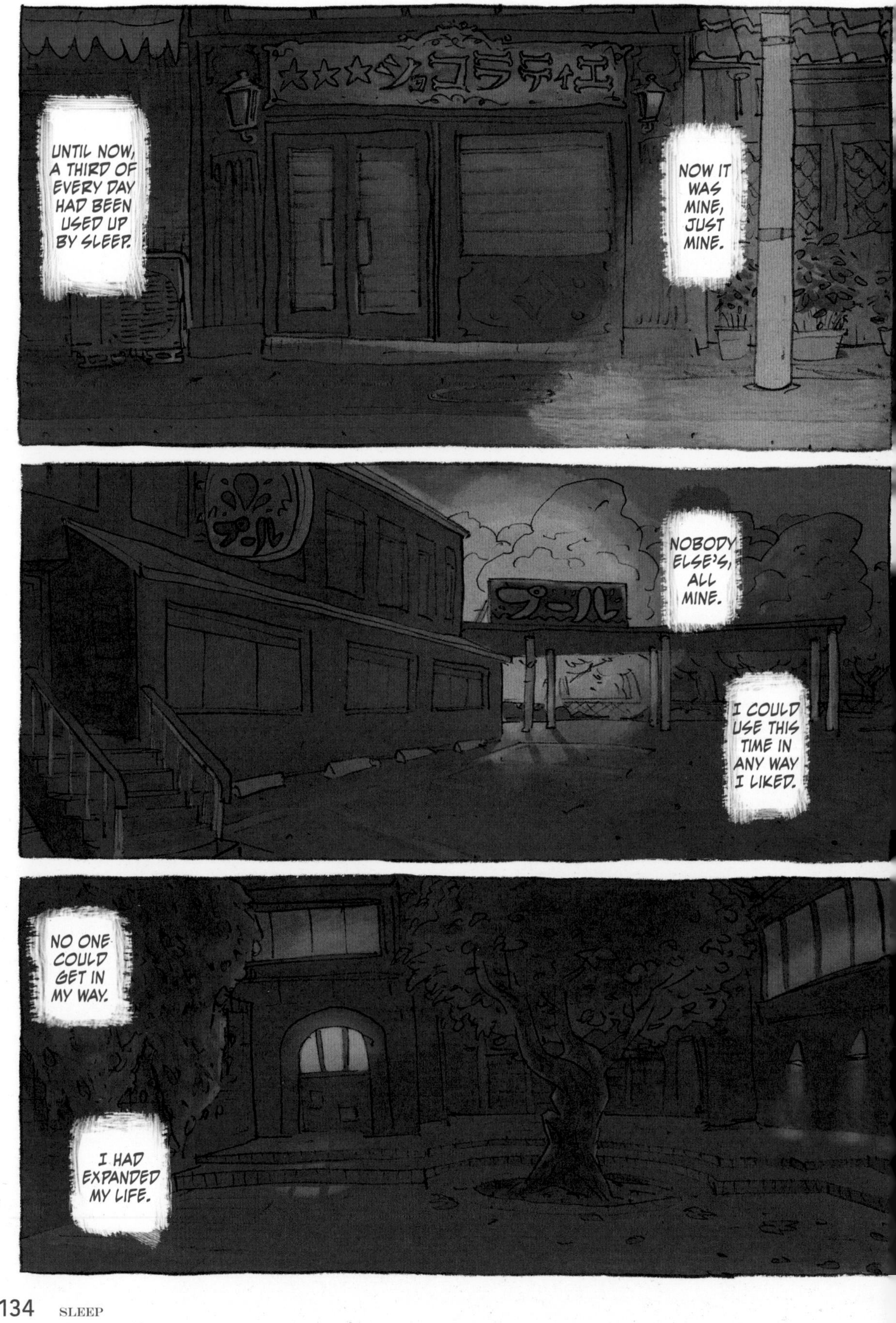
☆☆☆ショコラティエ
UNTIL NOW, A THIRD OF EVERY DAY HAD BEEN USED UP BY SLEEP.
NOW IT WAS MINE, JUST MINE.
プール
プール
NOBODY ELSE'S, ALL MINE.
I COULD USE THIS TIME IN ANY WAY I LIKED.
NO ONE COULD GET IN MY WAY.
I HAD EXPANDED MY LIFE.

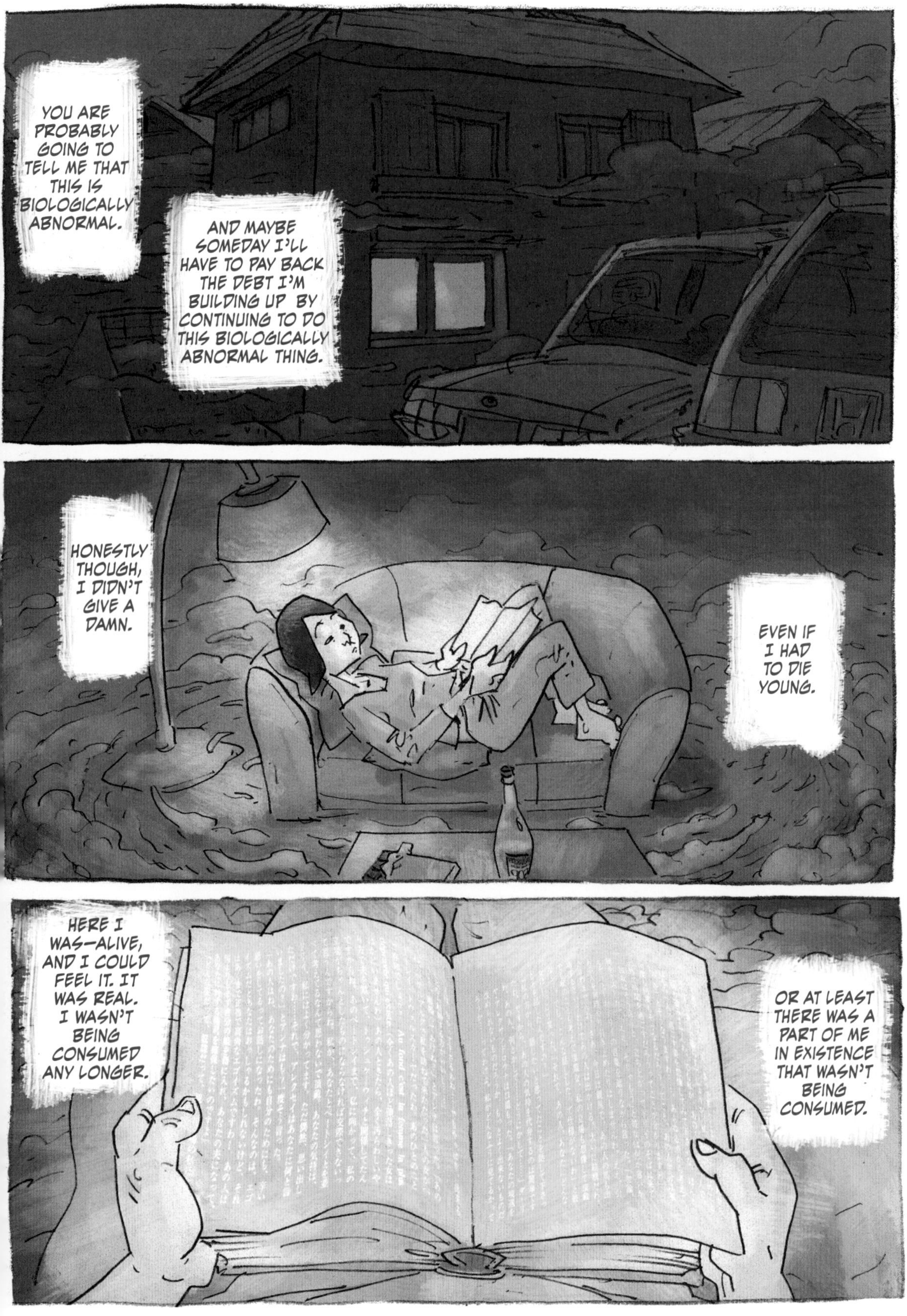
YOU ARE PROBABLY GOING TO TELL ME THAT THIS IS BIOLOGICALLY ABNORMAL.
AND MAYBE SOMEDAY I'LL HAVE TO PAY BACK THE DEBT I'M BUILDING UP BY CONTINUING TO DO THIS BIOLOGICALLY ABNORMAL THING.
HONESTLY THOUGH, I DIDN'T GIVE A DAMN.
EVEN IF I HAD TO DIE YOUNG.
HERE I WAS—ALIVE, AND I COULD FEEL IT. IT WAS REAL. I WASN'T BEING CONSUMED ANY LONGER.
OR AT LEAST THERE WAS A PART OF ME IN EXISTENCE THAT WASN'T BEING CONSUMED.

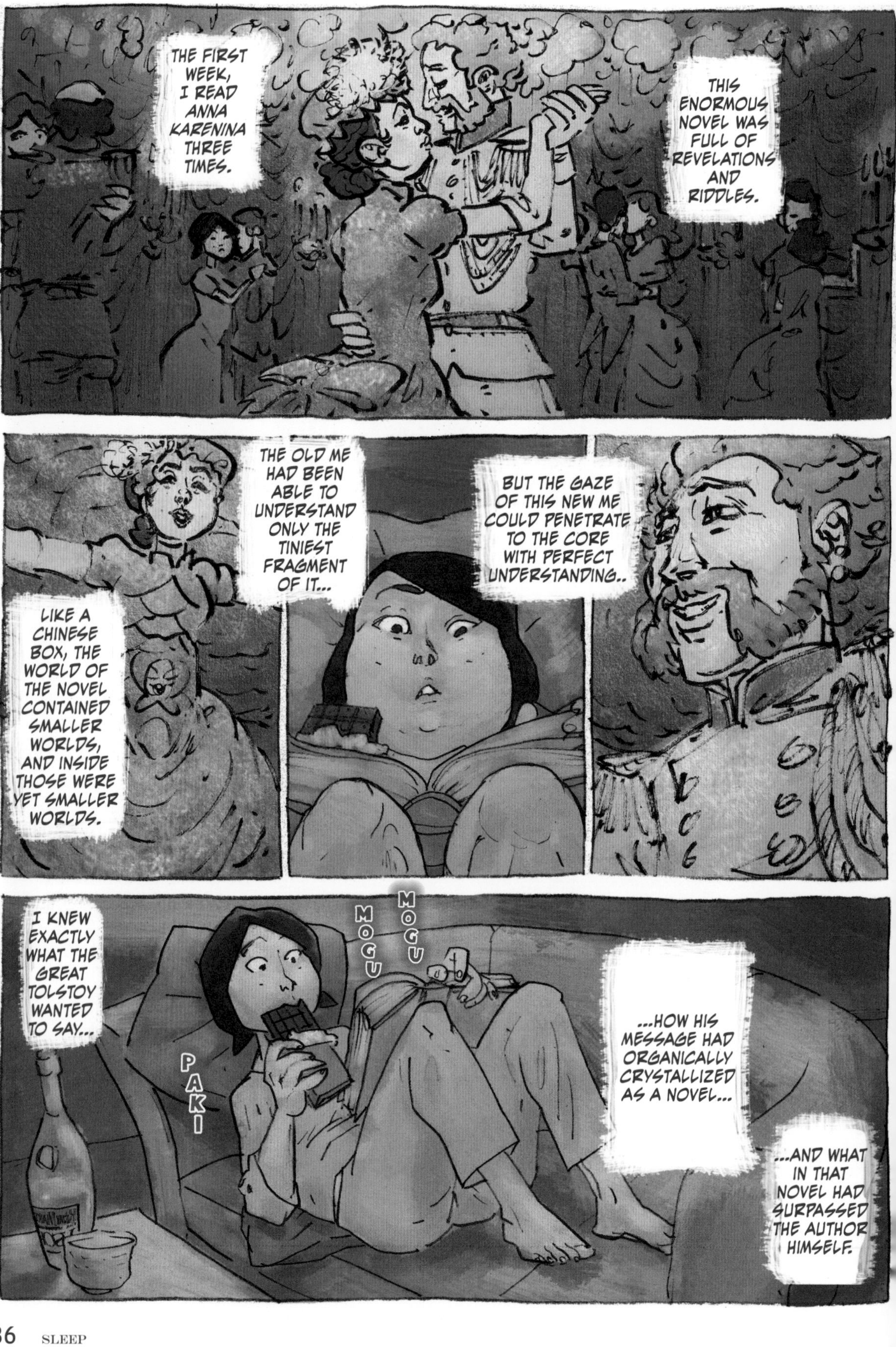
THE FIRST WEEK, I READ ANNA KARENINA THREE TIMES.
THIS ENORMOUS NOVEL WAS FULL OF REVELATIONS AND RIDDLES.
THE OLD ME HAD BEEN ABLE TO UNDERSTAND ONLY THE TINIEST FRAGMENT OF IT...
LIKE A CHINESE BOX, THE WORLD OF THE NOVEL CONTAINED SMALLER WORLDS, AND INSIDE THOSE WERE YET SMALLER WORLDS.
BUT THE GAZE OF THIS NEW ME COULD PENETRATE TO THE CORE WITH PERFECT UNDERSTANDING..
I KNEW EXACTLY WHAT THE GREAT TOLSTOY WANTED TO SAY...
MOGU
MOGU
PAKI
...HOW HIS MESSAGE HAD ORGANICALLY CRYSTALLIZED AS A NOVEL...
...AND WHAT IN THAT NOVEL HAD SURPASSED THE AUTHOR HIMSELF.

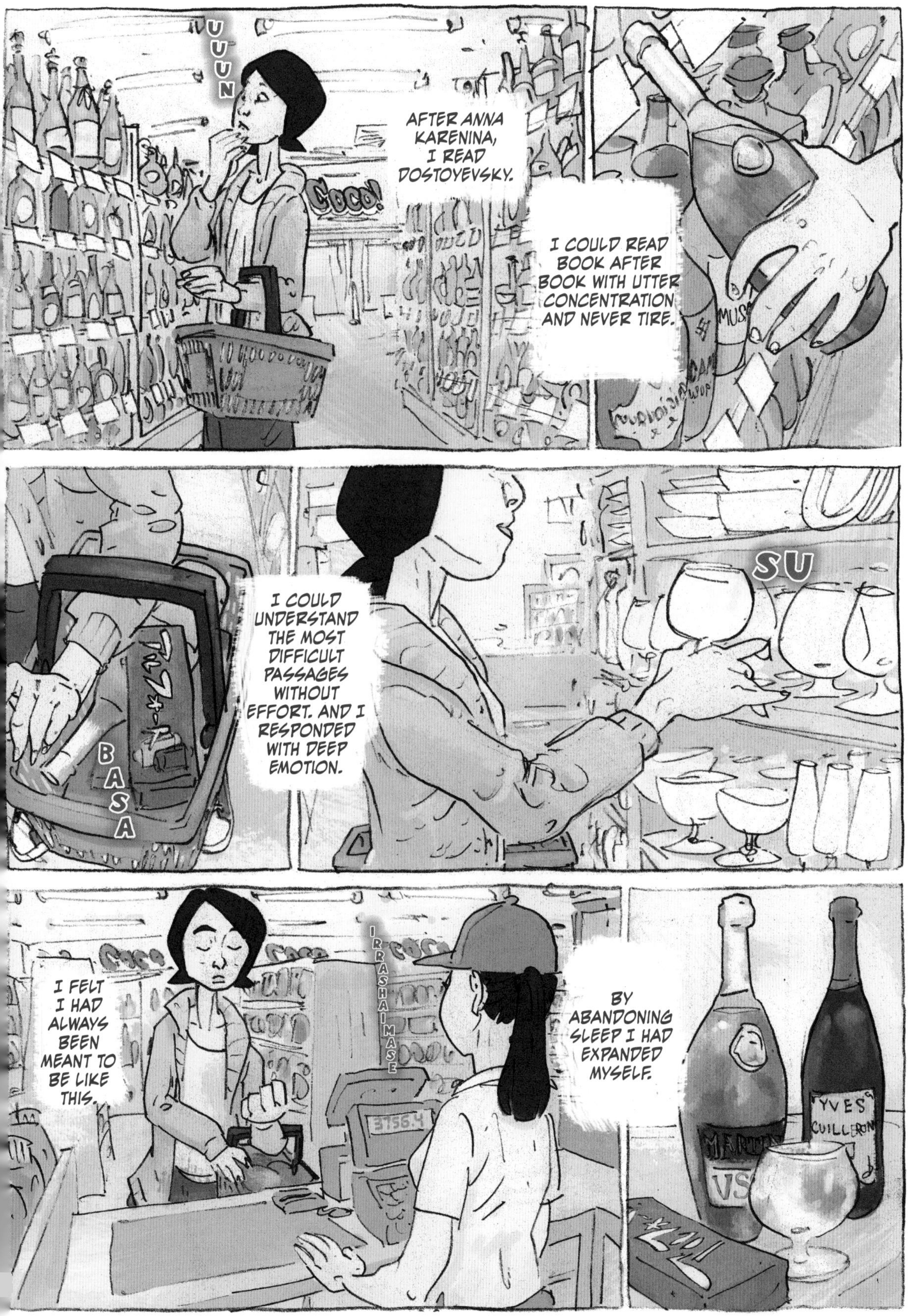
UUUN
AFTER ANNA KARENINA, I READ DOSTOYEVSKY.
COCO!
I COULD READ BOOK AFTER BOOK WITH UTTER CONCENTRATION AND NEVER TIRE.
I COULD UNDERSTAND THE MOST DIFFICULT PASSAGES WITHOUT EFFORT. AND I RESPONDED WITH DEEP EMOTION.
BASA
SU
I FELT I HAD ALWAYS BEEN MEANT TO BE LIKE THIS.
IRRASHAIMASE
BY ABANDONING SLEEP I HAD EXPANDED MYSELF.
YVES CUILLERON

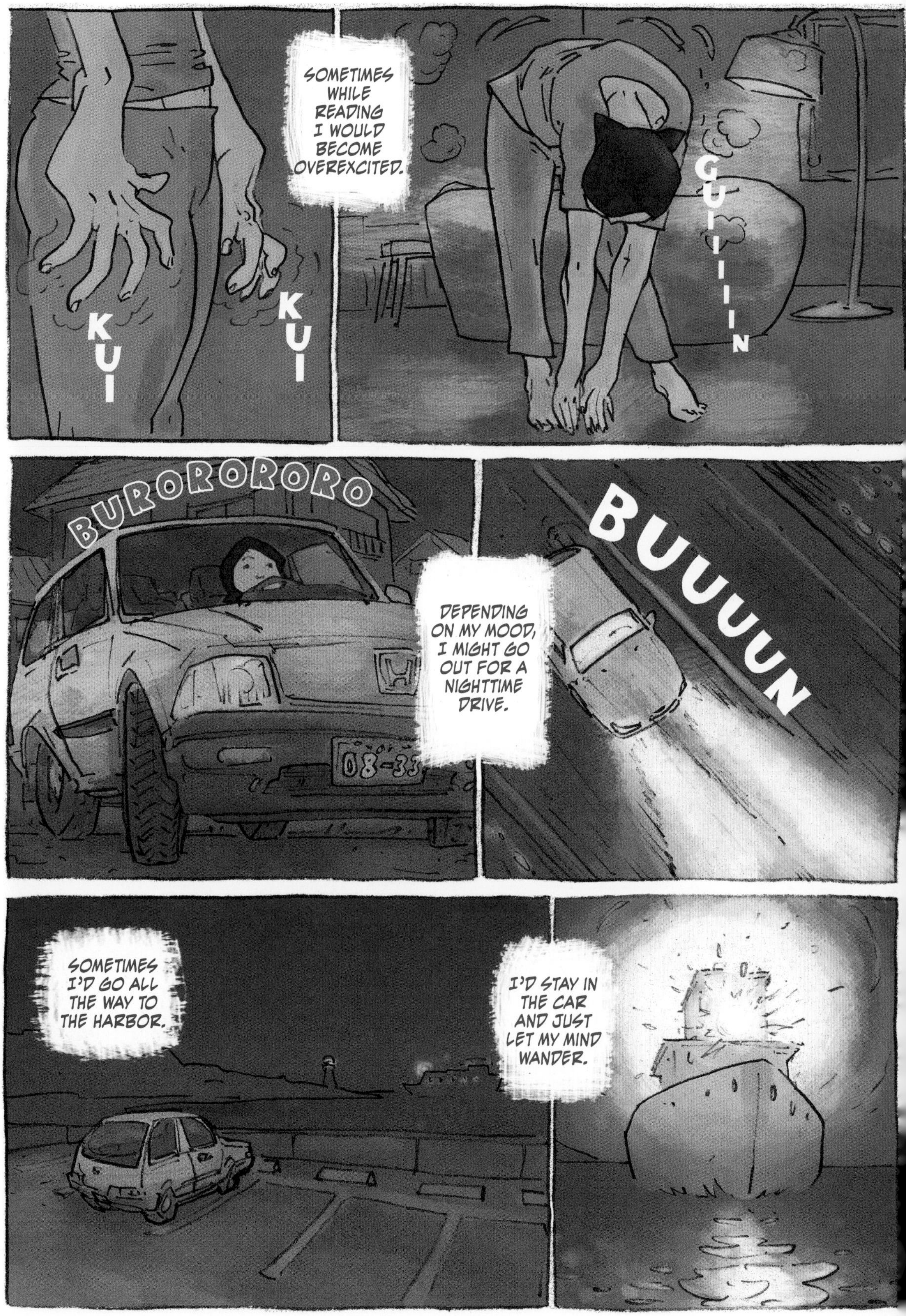
SOMETIMES WHILE READING I WOULD BECOME OVEREXCITED.
KUI
KUI
GUIIIIIN
BUROROROROROR
BUUUUN
DEPENDING ON MY MOOD, I MIGHT GO OUT FOR A NIGHTTIME DRIVE.
SOMETIMES I'D GO ALL THE WAY TO THE HARBOR.
I'D STAY IN THE CAR AND JUST LET MY MIND WANDER.

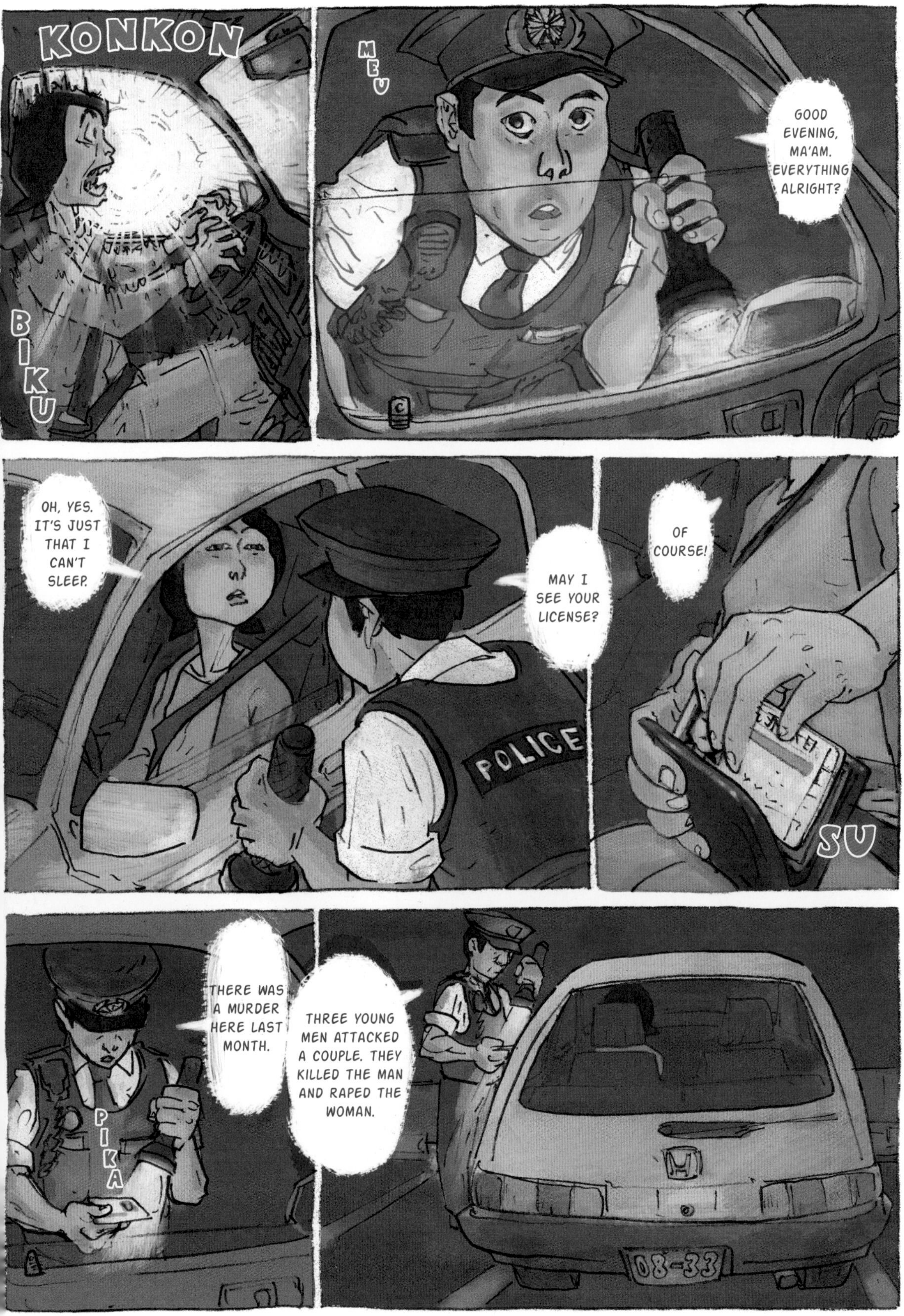
KONKON
BIKU
MEU
GOOD EVENING, MA'AM. EVERYTHING ALRIGHT?
OH, YES. IT'S JUST THAT I CAN'T SLEEP.
MAY I SEE YOUR LICENSE?
POLICE
OF COURSE!
SU
THERE WAS A MURDER HERE LAST MONTH.
PIKA
THREE YOUNG MEN ATTACKED A COUPLE. THEY KILLED THE MAN AND RAPED THE WOMAN.
08-33

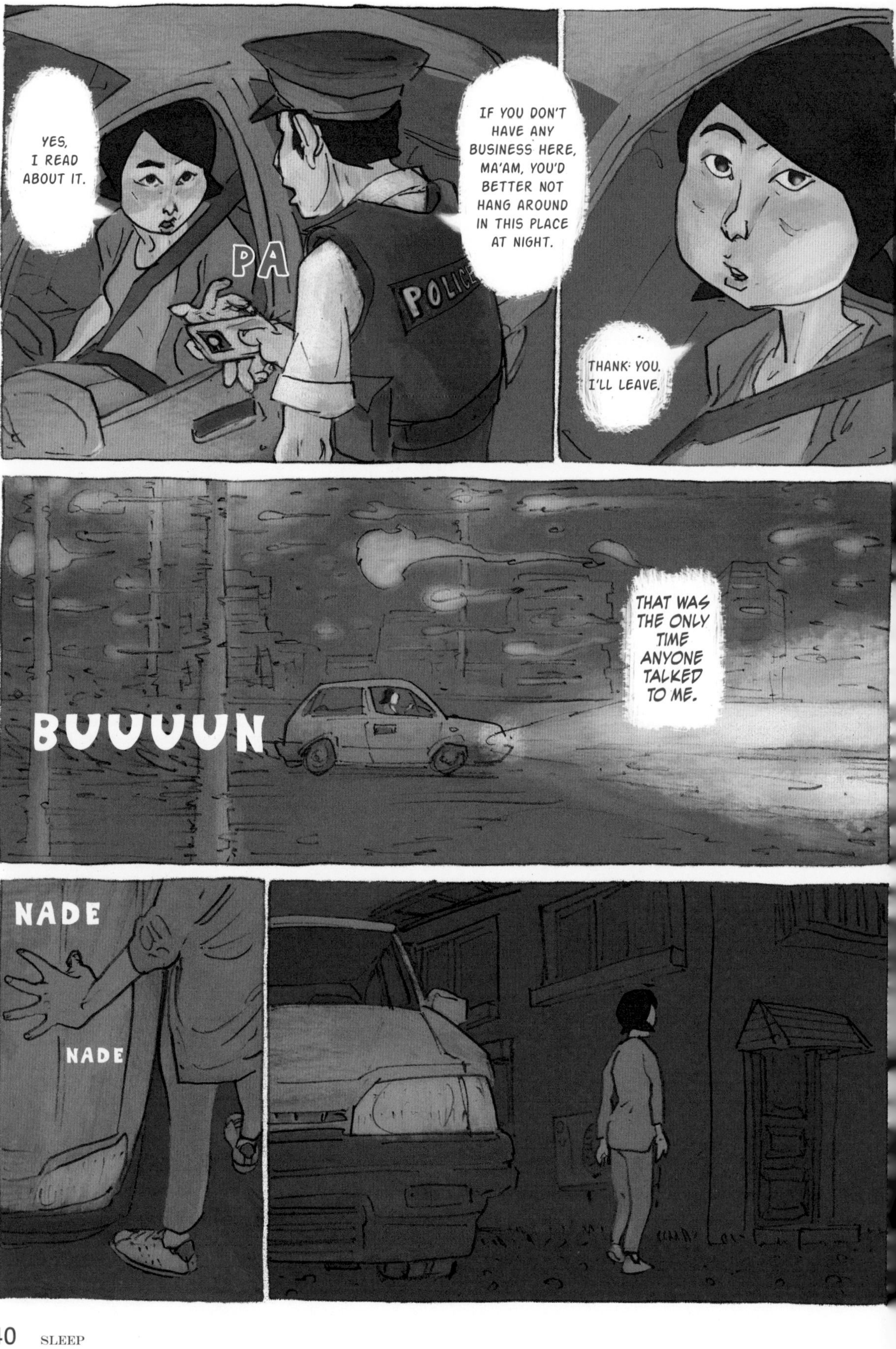
YES, I READ ABOUT IT.
PA
POLICE
IF YOU DON'T HAVE ANY BUSINESS HERE, MA'AM, YOU'D BETTER NOT HANG AROUND IN THIS PLACE AT NIGHT.
THANK YOU. I'LL LEAVE.
BUUUUN
THAT WAS THE ONLY TIME ANYONE TALKED TO ME.
NADE
NADE

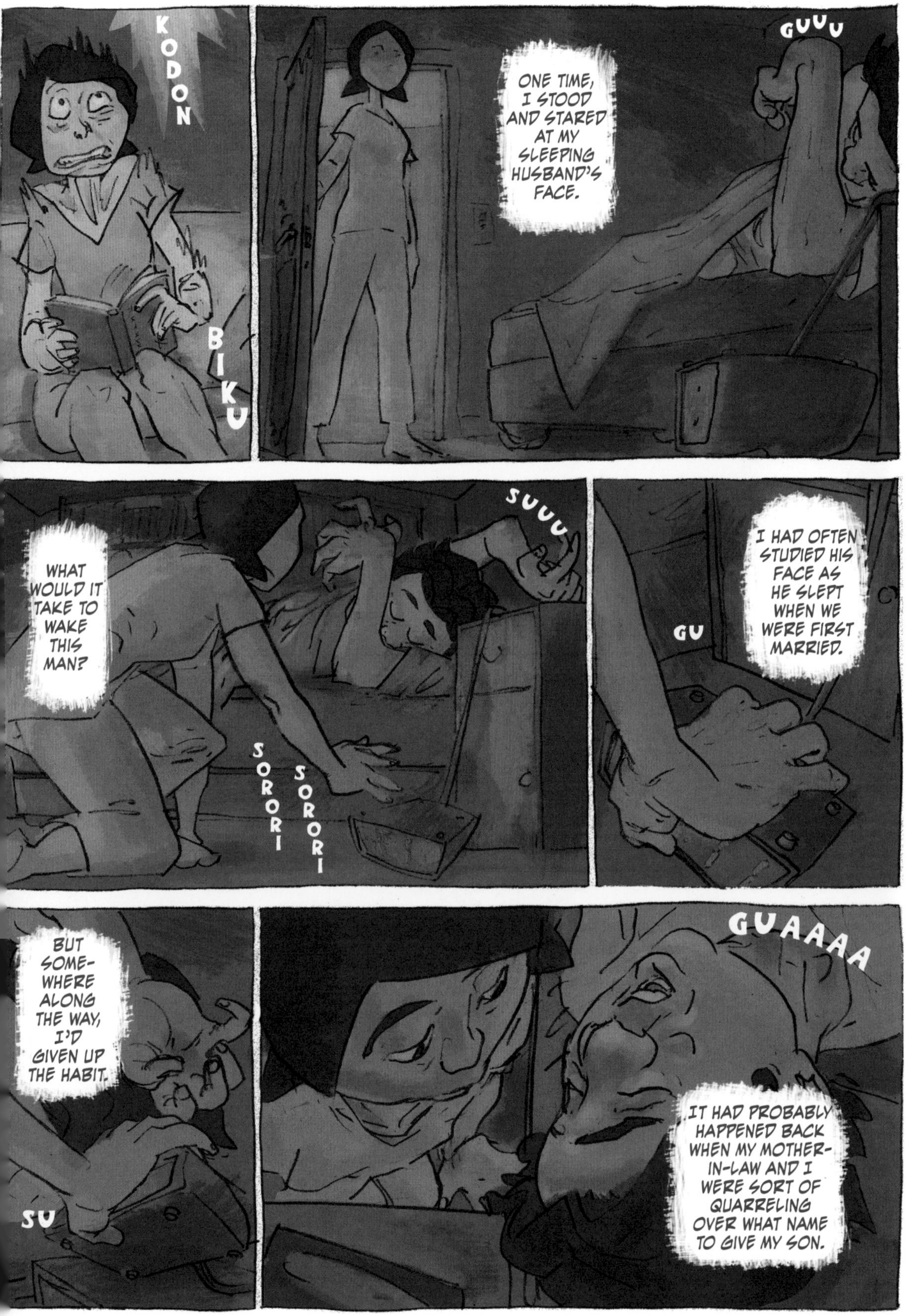
KODON
BIKU
ONE TIME, I STOOD AND STARED AT MY SLEEPING HUSBAND'S FACE.
GUUU
WHAT WOULD IT TAKE TO WAKE THIS MAN?
SUUU
SORORI SORORI
I HAD OFTEN STUDIED HIS FACE AS HE SLEPT WHEN WE WERE FIRST MARRIED.
GU
BUT SOME-WHERE ALONG THE WAY, I'D GIVEN UP THE HABIT.
SU
GUAAAA
IT HAD PROBABLY HAPPENED BACK WHEN MY MOTHER-IN-LAW AND I WERE SORT OF QUARRELING OVER WHAT NAME TO GIVE MY SON.

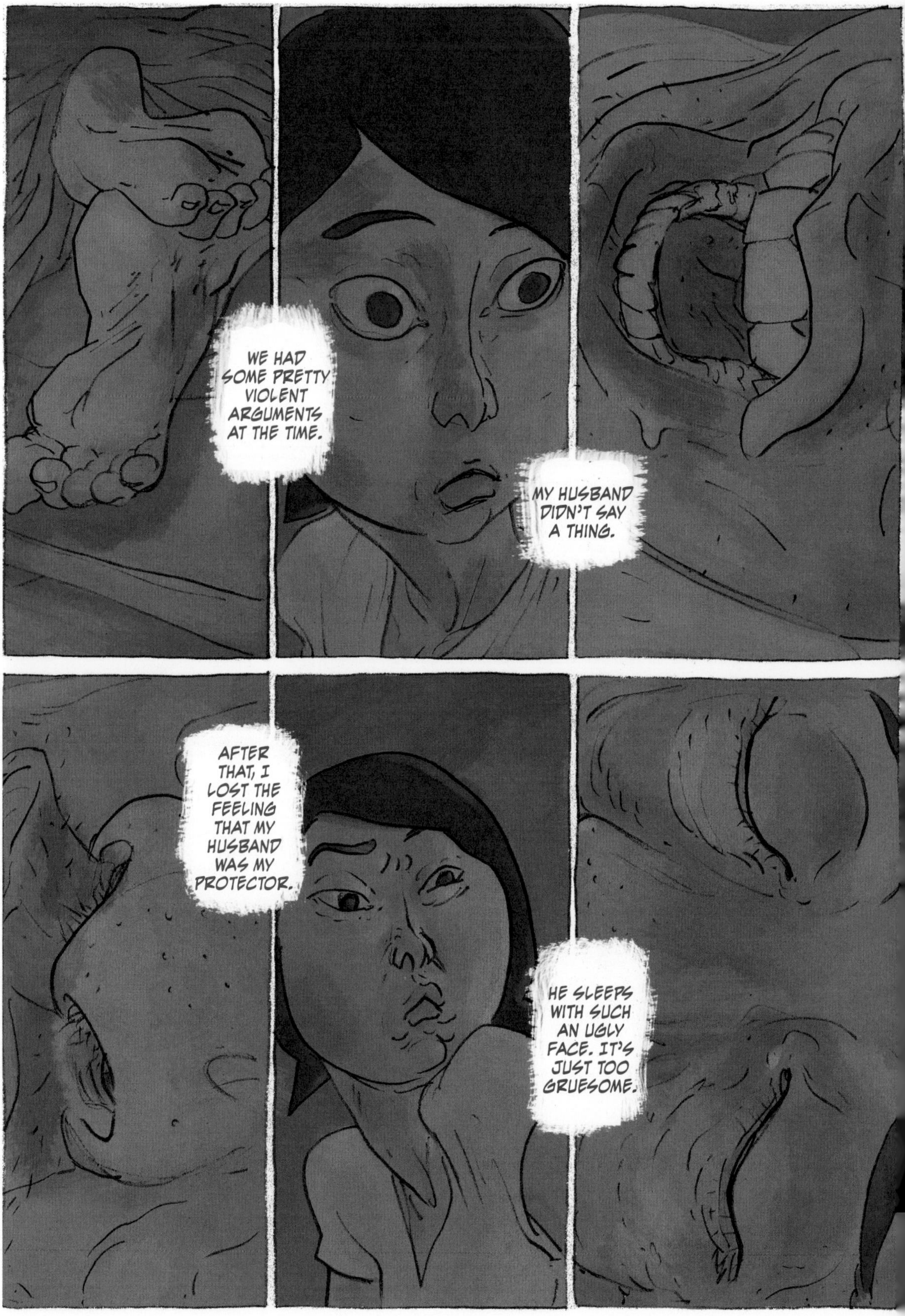
WE HAD SOME PRETTY VIOLENT ARGUMENTS AT THE TIME.
MY HUSBAND DIDN'T SAY A THING.
AFTER THAT, I LOST THE FEELING THAT MY HUSBAND WAS MY PROTECTOR.
HE SLEEPS WITH SUCH AN UGLY FACE. IT'S JUST TOO GRUESOME.

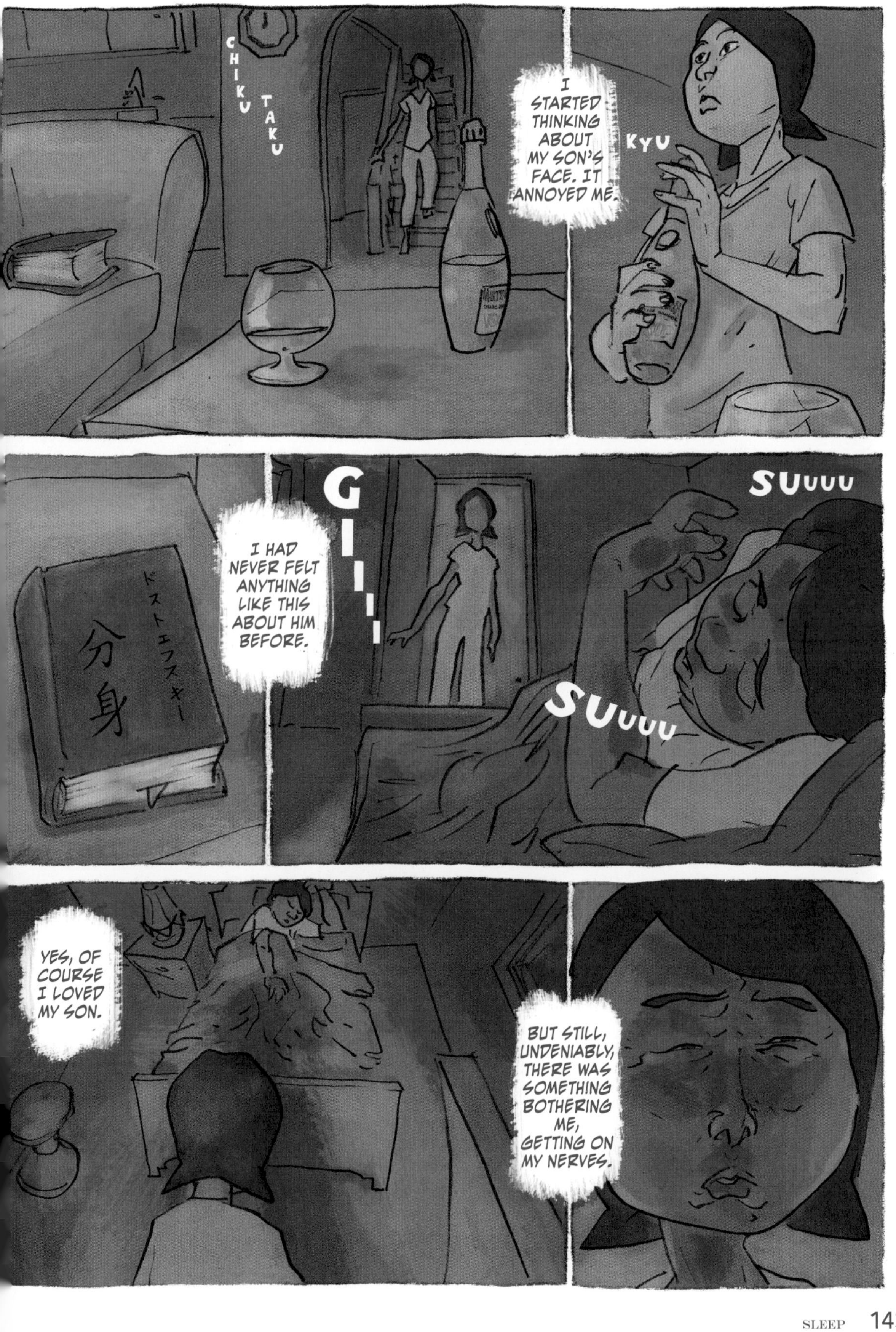
CHIKU
TAKU
I STARTED THINKING ABOUT MY SON'S FACE. IT ANNOYED ME.
KYU
I HAD NEVER FELT ANYTHING LIKE THIS ABOUT HIM BEFORE.
ドストエフスキー
分身
GIIII
SUUUU
SUUUU
YES, OF COURSE I LOVED MY SON.
BUT STILL, UNDENIABLY, THERE WAS SOMETHING BOTHERING ME, GETTING ON MY NERVES.

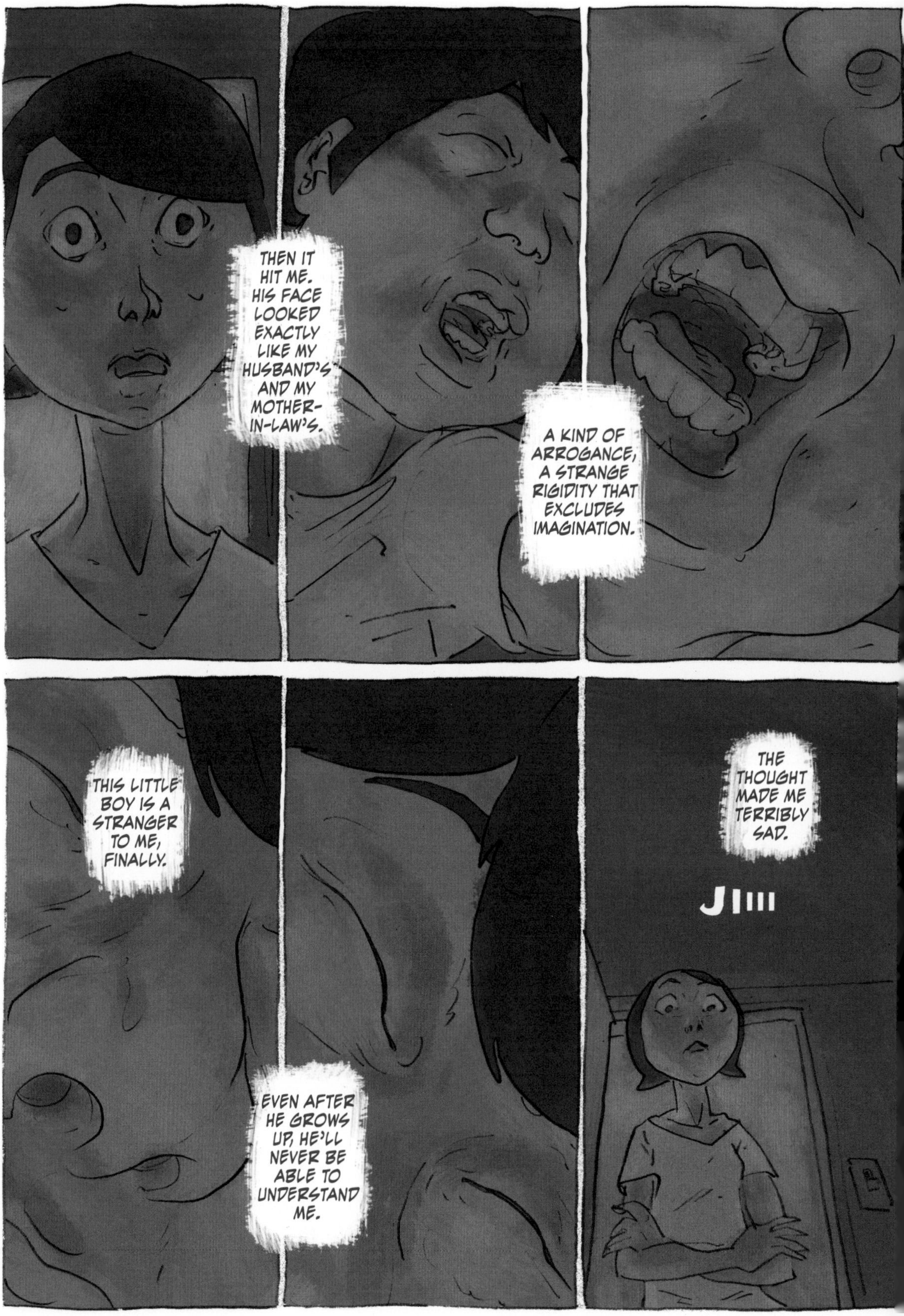
THEN IT HIT ME. HIS FACE LOOKED EXACTLY LIKE MY HUSBAND'S AND MY MOTHER-IN-LAW'S.
A KIND OF ARROGANCE, A STRANGE RIGIDITY THAT EXCLUDES IMAGINATION.
THIS LITTLE BOY IS A STRANGER TO ME, FINALLY.
EVEN AFTER HE GROWS UP, HE'LL NEVER BE ABLE TO UNDERSTAND ME.
THE THOUGHT MADE ME TERRIBLY SAD.
JIIII

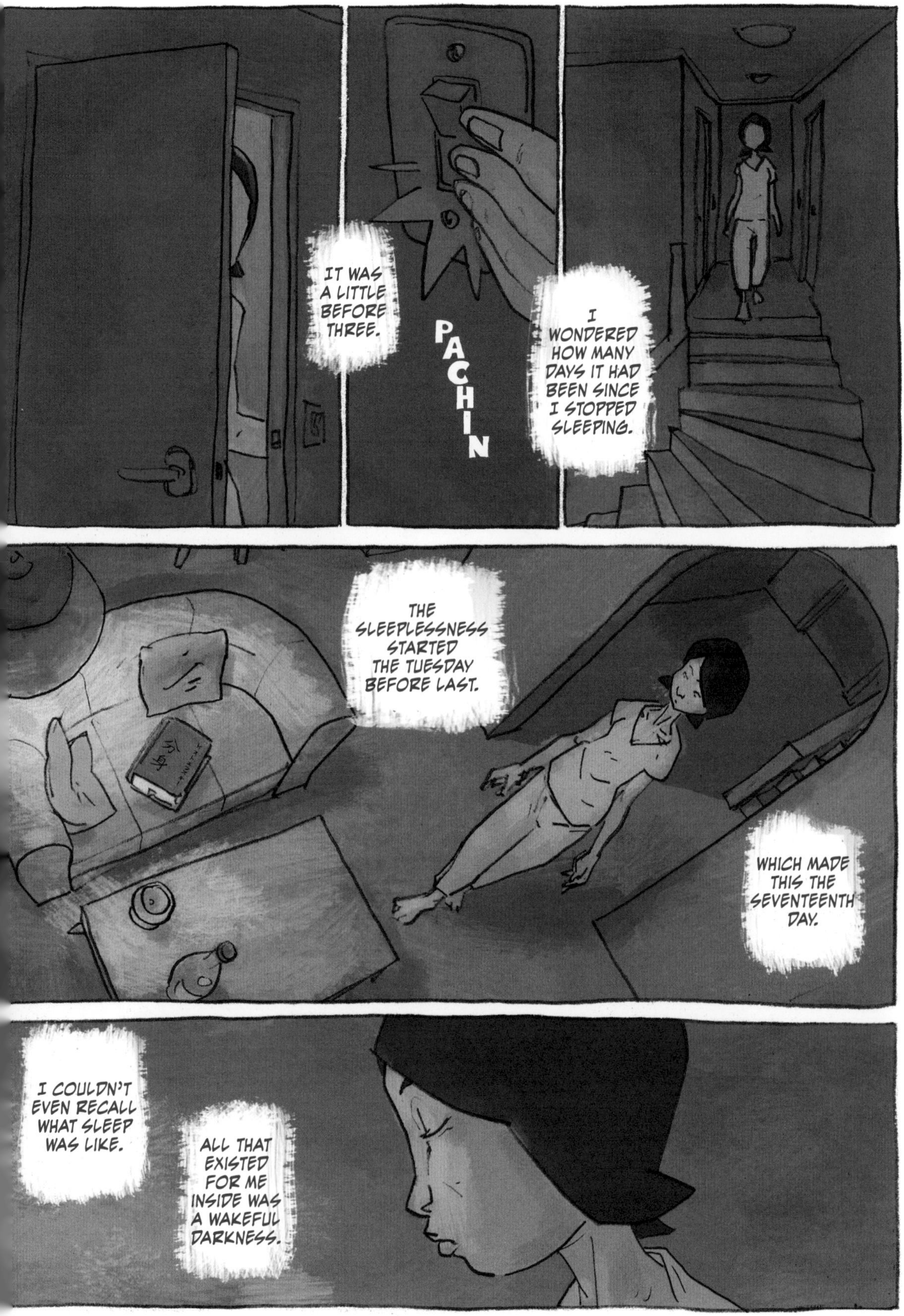
IT WAS A LITTLE BEFORE THREE.
PACHIN
I WONDERED HOW MANY DAYS IT HAD BEEN SINCE I STOPPED SLEEPING.
THE SLEEPLESSNESS STARTED THE TUESDAY BEFORE LAST.
WHICH MADE THIS THE SEVENTEENTH DAY.
I COULDN'T EVEN RECALL WHAT SLEEP WAS LIKE.
ALL THAT EXISTED FOR ME INSIDE WAS A WAKEFUL DARKNESS.

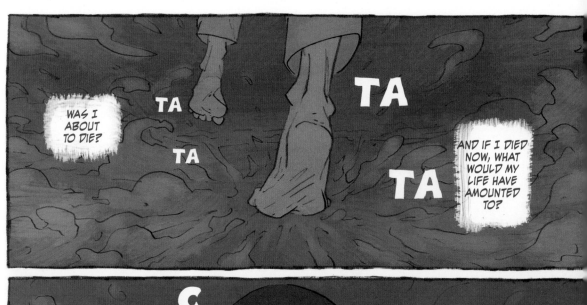

WAS I ABOUT TO DIE?

AND IF I DIED NOW, WHAT WOULD MY LIFE HAVE AMOUNTED TO?

UNTIL NOW, I HAD CONCEIVED OF SLEEP AS A KIND OF MODEL FOR DEATH.

BUT NOW I WONDERED IF I HAD BEEN WRONG.

PERHAPS DEATH WAS A STATE ENTIRELY UNLIKE SLEEP, SOMETHING THAT BELONGED TO A DIFFERENT CATEGORY ALTOGETHER?

LIKE THE DEEP, ENDLESS, WAKEFUL DARKNESS I WAS SEEING NOW.

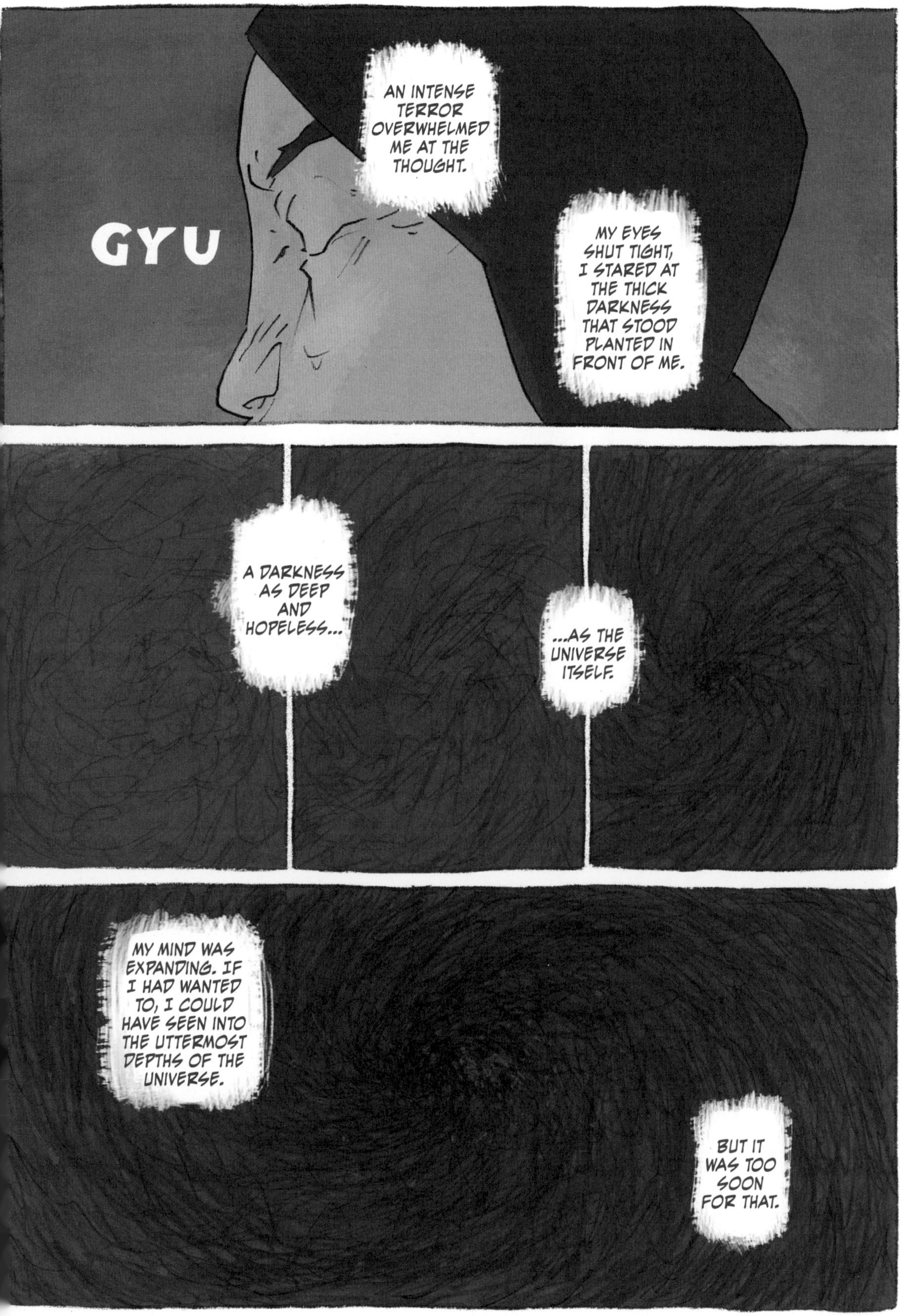
AN INTENSE TERROR OVERWHELMED ME AT THE THOUGHT.
MY EYES SHUT TIGHT, I STARED AT THE THICK DARKNESS THAT STOOD PLANTED IN FRONT OF ME.
GYU
A DARKNESS AS DEEP AND HOPELESS...
...AS THE UNIVERSE ITSELF.
MY MIND WAS EXPANDING. IF I HAD WANTED TO, I COULD HAVE SEEN INTO THE UTTERMOST DEPTHS OF THE UNIVERSE.
BUT IT WAS TOO SOON FOR THAT.

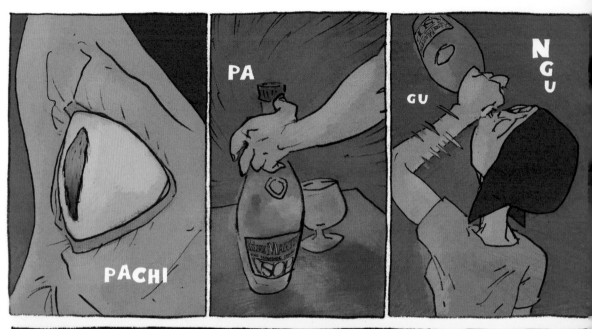

NGU

GU

PA

PACHI

SU

IF DEATH WAS
LIKE THIS,
BEING
ETERNALLY
AWAKE AND
STARING INTO
DARKNESS, WHAT
SHOULD I DO?

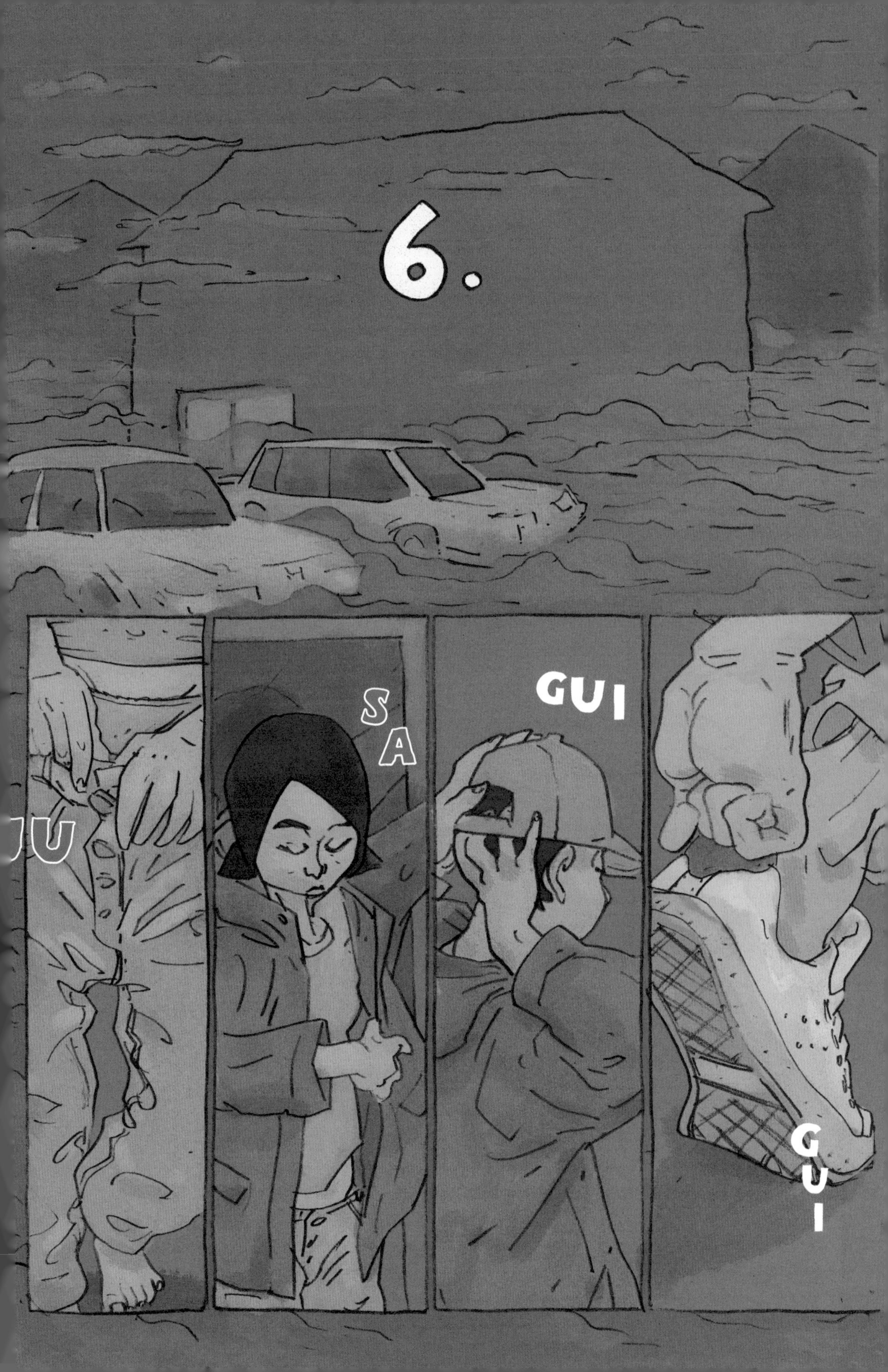
6.
JU
SA
GUI
GUI

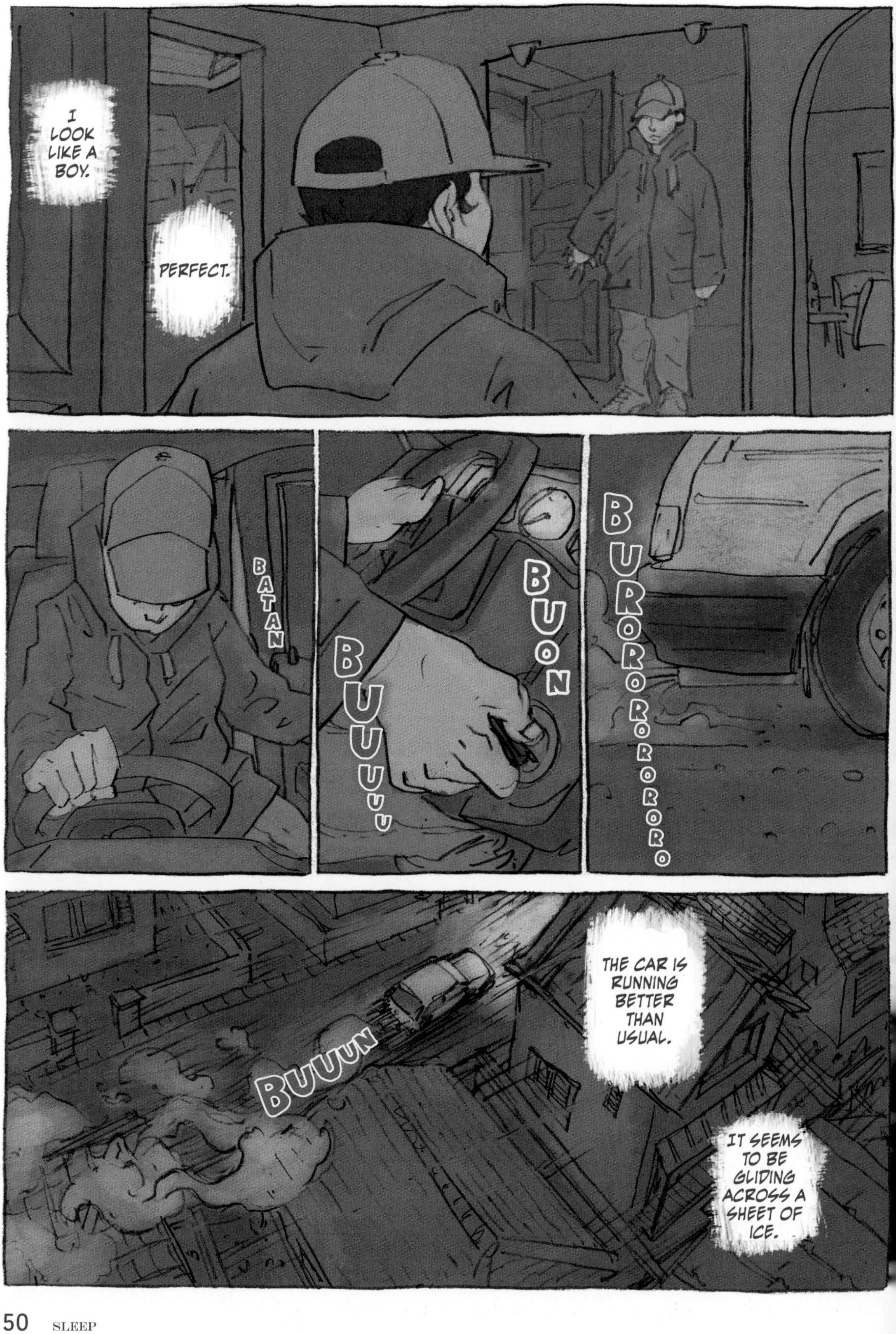

I LOOK LIKE A BOY.
PERFECT.
BATAN
BUON
BUUUUU
BURORORORORORO
BUUUN
THE CAR IS RUNNING BETTER THAN USUAL.
IT SEEMS TO BE GLIDING ACROSS A SHEET OF ICE.

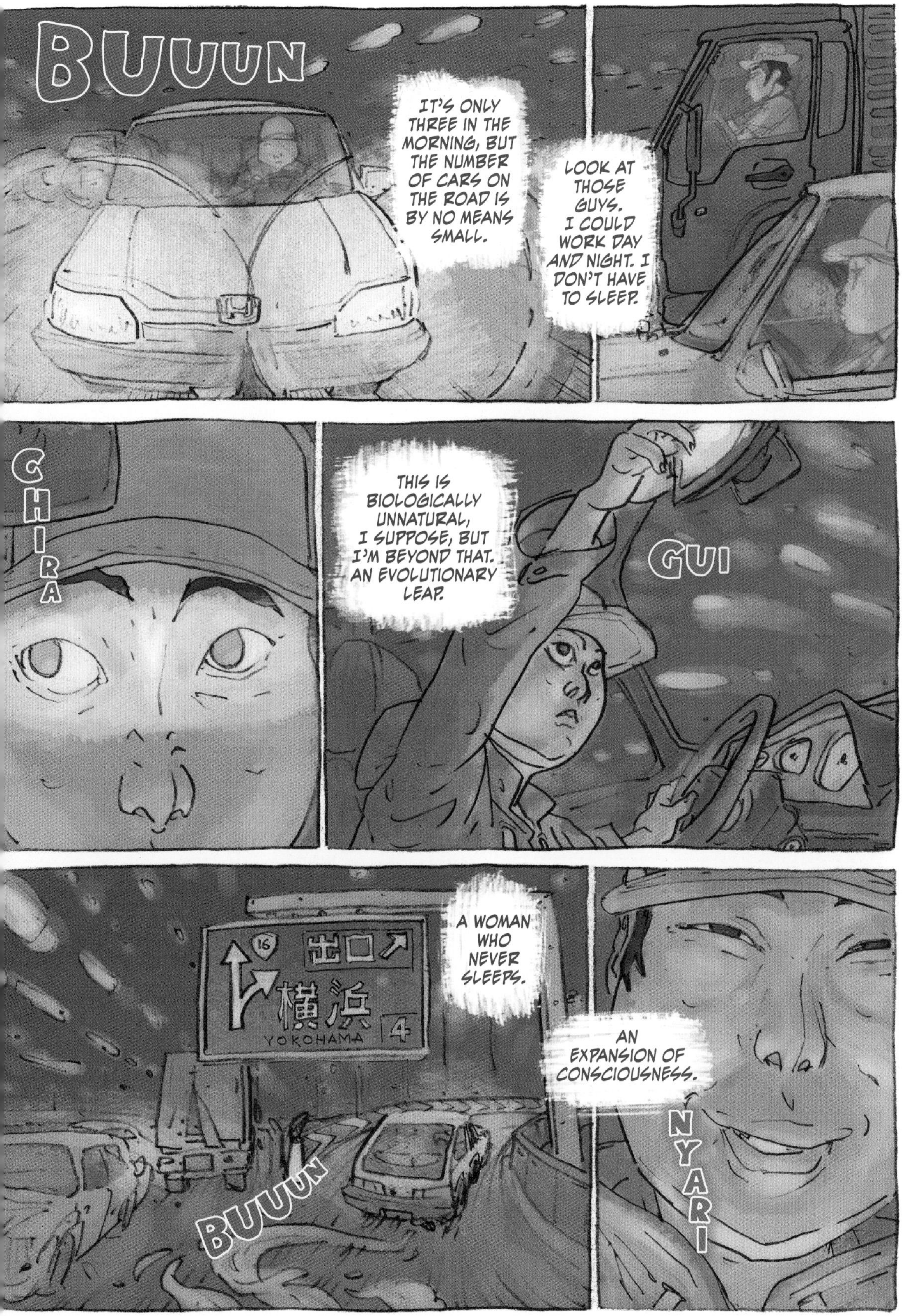
BUUUN
IT'S ONLY THREE IN THE MORNING, BUT THE NUMBER OF CARS ON THE ROAD IS BY NO MEANS SMALL.
LOOK AT THOSE GUYS. I COULD WORK DAY AND NIGHT. I DON'T HAVE TO SLEEP.
CHIRA
THIS IS BIOLOGICALLY UNNATURAL, I SUPPOSE, BUT I'M BEYOND THAT. AN EVOLUTIONARY LEAP.
GUI
16
出口
横浜
YOKOHAMA
4
BUUUN
A WOMAN WHO NEVER SLEEPS.
AN EXPANSION OF CONSCIOUSNESS.
NYARI

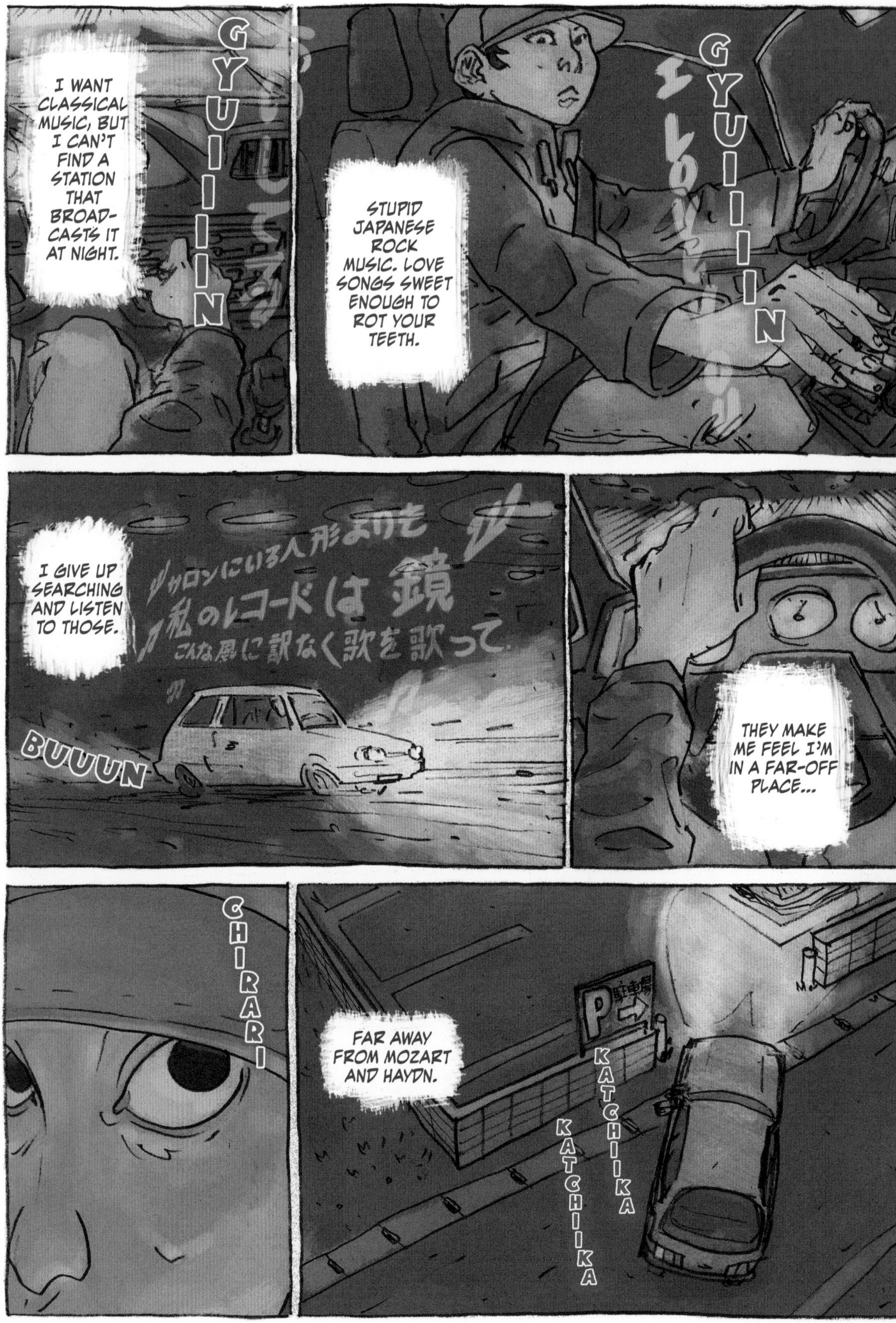
I WANT CLASSICAL MUSIC, BUT I CAN'T FIND A STATION THAT BROADCASTS IT AT NIGHT.
GYUIIIIN
STUPID JAPANESE ROCK MUSIC. LOVE SONGS SWEET ENOUGH TO ROT YOUR TEETH.
GYUIIIIN
I GIVE UP SEARCHING AND LISTEN TO THOSE.
サロンにいる人形よりも
私のレコードは鏡
こんな風に訳なく歌を歌って
BUUUN
THEY MAKE ME FEEL I'M IN A FAR-OFF PLACE...
CHIRARI
FAR AWAY FROM MOZART AND HAYDN.
P 駐車場
KATCHIKA
KATCHIKA

THERE'S ONLY ONE CAR IN THE PARKING LOT.

PROBABLY A COUPLE MAKING LOVE.

BURORORORO

I REMEMBER THE DRIVE I TOOK WITH MY COLLEGE BOYFRIEND. WE PARKED AND GOT INTO SOME HEAVY PETTING.

HE COULDN'T STOP, HE SAID, AND HE BEGGED ME TO LET HIM PUT IT IN.

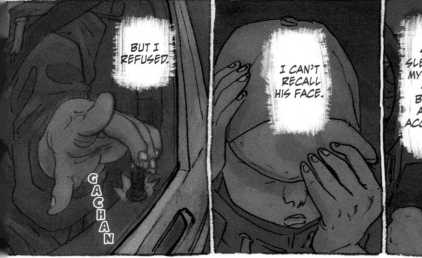

BUT I REFUSED.

I CAN'T RECALL HIS FACE.

GACHAN

SINCE I STOPPED SLEEPING, ALL MY MEMORIES SEEM TO BE MOVING AWAY WITH ACCELERATING SPEED.

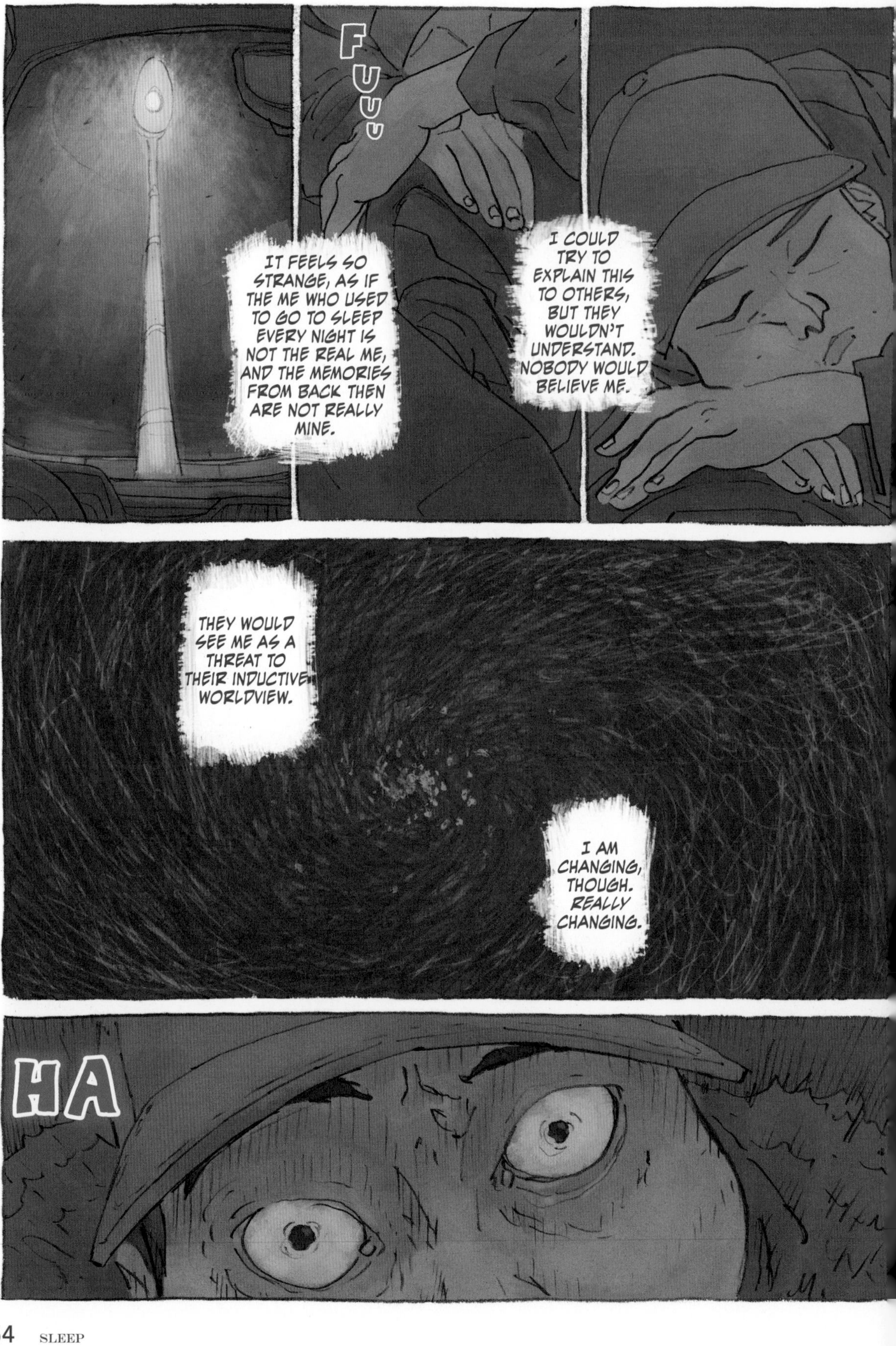
FUUU
IT FEELS SO STRANGE, AS IF THE ME WHO USED TO GO TO SLEEP EVERY NIGHT IS NOT THE REAL ME, AND THE MEMORIES FROM BACK THEN ARE NOT REALLY MINE.
I COULD TRY TO EXPLAIN THIS TO OTHERS, BUT THEY WOULDN'T UNDERSTAND. NOBODY WOULD BELIEVE ME.
THEY WOULD SEE ME AS A THREAT TO THEIR INDUCTIVE WORLDVIEW.
I AM CHANGING, THOUGH. REALLY CHANGING.
HA

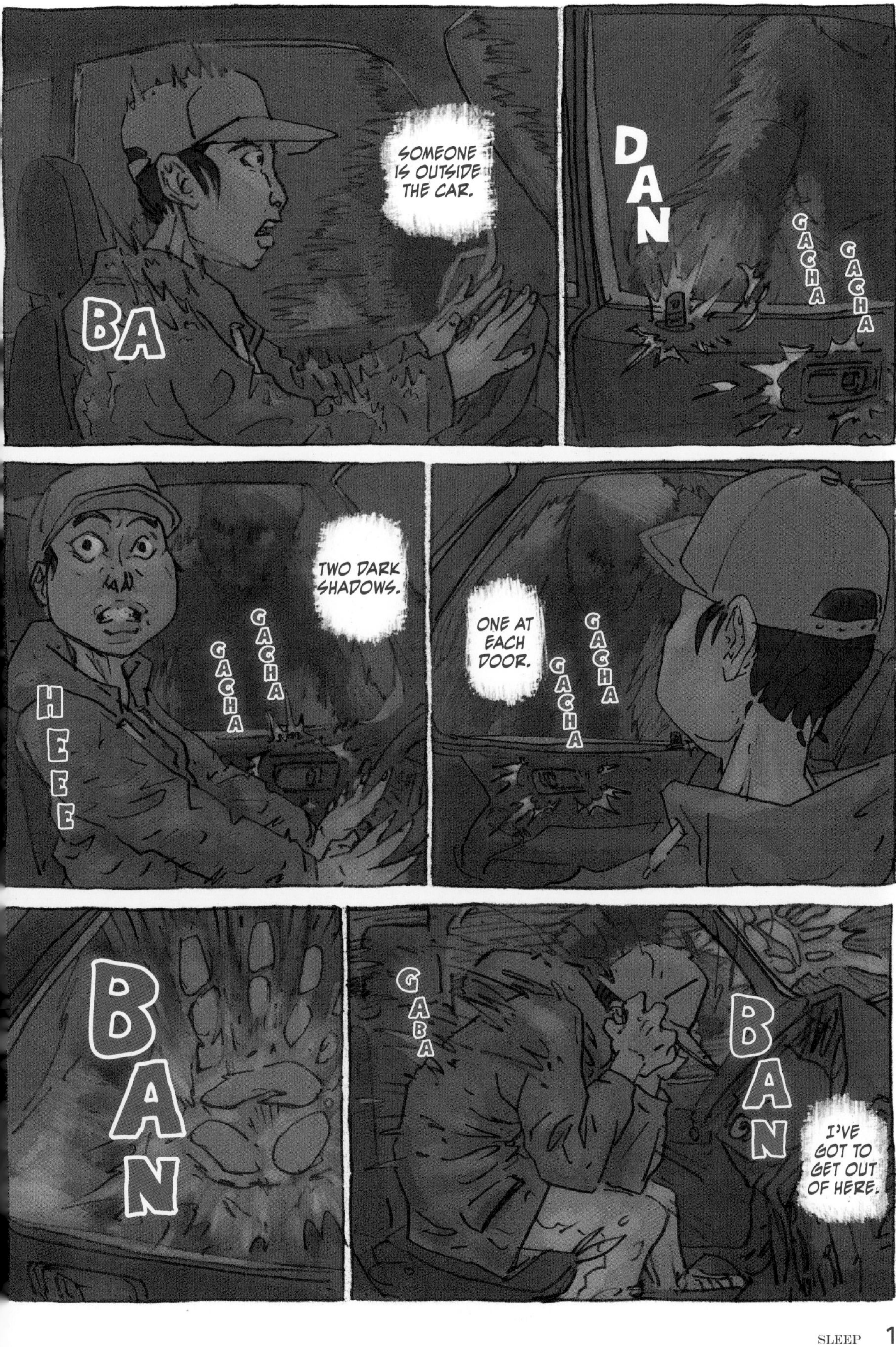
BA
SOMEONE IS OUTSIDE THE CAR.
DAN
GACHA GACHA
TWO DARK SHADOWS.
HEEE
GACHA GACHA
ONE AT EACH DOOR.
GACHA GACHA
BAN
GABA
BAN
I'VE GOT TO GET OUT OF HERE.

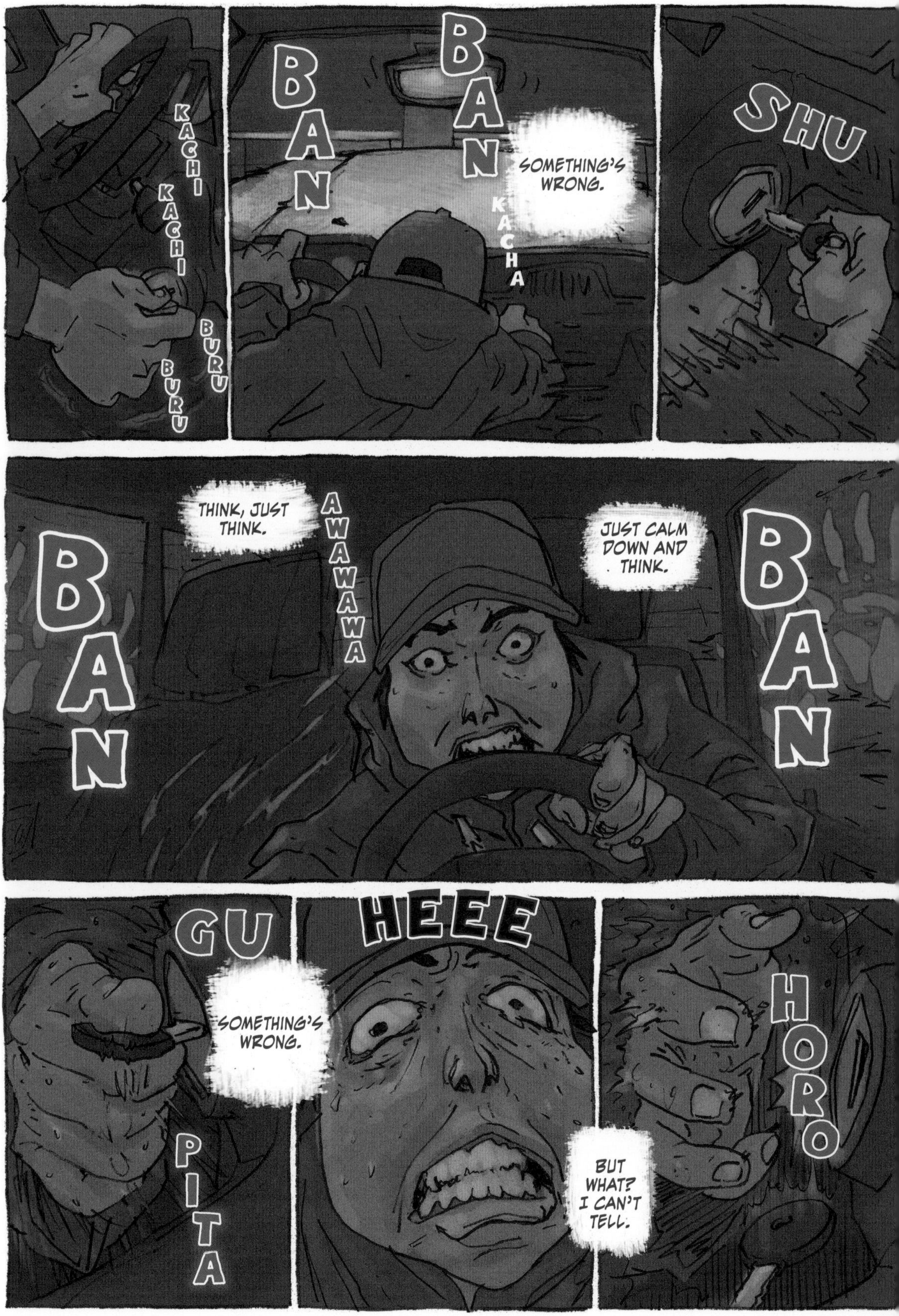
KACHI
KACHI
BURU
BURU
BAN
BAN
SOMETHING'S WRONG.
KACHA
SHU
BAN
THINK, JUST THINK.
AWAWAWA
JUST CALM DOWN AND THINK.
BAN
GU
SOMETHING'S WRONG.
PITA
HEEE
HORO
BUT WHAT? I CAN'T TELL.

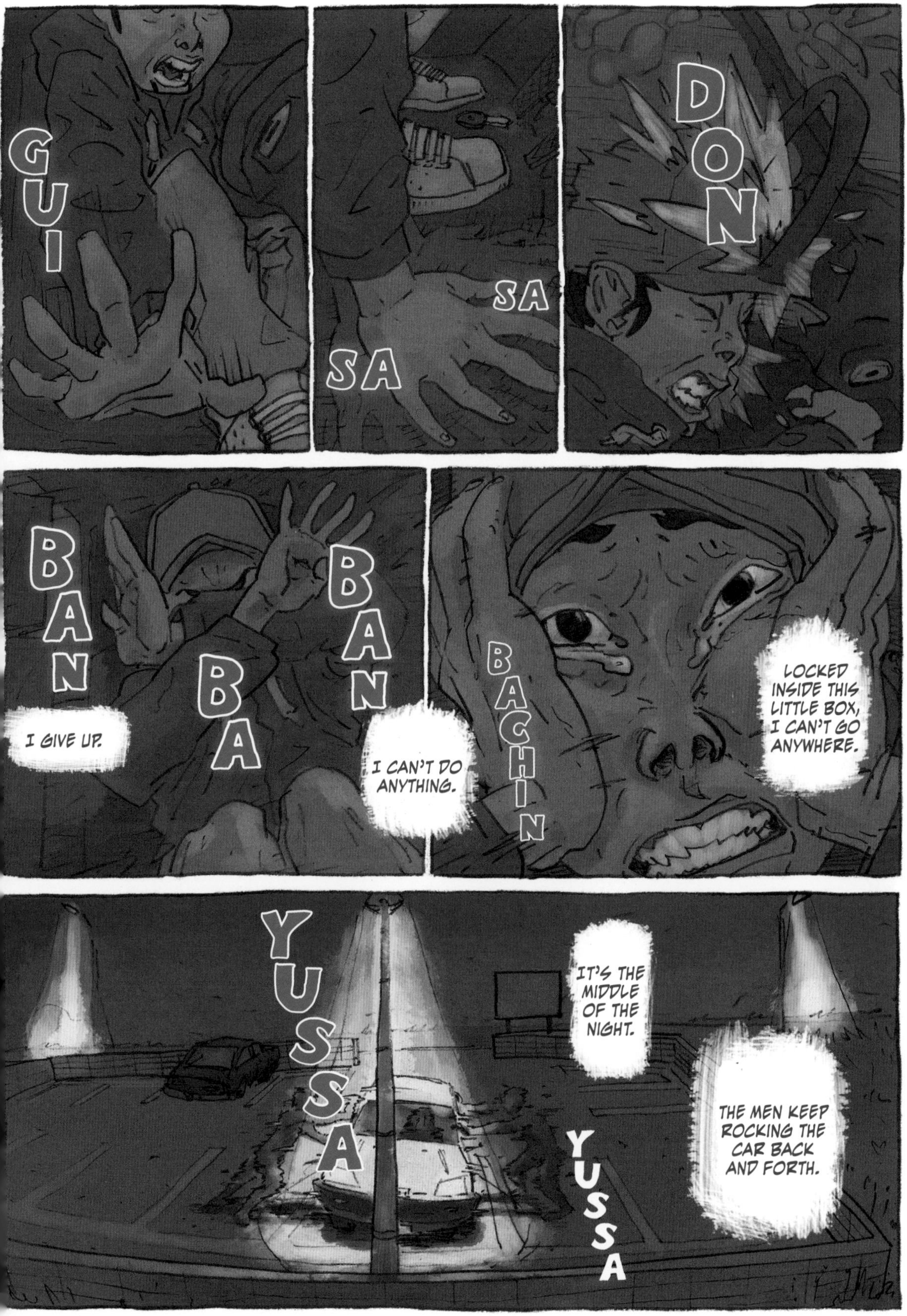
GUI
SA
SA
DON
BAN
BA
BAN
I GIVE UP.
I CAN'T DO ANYTHING.
BACHIN
LOCKED INSIDE THIS LITTLE BOX, I CAN'T GO ANYWHERE.
YUSSA
IT'S THE MIDDLE OF THE NIGHT.
YUSSA
THE MEN KEEP ROCKING THE CAR BACK AND FORTH.

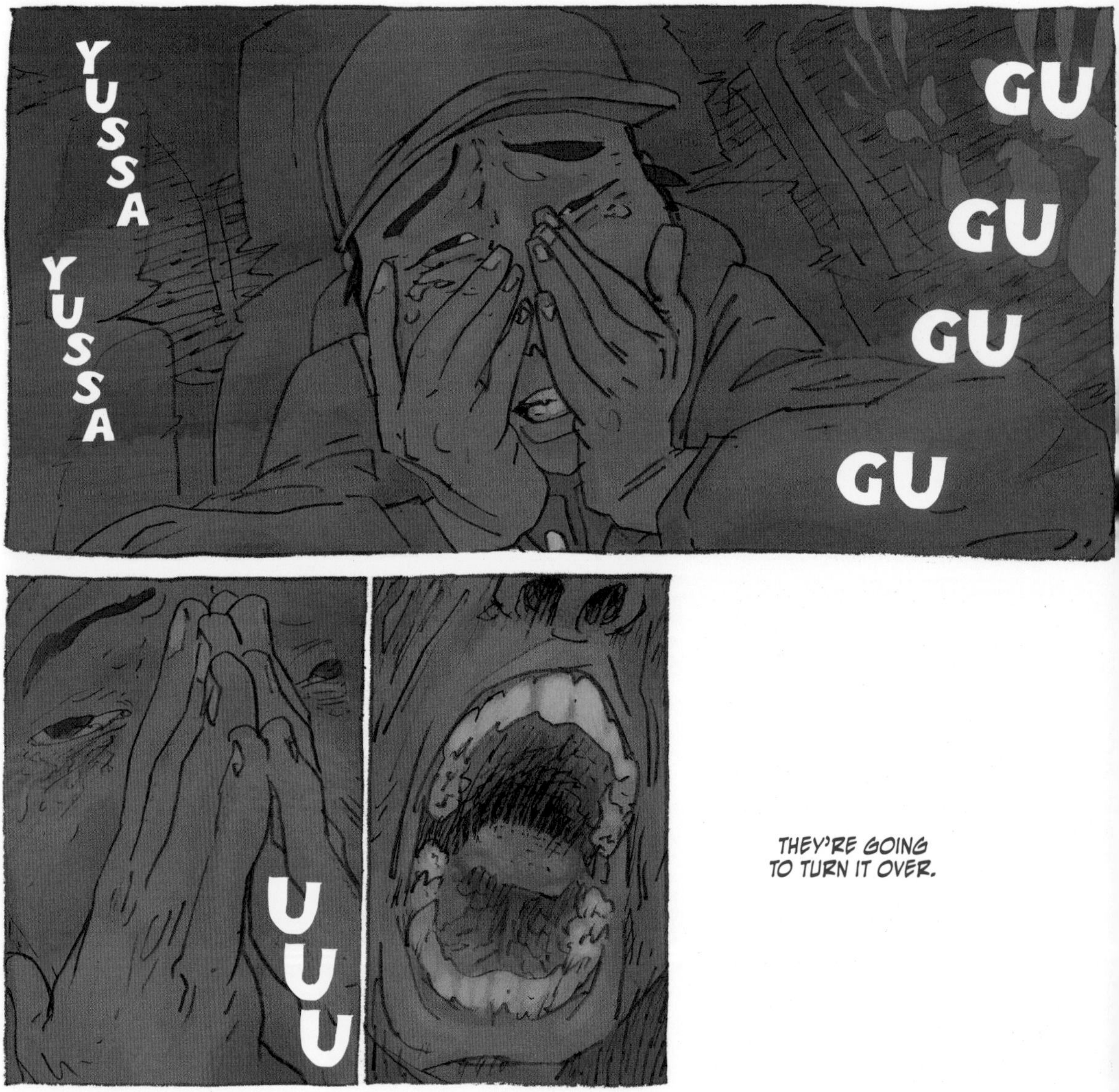
YUSSA
YUSSA
GU
GU
GU
GU
UUU
THEY'RE GOING TO TURN IT OVER.

"Books to Span the East and West"

Tuttle Publishing was founded in 1832 in the small New England town of Rutland, Vermont [USA]. Our core values remain as strong today as they were then—to publish best-in-class books which bring people together one page at a time. In 1948, we established a publishing outpost in Japan—and Tuttle is now a leader in publishing English-language books about the arts, languages and cultures of Asia. The world has become a much smaller place today and Asia's economic and cultural influence has grown. Yet the need for meaningful dialogue and information about this diverse region has never been greater. Over the past seven decades, Tuttle has published thousands of books on subjects ranging from martial arts and paper crafts to language learning and literature—and our talented authors, illustrators, designers and photographers have won many prestigious awards. We welcome you to explore the wealth of information available on Asia at **www.tuttlepublishing.com**.

Published by Tuttle Publishing, an imprint of Periplus Editions (HK) Ltd.

www.tuttlepublishing.com

Library of Congress Catalog-in-Publication Data in progress

ISBN 978-4-8053-1768-6

First edition, 2025

28 27 26 25   5 4 3 2 1

Printed in China   2409EP

TUTTLE PUBLISHING® is a registered trademark of Tuttle Publishing, a division of Periplus Editions (HK) Ltd.

Distributed by

North America, Latin America & Europe
Tuttle Publishing
364 Innovation Drive
North Clarendon,
VT 05759-9436 U.S.A.
Tel: 1 (802) 773-8930
Fax: 1 (802) 773-6993
info@tuttlepublishing.com
www.tuttlepublishing.com

Japan
Tuttle Publishing
Yaekari Building, 3rd Floor,
5-4-12 Osaki, Shinagawa-ku,
Tokyo 141 0032
Tel: (81) 3 5437-017
Fax: (81) 3 5437-0755
sales@tuttle.co.jp
www.tuttle.co.jp

Asia Pacific
Berkeley Books Pte. Ltd.
3 Kallang Sector #04-01
Singapore 349278
Tel: (65) 6741-2178
Fax: (65) 6741-2179
inquiries@periplus.com.sg
www.tuttlepublishing.com